ALL THE LITTLE LIES

S.J. SYLVIS

All the Little Lies
Special Edition
Copyright © 2022 S.J. Sylvis

Published: S.J. Sylvis 2020
sjsylvisbooks@gmail.com
Cover Design: Danah Logan
Editing: Jenn Lockwood Editing
ISBN: 979-8-9858020-2-3

AUTHOR'S NOTE

All the Little Lies is a full-length standalone high school bully romance intended for **MATURE** readers. Please be aware that it contains triggers that some readers may find bothersome.

ALL THE
LITTLE LIES

CHAPTER ONE

HAYLEY

I STARED down at my hand-me-down uniform. Plaid. Blue-and-white checkered fabric skittered along my skirt, hitting a few inches above my knees. The white stockings weren't as white as they were when they were first worn—I'm certain of that—but at least the worn holes were on the soles of my feet and not running up the sides of my calves. The white dress shirt was undoubtedly supposed to fit snug, but on my angular frame, it hung loose, making me appear childish—even more so with the girly bow-like tie that was tied around my neck. *If only it'd just strangle me all together.*

The gargoyles in front of the school stared at me with demonic eyes, and I almost shivered in my spot. I'd most definitely been in worse places, and everyone here, in all their ritzy glory, would realize that quickly when they got one good glance at my face. On the way here, I wondered if anyone would remember me. If they'd recognize me. If a certain *some-body* would recognize me. I was going to stick out like a sore thumb with the yellowing bruise on my eye and the healing cut on my lip. But I was a different girl now. My once glossy and long, ember-colored hair was now cut to my shoulders and dull—as if the life was sucked out of it, too. I was skinnier now, and although I went through puberty, my curves were almost nonexistent due to lack of nutrition. My stomach actually growled at the thought. All I had to do was make it to lunchtime so I could eat.

And by eat, I meant steal an apple or something when no one was looking at me. It wasn't as if Jill or Pete were going to give me any lunch money or pack me a nice peanut butter and jelly sandwich with a little love note in the shape of a heart that read *Have a great day at school!* I learned just what kind of people they truly were with a backhand right to my face last night. Great couple. The best. Definitely an A-plus for them as foster parents.

With a hesitant hand, I latched onto the willowy brass handle on the school's entrance. I was supposed to wait for Ann, my social worker, but I preferred to do this alone. If I'd learned anything in the last few years, it was that no one was going to look out for me as much as I'd look out for myself. Ann wasn't going to scowl at the group of catty cheerleaders when they snickered at my unfit clothing, and she wasn't going to stand her ground when a rich, preppy boy tried to cop a feel. It was all on me.

If I wanted to count on anyone in this world, all I had to do was look into a mirror.

"Hayley! Wait up!" Speak of the broad herself. Ann hurried up the cobblestone steps in her clacking heels, her auburn hair blowing in the early autumn breeze, and her coffee was literally spilling over the edge of the Styrofoam cup. My mouth watered at the sight of it, and she must have sensed that, because she gave me a half-smile and thrusted it in my direction.

I basked in its warmth as the creamy taste of hazelnut

landed in my empty belly. I was so grateful for the coffee I almost thanked her, but then I put up my shields and remembered that I wasn't exactly pleased with her. I know. *Typical.* Foster kid mad at their social worker. But as I glanced up at the skyscraper-tall prep school, I got angry all over again. It had been years since I'd attended English Prep Middle. My friends—and really, I meant *Christian*—had replaced me by now. We were seniors. He probably didn't even remember me from middle school. *Not true, and you know it.* I surely remembered him. And I'd have been lying if I said there wasn't a teeny, tiny part of me that longed for him to welcome me with open arms.

I understood why it was crucial for me to be here at English Prep. Ann pulled some major strings, and with the help of my stellar GPA, the headmaster allowed me in on a scholarship. I should have been behind everyone else here because I'd been to three different high schools in the last four years. It would take me a little while to catch up, but school was literally the only thing I had. If I wanted any chance at surviving and getting the hell out of this town, this vulgar place, I needed to get a scholarship to attend a great college. I needed out. I had to make it out alive. I had to.

"How were Jill and Pete last night? They seem like a really nice couple. Did you sleep well? How does your uniform fit? I tried my best to get you the size you needed. It goes against HR policy for me to use my own money to pay for things for you, so I had to get everything from the headmaster." I continued to stare at Ann as I gulped more coffee down. She was talking a mile a minute, eyes darting all around. "So? How was it? Do you like Jill and Pete?"

Did I like Jill and Pete? Ann had no idea how badly I wanted to say yes. She didn't have even an inkling as to how much I wished they were a nice couple like they seemed on the outside. But I was sure she knew as well as I did that there was much more to people than met the eye. And Jill and Pete? They had a little hell running in their veins.

"They were fine," I lied. There was no point in telling her they were spiteful, ugly people. I'd been with them for twelve hours, and I had already learned so much about them.

Jill catered to Pete. He whistled when his plate was empty or when he needed a beer, and she would come scurrying over the yellowing shag carpet to do whatever he wanted. I went ahead and excused myself last night when he asked her for a blowie—as if their new foster daughter wasn't sitting three feet away.

I couldn't complain too much, though. It beat the last foster home—and juvie.

Ann gave me a warm smile, and I almost caught myself latching onto it for dear life.

"Shall we go in?" Ann opened the clad door, and I realized I was holding my breath. Little black dots danced around my vision before I exhaled. The giant entryway was empty and smelled of cleaning supplies. The tile floor looked as if it belonged in some ornate gallery or museum. The ceilings were at least twenty feet high with large windows cut out, letting in the natural light. Pristine was the word that came to mind as I gazed into the large opening in front of me. Tall stone pillars were to the right of us, which I assumed, by the way Ann's heels were clacking in that direction, was the headmaster's office.

A small part of me was excited. What a breath of fresh air it would be to go to a school that prepared you for college, offering classes like British Literature and Astronomy instead of mundane classes consisting of how to use the proper grammatical form of the words *to, too, and two*. It'd be a change of pace to be around students who weren't trying to get you to join their gang or selling drugs behind the graffiti-covered bathroom stalls during lunch. Not only did I have to watch my back at whatever home I was currently in, but I also had to watch myself at school, too. Once you were labeled the "foster kid," a certain group emerged, and they tried their hardest to drag you under right with them. They thought you were just as broken as they were—and maybe I was. But that only made me run faster.

Keep your head down, Hayley. Keep to yourself, Hayley. Don't make a fuss. Don't make eye contact. Keep your mouth shut. The times I had mentally told myself those lines were far too many.

Ann cleared her throat as I tried to pull my skirt down. It was loose around my waist, so thankfully, it came down another half inch.

"Hello, I'm Ann Scova. I have a meeting with Headmaster Walton."

A small, dainty, older woman peeked up from her rich, oak desk and pulled her glasses down to the tip of her tiny nose. "Yes, one moment please."

Ann looked over at me with her glittering eyes and gave me a hopeful smile. *You and me both, sister.*

As soon as the door swung open, Ann rushed forward, and I followed after her. Once I stepped into Headmaster Walton's office, I fought the urge to let my jaw drop. His office was bigger than any bedroom I had ever had. In fact, I was pretty sure it was bigger than foster home number three —the one with the tiny orange bathroom. I could barely pee without my knees touching the shower curtain.

"Hello, Headmaster Walton. My name is Ann Scova; we talked on the phone a few days ago, discussing Hayley Smith." Ann stuck her hand out and shook the short, plump man's hand. He glanced at Ann, then to me, and then back to Ann.

"Yes, our scholarship student." He flipped through a file as he sat back down in his leather-backed chair. "Transferred from Oakland High, is it?"

Ann raised her perfectly plucked eyebrows at me. I cleared my throat as she and I both took a seat in the Cadillac-like chairs placed at the foot of his desk. "Yes, Oakland High."

"Mmmm." Headmaster Walton continued to read through my file, and I suddenly felt extremely self-conscious and vulnerable. I could only imagine what was in my file. "And I see you've attended a few other high schools in surrounding areas, yes?"

"Yes, sir." I held my tongue before I called him *Your Honor*. I kind of felt like I was back in the courtroom.

He clasped his hands after shutting the file, looking me square in the eye. Naturally, I wanted to cower, but I was no longer that girl. I didn't hide from confrontation; I pulled my shoulders back and held his stare confidently. "We have a zero-tolerance policy for violence, Ms. Smith." I swallowed, holding my tongue. "Although you come highly recommended by the staff at Oakland High, I worry our curriculum will be tough for you, considering your upbringing at local high schools. I'm well aware of your SAT scores, and of course of your situation, so I'm going to say this once and only once: if you fail to follow the rules in our school, you will be asked to leave. Your scholarship will go to the next willing student. You are smart. I'll give you that. But you may find that you don't fit in here."

His eyes flashed to the bruises on my face as the last sentence left his rosy lips. My nostrils flared, and I was one second from combusting with anger, but the rational part in my brain was quick to intervene. I knew what I looked like. I was homely looking. My face was ghastly, and my bruises were dark. The bags under my eyes were the color of ash, and the spark in my blue irises was dull. I looked like a troublemaker. My file surely described that—specifically, the last foster home incident. My attitude probably portrayed that I didn't give a shit, but I did. I actually cared. I wanted to succeed. I *needed* to succeed. If English Prep was my ticket out of this town and into a college where I could *survive*, then I'd bite my tongue. I'd swallow the harsh rebuttal that wanted to come out of my mouth.

"I understand, Headmaster Walton. You don't have to worry about me. I'm here for an education and to get into a decent college. That's all."

Headmaster Walton pursed his lips as if he wasn't convinced, but nonetheless, he nodded his head before standing up. Ann and I rose alongside him as he walked us over to the large oak door.

Ann said goodbye to him and thanked him once again for my scholarship. Before I followed her out, Headmaster Walton very briefly intoned, "I have high hopes for you, Ms. Smith. Don't make me regret my decision."

I swallowed back a lump in my throat. I recognized how pathetic it was that I wanted to cry because of hearing a statement like that from a complete stranger, but it had been a long time since anyone had said something so genuine to me.

Ann was waiting for me near the receptionist's desk with a cheery smile on her face as I pulled myself together. "Are you ready for this? I'm actually excited for you. Out of all the times I've had to check in on one of my foster kids, this is the first time I've actually been hopeful and excited. This school will be great for you, Hayley."

A tight smile came across my face.

Ann's face brightened up even more, the apples of her cheeks rising. "You've got this, Hayley. Go out there and make some normal friends. Try to be a normal senior, okay?" Her warm hands wrapped around my shoulders before she pulled me in for a hug. I stiffened almost immediately. If I thought that Headmaster Walton telling me he had high hopes for me was surprising, this definitely took the cake. I'd had three social workers since going into foster care, and honestly, I had hated every single one. But Ann? She was proving to be okay.

I wasn't sure if she actually cared about me, but after a small hug from her, I wasn't quite sure I cared.

"Thanks," I mumbled after she pulled away. My cheeks began to grow warm as I felt my walls falling down a little. *Don't get attached, Hayley. She's just a social worker.*

Right. Resuming back to my normal keep-everyone-at-arm's-length persona.

"Okay, well, I'll check in sometime this week. Let me know if you need anything at all, okay? It doesn't matter the time. Call me. You have my number."

A tight nod was my response, and she turned on her heel and walked out of the office. I didn't have the heart to remind her that, yes, I may have had her number, but I didn't have a cell phone, and there was absolutely no way I was asking Jill or Pete to use their landline. Chances were, Pete would ask for something in return, and *ha, sorry, but no thanks.*

After the small lady behind the desk gave me my class schedule and a map to English Prep, she walked me to my first class: American Literature and Poetry. Definitely a step up from Oakland High where we were learning how to write a five-page paragraph essay about a story I read in the seventh grade.

My heart tumbled in my chest as I blew out a shaky breath. I didn't think I'd be this nervous. The amount of times I'd walked into a new school should have prepared me for this moment. If I was good at anything, it was putting on a brave face in front of my new peers. Squaring my shoulders and straightening my spine was like second nature to me. But there was a pit deep in my belly. My bravery was wavering. I was standing on a cliff, looking down into the depths of fear and humiliation. Would Christian remember me? Would anyone? I wasn't popular by any means in middle school, but was anyone, really? We were all awkward and trying to find our footing in the midst of going through puberty. I might not have been memorable from middle school, but my parents surely were.

I remembered how these families worked. I knew that social hierarchies determined the food chain in this town. Screw the natural revolving of the world—the richest of the rich turned the planet on its axis. I used to be one of them. But now I wasn't.

My heart climbed into my throat as the door swung open. The small receptionist pushed me forward and mumbled something to the teacher. I kept my eyes locked onto the green chalkboard instead of swinging my gaze around the room. I reread the words "20th century poets: Sylvia Plath", but between each word I read, I silently muttered, *"If you show them fear, they'll eat you alive."* And if I looked at any of my new classmates in the eye right now, I'd blow my poker face. I needed to find my footing. The anxious and panicky girl inside of me was trying to claw her way out to find some type of anchor to hold her steady. And that was when I did it. That was when I let my eyes scan the room, and I found him almost instantly.

Christian Powell. My old best friend. Our eyes caught, and hope blossomed through my chest like a sunflower finding the sun. His eyes were the same shade of gray: stormy, grounding, always pinning me to my spot with comfort. But then his eyes narrowed, and his razor-sharp jaw became even sharper. The gray of his eyes turned to stone the very second the teacher introduced me.

"Class, this is Hayley Smith. She's new here; please welcome her and offer help when needed."

The entire classroom was silent. No one muttered a single

syllable. I didn't even think a breath was let out. Except for Christian. He was fuming in his seat. His fists clenched tightly. I wanted to turn around on my heel and go right back to Oakland High.

But I wasn't that girl anymore. I didn't bow down to anyone.

Welcome to English Prep, Hayley.

CHAPTER TWO

CHRISTIAN

TODAY WAS DESTINED to be a good fucking day. I knew that because when I'd woken up this morning and took my somnolent ass downstairs to snag leftover coffee from the day before, there was a fresh pot waiting for me. I could smell it from the stairwell. It dragged me from the top stair to the kitchen in record time. I was so blinded by the need for it that I almost didn't notice my father who was sitting at the large kitchen table—one that was rarely ever used—with his laptop propped open in front of him.

"Mornin', son," he said as I kept my bare back to him, pouring my coffee in a freshly washed mug, courtesy of—oh, that's right...*me*. The only person who did anything around here.

I grunted in acknowledgment, but really, I was fucking jumping around on the inside. My father being home meant one thing: I didn't have to parent today. I didn't have to walk back upstairs to drag Ollie out of his bed only to wait on his slow, hungover ass while he moseyed around in the shower, probably beating his dick, making us late for school. In fact, I may just leave without him this morning. I'd give my father the lovely duty of being an actual parent today. He could take Ollie to school himself.

"What brings you to this neck of the woods?" I asked, still keeping my back to him.

Silence encased the room. I was certain my father was feeling one of two things: anger or guilt. Maybe even both.

I was used to the never-ending letdowns when it came to him. He was never a present father, always buying us off— Mom included—and letting us fend for ourselves. Which wasn't much of a big deal a few years ago, but now that he was our *only* parent, it was pretty much just shitty parenting.

He gave zero fucks about Ollie and me.

He said he *trusted* us, and by us, he meant me. He shouldn't, though. He was misled. He mistook my silence and quiet, brooding nature as maturity, but the trust between us was nonexistent. He just couldn't quite see that.

Ollie and I were Irish twins: born within the same year. I was eleven months older. Yet, I held all the responsibility when it came to him.

But if I didn't, I had no idea where the hell he'd be.

Probably still facedown in Clementine's chest from last night's banger.

"Christian, I'm sorry. You know I wish I could be here more."

Lie.

I turned around and glared, but it was like looking into a fucking mirror. An ugly, warped mirror at that. We both had rich, dark-chestnut hair; our fair skin tone had a twinge of natural tan mixed in. Our jawlines were sharp and pointed, with our brow line heavy and defined. I used to hate that characteristic about him; I always felt like he was angry, even when his face was resting, but now I enjoyed seeing him aggravated. I all but salivated at the thought of pissing him off, though he never showed his cards. He simmered inside, raging and boiling so hot that his face would turn a heated shade of red, but he never lashed back out. He knew he was stuck. The guilt of having me raise myself and my brother outweighed any anger that I caused him to have.

"When are you leaving again?" I put my cup down on the counter, the clank a welcome break to the constant typing of computer keys.

He barely looked up from the screen. "This afternoon. How's Ollie doing?"

Sighing, I answered truthfully. "He's the same as he always is. Late for school, drowning in pussy and beer, still kicking ass on the team, in line to take my captain's spot next year. Oh, that's right..." I said, walking closer to him. I peered down, and he finally took his eyes off his computer. "What exactly are you going to do next year when I'm away at college and Ollie is here to fend for himself?"

My father scoffed. "I hardly think your brother being 17, almost 18, qualifies needing a babysitter, Christian."

"No, but he does qualify as needing a parent, *Dad*." And with that, I turned my back and began walking toward the stairwell. When I reached the bottom stair, I called out from behind, "He's all yours today. School starts at 8:05."

He mumbled something, but I chose not to listen, because *today was a good fucking day*.

As soon as I pulled my Charger into the parking lot, Eric pulled in beside me. Eric and I had been best friends since freshman year when we went head to head in the English Prep popularity contest. I won but wanted to lose. He lost but wanted to win. English Prep was one of the most prestigious schools in the United States. We were competitive in everything: academics, sports, extra-curriculars. But popularity goes by whoever's parents have the most money (ludicrous, I know, but I didn't make the rules), and Eric's father and mine have right around the same amount, plus their pull in the community. It wasn't long before girls started to take notice of us—even the upperclassmen. Then, the faculty and staff began treating us differently, too, mainly due to hefty donations to the school. It was only a matter of time before a new "king" was established.

After everything happened with my mom, it seemed I gained even more unwanted attention. First, I pushed everyone away, which only made things worse. Girls loved a jaded challenge, and jaded I was. I was angry all the time, which still lingered if I was being truthful, and pair that with picking fights with everyone—and winning—and I had girls fawning over the untouchable Christian, and the guys were afraid I'd break their neck. The teachers pitied me and let things slide, and mixing it all together with a smidge of my father's reputation and hefty donations, I all but ruled the school.

I loathed it at first, but it became the norm for me.

"What up, King?" Eric stepped out of his Range Rover with his Oakleys pulled over his eyes.

I grinned, walking over to him. "Rough night? Not even those sunglasses can hide the bags."

Eric and I began walking to the school entrance, him fixing his tie as he tucked a wrinkled shirt into his pants. I slung my backpack over my shoulder and walked alongside him. If Headmaster Walton saw the sloppiness of Eric's attire, he'd be pissed. But that was Eric. Ever since he came back from his father's the summer before last, he didn't care much about anything except partying. "You missed one hell of a party, dude. Missy did this thing with her ton—" Eric's sentence was cut off by the sight of Missy herself.

Missy was about a six on the hot scale. I, personally, thought her hair had too many different colors of blonde running through it (I didn't even know there were that many different shades), and her orange, tawny fake tan made me gag. She looked like she got into a fight with a spoiled can of orange spray paint that didn't quite get the job done.

"Hey, Eric. *Christian*." Missy walked past us after winking at Eric, which I assumed was meant to be seductive, and headed for the lockers.

"You were saying?" I prodded, watching Eric lust after Missy's swaying hips in her uniformed skirt.

Once I got to my locker and pulled on my navy blazer, a few other guys sauntered up to hear Eric's story.

"God, she took her tongue and licked every drop of cum my dick spit out. *Then,* she went back for more. She was a wild animal in the bedroom. I've never been so *into* it before."

Slamming my locker shut, I turned and looked at Eric. His eyes might as well have been glossed over while talking about Missy. Which was why I was going to say what I was about to say. "I've been sucked off by Missy before. It's nothing to write home about."

And just like that, Eric snapped out of it. He pulled his broad chest back and flexed his jaw. "Why do you always have to ruin it for me?"

The other guys chuckled and looked around at one another, most likely agreeing that I *did,* in fact, always ruin it for someone. There was a reason for my madness.

"Because while we're throwing the football, trying to win a championship, your head will be in the clouds as Missy's lips are around your dick. Love 'em and leave 'em, Eric. Focus on the game, not the player." That wasn't necessarily the reason I tried pulling him back from Missy. Eric got caught up in certain girls and was completely swallowed by them. He buried himself so deep in pussy and partying that I had a sense he was trying to escape something. I knew the feeling all too well.

He rolled his eyes as a few other people walked up to meet us at my locker, one of them being Madeline. If there were an actual hierarchy at English Prep, me being the king, then Madeline would have been the queen. That didn't necessarily mean we were "together", but everyone assumed, since she ruled the girls, that we were an item. We weren't. I was very clear in the beginning with her: I didn't have girlfriends. Madeline, however, was all about appearances and *the queen should be with the king, Christian*. Yeah, okay. What the fuck ever.

So, we were together for all intents and purposes: home-coming dances, prom, occasional keggers at Eric's cabin.

"Did you hear?" Madeline interrupted Eric's riveting story revolving around Missy's pussy.

She cozied up to me and grabbed my arm, placing it on her shoulders. Her nails scraped along my skin as all eyes were on her, ready to eat up her gossip.

"Did we hear what?" one of Madeline's follower's eyes grew wide, ready to hear whatever Madeline had to dish.

I stood back, my arm still stuck to her bony frame, and looked down the hall. My eyes scanned the shiny, silver lockers, glossing over the chess-club nerds standing awkwardly in their gray sweater vests. I passed by the smart girls who stared at our group like we were bullies on a playground (which we were). I was looking for Ollie, wondering if my father decided to wake him this morning or not.

Coming back to the present, I took my arm from Madeline.

That's enough of a show today, don't ya think? I said with my eyes as she gave me a glare. She quickly fixed her face and smiled, running her hands down her skirt and facing the group again. "Yep, that's what I heard."

Jace's grin etched upward. "Good. I hope she's a fuckin' babe who has a talented mouth. She'll be all over this." He ran his hands down his body slowly, looking like a fucking idiot. What girls saw in him, I had no idea. He was a wannabe. His parents weren't filthy rich like the rest of us; they were *just* wealthy enough for him to attend English Prep, which was why he tried so hard to fit in. The only reason he was in our group was because he played football. But nonetheless, a few of the girls started making catcalls and fanning themselves at his show.

Jace turned to Madeline. "What's her name?"

I glanced down the hall again; still no sign of Ollie. *Fucker better not be skipping school.* He had a test in Chemistry today, and if he didn't pass it, he'd be ineligible, and we fucking needed him on the team. He was fast as hell, and pairing that with my arm, we were likely to go to state. Coach would be so goddamn pissed if he skipped, and then I'd be the one who got chewed out.

The bell rang, drowning out Madeline's answer to Jace, and we all were on our way to class. My pulse quickened as each second passed that Ollie wasn't there. I pulled out my phone to text him when I took my seat in lit class, and that was when he walked in. The bags under his eyes were way worse than Eric's, but that was what happened when you drank half a bottle of Fireball and ended up with Clementine.

If I was my father's spitting image, Ollie was our mother's. We looked nothing alike. I got my father's dark features, and he got my mother's looks and personality. As a child, I was said to be shy. Then, when I grew older, I was often called out for appearing bored and uninterested. And now that I was only a few months from being an adult, people labeled me as brooding and a silent giant. Some even went as far as to say I had a dark and troubling soul, and who knew, that may have been correct after what happened with Mom. But Ollie? He was my mother, through and through. Sunny, radiant, the life of the party. Always. Even in his worst mood, he was still a bundle of fucking joy. It got to be annoying at times, but it was a nice reminder of her, and I didn't get those very often.

Ollie's blond hair looked darker as it was still damp from his shower, and his shirt was unbuttoned at the top with his tie hanging loosely around his neck. When he slammed into his desk, he whirled around and fixed me with a glare. "Fucker."

I barked out a laugh. "You're the fucker who made me pull your ass out of Eric's parents' room with your pants down to your ankles last night."

A smile broke out along his face. "I'm so fucking pissed I got that drunk. I can't even remember hooking up with Clem, but dammnnnn, the texts she already sent this morning." He looked up to the ceiling and mouthed a silent prayer, his hands coming together in the typical prayer hand manner.

"You need to be careful drinking that much, Ol." I bent my head down, keeping my voice low.

"Relax, brother. I'm fine," he muttered, pulling out his books. "You're not gonna believe who I saw in the office this morning."

I leaned back in my seat, fiddling with my pencil. "Who?"

As soon as the words left my mouth, the classroom door opened. My head turned in the direction of Ms. Boyd.

And just like that...

My blood boiled.

My fists clenched.

My jaw locked.

What the fuck is she doing here?

Ollie turned back to me and raised an eyebrow.

"Hayley Smith. That's who."

The organ in my chest thumped harder as my eyes passed over every inch of her body. It had been years since I'd seen her, but I'd recognize her anywhere. She had those eyes. Those piercing, suck-your-soul, icy-blue eyes. But just because her eyes were their normal color, that didn't mean she was the same girl. The same girl I used to trade my cookies with at lunch. The same girl that poured glue on Rebecca Lahey's hair for telling her that she was a tomboy. She wasn't the same girl. Not by a longshot.

There was something broken about her. I recognized it almost immediately. *Broken recognizes broken.*

Her dark hair was tangled at the bottom, and her uniform didn't fit like it should have. Her once rosy cheeks, tinted with color from laughing too much, were pure white. She reminded me of a porcelain china doll. Breakable. And by the looks of the bruises and cut on her face, someone already tried to test that out.

It didn't take long for her gaze to wander over to me. We always were drawn to one another, like moths to a flame. The hope in her eyes crawled over my skin like razor blades, cutting my very flesh, only for the hope to diminish and soothe those cuts when I shot her a glare. *Know your place. You don't belong here.*

If Hayley thought she had an ally here at English Prep, she was sorely mistaken. I'd break her just like she broke me. She was the start of a destructive avalanche that ruined my family.

Game on, China Doll.

CHAPTER THREE

HAYLEY

I'D BEEN at English Prep for approximately one and a half hours, and those one and a half hours felt like seven thousand years. I'd already learned so much, none of which was valuable or of any importance to furthering my education. I'd learned right off the bat that I was more alone in this school than I had been at Oakland High. At least at Oakland High I had Stacey and Matt. We were outcasts, but at least we were outcasts together.

At English Prep, I was the *only* outcast. It seemed everyone already had their "group", which made sense. I mean, these kids had been going to school together since the silver spoon was plopped in their mouths at age three, but not one of these wealthy kids had a friendly bone in their body. Noses had been upturned in my direction; wary glances were sent my way in the hallway; and let's not forget the moment I caught Christian's eye.

Chills broke out along my arms just thinking about it. I felt queasy, and I hated that. I didn't expect us to pick up right where we left off, but I also didn't expect him to hate me. And that was exactly what it was. Christian looked at me like I'd ripped his heart out and fed it to the wolves. His glare was steely, cold, and hit me right in the chest.

I blew out a breath and tried to think of anything else but him and his cold demeanor toward me. I lazily glanced around the lunchroom as I stood with my back against the wall. It was a quaint lunchroom; no more than fifty students were eating their fresh salads and grilled chicken that smelled heavenly. My mouth watered at the decadent scent. I was trying to come up with a plan to steal an apple or banana from the lunch line without being seen when something caught my eye from across the lunchroom.

Christian.

My head began to turn away, but I held my ground instead. *You're not that girl anymore, Hayley. Chin up.* I leveled my shoulders but kept my face neutral. I wasn't going to glare at him. I had no reason to. My heart moved in my chest as his gaze stayed in line with mine. There was plenty of chatter in the lunchroom, but it was muted as I locked onto those stormy eyes. His group of friends were in conversation, not noticing our little stare-off. It'd been years since I'd seen or heard from him, and yet, he still had some strange hold over me. I'd always felt tethered to him, even when he'd be halfway across the auditorium each morning before we'd depart to our classes in seventh grade. I felt my lips rising at the corners with the thought, but they stopped climbing when I felt a presence beside me. It took everything I had to tear my eyes away from my old friend, but whoever was beside me was standing entirely too close for comfort.

I slowly craned my neck and was met with a girl posse. You know the type: fake tans, too-white teeth, about a pound of makeup on, reeked of perfume.

"That's Christian," the Britney Spears look-alike said. I

knew she was the leader of the group, because she stepped forward as the rest of the girls stepped back. She was their ruler, and by the looks of her, she thought she ruled the entire school.

I smiled, the slice on my lip cracking open again. The taste of blood darted onto my tongue. "I know who he is."

Her face blanched for a millisecond before she recovered, popping her hip out at the same time her hand hit it. "He's mine."

I snorted, and a laugh followed it. I slowly turned my head back over to Christian, and he was still staring at me. I cocked an eyebrow. *Really?*

"I said he's mine, so you can stop staring at him, *Hayley*."

When my eyes met hers again, I eyed her suspiciously.

She flipped her blonde hair behind her shoulder. "*Yeah*, I know who you are. I know everything there is to know about you."

"I highly doubt that."

She turned back and looked at her friends, and, as if on cue, they all smiled creepily like a group of Cheshire cats. Just then, the girl raised her long arm in the air and snapped her fingers three times before the chatter of the cafeteria quieted.

Oh, great. A show. And I'm in the spotlight.

"Hello, fellow classmates. We have a newcomer, and I've decided to take it upon myself to introduce her." She walked over to a table full of boys who looked like they belonged in a chess club together and gave them one withering stare before they scattered like marbles being dropped on a freshly waxed floor. Another one of the girl's friends ran over quickly and pulled out a chair for her to climb on to stand in the middle of one of the lunch tables.

This is ridiculous.

I should have just walked out right then. I didn't have to be the butt of their joke. I didn't have to let her bully me. In fact, I could have ripped her hair out right then and called it a day, but then I would have been kicked out of this stuffy, prestigious school and sent back to Oakland High, and that would have been the end of me getting a scholarship to an Ivy League school. If I left now, it'd look like I was retreating, like I was backing down, and that wasn't me. I learned pretty quickly after my dad died that you couldn't run from trouble. It'd find you one way or another.

Running is what got him killed in the first place.

I had a hard exterior now. Whatever this bitch was going to say or do would be nothing compared to what I'd been through.

I crossed my arms over my chest, my back unmoving from the wall, ready to enjoy the show.

"English Prep, this is Hayley Smith. Our new classmate. Can we all give her a warm welcome?"

I willed my face to stay a neutral color. I had no idea if it got red, but I was praying to God it didn't.

Everyone in the lunchroom booed me. But I continued to keep my feet planted on the ground, watching from below.

The girl, who I now knew was Madeline from someone yelling her name in awe, spun around and mocked a smile in my direction. I cranked my neck up higher to stare into her eyes. She batted her thick eyelashes and puffed out her lips. "So, Hayley, would you like to tell everyone a little about yourself? Or should I do the honors?"

I didn't even bat an eyelash. I did, however, look around the room to see if any of the faculty members were witnessing this, because if they were, and they were letting it slide, they couldn't be trusted. But much to my surprise, there wasn't a single adult in the room except for a lunch lady who was too busy replacing tomatoes in the salad bar.

"No?" Madeline giggled. "Let me do the honors, then." She jumped down from the table, her skirt flying up so high everyone could see her classically pink thong, and came over to stand beside me. It took every ounce of willpower I had to keep my expression bored and my hands from knocking her on her ass.

"Hayley Smith," she started. The lunchroom was eerily quiet. It seemed everyone wanted to know my story. In any other circumstance, I might have felt flattered. But not this version of myself. My life was anything but ideal. "Hayley Smith has been in seven different foster homes in the last few years. Such a shame. But can you blame them? Who would want to keep such an ugly, poor, raggedy girl around?" She laughed, along with a few others, and I honestly couldn't believe there were girls like her that still existed. "Hayley's father was murdered when she was in middle school, and her mama took it a little hard." Madeline's eyes sliced over to mine as she trotted around the lunchroom, stopping by each table for a brief moment before moving to the next. "*Hard* as in...does the hard drugs now. But once again, can you blame her? Who wouldn't want to be high all the time with a daughter like that? After all, she's the reason her daddy was murdered."

My head twitched a fraction. My palms began to sweat. My feet were itching to move toward her. *How does she know all this, and why is she telling everyone?*

"Poor Hayley," she said, walking over to Christian's table. I was beginning to let my guard down. It was starting to get to me. My stomach hurt. My heart was aching with each beat against my rib cage. *No, don't let it in. Don't feel, Hayley. She finds you as a threat; that's why she's doing this.* I ground my teeth, pushing all thoughts of my parents away. My eyes began to gloss over, but I hurriedly blinked the tears away. "She's poor, guys, and I honestly have no idea why she's here in this school, but I feel kind of bad for her."

"Why exactly are you talking about me like I'm not in the

room?" I asked, my voice as steady as the three-hundred-year-old oak tree in the courtyard.

Madeline looked appalled that I had interrupted her story time. A few people snickered, and she shot them a look with her eyes no bigger than slits. "Because trash like you doesn't deserve to be talked to. Only about."

I shifted on my feet. "So, you like to spend your free time talking about trash? That seems strange."

Madeline's perfect round face formed angry wrinkles. Then, almost as if she had gotten a brilliant idea, her face lit up. She scooted closer to Christian, and I felt that tiny piece of jealousy creeping in. She sat on his lap, and my heart began to thud faster and faster. He leaned in close, his sharp jawline taunting me as he whispered something in her ear. She nodded with a conniving smile on her face. I noticed his hand creeping along her bare thigh beneath her skirt, and a chill ran down my spine. *Stop feeling. He's not yours.* And he never was mine—not in that way, at least.

Before I knew it, Madeline was standing up and walking over to me with a tray of food in her hands. It didn't take long for me to realize it was Christian's. Every guy sitting at his table was trying to hold back grins and laughs as Madeline approached me. I turned my neck and looked at her group of friends, and they were also trying to hide little smirks. I took half a second and met Christian's eye before Madeline leaned into my personal space.

"Ya know, since you're poor, do you want something to eat?" *Yes.* I did want something to eat. But I'd have rather chewed my arm off than admit that to these people. The entire cafeteria was under her thumb. I swiveled my head back to Christian. *Or his thumb.* What made me angry about this entire situation was the fact that Madeline knew I'd feel jealous with her sitting close to Christian. I was certain it was a lucky guess; I was sure every girl in this school wanted a piece of him, which was why she felt threatened in the first place. But she was right. It did bother me. Christian's looks alone were enough to lure any girl in.

"Nope. Not hungry," I said matter-of-factly. "Thanks, though."

And just like that, the entire tray of food was shoved into my chest with a thud. My stomach buckled forward as the tray clanked to the floor. Silverware ricocheted off the glossy tile and skittered over to the trash cans. My white shirt was covered in some kind of red sauce, and I was instantly pissed because of three things: One, I really could have used the food. What a waste. Two, I now had to figure out how to get a stain out of this shirt by tomorrow or else everyone would know just how bad off I was. And three, I somehow didn't see that coming.

Madeline whispered in my ear. "You don't belong here. And stay away from Christian." Then, she spun around and took a dramatic bow. Our peers wooed her, but I ignored them all. It wasn't the first time someone wanted to show their dominance to the new girl. But it did surprise me that Christian was a part of it. Back in middle school, when people would tease or bully his younger brother, Ollie, he'd shut them down within a blink of an eye. But here at English Prep, it didn't seem he cared much. In fact, it was as if he encouraged it. It was obvious that it was his idea for Madeline to pour *his* tray on my uniform. Christian was the bully now—or maybe he wasn't. Maybe he just stood up for people he cared about.

And he obviously didn't care about me anymore.

I left the lunchroom as slowly as possible to head for the bathrooms, not wanting anyone to think I was running away from Madeline or her threat. The girl's bathroom was as pristine as the rest of the school, the ceramic sinks sparkling as if they were scrubbed clean seconds before walking in here.

I glanced at my shirt and bit the inside of my cheek. *For fuck's sake.* I hurriedly untied the stupid bow around my neck and unbuttoned the front of my blouse. The air conditioner blew on my bare shoulders as I shrugged it off and began running it under water.

"Make sure that's cold water or else it'll stain worse." My eyes flicked up into the mirror, but I was only met with my own face and the navy stalls behind me. I began running the damaged cotton under the *cold* water and scrubbing some hand soap on it.

"Here," I heard the voice again. I dropped my head when something nudged my shoe. It was a stain removal pen, the kind that I'd expect only an old lady to keep in her purse.

Slowly, I bent down and grabbed it. "Thanks." The scent of fabric cleaner filled my nose when the creak of a stall door caught my attention. I kept my gaze on my shirt, respecting the girl's need to keep her face hidden.

"You're welcome," she answered, coming up beside me. I glanced at her out of the corner of my eye, and she smiled nervously. "You don't remember me, do you?"

This had me turning my head to get a good look at her face. I searched every curve, the jade color of her eyes, the pin-straight penny-colored hair. "Should I?" I asked, putting the cap back on her stain removal pen. I held it out to her, and she took it back slowly.

She snorted. "No, I'm not very... memorable."

I wished I could say the same about myself, but thanks to my parents, I'd always be remembered.

The girl tucked her hair behind her ears and shifted nervously on her feet. She was wearing expensive-looking black shoes, their shine catching my eye as she moved farther away from me. "We went to middle school together before you moved." She half-rolled her eyes. "I actually moved shortly after you but made it back here before my junior year."

"Oh," I muttered, wringing out my now stain-free blouse. *Fuck you, Madeline.*

"I'm not surprised you don't remember me."

"Why is that?" I walked over to the hand dryer but waited a beat so I could hear her answer.

She shrugged, staring at the bruise on my face. "You didn't seem to pay attention to anyone, except for..." I finished for her. "Christian."

She glanced over to my cut lip. "Yeah. Plus, I wasn't the most popular person."

I ran my blouse underneath the air dryer for a few seconds, getting some of the water to dry before putting it back on over my tank top.

"Well, I'm not the most popular either. Not anymore."

She gave me a half-smile, and I returned it. I didn't necessarily want a friend, but at the same time, it would be nice to have someone to go to for a stain removal pen, because ten out of ten times, the bully won't just strike once. I was certain Madeline would do something else to torment me. That was how girls like her worked. I'd been to four different high schools, and there was always one girl who enjoyed tearing down others. The school may change, but the girl never did.

"I know you already know me," I said, sticking my hand out, "but I'm Hayley."

Her smile grew as her palm collided with mine. "I'm Piper."

The bell rang, breaking our handshake. "What's your next class?" she asked.

"Poly sci," I answered. "With Mr. Lincoln."

"Follow me; I'll walk you."

"Only if I can use you as a human shield when Madeline throws more food on me."

Piper stopped and looked back at me with wide eyes. "That's who ruined your shirt? Sorry, but you're on your own with her. I was the butt of her jokes my entire junior year. I don't mess with them."

"Them?" I asked as we began walking again. I kept my eyes peeled for anyone else who wanted to mess with me, but no one even glanced in our direction.

Piper stopped in front of a classroom, and I assumed it was poly sci. "Yeah. The *it* crowd." She shook her head. "Meet me outside by the front doors after school. I'll drive you home and fill you in on English Prep. You didn't just walk into a prep school; you walked into a kingdom. And you and I? We're just peasants."

"Oh, I don't think you want to drive me home. I live—"

She shook her copper hair before I could finish. "After school. I'll see you by the doors." Then she turned around, disappearing into the hall. *Okay then.* When I moved to find a seat, my heart dipped when I was met with a familiar pair of blue eyes—Ollie.

Did he hate me as much as his big bro? He blinked once, twice, three times as I stood frozen at the door, waiting for his glare. But it never came. Relief pooled around my body. I didn't even know why I cared. I was here for education so I could get the heck out of this shitty town. I hadn't seen or talked to anyone in this world for several years. I shouldn't have cared what they thought. I shouldn't have cared that Christian hated my guts. *So what?*

If I allowed myself to feel, it would have hurt a little. Stung like a hornet on my very heart. But my feelings were off. *Always.*

My shoulder lurched forward as someone rammed into me from behind. I gasped when I turned around, but my anger was replaced by a surge of shock when I saw that it was Christian. He brushed past me quickly, the heat of his anger wafting all around us. Ollie looked from me then to Christian with a bemused expression. I was right there with him. *What is his problem?*

Nonetheless, I sucked it up and walked into the classroom with my shoulders square and spine intact.

I'm ready for round two.

CHAPTER FOUR

HAYLEY

BUSES SUCKED. Greyhound buses, school buses, and city buses. They all sucked. I was cautious of people now. Watchful and guarded, never sitting too close to a stranger. I remembered my mother teaching me what stranger danger was as a little girl, but up until those men entered our home when I was on the brink of turning thirteen, I didn't truly realize how dangerous strangers were. Since that day, I was constantly surrounded by them. Even my own mother grew to be a stranger.

So, the city bus ride to and from my foster home and English Prep shouldn't have been that big of a deal, but I still felt uneasy. The only benefit to the forty-minute bus ride every morning was that it got me out of the house sooner and back later. Pete was on his best behavior yesterday evening, even waving to Piper as she drove off in her convertible, and Jill left me half a plate of food on the stove. It was disgusting and tasted like cardboard, but at least it was food.

As much as my new foster home sucked, I was happy to

be there after school yesterday. I felt sick sitting in Piper's passenger seat while she gave me the rundown of the popularity contest at school. Here's what I learned: Christian was the "king" of English Prep, and Madeline was the "queen". I knew that much already from my brief encounter in the cafeteria. She filled me in on the other kids—popularity ranging from whose parents had the most money. It seemed as if English Prep was more of a breeding ground than anything. She told me where the best keggers were and how they were thrown after every football game. It was all very normal in terms of high school, except Piper mentioned that they all held themselves to a higher standard because their families were treated like royalty in town. There was even a rumor that Christian's father had the police force in his pocket. That wasn't the first time I'd heard of someone having the police on their side, even if they weren't technically on the *good* side.

I held my tongue before my mouth blurted the question I didn't want to care about: *Were Christian and Madeline dating?* I shouldn't have cared. I didn't have room in my life to care, but I did. Jealousy surged through me, and I had no right. Christian and I were close before my life was turned upside down, but he was never really mine. We weren't an *item*, per se. We never kissed or any of that. But we were close, and everyone knew it. We were drawn to one another. Spent most of our free time together in his fancy treehouse behind his mansion-like home. But I still had no right.

I argued with myself the entire night about why I cared. As I lay there on my pitiful mattress on the floor of a bedroom that felt more alien to me than anything, I couldn't stop replaying Christian's glare and repeating everything the Wicked Witch of the West spewed in the cafeteria. Piper ended up giving me the answer to my question without me even asking. She completely warned me off Christian. "*Made-*

line and Christian aren't together, not officially. But unofficially? Yes. Unofficially, Madeline sucks his dick whenever he snaps his fingers, so she claims him on a daily basis. And if she senses a threat, it's hard to tell what she'll do." My stomach tightened at the thought. There was something about the past and Christian that caused a spark inside of me to burn bright. I knew the hurt was creeping in, but I pushed it down. Instead, I replaced it with anger. Christian had *no* right to shoot me dirty glares and sick his psycho, unofficial girlfriend on me. Every time I thought of him after I got out of Piper's car, I saw red. The weepy, sad part of my soul that was forever hung up on Christian and my twelve-year-old self's feelings, was gone. That was the old Hayley. The new Hayley had no feelings and didn't think of the past.

The bus lurched to a stop on the corner of the street where English Prep, in all its mass glory, laid. The stone building was built in the early 1800's, which explained its cobblestone entryway and dramatic medieval archways. It started off as a mansion, owned by a very wealthy businessman named Edward Brown, and then later transformed into a preparatory school founded by Edward's heirs.

It was a beautiful building. Just by looking at it, I could taste the freedom the education would allow me. Graduating from a school like English Prep, along with my SAT scores, could grant me a seat at an Ivy League school with a scholarship. This year was all that stood between me, a former rich girl turned foster kid, and a ticket out of this hellhole. This place could give me the wings I needed to fly far, far away from the reminders that tainted my life.

I just had to get past the haters.

Piper stepped in line with me as we began walking over the threshold of regular asphalt to cobblestone. The iron gates were wide open and welcoming. "I wish you would let me pick you up in the mornings."

I turned and looked at her bright face, free of any makeup, like mine. Except, her face was free of bruises —*unlike* mine. The memory of how I got them started to creep in, my stomach lurching to a halt, but I shoved them clear away. *No.*

A small, raspy cough came out of my mouth. "I appreciate it." I looked away. "But it's a long drive, and I wouldn't feel right having you pick me up without giving you gas money, and I don't have any money." *At all.*

"I don't need gas money. My parents pay for my gas, so it's not even like it's a big deal. I know they don't know you, but if they saw where you lived and how you had to take a city bus to school, they'd be happy to help."

I shook my head as we reached the doors. I quickly scanned the faces of students, but thankfully, I didn't see anyone who wished I was dead on the spot. "It's not so bad." I shrugged, holding onto the straps of my worn backpack. This backpack had been with me since the very beginning. It was one of the only things I took when CPS showed up. I remember my mom looking at it on my back as I walked out of the trailer. My dad had given it to me on the first day of middle school. It was expensive and had my name stitched on the front. I assumed she'd tell me to leave it so she could sell it, but then she realized my name was on the front, and how many Hayley's did she know? Her shoulders sagged when she made the connection. Then, her back was turned on me and that was that. If I truly thought about that moment, it stung. My mother had never been the super loving and caring type, but after my father died, it was like I never even existed.

Piper stood beside me as I began rummaging through my locker, trying to remember which class I had first. The course load was way more than Oakland High, but considering Jill and Pete weren't really the "Let's have a family game night!" type of foster parents, I had plenty of free time to get everything done after eating the cardboard dinner. "It is a big deal, Hayley."

I paused and peeked at her through my dark hair. "Why do you care so much? You just met me. I have bruises and a cut on my face, which I know bother you, because you stare at them. I'm definitely an outcast at this school, and being friends with me is quite possibly a very stupid idea. So why?"

My words were harsh, and I didn't mean for them to be. I just didn't know how to do this. How to be *friends*. Real friends. Not the you're-a-foster-kid-and-so-am-I type of friend. Piper was the kind of girl who wanted to have sleep-overs and paint each other's nails. I didn't know how to act. I didn't know how to feel about it.

That's a lie. You feel happy. You're just afraid to feel happy.

Piper stuttered, "I—I, well, to be honest, you looked like you needed a friend, and most of the girls here are catty and up Madeline's bleached asshole or in a serious relationship with their boyfriend, which leaves no room for a friend. My best friend moved a year ago, shortly after I started to attend English Prep, and I've been kind of lost since."

That sucked. I knew how it felt to lose a best friend. Just as the thought entered my head, his face appeared down the hall. Christian's beautifully, devastatingly chiseled face. It was like a sucker-punch. I quickly averted my eyes back to Piper so I wouldn't risk meeting another one of his scowls.

"I'm sorry," I breathed out. I shut my locker, holding onto my English book. "I just..." I looked down at my ratty Converse (which looked ridiculous paired with my school uniform). "I haven't had a real friend in a long time. Everyone and everything eventually gets taken from me, so it's hard for me to get attached. But you're right." I stared at her jade eyes. "I *do* need a friend."

She smiled. "Then you've got one."

A real, genuine smile had my cheeks rising as she locked

her arm with mine. Before we parted ways to our different classes, she gave me a sideways glance. "But truthfully? Your bruises don't bother me; I'm just curious."

I swallowed, and it felt like knives lodged in my throat. "Let's just say...someone tried to take something that wasn't theirs, and I retaliated."

Piper's head twitched a fraction as we stood a few feet from the wooden door to English class. "Like what, money or something?"

I looked her dead in the eye. "No."

Her eyes showed pure innocence for a moment, as if she couldn't even conjure up the idea of what else someone could take from me. But then it clicked, and her light eyes grew dark. "Oh."

I smirked. "Don't worry. He looks a lot worse than I do." *Thank God his parents dropped the charges.*

She nodded sternly, as if she was proud. And then we went in opposite directions. I took a deep breath before entering the classroom. My eyes were staying trained to the front of the class and my book at all times. Christian was in this class and my poly sci class. And Madeline was in my world language class (I absolutely made it a pact to learn how to disrespect her in Mandarin) and PE. If I could get through those few classes without Christian knotting his face into a scowl and Madeline keeping her insults to a minimum, I might actually have a chance at this school.

Hope filled my chest at the thought. My limbs grew tingly, and a smile was dancing on my lips.

And then I made the mistake of peering to my right. Christian had sat down, his pale, smooth skin turning splotchy with red, his jaw set in a firm line, his hand clenching his pencil so tightly it snapped.

I swallowed my thick spit and turned to face the blackboard. My heart sped up, and I tried for the life of me to rack my brain further into the past to dig up my last encounter with Christian, but I had a hard time finding that memory.

Too much had happened.

Too much that I *couldn't* think about.

Too much that I *wouldn't* think about.

Christian could keep glaring at me like I'd committed some insane crime toward him. Nothing, not even Christian, could get me to unlock the past.

Absolutely not.

CHAPTER FIVE

CHRISTIAN

I STARED at Hayley from across the lunchroom. She was sitting with some girl I'd never even seen before. The two of them huddled together, whispering back and forth. Her dark hair framed her smooth, pale face, and in contrast, those bruises stuck out like a red flag: trouble. *She* was trouble.

The bruises interested me, but not because I felt bad for her or felt the need to snap someone in half for putting them there. I just wanted to know who else Hayley had a vendetta with.

"I need you," I bent down and grumbled in my brother's ear. "Bring Eric and Jake, too."

I didn't wait for a response. I knew he'd follow through. I stood up, scooting my chair back, and walked slowly through the cafeteria. My peers stopped talking and taking bites of their lunches when I passed their tables, as if they thought I was going to sit down and have a conversation with them. Or maybe they were afraid I'd take their tray and dump it all over their pristine uniform like I'd told Madeline to do to Hayley yesterday.

Madeline was a vindictive girl. I knew she'd jump at the chance to embarrass Hayley. It was just too easy, if I was being honest.

I didn't bother to give Hayley a glance as I passed by her table, but I did notice that she didn't stop talking like the rest of the cafeteria did. It was as if she didn't even notice me passing, which was complete bullshit. She could feel my presence from across the lunchroom, just like me with her. She was just making it a point *not* to notice me.

"Where we going?" Ollie asked, catching up to me. My father had left early yesterday evening, which wasn't a surprise, but that meant I had to drag Ollie's ass out of bed ten minutes before we had to leave this morning. Pissed me off.

"There's something I need to do."

We continued down the hallway, Ollie beside me, and Jake and Eric trailing. They were talking about the game this weekend as we stopped in front of the office.

"Jake," I barked. "I need you to punch Eric in the face. I need a diversion to get into Headmaster Walton's office."

"Whoa, whoa, whoa," Ollie interjected, getting in my face. "What the fuck? We have a game Friday. They can't fight! They'll be benched."

I shook my head. "Relax. I'll handle it. No one is getting benched." I glanced at Jake and Eric, who really didn't seem to give a fuck either way—precisely why I chose them. "You punch Eric then, Eric, you punch Jake. We'll drag you guys in there. Sit you down in front of Ms. Boyd. Ollie, you'll work your magic with her while pretending to keep an eye on these two. I'll go into Headmaster Walton's office and get what I need to get."

"Which is?" Ollie crossed his arms over his chest, raising

an eyebrow. I hated when he fucking did that. He looked just like Mom. She always raised one eyebrow at me when I was lying about something.

I thought about not telling him and giving him a bald-faced lie, but that would mean I cared more than I did, like I was harboring a secret and being covert with my intentions regarding Hayley. That wasn't the case. I wanted the entire school to know I hated her and had plans to break her in half.

"I want to know why *she's* here, and more importantly,"—I turned around, giving them my back as I reached for the years-old doorknob to the office— "I want to know her weaknesses."

"Brother," Ollie warned from behind. "Leave the poor girl alone. Hasn't she been through enough? I mean, did you see her face? And she's skinny as fuck. Doesn't look like she even eats. And that shit that went down with her dad?"

I spun around forcefully, something clawing at me from the inside. "Why do you care?" I was seething underneath my cool composure. Ollie could probably sense it because he knew me better than anyone, but he didn't know about *this*. He didn't know that I blamed her. There was power in keeping secrets—no one could destroy you if they didn't know how.

He held his hands up in protest, dropping his head for a second before catching my eye. "I'm just trying to figure you out. You two used to be inseparable. I think I was even jealous of her at one point in our lives. I distinctly remember you choosing her to be on your dodgeball team in the seventh grade. That hurt, bro." He smirked before growing serious again. "And now you hate her? So much that you had Madeline embarrass her in front of the entire school like the catty bitch that she is. You hate that type of shit. So why?"

I strode over to him, erasing the distance between us. Jake

and Eric were both staring at us indifferently, most likely wondering the same thing. My brother and I were the same height and build. Tall with a broad upper body and cut muscles from football conditioning. The only difference was my arms were bigger and his legs were faster. A battle we often tried to remedy. "None of your fucking business."

We stared at each other for so long that I felt my plan slipping through my fingers as the clock continued to tick. I finally shrugged him off and sent a look toward Eric. That was all it took. Eric wound back before Jake took an uppercut to the jaw.

"You fucker," he spat with a hit back. Ollie instantly got in between them before they got too invested and neglected that this was planned and not an actual fight. Jake's lip was busted, blood dripping down to his chin, and Eric's eye was forming a welt. *Those are my boys.*

"Good shit. Follow my cue." I gestured toward the door but stopped right before I opened it. I looked back at all three of them. "And stay the fuck away from Hayley."

Jake formed a frown, and Eric nodded. Ollie only stared at me, but I knew he'd listen. We may not have always agreed, but he wouldn't defy me on this. Not when a girl was involved.

Once I opened the door, the scent of old, dusty books wafted around. I crooked a smile in Ms. Boyd's direction.

Show time.

It only took three compliments, a hefty dose of flirting, and a dazzling smile to get Ms. Boyd to let me in the Head-master's office.

Headmaster Walton was at lunch—which I already knew —and due back within the next ten minutes, so I had to act fast. I rounded his large, mahogany desk and roamed my gaze around the stupid, ancient globe, a framed picture of him and his wife, the row of expensive pens that were in a perfect line... *Bingo*. A large folder sat near the edge of his desk, underneath a pile of useless papers. The name Hayley Smith was written on the tab in permanent marker.

I took the folder and placed my ear against the door for a moment, hearing Jake and Eric arguing over their "fight", which caused me to smirk. *Damn good friends they are.*

I scanned the contents quickly, sucking in all the information I could regarding Hayley.

Seven foster homes since seventh grade. *Hmm. I thought Madeline was making that up to embellish her story...guess not.* Three different high schools. Her current foster home was two towns over. *Interesting.* I took my phone out and snapped a picture of her address. *Might come in handy one day.* She was in juvie for assault before she came here, but the charges were dropped. *Now that's perplexing.* My eyebrow hitched as I glanced at her school credentials: 1560 SAT score. *Damn.* Even though I hated her, that was a damn good score. She always was smart.

I flipped through a few more futile pages, and my hand stilled on the last page. It was a handwritten letter from someone named Ann.

Dear Headmaster Walton,

My name is Ann Scova, and I am Hayley Smith's social worker. I am writing to you personally to ask if your board would reconsider opening up one more scholarship this year. Hayley is a bright child. The brightest I have ever worked with. Her life was ripped away from her at the age of twelve, and since then, her studies have never taken a hit. Personally, I feel that she excels so well in school because it is the only thing she can control.

Unfortunately, Hayley's father, Jim Smith, was a very wealthy man up until the night he was murdered. He was murdered in the home that Hayley resided in, and from the bits and pieces I've gathered from Hayley's past social workers, Hayley actually witnessed the murder with her own eyes, and she may have been the reason the murder took place after her call to the authorities. After Hayley's father passed, revealing the serious and illegal crimes he was a part of, Hayley and her mother moved to a trailer park south of Pike Valley. After a short while, CPS got a call, and Hayley was taken into the state's care immediately due to her unfortunate living conditions. But like I've said, although Hayley has been through troubling times and on her own in most senses, she's never let go of her goal. She wants to graduate and go to an Ivy League college, with hopes of a scholarship. I don't think she'll get that going to a public school.

Please reconsider your scholarship program. Just this once. Hayley doesn't have many people fighting for her, and I'd love if we could do that together.

Thank you,
Ann Scova
LSW

The paper crumpled in my hand as I read the letter. If it were anyone else, I'd maybe feel bad for them. It sounded like a fucked-up life. One parent dead, the other unable to care for you. I chuckled. *Sounded a little like my life.* And I had Hayley to thank for that.

It all boiled down to one unanswered phone call. All she had to do was mutter one fucking word and things would have played out differently. She was the catalyst that caused everything in my life to change.

I carried around a hatred for her that was so heavy it felt

like chains were tied to my ankles. And the hatred I carried for myself was almost just as heavy. It was what kept me from untying those chains in the first place. If I untied those chains, I'd be met with guilt, and I much preferred the former.

I shut Hayley's folder and shoved it back onto Head-master Walton's desk as I heard his gruff voice outside the door. I made myself comfortable in the leather chair perched in front of his desk, ready to put on the charade to "punish" Eric and Jake on my own, considering I was the football captain. While I waited, I tried pushing away the swirling thoughts of Hayley.

Remember, Mom died because of the spiral you and Hayley created. Hayley may not have known it yet, but she wasn't just responsible for her father's death, but my mother's, too.

CHAPTER SIX

HAYLEY

THE NEXT FEW days passed by, and to my surprise, everyone was quiet. Christian didn't do anything out of the ordinary—so, nothing more than some glowering in my direction. Madeline turned her nose up at me and snickered at my too-big uniform after gym class, which ended with a rude remark, but so far, there had been no casualties.

Things were okay at English Prep, but Pete found me sneaking food into my room a couple of nights ago, so now I had a lovely lock on my door. This wasn't the first time a foster parent had locked my door at night, and it was partly my fault. I should have known better. My number one rule in foster care was to never let your guard down, no matter how nice the family seemed. I learned that *very* quickly after Gabe.

"So, plans for tonight?" Piper slid in beside me at lunch, her tray a colorful assortment of fresh veggies and fruit with a nice, juicy hamburger. My mouth watered at the sight of it. Then, as if on cue, my stomach growled, too. I placed my hand on my front to drown out the sound, but Piper's eyes lowered until she saw my hand.

"Why don't you ever eat lunch?"

I shrugged. "Not hungry." I didn't want to tell her I didn't have lunch money. The scholarship didn't cover lunch, only the tuition fee, and the headmaster was nice enough to lend me the bits and pieces of lost-and-found clothing to make up a couple of uniforms.

Piper gave me a weird look as she bit into her hamburger. I knew what she would do if I told her the truth. She'd offer to pay, but I already felt guilty because she kept driving me home from school. Regardless if her parents paid for her gas, I hated taking handouts. I also didn't want her to think I was only being her friend because she kept giving me things.

"I'm going to go to the library to study before world language," I muttered, standing up quickly, trying to escape the conversation before it started. I smoothed out the stupid schoolgirl uniform and gathered my backpack.

"Hey! Wait!" Piper said, grabbing onto my wrist. "Do you want to go to a party with me tonight?"

Her green eyes twinkled with hope above the sprinkle of freckles on her nose.

A party? With these people? I'd rather stay locked in my room, listening to Jill suck Pete off in the next room.

Piper shook her head as if she read my thoughts. "It's the next town over. Have you heard of Wellington Prep?"

Still standing, holding my backpack straps, I responded, "Um, yeah, sounds familiar."

I knew exactly what Wellington Prep was. It was English Prep's rivalry school. Their academics were just as good, the families just as rich. It was on the other side of this messed-up town. Pike Valley had exactly that: valleys. There were the two wealthy valleys where English Prep and Wellington Prep resided, then the rest of the valleys consisted of the middle class and the straight, dirty-begging-for-pennies poor. I'd lived in every one of them, except Wellington Prep.

"Well, my cousin, Andrew, throws parties almost every weekend. It's where I hang most weekends since it was my old school and all. My parents travel a lot, leaving me home alone, and after bingeing *Gossip Girl* for the twentieth time, I decided I needed some sort of social life, even if at the wrong school."

I frowned. "I'm not sure my foster parents will just let me go to a party three towns over." *No, they'd rather just lock me in my room and pretend I don't exist.*

Pete and Jill couldn't afford me getting into trouble. If I got into trouble, the state (Ann) would investigate, and they wouldn't get their precious foster-parent paycheck. That was all I was to them: a check. Money was the root of the world's problems, I swore it.

Piper gave me a half-smile. "Well, if you change your mind, text me."

Embarrassed, I dropped my head. "I don't have a phone."

Her face blanched as she dipped her fork into her salad. "Oh, that's right. Well, you have your laptop, right?"

I nodded, tugging my backpack close. My laptop was five years old but still worked like a gem. It was the only thing in my backpack that I had brought from my house when CPS took me. That, some clothes, and the locket I wore around my neck.

"Just email me through our school email address. Okay?"

Piper bit into her ranch-covered lettuce, and I nodded with a fake smile on my face. "If I change my mind, I will. I'll see you later."

And what I meant by change my mind was *if Jill and Pete decide to be nice human beings in the next eight hours, then yes, I'll email you.*

I slowly backed away from Piper and turned around. I

walked over to where the food was and waited a beat before I
felt I could blend in with the other students grabbing trays
and filling their plates with food. Leisurely, I stepped in line,
pretending to grab a tray, and stood behind one of the tallest
boys I could find. I swept my gaze to Piper, and she had her
back to me, thinking I'd gone up to the library—which I
planned to do right after I grabbed something small and
discreet from the buffet. From what I could gather, no one
was paying any attention to me, so I hurriedly swiped an
apple and stepped out of line. I bent down beside a cluster of
students and pretended to tie my shoe while simultaneously
pulling my backpack off my back to shove the apple inside. *I
just need some calories.* It was hard to tell if Jill and Pete would
leave a plate for me this evening, especially after stealing
some food from their pantry.

Right as I unzipped the zipper, a pair of black shoes
appeared so close to me I thought they were going to step on
me. I angled my chin up, my hair falling past my shoulders.
My eyes went past a pair of khakis and a filled-out navy blazer
as I sucked in a breath. Christian tilted his head a fraction
and clenched his jaw.

My chest grew tight. Nerves trickled down my spine.

Cool, gray, hooded eyes were staring down at me, and I
swore it was just the two of us in the cafeteria. The chatter
and clanking of dishes was nonexistent. I felt like I was
looking through a tunnel and Christian was at the very end.

I swallowed, licked my lips, and continued to stare at him.
Don't look away. Almost as if it were a challenge, he flicked his
eyebrow and he narrowed his eyes. He lazily crouched down
so we were eye level. My heart was beating a thousand beats
per second, and the only thing I could think was, *He's painfully
beautiful.* Christian's jaw was as sharp as glass, his skin free of
flaws, his nose strong and straight, and his eyes could suck
the life right out of me.

My mouth parted as he leaned in closer, his intoxicating smell putting a spell on me. Then, I felt his hand cover my apple, and he plucked it right out of my palm.

I gasped, the action bringing me back to reality.

"Like father, like daughter?" He took a big bite of the glossy, red skin. The juice dripped down onto the floor below us. His jaw worked up and down as he chewed, and after he swallowed, he stared me right in the eye and whispered, "We don't steal at my school, *thief*." Then, he stood up, threw my apple in the trash, and walked away.

I gave myself three seconds to gather my emotions and threw them right in the trash along with my lunch.

Fuck him. This wasn't his school, because if it was, and he truly did "rule" it like everyone said, then I wouldn't still be here.

"Thanks, Piper. Again, you really don't have to drive me home." Piper smashed her lips together as she looked at the small, smokey-colored house I now called home. It actually looked bigger than what it was. There were three bedrooms and two tiny bathrooms. My room was the smallest—no surprise there—and my bathroom was, thankfully, only used by me. Jill and Pete used their master bathroom from what I observed. When Ann and I first came to the house, it was sparkling clean, the smell of Pine-Sol wafting throughout. The floors were shiny, and the kitchen counters were wiped off. Pete's chair was empty as he and Jill answered the door with smiling faces.

But as soon as Ann was gone and we all sat down to eat, they laid down the rules of the house. I was to be quiet, keep my nose out of their business, eat what they gave me, and I was limited to six-minute showers, and I got the laundry machine on Tuesdays and Saturdays. They would not be giving me a phone or an allowance, and no rides, either, unless it was to check in with Ann. If I followed their rules, I could continue staying with them after I turned eighteen and until I went off to college (of course, I'd have to give them the grant I'd apply for with the state or get a job and pay them). Otherwise, I'd be thrown out and shit out of luck. If I got thrown out before I was eighteen, I'd go to a group home. And after? I'd be homeless.

I knew they weren't being nice people by letting me stay until I started college; they just wanted to continue getting extra income. But what choice did I have?

"Are you sure you don't want to go to the party with me? Maybe bring me inside and we could say we're staying at my house for the weekend?"

The thought made my stomach hurt. I didn't want to ask Jill and Pete for anything, even staying the night with a friend. If it were just Jill, maybe, but Pete? No way. He was a mega-asshole who liked to control everything.

"You don't want to go inside there," I all but whispered, staring at the house. "I'll see what kind of mood they're in and ask if I can. But don't count on it." *Lie.* I pulled the door open and began to climb out. "Thanks for inviting me, though." I smiled. "And the ride. You're a good friend, Piper."

And she was. I was just too afraid to get attached.

She smiled brightly, the freckles on her cheeks meeting her eyes. "Email me anyway, okay? Just so I know you're okay over the weekend." She glanced back at the house. "I have a feeling you try to make things seem like they're okay, even when they're not."

I stared at her for a beat before giving her another lift of my lips. "I promise I'll email you later. Have fun at the party."

She nodded as I closed the door and began walking up

the broken concrete steps to the house. Piper was right. I did try to make things seem okay when they weren't. Which was exactly why I didn't tell her what happened with Christian earlier.

Something had happened during our five-year hiatus that made him hate me, and it was driving me crazy. The glares he gave me were one thing. His bitchy "non-girlfriend" was another. But taking my food? My only source of nutrition? It was about to be game on. I did nothing to him. Nothing. There was absolutely no reason I deserved to be treated that way.

And yet, I somehow always found myself in this position. Getting shit on by people who thought they were better than me.

So lost in my raging thoughts of Christian, I didn't realize I was inside the house until Pete barked at me. "What are you doing standing there with the door wide open? Shut the fucking thing."

I jumped in my skin and shut the door behind me. My pulse was climbing in speed as I rushed past him and to the stairs. Jill bent down and whispered something in Pete's ear as I turned my head, and then I flinched when I heard skin slap skin. I paused, my hand on the handrail, ready to retreat upstairs.

"You're a dumb bitch. No, she isn't getting food tonight. I caught her stealing out of our pantry last night. This is her punishment."

I spun around slowly and eyed Pete in his white under-shirt that was a hair too small. He wore his black pants that still smelled of engine oil from working at the mechanic shop. He looked crazed. Spotting the beer can beside his chair, I clenched my teeth. *Pete must be a little heavy into the alcohol.* A bead of sweat crawled down his red face. Jill was standing beside him, holding the side of her reddening cheek. There was a fire in her eyes. I recognized that look, but in the end, she kept her mouth shut.

Jill was wearing a pair of light-blue scrubs with her purse draped over her shoulder. My heart studded to a stop. *Is she going to work?* She was leaving me here with him all night? Alone? Fear was climbing in the back of my throat, but I swallowed it down. *You've been in worse circumstances.* Fear meant weakness, and I had no room to be weak in a life like this.

"Are you going to work?" I asked quietly, still standing by the stairwell.

Jill nodded once. "Sometimes I work the night shift. I'll be back in the morning."

I took a deep breath, slowly exhaling so Pete wouldn't notice and demand I stop breathing his air or something. "Okay," I answered, turning around to walk upstairs.

Pete yelled from down below, "No dinner tonight, and I'm locking your door at 8pm sharp, so get your business done before then."

I didn't answer. Instead, I ran up the stairs and shut the door. I sunk down against the wall and stared at the mattress on the floor with stained sheets from who knew what. I squeezed my eyes shut and counted to ten.

One, two, three. *You've been in worse places, Hayley. Suck it up.* Four, five, six. *Calm your heart.* Seven, eight. *It was worse when living with Mom.* Nine, ten.

Reaching into my backpack, I let out a shaky breath. I heard the door bang against the wall downstairs, and suddenly, I was twelve years old again, sitting in a stairwell on the phone with the police as my father was shot in our living room.

My hands were trembling as I opened up my laptop and the browser. It only took me three seconds to decide I didn't want to be locked in my room all night to think of things that had no part residing in my brain anymore. Christian included.

Piper emailed me back within minutes.

She'd be here at ten, and all I had to do was figure out how to climb down the side of the house from my window without breaking my neck. But honestly? Would that even have been a bad thing?

CHAPTER SEVEN

HAYLEY

THE FADED WHITE lattice with overgrown, tangled vines scratched my stomach as I shimmied down to the ground. Once my black Converse crunched the crispy leaves, I let out a sigh of relief. My stomach was cut, I think, but I didn't care. I felt ten times lighter after being in that house with Pete's blaring TV downstairs. My door was locked at 8pm sharp, just like Pete said. I just hoped he didn't check on me through the night, but by the looks of him through the living room window, he wouldn't, as he was passed out with a slice of pizza resting on his belly and a pile of crumpled beer cans on the floor. *What a sight.*

I spotted Piper's BMW down the street with the headlights off, like I told her, and hurried over. I tapped on the window twice to signal it was me.

The lock unlatched, and I climbed inside, buckling my seatbelt.

She opened her mouth to say something, but I stopped her by putting my hand up.

"I need to say something," I rambled, pulling my thick hair down from my ponytail. Piper leaned back in her seat and angled her body toward mine. Her glittering eyes stared at me intently. "I don't know how to be a friend. I have a hard time letting people in because I'm scared. And it takes a lot for me to admit I'm scared. Everyone and everything has been ripped away from me at some point, and it sucks. That house I'm living in? It sucks. They lock my door at night. I haven't had dinner because I'm being punished for taking food out of the pantry when they were asleep. I don't eat lunch because I don't have lunch money." I took a deep breath, realizing I was talking a mile a minute. "I emailed you because I realized I need a friend in the worst way. So, I'm sorry if I end up sucking at being your friend in the end. Just know, I'm trying."

A huge smile worked its way onto Piper's face as the words tumbled out of my mouth. It was dark in her car, the lights on the dashboard the only thing illuminating our faces. A bluish glow danced along her cheeks, and I felt myself relaxing. She reached over and squeezed my hand. "You're doing just fine. I need a friend, too. My old best friend just *had* to move with her family. The nerve."

She snickered, and I did, too. Then, we were full-on laughing. I felt like a thousand bricks had been lifted off my shoulders, but as soon as we pulled up to the party after Piper stopped and got us tacos in a drive thru—which I basically inhaled—the nerves were right back where they started.

"You look great." Piper stepped up beside me as we began walking to the tall house. I crooked my head up so high I could see the glittering stars playing peekaboo behind its roof.

Piper was wearing distressed skinny jeans and a chunky sweater that probably cost more than all of my attire combined. I glanced down at my outfit: black Converse, black skinny jeans with holes in them—only mine were distressed from actual wear and tear—a white band t-shirt I stole from a past boyfriend, and my jean jacket that was also distressed from wear and tear. I shrugged. "I don't have a whole lot to work with. I hope I don't stand out too much."

Piper smirked, shoving her braid off her shoulder. "You were born to stand out, Hayley. And that has nothing to do with your outfit."

Not sure what she meant, but I didn't have time to ask as we were suddenly walking through the threshold of a house that looked lavish on the outside and even more extravagant on the inside. Glossy tile floors were at our feet, and strange, headless statues stood along the walls, as if the intricate chiseled bodies were part of the welcoming committee.

"Come on, Andrew and his friends are on the second floor."

Piper pulled me along and gave me a rundown of the Wellington Prep gang. Andrew was basically the leader of the school, and Piper pretty much compared him to Christian, except she said Andrew wouldn't be a world-class dick to me. Then, there were the girls of the school, but since I was with Piper, they'd be on their best behavior since she was Andrew's cousin and they were all friends at one point or another.

"Then there are Andrew's guy friends." Piper blushed a little as we climbed the stairs. "You've got Chase, Will, Cole, and Harrison. Then a few random guys here and there, but those are Andrew's closest friends and part of the 'in' circle."

"The 'in' circle?" I asked as we rounded the landing. I could hear a rap song playing and girls squealing. *This oughta be fun.*

We stopped a few feet away from a large room that had strobe lights interchanging in color and loud music blaring from speakers. I spotted some dancing girls holding drinks above their head when Piper stepped into my line of vision.

"Yeah, you know how Christian has Ollie and Eric, and a few others, always trailing behind him?"

I nodded briefly, although I didn't want to admit that I'd noticed Christian and his gang. It was hard to miss them striding down the halls, though. They thought they were divine superhumans or something.

"Well, Chase, Will, Cole, and Harrison are the guys that trail Andrew."

I formed an O with my mouth. Piper's hand landed on my wrist, and her face turned somber. "Stay away from Cole, though."

I furrowed my brow, but before I could ask why, she pulled me into the party.

Alrighty then. Let's do this. Time to be a normal teenager, for once.

CHAPTER EIGHT

CHRISTIAN

ERIC PASSED the blunt off to Ollie, and I had to force myself to keep my hands on my lap. I was seconds from ripping the damn thing from his arrogant mouth, but I also realized I was a little on edge lately.

We had won the game tonight, and my teammates deserved to celebrate, me included, but I didn't want to do that shit right now. I was too worked up and inside my own head. My thoughts weren't clear enough as it was. They were muddled with visions of oceanic eyes peering up at me from below.

"Bro, just take a fuckin' hit. You need to lighten up." Ollie puffed out some smoke and tried to hand me the joint.

"I can help you lighten up," April purred from my right, and I glanced over at her. If I closed one eye and turned my head, she was attractive, I guessed. It might help me calm down, too.

I broke my silence today. I'd been simmering the entire week on what to do about a certain someone named Hayley.

Did I continue tormenting her? Did I come right out and tell her to get the fuck out of my school? Did I yell at her and tell her I hated her? The choices were endless. I couldn't decide what route to go.

Then I saw her stealing an apple, and I jumped at the opportunity. I was alone. No one would give me shit about it. Ollie wouldn't give me that disapproving look. Jake wouldn't mouth off that she was "hella fine, even with those bruises." So, I swooped in and got entirely too close to her face. She smelled good. Sweet, like vanilla. She smelled nothing like Madeline with her overpriced perfume, or April who had somehow found her way onto my lap.

April laid soft kisses on my neck as I leaned away from her. Ollie and the rest of the guys were talking about Wellington Prep, the school we beat to the ground—in the rain, nonetheless—when Madeline stormed into the cabin.

She instantly searched for me, and when she spotted me, she scowled, but only for a moment. Her blonde hair was tied in a bun, and it bobbled on top of her head as she stomped over to me and April.

"We need to talk. *Now*."

"Relax, Madeline," April said, sliding off my lap. "Nothing happened."

Madeline rolled her eyes before turning her back. "What happened was you just got kicked off the cheer squad for being a backstabbing slut. Christian, come on."

April gasped as I stood up. "You can't do that!" she shouted, but her yells were drowned out when I followed Madeline into the downstairs den.

"What?" I asked, a snip in my voice. My eyes immediately followed Madeline's gaze as she looked over to the couch. Two other girls were sitting there, both of whom I recognized but didn't care to know their names.

"We have a problem, and I'm certain you'll take care of it."

I followed Madeline farther into the den, unease settling in. "What's the problem?" I treaded lightly. Madeline had a knack for making shit seem much worse than it was. She was dramatic, and that was speaking lightly.

"Wellington Prep boys put their hands on Cara, and it wasn't with her permission."

I paused, flicked my eyes over to the girl I presumed to be *Cara,* and then back to Madeline. "Tell me everything."

Once I rounded up the boys, we drove the thirty minutes it took to get to Wellington's side of Pike Valley. I told Madeline to stay with Cara, the girl who confessed that a Wellington Prep boy went a little too far with her after the game tonight.

Eric and Jake were yammering in the back of my Charger, hyped up to beat ass. Only, they weren't the ones who were going to do the beating. I was.

Not only was I fucking pissed that Wellington Prep had hit on our girls, but to do it without their permission? No. I didn't stand for that shit at English Prep, and I wouldn't at their school either. I was an asshole, I knew that—an arrogant asshole, at that—but *this* wasn't okay.

Did I treat girls like royalty? No. Did I worship the ground they walked on? Also no. But did I disrespect them in a way so vulgar as to take away their right to say *no*? Absolutely not. I knew where to draw the line, and I wouldn't dare cross it.

We pulled up to a large home much like the ones in my

neighborhood. Ollie shifted in his seat, rubbing his hands down his jeans. "What's the plan?"

I turned my car off and took several, calm breaths. I wasn't fazed by this at all. Beating this motherfucker, *Cole*, sounded like exactly what I needed. It was a nice distraction. Earlier, I was hyped, jittery, couldn't stop thinking about that fine little china doll I wanted to break in half. Thoughts of Mom blurred my vision every time I thought of Hayley, and that wasn't settling well with me. But this? This felt right.

"Follow my cue as always, brother. I'm going to make Cole Johnson my bitch, just like he tried to do with Cara."

"So, you're gonna try to fuck him?" Ollie laughed at his own joke. I glared at him, and he quickly shut his mouth.

"Let's go, boys," I said as I climbed out of my car.

Jake yelled, "Fuck yeah! Let's teach these Wellington Prep tools that they need to stay the fuck away from English Prep."

That was exactly what we were going to do.

CHAPTER NINE

HAYLEY

Piper went to get some sodas for us two minutes ago, but it felt like an hour. I stood along the far wall, watching the drunken girls dance their asses off in the middle of the room. They were dressed in barely any clothing, and most of the boys were drooling with their eyes in the shapes of hearts.

I wished I could have been like those girls.

Happy.

"I don't think I've seen you around here before," a sly voice slithered up beside me, and I felt it all the way to my bones.

His voice was creepy. Breathy and warm on the side of my neck. I took a step to the left before answering. "You haven't. I'm new. I'm here with Piper."

"Ah." He smirked. "Piper's friend. The untouchable Piper." He dipped his head low, his eyes hooded. "Per her cousin's words."

I shrugged, dancing my gaze all around this guy's features.

He was tall—so tall I had to look up at him. His dark hair was short on the sides and a bit longer on top. He was attractive, but in the I'm-rich-and-my-parents-give-me-everything type of way. Preppy. His hair had too much gel on top—so much that the dancing strobe lights glistened off the shiny strands.

"So, you go to English Prep?" He was in my space again, even though I'd stepped to the left.

I swallowed and answered, "Yep."

"And how do you like it?" He eyed me suspiciously, his baby blues flicking down to my mouth a couple of times. My skin crawled. *It was not on my to-do list to get hit on.* But this did beat being locked in my bedroom, so what the hell. "I bet you hate it."

Glancing out of my peripheral vision, I responded, "What makes you say that?"

His hand reached out, and he brushed my hair behind my shoulder. I froze, planting my feet to the ground. I hated the way my heart thumped in my chest. My stomach grew tight, and I had to bite down on my lip to keep myself from over-reacting.

He isn't Gabe.

"You look like you don't belong."

That had me turning my head. And he gave me a lopsided grin. "That isn't a dig, sweetheart. That's a compliment."

Just then, his gasoline—aka vodka—breath hit me in the face as his hand wrapped around my wrist. Chills ran up my arms, and my vision started to get blurry on the sides. *Where is Piper?* "Why don't we go upstairs and talk a bit? It doesn't seem like this is your scene anyway."

"What's your name?" I asked, keeping my feet glued to the floor.

He gave me his lopsided grin again. "Cole."

My insides churned. I pulled on my wrist for him to

release me, but his grip got harder. "Oh, relax. Whatever you heard about me isn't true."

The nervous feeling deep within my belly quickly grew to anger. I leaned into his space and felt like a queen looking down at a lout. "I know guys like you, Cole. I didn't hear anything about you. Your character says plenty. Now, let go of me before I bang your face off the backside of this wall."

His eyes narrowed, but he didn't move. So, I acted fast. I grabbed his arm with my other hand and bent his wrist backward. He screamed out, surprised that I wasn't kidding, as I turned him around and pushed him with all my might toward the wall. He wasn't hard to move, because I'd caught him off guard, but if he wanted to, he could probably knock me down within a second.

I wanted to push my knee into his back to teach him a lesson about laying his hands on a girl, but he was suddenly ripped from my sight.

Just then, Ollie stepped in front of me. I looked up, shocked that he had somehow appeared out of thin air. "Sorry, scrapper. Christian came here to beat that fucker's ass, and I have a feeling he's gonna go a lot harder since he just saw that little scene."

I ignored the way my heart hiccupped at the sound of Christian's name. "Move," I demanded, crossing my arms. "I can take care of myself."

He threw his head back and laughed. It was a boyish laugh, a youthful I-don't-have-a-care-in-the-world laugh. It brought back memories of the past that I quickly shoved away. "I don't doubt that for a second, Hayley."

I had no idea where Christian took Cole, and when Piper came back to find me, she was completely confused to see Ollie guarding me by the wall. No one else in the room seemed to notice the commotion, which was probably the way Christian wanted it.

"What the hell? I leave you for three minutes and all hell breaks loose!" Piper looked from me, to Ollie, then back to me.

"Move, Ollie. Or I'll take you down, too."

Ollie laughed again, and right when he threw his head back, I kicked my leg out and swept him right off his feet. He landed with a thud, and I rushed past him.

I heard him and Piper bantering back and forth.

"Go get your stupid friend, Piper."

"Oooh, so he *does* know my name."

"Of course I know your name. Your tits are talked about often in the locker room. You may be quiet, but those hips talk, baby."

Their voices trailed as I made my way around the end of the hallway and pushed my hair behind my ear to have a listen. It wasn't long before I heard grunting and flesh on flesh.

Running on the lush carpet, I came to an open living room with two of Christian's friends standing guard, watching the fight unfold. Christian was rearing his arm back, ready to punch an already bloody and barely conscious Cole even more.

"Stop him!" I shouted. "Cole's eyes aren't even open!" *Is he even conscious? He's going to kill him!* My body grew warm, a sickly feeling hitting me head-on.

"No can do, New Girl."

I stepped forward, ready to put an end to the brawl, but one of Christian's friends—Eric, I think was his name—met me halfway.

"He's going to kill him!"

Eric glanced back and shrugged. "He knows when to stop."

No, he doesn't. Christian was out of control. He was on a

different planet called *I want to go to jail a few days before my birthday.*

I peered up over Eric's shoulder, and unease was settling in my bones. I wasn't really in the mood to watch *another* murder or for my ex-best friend to become a convicted felon. No matter if he hated me or not.

"Stop him!" I growled through my teeth.

Eric didn't even bat an eye, but the other friend was beginning to look anxious. He worked his jaw back and forth and glanced at Eric with pleading eyes.

Go stop him, I urged silently as he peered at me. I didn't wait for him to consider my urgency. Instead, I darted around Eric, too fast for him to even realize what happened, and I yelled, "Christian!"

The room fell quiet. Christian, with his arm reared back and a murderous look on his chiseled face, stopped and looked me dead in the eye. His eyes were cold and demeaning, but they were there, locked onto me.

"That's enough! He isn't even conscious."

I heard whispering from behind me.

"Did she just get him to stop by only saying his name?"

"Yeah, bro. It usually takes two of us to pull him out of something like that."

"Interesting..." The last one was Ollie.

Still holding a blood-stained Cole, Christian spat, "You care about this fucking piece of shit who puts his hands on girls without their permission? Huh? Are you *that* fucked up, Hayley?"

I ground my teeth, spitting right back, "Probably, but to be honest, I really just didn't want to watch another person get murdered in front of my eyes."

It was so quiet in the room I could hear my own beating heart. It was pounding underneath my skin, anger blurring along with irrational behavior. I wanted to take Christian by his ear and drag him into another room and demand to know what his problem was with me.

"We need to talk," Christian ordered, storming out of the room.

Yes, we freaking do!

CHAPTER TEN

CHRISTIAN

I REMEMBERED the last time we were in a room alone together. It was under much different circumstances. My life was good then. I mean, compared to what it was now. Dad still worked a shit ton, and Mom was out with her friends more often than not, but at least she was alive and I didn't have this suffocating feeling of guilt at every corner I turned, especially with a dark-haired girl standing there, reminding me of the one thing I did wrong.

I would never in a million fucking years say this aloud, but part of the reason I thought my life wasn't so bad back then was because of her. The second we met in fifth grade, we were almost inseparable. Something about her was magnetic. I was drawn to her. She always wore a frown unless I was around, and that made me feel good. Worthy. Like I meant something.

"This is so dumb," Hayley said from beside me. I wanted to agree with her, but I didn't think it was dumb. I liked being this close to her; it did something to my insides. Jumbled them all up, but in a

good way. I felt nervous but calm, too. That was what Hayley did to me.

"Why is it dumb? Let them think we're in here making out all hot and heavy."

She shifted around on her butt, unknowingly scooting closer to me. "I don't know. Everyone knows you already know how to make out. And everyone knows that I don't know how."

I tried to adjust my eyes in the darkness so I could see her face. "Who said I knew how to make out?"

She laughed lightly. "Um, let's see. April, Carrie, the two older girls that are in high school now..."

I stopped her. "Okay, okay, okay. I get it. But so what? I have a reputation to uphold."

She scoffed, her warm, minty breath hitting my face. "Yeah, I know. I'm only popular because we're friends."

"That's not the only reason. All the guys want to take you to the sweethearts dance."

"Well, none of them have asked me."

Yeah, I knew that because I had told them not to. It was on the tip of my tongue to ask her. Maybe I shouldn't. What if she says no? What if she finds out I sabotaged every opportunity she had to go with basically every single seventh grader? Even Ollie wanted to ask her. Over my dead body.

"I was think—" Just then, the closet door opened, and April's face appeared.

"Your seven minutes in heaven are all up. And..."—she looked between the pair of us—"you two don't look like you spent any time in heaven at all. Did you even kiss her, Christian?"

Hayley shifted nervously, looking down at her bent knees. She didn't even want to come to this birthday party. Neither did I, but my mom made me, therefore I made Hayley.

"Yeah, we did," I answered, standing up and holding my hand out for Hayley. "And guess what, April? Hayley is a much better kisser than you."

Hayley gave me a thankful smile, and I felt like I was on top of the world again. Something about having her by my side made me feel whole.

But that was then, and this was now.

Things had changed.

Hayley stormed past me, her little body quaking with anger.

I was still feeling the effects of smashing Cole's face in. My adrenaline was pumping, and my blood was rushing fast. My heart sputtered inside the walls of my rib cage, and seeing Hayley was making things that much worse.

What the fuck was she doing talking to Cole? What the fuck was she even doing here? The second I saw her, my blood ran cold. The seventh grader inside of me was jealous for a moment, and then I remembered everything that came after seventh grade, and I wanted to kill them both.

After finding a light switch, I slammed the door shut behind me with my foot, drowning out my brother's annoying voice and Hayley's friend's shrill demand for us to leave the party. Cole was moaning on the floor, and it took everything inside of me not to go back out there and fully knock him out again.

I danced my gaze around the room and realized Hayley and I were in a random bedroom. It looked suited for a princess as it had a huge canopy-type bed in the middle and frilly lampshades on the tables.

"What the hell is wrong with you, Christian?"

I glared at Hayley in her ripped-up black jeans, pacing back and forth. This was the first time she'd spoken to me since coming to English Prep.

"You could have killed him! And by the way,"—she faced me now, only a yard away, putting her hands on her waist—"I had it handled. You swooped in like some stupid hero and snatched him away right before I was going to take him down."

I laughed. It wasn't a humorous laugh. It was condescending and laced with anger. My chest was rising and falling fast, sweat still glistening on my forehead. "You think I was swooping in there to save you?" I laughed again as her eyes narrowed. "I couldn't give a fuck what happened to you. Cole laid his hands on one of English Prep's girls without her permission, and he needed to be taught a lesson. He's fucking lucky I didn't kill him."

Hayley didn't say anything. The room grew tense. I could tell she was clenching her teeth together, and I was doing the same.

"I want you gone," I said, still glaring.

She shook her head, her dark locks a curtain in front of her face. The bruises from the first day of school had healed, her skin looking flawless and angelic. But she wasn't an angel, that was for certain.

"Why?" Hayley's blue eyes connected with mine, and the anger was gone. She looked vulnerable, her pouty mouth frowning, her cheeks looking hollow. "Why, Christian?" she asked again. The sound of her voice felt like thorns pricking right through my skin.

I strode over to her, angry that she was having an effect on me. She didn't move a muscle. She stayed right in her spot, not giving a damn that I was an inch away. She wouldn't move unless I ran her over with my body. That was how stubborn she was. Always had been. I peered down into her face, and she angled her chin to mine. "Because I don't want to see your fucking face every five seconds." *Because I don't want a reminder of the past—the good and the bad.*

She shook her head lightly, never taking her eyes off mine. I dropped my gaze to her mouth when she spoke. "That's not a good enough answer. Something changed in you. Something happened in the last five years. Something that made you hate me, and I want to know what it is."

My mouth went dry. My throat felt like it was beginning to close. The words were bubbling up and threatening to come out.

She pushed her body closer, her rising chest touching me now. My breathing sped up. I wanted to wrap my hands around her arms and pull her into my body, but in the same breath, I wanted to scream and push her away. But instead of doing either of those things, I peered down into her eyes lethally. "Seeing you makes me think of the past, and I don't need that fucking reminder," I growled.

Her face blanched. "But why? Are you angry that I didn't say goodbye? That I didn't keep in touch?" She scoffed, clearly growing angry. "Well, I'm freaking sorry, but I was a little preoccupied with watching my dad get murdered and having psychotic men in masks promise that they'd be back to collect *me* for a settlement when I grew some tits. Oh, and let's not forget about my mother going off the fucking deep end, which landed me in foster care!" Hayley was yelling by the end of her rant, but I kept my voice nice and steady. Cold.

"I wish I had never cared about you." She kept her face unmoving, but I could tell she was bothered by what I'd said. "Do you want to know why? *You* are part of the reason my mom is dead." Her face was as white as a ghost, and her mouth parted as she gasped. "And guess what, Hayley. I don't give a fuck about your sob story. You're not the only one who watched a parent die." I quieted my voice; it was damn-near a whisper. "I guess we both have some guilt running around in our veins. The only difference is, you played a part in two deaths, not just one."

I knew it wasn't her fault entirely. She had no idea her phone call that night would kickstart a spiral of fucked-up shit. But whether she believed it or not, she was the start of the end to my mother. I tried to save Hayley that night, and instead, I ended up killing my mom in the process. The more I blamed Hayley, the less I blamed myself. And that was how I had to keep it.

"Now stay the fuck out of my way," I seethed and turned around and left her all alone.

CHAPTER ELEVEN

HAYLEY

I DIDN'T REMEMBER LEAVING the party. I didn't remember climbing into Piper's BMW. I had no idea how we ended up back on my street, but looking up at the darkened sky through the windshield, I saw the drab gray house I called home.

"Hayley," Piper's voice startled me, and I met her worried face. "You're kind of scaring me. You haven't said a word since you talked to Christian."

"How did his mom die?" I barely recognized the sound of my own voice.

Piper looked around the interior of her car, lost in thought. "Christian's mom?"

I nodded, bringing my knees up to my chin. I felt so small and so weak after talking to him. He tore me down with just a few words, and that didn't sit well with me. I was stronger than that.

"She overdosed when we were in eighth grade. It was right before I moved to Wellington Prep."

Overdosed? I had no idea his mom had died. I always liked his mom. She used to give me rides back to my house when Christian and I were hanging out and it grew past dark. She was nice—which was more than I could say about my own mom, even more so now.

"I don't get it," I whispered, racking my brain. "How is that my fault?"

"You're not making any sense."

I looked at Piper. Her face was a mask of confusion. "He said it was my fault."

"What?" She blew breath out of her mouth and turned her body to face mine, getting comfortable in her car. "Okay, listen. You said earlier you didn't know how to be a friend, so I'm going to teach you. Right now, you would tell me everything that happened with you and Christian, and then we'd spend the rest of the night trying to dissect everything and figure it out."

Was that what friends did? I wasn't used to this. The thought of sharing anything with anyone made me queasy. I'd rather suck Pete's dick than take someone up on their offer for help. *Okay, that's not true at all.*

A shaky breath left my lips. "Okay, I'll start from the beginning."

After taking a full thirty minutes to fill Piper in on all things Christian related and answering her incessant questions, we were both lying back in her BMW seats (which were more comfortable than my mattress at Pete and Jill's), still pretty far from understanding what Christian meant.

"Are you sure he said it was your fault?"

I laughed sarcastically. "Yeah, pretty much. His exact words were '*You're part of the reason my mom is dead.*'"

"That makes no sense."

No, it didn't. It didn't make sense at all. I glanced at the dashboard, seeing that it was 3 am. I swung my gaze over to the glowing light of the TV shining through the living room window.

"I should get back inside."

Piper looked at the house and nodded. "Okay." Then she glanced at me. "You have Wi-Fi, right?"

"Yeah. That's the one thing Jill and Pete actually allow me to use, for school work."

She gave me a soft smile. "Good. Google Christian. His father. His mother. Everyone. Gather all the information you can, and we'll talk more on Monday. We will figure this out."

I nodded. "Good idea." I reached for the door handle, and before getting out, Piper spoke up.

"I'm picking you up at 7am on Monday. No excuses. I'll honk when I'm here."

I opened my mouth to protest, but she gave me a look, raising her eyebrows and shaking her head no.

I didn't let myself smile until I was safely back in my crappy room. At least I had one friend at English Prep, right?

On Monday, Piper slid in beside me during lunch and whispered, "Any luck?"

I closed my world language book and placed it in my bag. "Nope." Piper and I had spent the entire forty minutes it took to get to school trying to figure out what Christian meant. I searched him and his family online, but not a whole lot popped up. There was a brief article about a car accident, but there were no fatalities, so that didn't make any sense either. It was a mystery.

"I've been trying not to think about it, honestly. I have too much other shit in my life to worry about other than

Christian thinking I had something to do with his mother's overdose. That's insane. *He's* insane."

Piper was nodding along with my rant as she picked at the contents on her tray. Before I knew what she was doing, she was placing food on a separate plate and sliding it over to me.

"No," I said, shoving the plate back over to her.

She gave me a pointed look, her green eyes peering up at me through her thick eyelashes. "*Yes.* Now eat."

I shook my head. "Piper, I appreciate this, but you already conned me into allowing you to give me rides to school every day. I'm not taking your food, too." But my stomach protested as the aroma filled my nose. *Just take the food, Hayley.*

She pushed the plate back in my direction. "Hayley, can you just let someone help you? I want to do this. I don't like the thought of anyone, not just my friend, going without food. I volunteer at the soup kitchen on Saturday mornings, and I donate all my old clothes to charity. I *like* helping people. Especially if they're my friends. So please, eat."

I gazed into her genuine, doe-like eyes as they pleaded with me. I fiddled with my skirt, trying to keep my emotions in check. I wasn't an emotional person by any means. I never cried. I pushed every feeling down the second it came into view. I didn't *feel.* Feelings made you weak and vulnerable, and that wasn't something I wanted to feel. That was why it made me so angry that Christian got to me. Those stormy eyes and steely jaw were a vision in my head I couldn't ignore. His grainy words were on repeat.

"Thank you, Piper," I barely squeaked out. "But let me repay you with something. Do you need a tutor? Or um..." I thought for a moment. *What the hell did I have to offer?* "A car wash? Although, I'd have to use your water and your soap... at your house."

Piper laughed, plucking a French fry from her plate.

"Hmm, maybe go to the next home football game with me? I haven't been to one since Callie moved away, and I feel like a loser because it's my senior year and I haven't been to any of the games."

"Deal," I said as I snatched my own fry and plopped it into my mouth. "As long as Jill and Pete say it's okay."

Piper's eyes twinkled as she squealed and threw her arms around my neck briefly. I smiled when she released me, and it was a genuine one. I allowed a tiny piece of happiness to creep into my heart for a second—that was, until I happened to glance up to see Christian glaring at me.

And that was how the rest of the week went: Piper and me laughing together at our table while I tried to pretend that Christian and his angry, smoldering looks weren't bothering me. He ignored me completely in our classes together. I hid in the back like a coward as he commanded all the attention in the front. If I had any spare time in class, I spent it doing homework, which kind of backfired as I usually did all my homework when I got home so I could have a distraction from Pete's drinking and Jill's pleads for him to be nicer to her.

Although I hated my foster home, it wasn't the worst one I'd been in. That didn't mean it was great by any means, as Pete was still locking my door, but I was surviving. And despite the whole Christian fiasco and either being ignored completely by my peers or sneered at, I actually enjoyed English Prep. I liked the extensive curriculum. It occupied my mind when it wanted to wander and took up a lot of my free time. Sure, Christian hated me, and Ollie wouldn't look in my direction. I was among the peasants in the hierarchy of royally popular kids, but at least I had made one true friend, and that was more than I could have said for any other high school I had gone to in the last few years.

Even Madeline had left me alone, which was surprising. If you didn't poke the bear, it wouldn't wake up, I guess.

Slipping off my gym shirt in the girl's locker room, I listened to the gossiping occurring around me. Gym was my last period of the day, so as soon as I got dressed, I was able to leave. I always thought guy locker room talk was a thing people often talked about, but girl locker room talk? It made my head spin.

"Did you hear that Madeline kicked April off the cheer squad?"

"Did I hear my name?" That was Madeline speaking.

"Yeah, we were talking about how pathetic April has been since you booted her hoe ass off the squad."

Shrill, ear-piercing laughter. God, girls were so mean and catty—vindictive, at best. I was almost thankful I'd been such a loner all these years. Girls like them were awful.

As I bent down to gather my uniform, it was suddenly snatched out of my grasp. *I spoke too freaking soon.* I sighed as my nostrils flared with annoyance. *One guess.* I had one guess at who would be stupid enough to take my uniform as I stood there in my bra and underwear.

I slowly turned around, and there she was. Madeline, with her bleached hair and fake tan. She was smiling connivingly, her posse not far behind her, all sharing equally bitchy smiles. They were all back in their school uniforms, whereas I stood half-naked.

They had the upper hand.

Lovely.

I had let my guard down. I had gone a few days without anyone bothering me, and that was my first mistake. If you take down your trap, the wolves will tear your shelter down eventually.

Not bothering to cover my skin, I inched an eyebrow upward at Madeline. She thought she was the queen of this school, but didn't she realize that queens were often overthrown from their throne? Being a queen didn't mean anything if people feared you more than they loved you. The only reason those girls were standing behind her was because they didn't want to stand in front of her, much like I was.

"Like what you see?" I asked, planting a sly smile on my face.

Madeline's face twisted with disgust.

"Are you kidding? You're nothing but a piece of filthy trash covered with skin and bones."

I shrugged. "Skin and bones? Isn't that why you and the rest of your clan refuse to eat carbs? I thought you wanted to be skinny? Otherwise, you wouldn't fit into that cute little cheer uniform. Am I right?" I tilted my head. "When *was* the last time you had bread, Maddie?"

I snickered. Her face twitched a fraction, and I knew I struck a chord. Girls like her were the same across all high schools. Cutting out carbs, trying to be a size zero when they *should* be a healthy size five. There was nothing wrong with having curves. Why couldn't they see that? I heard her scolding one of her friends two days ago in the lunchroom— in front of everyone, of course. *"Put down that potato, Ariana, or else you'll look like a potato and be at the bottom of the pyramid."*

"I thought I told you to stay away from Christian," she snarled at me, holding my uniform in her hands, close to her chest.

My eyebrows rose. "No problem there. He's all yours."

She narrowed her eyes like a cat, her friends all looking back and forth to one another. I was sensing the climax coming soon, and I was really hoping I could rip my clothes out of her hand at some point, because I was starting to get chilly with the draft from the air conditioning breathing down my bare back. And not to mention, Piper was probably wondering where I was.

"See, I heard differently. I heard you two were leaving a

room together the other night after I sent him on my errand."

"Your errand?" I asked, confused. *Was she the girl Cole messed around with? Who cares, Hayley! Grab your clothes!*

I inched toward her, but she was smarter than I gave her credit for. She laughed and handed my clothes off to one of her friends. *Dang it.*

"I sent him to teach Cole a lesson. See, Cole dissed me, and I knew that if I said he touched one of my friends without permission, Christian would go crazy. Especially considering Cole went to Wellington Prep." She threw her head back and cackled like a wicked witch.

"So, let me get this straight," I started, keeping my voice even. "You wanted to get with Cole, and he took a hard pass —can't say I blame him—and you told Christian...that he raped someone...just to get him beat up?" *What kind of world am I living in?*

It was pure silence in the locker room. So silent that you could hear the guys getting rowdy in their locker room through the vents.

Madeline shot me another dirty look, throwing her hair over her shoulder and popping her hip out. "I find it funny that you think you're in a position to judge someone, Hayley. Have you seen yourself? Your daddy got murdered because he was such a loser, and your own mother didn't want to take care of you. Save the judgments for yourself. You're likely to end up on a stripper pole, begging men to fuck you so you can feel worthy."

"Funny coming from someone who just tried to fuck a Wellington Prep boy."

It took every ounce of restraint I had in my body not to lay her flat on her ass. I envisioned it. Me pulling back my fist and punching her in her perfect, flawless face. Her body flying backwards and landing on the cool, concrete floor. But

I couldn't do that. If I got in trouble at this school, there would be no detention. There would be no punishment. I'd be kicked out. Back at Oakland High. Unable to get the hell out of this shitty town, and not to mention, back where Gabe was.

Instead of punching her lights out or giving her any satisfaction that she had wounded me, I put on a brave face, reached down and put on my Converse, and walked right past her and her fucked-up girl gang. If I showed one ounce of fear or hurt, these vultures would eat me alive. I made it seem like I wasn't affected by her words.

But I was.

They stung.

I'd been hit before, slapped around more than I cared to think about, but words? Those stuck with you.

Your own mother didn't want to take care of you. That was a true statement. She didn't. My own mother told me she hated me. *"It's your fault we're in this position. It's your fault your father is dead. He had it under control, and you had to go and call the police. Now look at us!"*

I shivered as the memory ran through my brain. My eyes glossed over, but I sucked the unshed tears back in.

What doesn't kill you makes you stronger.

And walking down the hall in search of clothes wasn't going to kill me.

Not today.

CHAPTER TWELVE

CHRISTIAN

MY FATHER HADN'T BEEN HOME for two weeks, except for a few hours last weekend. This was nothing out of the norm for Ollie and me, but lately, I'd been extra thankful for Ms. Porter. Once a week, when Ollie and I went to school, our maid/nanny/housekeeper, Ms. Porter, would come and do all the laundry in the house and make sure the fridge was stocked. It was a small gesture on my father's part to hire her a couple of years ago, and I was glad. I couldn't imagine slaving myself on the field, looking after Ollie's childish ass, *and* acting like a Stepford wife, busying myself with laundry and cooking at home. That was what I was thinking about when I began throwing on my shorts and shirt that I wore during practice. Two more weeks and we faced our biggest competitor, and Coach was working us so hard I didn't even have time to think about anything extra, let alone *do* anything extra.

Thank fuck. Even if I found football to be unavailing some days, at least it served as a welcomed distraction.

Out of nowhere, Kyle came flying into the locker room, slipping on his ass before sprinting up with a stunned look on his face. "HOLY SHIT."

"Did you forget your ADHD meds again, Voorhies?" A few of my teammates laughed, but I was being serious.

He looked at me, surprise still etched on his face. "I just saw New Girl walking down the hall in her bra and panties, rocking those kickass Converse she wears every day. I don't know where the fuck her uniform is, but *damn!* You all have to go look. My spank bank is now full of New Girl images."

Pure anger rose out of my chest, and I couldn't figure out if it was because Voorhies said his spank bank was filled with my old best friend or if it was because I was pissed that she was parading around the halls like a stripper. Regardless, it didn't matter. My legs were sprinting out of the locker room, not giving a shit that Coach was going to bitch that I was late for practice.

What the fuck is she thinking? Walking around my school half-naked. Jesus Christ.

I heard Ollie yell my name as guys tried to plow out of the locker room.

"I'll take care of this. Cover for me," I shouted back.

If it had been any other girl, I wouldn't have cared nearly as much, but Hayley? No. I was looking for a reason to get her kicked out of this school, and I thought I had just found it, especially with the tinge of jealousy that I just felt.

I knew what Ollie thought when I'd told him I'd take care of this. He thought I was trying to do damage control, to keep things under control and running smoothly like I'd done for the last two years in this school. After all, he had no idea how much I truly hated Hayley and wanted her gone. He didn't know what was said between us the other night. For all I knew, he thought we were making amends. Or hell, there was even a rumor going around that I was in there fucking her. Madeline would surely shut that down soon.

My blood pumped as I jogged the hallway, and when I rounded the corner, my breath hitched. My knees buckled. A perfect, round ass stared back at me. *Jesus. Christ.*

"What the hell are you doing?" I seethed as I caught up to her. I rested my hand on her forearm and quickly spun her around. Hayley yelped and jerked her arm out of my grasp and flew backwards into the lockers, a loud clang echoing in the hallway.

Fucking shit.

"Get in here," I chastised, opening the door to the stairwell. Hayley reluctantly followed me inside but put a clear distance between us. Her shoulders, which were bare besides a tiny strap from her bra, stiffened, but her face...it wasn't the brave, unemotional, bored expression she wore every time I caught her in the hallway. It wasn't the I-hate-the-world expression, either. She was wounded. There were worry lines around the crinkles of her eyes.

"What the fuck are you doing walking around like that?" I asked, placing my hands on my hips. "Do you want the entire school to see you half-naked? What is this? Proving something?"

She rolled her eyes. "What on earth would I be trying to prove by walking around like this?" She gestured to her body, and I couldn't keep my eyes off her. I traced the curve of her perky boobs down to her flat belly, and I had already gotten a glimpse of her ass. My chest grew tight, and I had to internally shake myself to remember who she was and what one look at her from across the room made me feel.

Guilt.

I felt even more guilty thinking she was the hottest thing I'd ever seen.

Because fucking shit, she was.

"Then what gives? Wanting to get kicked out of English Prep to put you out of your misery?" I asked, erasing a few feet she had put in between us.

"Why are you so concerned?" She erased the rest of the space between us, peering up into my face. "Afraid to see me go?"

I laughed sarcastically. "Quite the opposite. I'm marching your ass to Headmaster Walton's office right now. I just wanted to be present when he booted you back to Oakland High."

Something flickered across her face. *Fear?* I recognized that look. Her blue eyes grew distant, her arms going around her middle. She nibbled on her bottom lip, and naturally, my eyes zeroed in on them.

"*No,*" she breathed out, keeping her gaze fixed to mine.

For a moment, I forgot I hated her. It was like I was under a trance, under the same spell she had put on the rest of the guys in this school. They all talked about her—no longer in front of me after I threatened them all, but there was still distant chatter. Hayley was mysterious, different. But she'd always been that way to me. *Different.* In the best of ways.

But I no longer knew Hayley, and she no longer knew me.

"*Yes,*" I ground out. "I want you gone, Hayley." *Scratch that. I need her gone.* "Now, you and I are going to walk to Headmaster Walton's office, and I'm going to tell him I found you trying to seduce the guys on the football team by walking around like that." I pointed with my chin down to her body. "And then you'll be gone. My word against yours, and we both know I'm the powerful one here."

She let out a hiccup of air. "I can't go back to Oakland High. I know you hate me. But I can't go back there, Christian."

Why did hearing my name on her lips cause a war inside

my body? It erased the past, jumbled up the present, and somehow predicted the future.

Hayley's pink-tinged cheeks were now ghostly white. Her blue eyes were no longer distant, but instead, wide-eyed and crazed with fear.

Her words rushed out. "I know something; something you'll want to know. But I'll only tell you if you keep this under wraps and let me stay."

Intriguing, yes. Worth me letting her go scot-free and having to deal with seeing her face every day, given what it does to me? No. "I'll decide after you tell me," I countered, still towering over her. At least from this angle, I could keep my eyes on her face and not her body. Teenage hormones were a goddamn bitch sometimes. My dick didn't care that I hated her. In fact, it made her even more tempting.

She thought for a moment and realized she didn't have another choice.

"Madeline was the one who took my clothes." Her tongue darted out to lick her lips. She kept her eyes off mine as she spoke. "She said she found out we were in a room alone together at the Wellington Prep party....and..." Hayley swallowed, crossing her arms over her pink bra.

"And what?"

"She said she made up the part about Cole messing with her friend so you'd beat him up."

I laughed. "You're lying."

She shook her head, her dark hair covering her face for a moment before she looked at me. "She said Cole passed her up and she wanted to get back at him, and she knew you'd react if she told you he messed with one of her friends...*inappropriately*."

I paused, thought for a moment, and then my blood began to boil even hotter than it did when I saw Hayley a few moments ago.

Before I knew what I was doing, I was ripping the shirt off my back and flinging it toward her. She hesitantly took it with a shaky hand.

"Put it on."

She didn't even think twice. After she pulled it over her slender body, moving her hair to the side, I put my hand underneath her chin and brought her gaze up to mine.

"This means *nothing*."

She tore her face from my grasp and all but snarled at me.

I left her alone in the stairwell and tried to calm myself before getting back to practice.

I still hated Hayley Smith with all of my might, but maybe even a little more now because I knew what she looked like underneath her school uniform. And let me tell you, it was far better than what my twelve-year-old self conjured up before she left town.

The next day of school came too quickly. After practice last night, I went straight home and holed myself up in my bedroom, even through Ollie's protests and asking what had happened with Hayley. He tried to get a rise out of me by asking, *"Did she look as hot as Kyle said she did?"* I gave him a death glare and slammed the door in his face.

I had to dissect my thoughts. I tossed around a stupid kid's basketball from the hoop I got for my tenth birthday. My room was the same as it was then: a blue comforter, navy walls, the pitiful basketball hoop on the back of my closet door. Nothing in our house had changed since Mom died. Not even her vanity with her expensive jewelry. Dad wasn't home enough to even care, or maybe that was why he wasn't home to begin with. Too many reminders. I understood that; I couldn't even stomach going in their room.

It felt wrong to change anything in the house, and as vast and expansive as it was, it was easy to hide out in my bedroom alone.

I tried to shove away my thoughts of Hayley and focus more on Madeline. *What to do, what to do.* It didn't bother me at all that she was fucking with someone else—or attempting to. We weren't exclusive and were never in an actual relationship, and I hadn't fucked her in a long, long time. She hadn't sucked my dick in a while, either. But to lie to me and tell me he fucked with one of her friends so I'd beat his ass so she'd have a way to retaliate? That was crossing a fucking line.

Did he deserve to get his ass beat? After seeing him try to man-handle Hayley, probably. And who knew, maybe he had fucked with a girl against her will a time or two, but it sent me straight to the red at the thought of me plummeting my fist into his face over the fact that he didn't want Madeline's pussy. The entire situation made me look like a complete fucking idiot, and that didn't sit well with me.

It also didn't sit well with me that I took Hayley's word right off the bat. I knew she wasn't lying to me, and the fact that I didn't feel the need to fact-check her story proved a small part of me trusted her, which went against everything I stood for when it came to her.

I needed her gone, and the one chance I got, I forfeited it.

I looked over at her in class this morning, waiting for the familiar feeling of anger to pop up. I needed that feeling of resentment to seep in so I could bask in the comfort of knowing our up-close-and-personal conversation yesterday meant nothing. *Remember, she started the spiral, Christian. She was the start of it all.*

The past tried to creep into my head, begging me to remember who she was before everything happened.

She tucked her hair behind her ear, showing off her naturally pink-tinted cheeks and clean face. She reached up and adjusted the little bow tied around her neck, scratching at the material. I hated that she was so mesmerizing. Was it the mysterious vibe she held? Was it because she was a little rough around the edges but also had a sort of silent beauty about her? Or was it because she appeared perfect on the outside, but I knew she was tainted with flaws on the inside?

I wasn't the only one in the room staring at her. Voorhies was licking his lips while tracing his eyes up and down her body, and Clayton and Zach had their heads huddled together, whispering about her. Annoyance slithered up, and I shoved my book off my desk and onto the floor, causing a loud bang to go throughout the room. All eyes were on me, and I gave each of them a glare. Voorhies rolled his eyes, but Zach and Clayton were oblivious to my nonverbal threat. *Quit fucking looking at her, and quit fucking lusting over her,* my eyes said. I slowly slid my gaze back over to her, and she was staring at my book on the floor. Her rosy cheeks were replaced with a whiteness that matched her shirt. She let out a shaky breath.

My eyebrows clustered together as I bent down to gather my book. Ollie had a smirk on his face and eyed me suspiciously. I ignored him as I came upright at my desk again.

Class hadn't even started yet when Ms. Boyd buzzed into the intercom and asked for me, Ollie, and Hayley to come to the office. Hayley's head snapped over to mine, and I swore, the blue hue of her eyes was replaced with a simmering red. I knew what she thought. She thought I went back on my word, that I told Headmaster Walton about the half-naked debacle from yesterday. Her eyes portrayed just that.

As soon as the three of us were out of the classroom,

whispers floating all around us, Hayley jerked in front of me and poked my chest. "I guess I should have listened to you when you said nothing had changed!"

I looked down at her finger on my chest, poking my tie, and then back at her face. I smirked. I had no idea why the three of us were called down to the office, as I didn't tell Headmaster Walton anything. In fact, no one really knew anything other than Hayley and me, but letting her sweat was fun.

I liked seeing her bothered.

Hayley backed away slowly, the anger receding rapidly. Ollie stood and looked back and forth between us, trying to figure us out. Hayley began to shake her head, wrapping her arms around her body. She mumbled, "Shit." Then her gaze traveled to her shoes. I followed her every move. My ears perked for more of her mumbling. "I can't go back there. I'll just have to ask Ann to transfer me. She'll understand."

"She'll understand what?" I asked, divulging in her hidden world. The need to know more was eating at me. I liked control, and Hayley was too far out of reach.

"None of your business!" she all but shouted. Hayley took several breaths, but it was almost as if she were gasping for air. Ollie took a step closer to her cautiously, toeing the tiles one by one until he was right in front of her.

He looked at me, and his worried expression bugged me. I growled, striding to the pair of them and stopping right in front of her. "She's having a panic attack."

Ollie kept his eyes on her. "I know." Then, he brought his attention to me for a second. "I recognize it. She's doing exactly what you used to do."

My teeth clanged together. I hated thinking about a time when I was the weaker link. For a year after Mom passed, I'd have random panic attacks. My heart would speed up, viciously trying to climb right out of my chest, my vision would get spotty, and I couldn't breathe. Ollie was always the one to calm me. He was my anchor.

"Hayley." He bent down to her level. She somehow slid to the floor and had her back resting along the lockers. "Tell me something you smell."

Her breathing was still rapid, her chest rising and falling quickly. I found my own chest rising a little faster, watching her.

Ollie spoke again. "Hayley, focus!"

It was like Ollie wasn't even there. My pulse quickened with every passing second. I was becoming more and more bothered at the sight of her. I thought back to her file that I had momentarily stolen. *Did it say anything about Oakland High? What the fuck happened there?*

Finally, I could no longer take it. I bent down and snapped my fingers. "Hayley!"

Just like that, she jerked her chin and met my eye. "Tell me something you smell."

Through her gasps, she said, "Wh—what?"

I drove my eyes into hers. "What do you smell?"

"Woodsy...pine... cologne. *You*."

I nodded. "Tell me something you feel."

Her breaths became a little steadier. "Cool tiles." Her fingers brushed over the floor.

"Tell me something you see."

"You. I see you."

We stared at each other. Her eyes connected to mine, mine connected to hers. The color was coming back to her face, and her body became more relaxed. Her breaths evened out. *There you are.*

"You good now, Scrapper?" Ollie asked. *Shit. I forgot he was here.*

I stood up quickly and fought the urge to run in the other direction. Hayley nodded, peering up into his face. She slowly gathered herself and pulled herself up using his hand, smoothing out her not-long-enough skirt. My eyes lingered on her legs for a fraction too long. That didn't sit well with me, either. None of this did.

Shit. Maybe I should tell the headmaster that she tried to seduce the football team and get her a one-way ticket out of English Prep. *No, not before figuring out what she's so damn afraid of at Oakland High.*

Her voice was soft, like a feather floating to the ground. "Yeah, thanks. I'm fine."

"So, what the fuck are we all three doing going to the headmaster's office?" Ollie asked as he stepped back, giving Hayley some space.

She puffed a lock of hair out of her face. "Ask him."

I scowled in her direction. "Fuck if I know. I didn't go to him like you think."

A sarcastic laugh fell out of her mouth. "I don't believe you. You'd do anything to get me out of your *kingdom.*"

Ollie threw his head back and howled with laughter. "Kingdom?"

She crossed her arms. "Not my words. But regardless, Christian likes to think he's the king of this school, so..."

I snarled. "Well, if the crown fucking fits..."

Ollie laughed harder this time, and I pushed past both of them, heading straight to the headmaster's office.

I glanced back and saw that he had flung his arm over her shoulders as they trailed me. *He better not even think of befriending her.* She was the enemy, and that was how it had to stay.

CHAPTER THIRTEEN

HAYLEY

MY LEG BOUNCED up and down as I sat beside Ollie in the waiting area. Christian was asked to go into Headmaster Walton's office alone, so Ollie and I had to stay out here.

If I had to go back to Oakland High and be around Gabe, I'd lose it. This wasn't even about not getting into an Ivy League, or scholarships, or the great faculty recommendations from a school like English Prep. This was wholeheartedly based around survival. The mere thought of being around Gabe sent me straight into a spiral of panic.

"So, why does my brother hate you?" Ollie whispered as he kept his eyes on Ms. Boyd who kept glancing at us from atop her tiny, gold-framed glasses.

"He didn't tell you?" I whispered back, my leg still bouncing.

Ollie placed his palm on my leg to stop it from jiggling. Normally, a random touch from someone would have made me recoil, but with Ollie, all it did was calm me. Ollie had always been the sweet brother, the caring one. Whereas Christian was the hothead who never backed down from a fight, Ollie was the one who thought things through. He always seemed to have a plan back when we were kids. "Not a single word. But that's not surprising. Christian isn't exactly an open book. Never has been—and especially not after Mom died."

I thought back to when we were younger. Ollie was cute and constantly wanted to hang out with Christian and me. His light hair was usually messy, and his face was always stained with dirt. He'd had crooked teeth, but those were fixed now. I didn't think anyone could deny that he was attractive. He and Christian didn't look a whole lot alike, but they were both cut from the same perfect stone.

My heart ached. "I'm sorry about your mom, Ollie."

His hand squeezed my leg gently. "I'm sorry about your dad."

"Ollie?" I asked, feeling a bit braver around him than I did with Christian.

He tipped his chin after checking to make sure Ms. Boyd wasn't looking at us.

"What did I have to do with your mother's death?"

"What?"

"Christian said that I was the start of it all. How?"

Ollie's eyebrows drew together. "He said that?"

I nodded, but before I could elaborate any further, Headmaster Walton's door flew open, and Christian walked out looking like the hot, smug bastard he was. His eyes instantly fell to Ollie's hand on my leg, and I could have sworn his nostrils flared, but I didn't dare look him in the eye. Not only was I embarrassed I had a slight breakdown in front of him, but even more so as his voice was the only thing I could focus on to get me to calm down. Talk about pathetic.

The headmaster appeared behind Christian. "Ms. Smith, I'd like to talk to you for a moment. Ollie, you're free to go back to class with Christian, but in the future, please don't punch your teammates while they're trying to leave the locker room, even if you are trying to protect someone's privacy."

Someone = me.

I hurriedly stood up, Ollie's hand falling from my leg. I passed by Christian without sparing him a glance.

This could go either way. Christian could have walked in there and told Headmaster Walton a lie, and I'd be getting thrown out of English Prep, or he could have told the truth, and Madeline would make my life a living hell.

I wasn't sure which was the better option at this point.

"Ms. Smith, please take a seat."

Sinking down into the leather chair, I felt my heart slide to the ground. Headmaster Walton waltzed over to his seat and sat down, smoothing his hand over his tie. "I was made aware of the little situation that occurred yesterday."

This is it. I'm getting thrown out of English Prep.

"I want you to fully understand the severity of this." I began to nod as he continued. "Bullying is not okay. I will be having words with Madeline later today about stealing your uniform, and if something like this occurs again, please make it a priority to tell me. Or Christian."

Or Christian? I would most definitely not be telling either of them, but especially not Christian.

"I understand," I answered. My chest was beginning to feel less constricted. "So, just to be clear, I'm not getting thrown out of English Prep?"

Headmaster Walton gave me a genuine smile and shook his head. "No, and I'm very pleased with what your teachers have been saying about you, Ms. Smith. You've been here for two weeks and they're already saying you're one of the brightest students they've ever had."

Pride swelled in my chest, and it felt good. It soothed the panic and distress I'd been feeling just moments ago. I'd had a whirlwind of emotions today, and it was only nine in the morning.

"You may be dismissed back to class now. Stop at Ms. Boyd's desk, and she'll write you a note."

I gave him a small smile and stood up, smoothing out my skirt. "Oh, and Hayley?"

"Yes?" I asked.

"Madeline and her parents will be paying for a new uniform if she can't seem to locate the one she stole yesterday. And"—he looked down at my folder for a moment—"I do need to report this incident to your social worker. I just wanted to inform you."

I ground my teeth and gave him a curt nod.

Great.

Piper pulled up to the curb and put her car in park. We'd spent the entire drive to my house dissecting Christian and my slight meltdown.

"I hate to say it, Hay."

I unbuckled my seatbelt, leery of her expression. "What?"

Her pink lip curved upward. "I think Christian *wants* to hate you...but he can't."

I scoffed. "He definitely hates me, Piper. Trust me."

The cold, demeaning stare he gave me the first day he saw me proved that much. Yes, he talked me out of a panic attack earlier, and yes, he very well could have had me thrown out of English Prep this morning if he really wanted, but he still hated me. In fact, he basically told me so.

"Who is that?" I followed Piper's line of sight and sunk back into the passenger seat.

I groaned. "Ugh. That's Ann. My social worker."

Her mouth formed an O. "She looks nice."

Ann was on the nice side—for social workers, that was. She was actually the nicest social worker I'd ever had. After the incident with Gabe, they replaced my old social worker, Daniel, with Ann. They thought I'd respond better to a woman versus a man, and they were right.

I still didn't let myself get too close to her, though. It wasn't like she was trying to be my fairy godmother or anything. She was only in charge of me because the state said so. Confiding in a social worker was a lot like crying wolf. You couldn't complain about much of anything because no one would believe you, and not to mention, it usually made things worse.

You'd just continue to suffer, *alone,* until you aged out.

"I gotta go in there and do damage control. She's probably filling in Asshole One and Two about Madeline taking my clothes and the 'bullying'."

Madeline didn't so much as spare me a glance for the rest of the day, but I knew she wanted to. I could sense her anger from across the cafeteria and even more so during our classes together. A mysterious dodgeball hit me in the head during PE, too, and I was certain it was from her.

Piper gave me a comforting smile. "Okay, well, email me later if you get bored after homework and stuff. Or maybe, like, be a normal teenager and create a social media account, and we can chat on there."

I gave her a fake laugh and climbed out of her car. Social media wasn't the safest thing for someone like me to utilize, but I wasn't about to say that to her. Instead, I bent down at the last second. "I'll wash your uniform and give it back after Madeline replaces mine."

She shook her auburn hair out. "Don't worry about it. I have, like, five hundred uniforms. Keep it in case you find yourself walking down the hall half-naked again." I glanced down at the skirt, and she interjected. "*But* if it makes you feel better giving it back, that's fine, too."

This time I smiled for real. "Now you're learning."

She laughed as I slammed the door and crossed the street. I glanced back once at Piper and watched her fading headlights. I took a deep breath but paused before I went inside to face Ann, Pete, and Jill. My eyes zeroed in on an all-blacked-out Escalade parked at the end of the road.

Talk about sticking out like a sore thumb. This was a shitty neighborhood. I was half-worried Piper's car would get messed with the night I snuck out to the party.

I rolled my eyes as I continued to stall. *Go on and get it over with.*

I squared my shoulders, flipped my dark hair out of my face, and went inside.

"Oh, great. You're back from school." Ann stood up from the couch and dusted her skirt off. *If only she knew that Jill had sucked Pete off in that exact spot a few days ago.* My body shivered at the thought. *Gross.*

"Hi." Old cigarette smoke burnt my nostrils as I walked through the threshold. Pete was all but glaring at me, no doubt pissed that Ann had stopped by. His hair was as greasy as the engine oil on his mechanic's shirt. Jill wasn't home; she must have been on second shift at the nursing home today.

"I just came to check in with Pete. I had a call from Headmaster Walton this morning."

Silence erupted throughout the room. Pete was still staring daggers in my direction. Ann was waiting for me to say something, but I kept my mouth shut. I had learned that it was always better to say nothing at all.

"Pete said he had no idea you were getting bullied at

English Prep." She shot him a displeased look, and he brought his eyes to the floor.

Trying to cover my tracks with him, I shrugged. "It was the first time, so I didn't tell him or Jill. It's not a big deal. I've handled worse."

Ann walked toward me. "Why don't you and I go out front to talk?"

She brushed past me, her flowery scent a nice break in the stale-cigarette smell from Pete. I flicked my eyes to his, and he glowered at me. *He was definitely mad. Great.*

The screen door slammed when I stepped onto the porch. Ann had her arms crossed over her yellow blouse with her phone and keys clenched in her hands. "So, how are things really, Hayley? You obviously don't want to talk in front of Pete, which has red flags popping up everywhere."

I could sense Pete staring at me through the screen door without even looking. The cold rawness in his glare seconds ago felt like a snake wrapping around my neck and cutting off my circulation.

"Things are fine, Ann. I'd tell you if they weren't. Pete and Jill are great foster parents. I didn't tell them about Madeline because it wasn't that big of a deal."

She stared at me, her mouth in a straight line. I looked away before she could see right through me. *Hmm. The Escalade is gone.* Drug deal?

"Who is this Christian boy the headmaster talked about? Seemed like he had your best interest at heart. Boyfriend?"

I laughed out loud, cutting my attention back to Ann. Not only was it funny that she thought Christian was my boyfriend, but also because she was obviously trying hard to find a common ground with me so I'd trust her. *No, Ann. We're not going to talk boys together like we're besties.*

"We should cut the bullshit, Ann."

She leveled me with a stare. "I agree. So, tell me, how is it really living here?"

Why was she doing this? Why was she acting like she cared or that she had some magical wand that would change the way my life was?

"Does it matter?" I asked, shifting on my feet. I reached up and untied the bow around my neck, sliding it from my skin. The autumn breeze gave me goosebumps.

Ann's face softened. Her mouth set into a frown. "Of course it matters, Hayley."

I laughed sarcastically as I looked out into the near-empty street again, Pete's beat-up truck sitting close to the curb. "No, it doesn't, Ann. You heard the judge. If I mess this up, I'm going to a group home. I turn eighteen next month. If I'm in a group home when I age out, there is no going back. They don't keep you when you turn eighteen. I'll still get a small chunk of money from the state, but the group home won't take it as room and board. Jill and Pete are my last hope; they'll take my stipend money and let me stay until college. Even if things *were* terrible here"—I gave her a pointed look, raising my voice—"which they aren't, there is no other option. So, with that said, things are just dandy. The best house I've been in yet. School is a breeze. The end."

The muscles along her heart-shaped face teetered back and forth. She knew I was right. This *was* my last chance. I had no other options. It was torture knowing things could slip right out of my grasp if the wrong move was made, but it had been like that for the last five years.

I could be sent back to Oakland High with the snap of Christian's finger. One mess up and the headmaster would likely turn his back on me. One wrong move with Jill and Pete and I could end up homeless before I even graduated high school. I felt like I was constantly teetering back and forth over a cliff.

Ann inched a little closer to me and whispered, knowing very well that Pete was probably listening, "If it gets bad enough, Hayley...tell me. I'll do everything I can to help you. You know that, right?"

I wanted to believe her. I really, really did. I was desperate to believe her. But I'd been burned one too many times.

"Yes," I answered. Then I turned around and walked through the front door and waited for her to leave as I stood back and watched through the window.

Part of me wanted to dart up to my room, but instead, I stayed in the living room with Pete, wanting to get it over with. I knew he'd have something to say. There was no point in running.

I kept my gaze on the glossy window, feeling the devil behind my back. "Spit it out, Pete. I have homework to do."

My heart beat fiercely; my skin prickled with fear. I didn't know why I mouthed off, but I suddenly wished I could suck the words back in.

"She didn't believe a fucking word you said. Now she's going to be checking in every other fucking day." Pete grew closer to me, his voice loud and mean.

I spun around and leveled his sweaty face with a glare. "Let's be real here. I could have told her that you have your wife suck your dick every night while I'm in the next room. Or I could have told her that you lock me in my room like some caged animal. Or maybe I could have told her that you only feed me leftover scraps from dinner and that you drink beer all night long and slap Jill around." Pete's face was redder than a tomato, his eyes blazing with anger. "But I didn't. I didn't because I need you just as much as you need me."

He spat as he yelled, "I don't need you. You're an ungrateful little bitch. I could have you kicked out of here and replace you with a new foster kid if I wanted."

I tilted my head and narrowed my eyes. "But could you

really, Pete? I'm guessing you've been under suspicion before, which is why they placed *me* with you. The girl that no one wanted. I was your last resort." My mouth kept rambling even though my brain was screaming at me to stop before he snapped. "What is it? What do you need the foster money for? Gambling? Some kind of crazy debt? You better watch yourself. Debt is what got my dad killed."

I saw him lose it right in front of me. His eyes grew crazed, and I knew I'd just awakened the beast. The smart thing would have been to put some kind of barrier between us, but I didn't. Before I could even think to defend myself, he swept me off my feet and kicked my ribs while I was down on the dirty floor. I yelled out a grunt as his boot connected with my side. I curled into a ball, knowing very well that I needed to stay down. He was much bigger than me. Even if I got back to my feet, he'd easily knock me down again.

My side burned with raging pain. Tears threatened to spill at the corners of my eyes. I bit my lower lip to stop it from trembling.

Pete bent down, but I kept my vision on the couch leg, not daring to look up at him. "You have it backwards. You need me much more than I need you. Mouth off again and I'll throw you out on your ass faster than you can say your farewell." Pete stormed away, stomping to the kitchen. I heard the fridge door clank open and the pop of a beer tab.

He shouted, "Door's getting locked at seven tonight. And no fucking dinner."

I slowly pulled myself up and grabbed my bag, basically limping upstairs.

Not one single tear was shed. Not even from the dull ache in my side or from the fast-approaching purple bruise.

I didn't cry for men like him.

I didn't cry when my father died.

I didn't cry when Gabe proved to be someone he wasn't.

I didn't cry when Christian told me he hated me.

And I wasn't going to cry because Pete kicked me like I was a dog.

Instead, I opened up my laptop, finished my homework, and applied to another college far, far away from this town.

CHAPTER FOURTEEN

CHRISTIAN

MY ROOM WAS pitch black when I tore my eyes open. I knew what day it was, but I had no intention of indulging in it. Birthdays lost their meaning over time, and it was the one thing Mom always went all out on. She may have been absent every other day of the year, but when Ollie's and my birthdays came around, she pulled out all the stops.

I used to look forward to the chocolatey cake and her high-pitched voice singing "Happy Birthday." My father would even join in on the occasion. But today, the only thing I was looking forward to, at least right now, was the coffee waiting for me downstairs.

As soon as I reached the kitchen in my drowsy state, I paused. There was a steaming pot of coffee already brewed. *Ollie?* I guessed it *would* be nice of him to actually get himself up to make coffee on my birthday. His silent gift to me, knowing very well I hated celebrating.

"Mornin', son."

My hand froze in mid-air as I reached for a mug.

"Happy birthday," he said, coming further into the kitchen.

I inhaled and poured my coffee before turning around. "Thanks. Didn't know you knew when my birthday was or that you'd be home today."

My father was wearing a plain T-shirt and running shorts, like he was about to go for a run. Maybe that was his norm? Wake up. Get coffee. Run. I wouldn't know. He wasn't here long enough for me to pinpoint a routine.

He sat at the breakfast bar and placed his hands on the marble top. "I didn't want to miss your birthday. It's the big one. The big eighteen." He grinned, ignoring my first comment. "I remember when I turned eighteen. I thought I was on top of the world. Finally an adult." He glanced down and shook his head back and forth. Then, he brought his attention to me. "I was nothing like you at age eighteen. I was an immature kid who felt he was entitled to everything."

I took a gulp of my coffee, ignoring the way it burnt my mouth and the desperate attempt of my father trying to have a conversation with me.

"Your mother never wanted to spoil you and Ollie. She wanted to make sure you two weren't entitled to everything. Materialistic. I've probably failed a little at that in the last few years, but you really don't ask for much." A smile reached his eyes. "You're everything your mother would have wanted you to be. You're mature beyond your years. You've been that way since the moment your mom passed."

I clanked my teeth together hard. This was not on my list of things to talk about at 6:30 in the fucking morning—or ever.

Resentment was creeping down my limbs; words I didn't want to say were on the tip of my tongue. I squeezed my eyes shut for a moment, and when they opened, I saw something I'd never truly seen before. My father was a shell of a man. I used to look up to him. The days he would come home from a business trip were my all-time favorite. I'd no longer be the man of the house, which was what he'd always told me when he departed for a trip. The second he was home, he'd dote on Mom, wait on her hand and foot. Her cheeks would be rosy from blushing, and her smile would be as bright as the sun. He'd spend nights wrestling with me and Ollie and let us stay up past our bedtime playing football in the backyard. Then he'd leave again on another trip, and things would go back to normal.

And then the crash happened, and nothing was ever normal again.

Maybe it affected him more than I gave him credit for. But that didn't excuse his lack of parenting. It didn't justify his decision to forget about his sons. Ollie and I had raised ourselves. He put a roof over our head, paid someone to clean the house and fill the pantry, gave us expensive cars and phones and a credit card with a hefty limit on it, but that wasn't what we needed, especially after Mom died.

My father kept talking, but I was too busy pushing my thoughts away to hear what he had said. I came in on the tail end of the conversation.

"Ollie said that's what you wanted, so I'll go ahead and install it while you're in school. I thought maybe I'd stay for your game, too, before going back to China for the week."

I drew my eyebrows together. "Ollie said I wanted what? And you're staying for our game?"

"The new gaming system. Isn't that what you wanted?"

I chuckled, feeling some of my anger loosen. I took another sip of my coffee. "I know you're never truly present when you're home, but you should know by now that I'd never want something like a gaming system for my birthday. That's something Ollie would want."

My dad shook his head. "That little shit."

I laughed, and for a moment, things seemed normal. Things seemed *all right*. My dad and me, sitting in the kitchen, drinking coffee and laughing about my younger brother. The only thing missing was Mom. It was such a small glimpse of the life we didn't have, but it felt good while it lasted.

Ollie popped downstairs, already wearing his uniform, freshly showered and ready to go. "Who's a little shit?" He slid past me and my father, searching for something to eat in the fridge. He opted for a premade breakfast smoothie that lined the shelves inside.

"You," my dad and I said at the same time.

I walked over to him and plucked the smoothie out of his hands. He yelled, but I smacked him upside the head. "Thanks for the gaming system. I'll make sure you never use it."

"Oh, now come on!" he whined, throwing his hands out. "I knew you'd say you wanted nothing for your birthday like you've been doing for the last three years. Why let a perfect birthday go to waste?"

My dad listened to Ollie and me banter back and forth for a while before he excused himself to go on his run. As soon as he was out the door, Ollie snapped his head over to me. "What got into him? He never cares when it's one of our birthdays. Gets a lame gift and has someone from the store wrap it."

I shrugged, finishing off the smoothie. "I don't know, and I don't really care."

Ollie's face remained unreadable. "You're too hard on him sometimes."

I said nothing in response. Ollie wasn't nearly as pissed off at our father as I was. I was the cold son; he was the warm one. That was how it had been since Mom died.

"I heard him say he was coming to the game Friday."

I shrugged, clearly wanting to put a cease and desist order on the conversation.

Ollie ran his hand through his hair. "I don't think he's watched us play a single game since before..." I let out a hefty breath as he paused. It'd been four years since Mom died, and Ollie still struggled to say the words, and I did, too, at times. Four years was a long time, relatively speaking, but time didn't work that way when it came to death. Those memories surfaced whenever they wanted, and they cut just the same.

"Okay...onto better things," he started, shutting down the previous conversation. "I...wanna know..."—Ollie was dragging his words out in a sing-song voice that made him sound like a little schoolgirl—"why you told Hayley it was her fault Mom died, and also, I'd like to know what the fuck happened between you two in the stairwell."

I began to shake my head, but Ollie's voice grew stern—something he was never described as. "Before you say 'nothing' and brush me off again, just know I won't stop pestering you. Every single moment of every single day, I'll ask again and again." He dipped his head down. "And you know how annoying I can be."

I rested my arms on top of the marble counter, hanging my head. *For fuck's sake.* "Madeline lied. Cole didn't rape her friend or try to do anything like that. He dissed her when she made a pass at him, and she wanted to get even. That was what Hayley told me, and she only told me because I agreed not to tell the headmaster a lie that would get her kicked out of English Prep. Madeline stole her clothes because she's goddamn psycho."

Ollie paused, taking in my words, and then threw his head back and laughed. "Madeline *is* a goddamn psycho. What are you going to do?"

I ran my hand feebly down my face. "I'm gonna embarrass the fuck out of her tonight at the birthday party you put together."

He groaned, smacking his hand on the counter. "It was supposed to be a surprise! Who told you?"

I snickered, walking out of the kitchen. Over my shoulder, I yelled, "You just did, *idiot*."

He shouted back. "Don't think I don't know that you're avoiding the first question. I'll keep pestering you, brother. And I'm nothing but determined."

I ignored him as he yelled through the bathroom door as I showered and again when I got dressed. I also ignored him the entire drive to school as he drove beside me the entire time, waving his hands out the window. Every time I looked at him, he'd mouth the words *Tell me!*

He was the most annoying fucking person on this planet.

Once we got to school and in with our group of friends, he finally stopped asking. I'd never been more thankful to be surrounded by a group of people than in that moment.

In the middle of gathering some books out of my locker, everyone chatting around me, I heard Eric say, "Happy birthday to our king." When I shut my locker and turned my head over to him slightly, I saw he was on his knee, bowing in front of me, causing everyone to laugh.

"Get up, fucker." I smirked, shaking my head.

"The birthday boy's party is gonna be *lit* tonight. Right after we give Kerrington High a run for their money."

I fist-bumped him and nodded. Madeline was down the hall with her friends, and she gave me a wink. I winked back, even though an angry fire was erupting inside. I had to play nice until tonight when I brought her down to her knees. The queen of the school was now on the king's shit list. She may even have stolen the number one hate spot from Hayley.

And speak of the china doll herself. I'd been pushing her out of my head since yesterday morning when she'd accused me of telling Headmaster Walton about her little half-naked show. I didn't want to think about her or continue to picture her with her bra and panties on while I jerked off in the shower. I wanted to hate her and be done with it. So that was what I tried to focus on. I was no longer trying to figure her out. I was ignoring her and hating her all together.

She didn't exist.

Therefore, the guilt didn't exist.

But... I kept my face stoic, pretending I was listening to Eric and Ollie going on about making jungle juice for the party. There was talk about potential lap dances lined up for me, alone time in the hot tub with Madeline (Ollie laughed at that idea), and yet, my eyes still wandered over to Hayley.

Snow White. That was the perfect nickname for her. A porcelain Snow White doll. Dark hair. Fair skin. Ruby lips that were naturally stained that color.

I kept watching as the redhead that seemed to be Hayley's friend placed her hand on Hayley's wrist. Their heads were huddled together. Hayley was trying to brush something off. She shook her head and shrugged a few times. Then, I watched as her friend reached for Hayley's uniform shirt. It was half untucked before Hayley took a step back and bristled. She looked around the hallway, seeing if anyone had noticed. Her eyes caught mine, and they grew wide. Then, she looked back at her friend and grabbed her arm, dragging her to the bathroom.

It was like I was sucked into a reality show titled "What Was Hayley Smith Up To?"

"Enjoying the show, brother?" Ollie was standing beside me now, his voice low.

I snapped my attention to him. His green eyes danced with humor.

"Fuck off," I said as I stormed down the hall and entered

my first class, bypassing Madeline, and her crew, and
everyone who wished me a happy birthday.

It took everything I had not to rip open the door of the
girl's bathroom to see what Hayley's friend was so persistent
about and why she was lifting her shirt.

I wanted to bang my head off the wall. *Why the fuck am I
thinking about the girl that drives me to the edge of insanity?*

That was what I was.

Insane.

We had almost lost the game tonight. Coach yelled—mainly
at me—because we were fucking up passes left and right. He
pulled me aside after the locker room was empty, everyone
already on their way to Eric's parents' cabin for the party.

"Where the hell was your head at tonight, Christian?"
His red-rimmed eyes were laced with anger and disappoint-
ment. He rubbed the scruff on his face. "You're lucky the
scouts weren't here tonight. You've got scholarships to think
about. What the hell was that?"

I knew what it was. My chest grew tight. My shoulders
tensed. I wanted to throw my Nikes on and go for a three-
mile run in the cool October air so I could clear my head,
stop thinking about Hayley, and chill the hell out.

All day I watched her. I couldn't stop myself. I saw her
wince during lunch. I watched as she and her friend talked
with their heads jammed together like they were sharing
secrets. There were big bags underneath her eyes. Something
was off with her, and this weird, fucked-up part of me
couldn't think straight until I knew what.

I had no idea why. Maybe it was because I felt like Hayley
was out of my control. She stirred something up inside of me,
and it drove me mad. Or maybe it was because there was a

time when I would have done anything to protect the girl that made me feel alive.

Coach barked at me again, and I cleared my thoughts. I said the first thing that came to mind. "My dad was supposed to show tonight, but he ditched at the last minute. Had to catch an earlier flight. That's why I was playing like shit. My head was preoccupied. It won't happen again."

"You're damn right it won't. Next week is our game against Oakland High. Scouts will be here. The good ones. You need to play your very best." He grabbed my shoulder and gave it a squeeze. "If anything, make *me* proud."

I gave him a curt nod and threw my shirt over my head, and we both exited the locker room. Once I was out by my car, underneath the darkened sky scattered with nighttime stars, I stared out into the abyss. *There is no room in your head for Hayley. Not tonight.*

And just like that, I pushed her away and climbed in my car. I was going to Eric's for my birthday, and after I brutally shamed Madeline for being a world-class bitch and a terrible human being, I was going to let go and have fun. I was getting back to the old version of myself—the one who didn't allow himself to get preoccupied with the past.

CHAPTER FIFTEEN

CHRISTIAN

ERIC'S CABIN was at full capacity. His parents had just as much money as my father did, so their lake cabin was bigger than most people's homes. His parents knew we used it as a party spot, and as long as we cleaned up the next day and things didn't get broken, they didn't give any fucks. Perks of having detached, wealthy parents.

When I walked in, the entire room full of people yelled "surprise" which was stupid considering it wasn't a surprise party. Eric came out of the kitchen and yelled, "YEE HAW. The birthday boy is here! Time to drop your panties, girls."

I rolled my eyes as a smirk inched its way onto my face. And not to my surprise, several girls appeared in front of me, lifting their shirts and flashing me their tits. I cocked an eyebrow, giving each girl an equal amount of attention, and then I sauntered off to the kitchen to grab a drink. Ollie was standing there with his back against the counter, wearing a black t-shirt. He was talking to Bristol, a pussy he often frequented when he was in between girls.

Once he saw me, he lifted his cheek. "Happy birthday, bro. Madeline is in the living room, waiting for you."

My face twitched. *Show time. I'll teach her to fuck with Hayley and me.*

My steps faltered as Hayley entered my mind. *No, Madeline doesn't fuck with me.* She could fuck with Hayley anytime she wanted. I didn't care.

Ollie whispered something in Bristol's ear, and before I knew it, she was going around and gathering everyone to follow me into the living room. Madeline was sitting on the couch, a drink in her hand, wearing a scandalous outfit that showed her flat midriff.

She was the shallowest person I knew. Vain. Mean. A liar. The only good thing about her was that she was always eager to please me, dropping to her knees without even asking her to. But just because she was good at sucking my dick, or we were compatible in the bedroom, that didn't mean I'd humor her with this charade of being her date to prom or the king to her highness. She went too far for my liking. Lying about something like rape was dangerous and downright dirty. Didn't Madeline know I hated liars?

"There's the birthday boy," she purred, sitting up a little taller. Her friends shrunk away as I inched closer. The room was hyped, music pouring from the speakers.

I wanted to put on a show and teach her a lesson. What she did was fucked up. And her friend who went along with it? I'd say she was just as much to blame, but I was 100% certain Madeline had blackmailed her into lying. That was how malicious she was.

Once I got in front of Madeline, she stood up and rose to her tiptoes, looking around the room to make sure all eyes were on us, and tried to kiss me. Right at the last second, I turned my head, and her lips landed on my jawline. She pulled back instantly with a gasp.

"Sorry, *babe*. I'm just not feeling you tonight."

She paused, her fingers tightening around my bicep. "Um, what?"

The room quieted a bit, and someone had turned down the music. Ollie met my eye from across the room, and he grinned. People were muttering, clearly confused.

"You know," I started, peeling her dirty fingers from around my arm. "I was kind of feeling the hot tub tonight."

Her face brightened, her pink lips splitting into a smile. "Yeah, it was reserved for us." A long fingernail trailed the outline of my pecs, and I grabbed onto her hand and pushed it away.

I took a step back. "Actually, Madeline. It was reserved for *me*. And I don't think I want you anywhere near me tonight." I thought for a moment, glancing around the room, looking at our audience. "Or ever."

This was like social murder for Madeline. Me openly striking her like this. But when you fucked with me, I fucked right back.

That was how I became respected at English Prep. Sure, having the money and last name helped matters, but putting those who did the wrong thing in their place gained me attention. It was the reason I was captain of the football team and why I had the headmaster in my pocket.

"Um, what?" she asked again nervously. The music was cut off completely now. Everyone was at the edge of their seats to hear what I was going to say.

I plucked the drink from her hand and brought it up to my lips, chugging the warm beer that swirled inside. Once I was finished, I handed her back the cup, and she took it with a wary expression on her face.

"See, when you said that Cole had tried to rape your friend, you knew I'd retaliate. Not only because it was Wellington Prep, but because that's something I'd never stand for in any situation—Wellington Prep or not." Madeline's eyes narrowed as our friends started to whisper. Her eyes were saying, *"Don't you dare."* But did I ever. I took languid steps over to April, the girl that Madeline kicked off the cheer squad for cozying up to me a couple of weekends ago, because I knew that'd sting the most, and draped my arm over her dainty shoulder. "I heard that was all a lie. I heard Cole didn't do the things you accused him of, but that you were wounded because he didn't want anything to do with you when you tried spreading your legs for him."

Madeline's nostrils flared, and she started to shake her head so hard her blonde hair was flapping around her face. "That bitch. She's lying."

From underneath my arm, April spoke up.

"Hayley isn't lying. I heard you tell her that after you stole her clothes in PE the other day." April's lips curved upward. "Did you forget that I was in PE with you, too? Careful, Madeline. You're burning bridges left and right lately."

A high-pitched growl left Madeline's mouth. She looked as if she were ready to pounce on April.

"Get out," I said calmly.

"You're making a mistake, Christian."

I slowly walked over to her like a lion on the prowl. "No, you made a mistake when you tried to play me. I don't like liars, Madeline. Now get out. It's my fucking birthday, and seeing your face makes me want to vomit."

She rolled her eyes and stood back, trying to appear like she wasn't fazed, but I knew better. I could see right through her; she was all sorts of nervous on the inside. Her words came out rushed. "Funny you say that. You seemed to like my face last time we fucked."

I tilted my head. "Did I? I could have sworn I took you from behind for that *exact* reason."

She gasped softly, her face turning red. People snickered around us, and someone yelled, *"Oooh. Burn, baby, burn."*

I leaned down into her personal space, looking her dead in the eye. "What you did was dirty, Madeline. And I never want to get my hands dirty again." I turned around and walked over to April, claiming her hand in mine. Then, I looked over my shoulder before heading out to the hot tub. "And if you ever fucking mess with Hayley again, you'll find yourself at Wellington Prep with the accused rapist, and let me tell you, he knows *exactly* what you did."

Her mouth opened in shock, and mine almost did, too. *Did I just fucking stand up for Hayley in front of everyone?*

Eager to erase the moment, I pulled April through the back door, letting it slam behind me. Everyone could see through the thin layer of glass separating us from the rest of the party as I pushed her body up against it and claimed her with my mouth, not even giving a fuck that this wasn't part of my plan. I meant to use April as a way to push Madeline further into rage, taunting her with an enemy, but now I was taking it a step further because I was desperate to make up for my thoughts of Hayley.

I was infuriated with myself and eager to replace all the images of Hayley I'd subconsciously taken throughout the day and stored away for later. My tongue pushed into April's warm mouth, her cherry-tasting lips only distracting me for a second. Her jean-clad leg wrapped around my hip, pushing me closer to her center. She moaned out a noise and tangled her fingers through my hair.

Get. Out. Of. My. Head.

I ground my dick against her, needing more pressure—anything to get me to stop thinking. But it didn't work.

Why did Hayley look so worried when her friend tried to lift her shirt?

I groaned and pushed away from April. I turned my back

and walked farther into the autumn night, the leaves crunching underneath my shoes.

"Christian?" she asked, tip-toeing after me. "What happened? Things were just getting good."

Not good enough.

"There's something I need to do." I walked back into the cabin after mumbling a half-assed sorry to April. My chest was heaving, and my hands ached from clenching my fists so tightly.

I ignored everyone who tried to stop me to talk about Madeline and our little show and stepped in front of Ollie, who was doing his best at getting into Bristol's pants for the evening. He grinned when he looked up at me. "Bro, nice show. Madeline stormed out of here faster than Andrews scored that last touchdown."

"There's something I need to do, and I need your help."

His grin fell. "What? Right now?" He swept his gaze back and forth between me and Bristol and groaned. "Fine. But only because it's your fucking birthday."

He winked at Bristol and then began to follow me out of the kitchen. Once we were through the threshold of the house, I unlocked my car, but he stopped at the last second. "Wait, we're leaving? We're leaving *your* party?"

I ignored the question and opened my door to slide in. "Who is that girl that Hayley always hangs out with?"

Ollie climbed in after me. "The hot redhead? That's Piper Jacobs. Why?"

I looked over at him, the rumble of my car in the background. "Do you have her number?"

He shook his head. "No, she's way too uptight for me to pursue. Although, I would love to find out if she's a natural redhead, if you're catching my drift." He wiggled his eyebrows up and down.

I was being unpredictable right now, running on instinct

and instinct only. "Find her online. Find out where she is. I need to see Hayley."

Ollie didn't move to grab his phone. He didn't do much of anything but blink.

"What?" I barked. I wished I knew Piper myself; I'd have left Ollie here and hunted her down alone and demanded she tell me what was going on with Hayley.

I had no idea why I cared. I didn't want to—not even in the slightest. I wanted to hold onto the resentful feeling I had for her. But there was something burning inside of me, urging me to dig deeper. To learn all of her secrets and hold them close.

"I'll help you," Ollie finally said, leaning back in his seat, but he made no attempt at digging out his phone to search for where Piper might have been tonight. "But you're going to tell me why. You're going to tell me why you told Hayley it was her fault Mom died." He stared me down, his usual humor gone. "Because unless Hayley was shoving the pain pills down Mom's throat...it wasn't her fault."

It felt like my rib cage was wedged open and it was seeping the bloody truth all over my clothes.

I placed my hand on the steering wheel and started to back down the gravel road. I swallowed the thick spit lodged in the back of my throat. "I'll tell you on the way."

"On the way to where?" he asked, pulling out his phone.

"On the way to wherever Piper is. And then to Hayley."

They say the truth will set you free, but I highly doubted that. Apparently, it was sending me straight to Hayley.

Why won't she pick up the phone? I paced back and forth in my bedroom, tripping over the stupid basketball on the floor. It'd been two hours since she called me frantically, saying her parents were fighting again. When I'd asked what they were fighting about, she said she was going to get a better listen and she'd call me back later.

She still hadn't called back.

I worried about Hayley. Not just because I had a crush on her, but because she was my friend, too. One of my best friends. She played video games with me and happily hung out with Ollie even when he was being annoying. She said she had always wanted a sibling, someone she could hang out with when her parents were fighting, so letting him hang out with us was a must.

I blew air out of my mouth and left my room. Echoes of a cooking show were hitting my ears as I climbed down the stairs and entered the kitchen. There was Mom, baking something for our school's bake sale, which was a nice sight since she'd been out with friends the last few nights. She had flour smeared on her face when she turned around, and her light hair was tied in a bundle above her head. "Hi, honey, what's up?"

"Mom, can you drive me to Hayley's?"

She looked concerned for a second. "Why? It's almost 8:00. You should be getting to bed soon. You can see her tomorrow."

Fear prickled at the back of my neck. "No, I think something is wrong with her. She called me about her parents, and now she won't answer."

Mom measured out some sugar in a cup and poured it into the bowl, not looking up at me. Thunder boomed in the background, and it did nothing but heighten my anxiety.

"Christian. I'm sure she's fine. Doesn't she call you all the time about her parents?" She sighed. "I'm sure Hayley is fine."

"Mom," I urged. "Something is wrong. I can tell."

She shook her head. "Christian. It's almost time for bed. I'm in the middle of baking, Ollie is upstairs in the shower, and—" Another bang of thunder. She pointed to the window with her spatula. "It's raining. The answer is no."

Anger clawed at me. Something was wrong, I could tell. I pulled *out my cell phone again and tried to call. This time, it went straight to voicemail.*

"Mom, please!" I begged. My stomach began to tighten.

"No!" she shouted. "Now, stop. Go see if Ollie is out of the shower. You need to get ready for bed, too."

"Fine. I'll freaking go by myself!"

I hurriedly ran over to the door, pulled my shoes onto my feet, ignoring my mom's protests, and pulled my jacket on. If she wasn't going to drive me over there, then fine. I'd take my bike.

I jumped on the seat and tore out of the garage, flying down our cobblestone driveway and heading for the gates of our neighborhood. Rain danced in front of my vision, and my wheels were sliding everywhere along the slick asphalt, but I didn't care. I could feel it in my bones.

Something was wrong with Hayley.

Something *was* wrong with Hayley that night. She watched her father get murdered.

And I watched my mother get hit head-on by a Trailblazer as she drove through the storm to find me. I was the one who left that night, ignoring her. If Hayley would have just kept her business to herself or answered the phone when I had called back, I never would have left. I never would have disobeyed my mom, and the crash never would have happened. My mom wouldn't have been prescribed pain pills for her injuries, and she never would've gotten addicted.

And she never would have overdosed.

I glanced at Ollie in the passenger seat, and he looked as if he was barely breathing when I finished telling him. He was probably too fearful to do anything, afraid I'd stop spilling the ugly fucking truth. We were parked outside of the same house we came to last weekend when I'd come to teach Cole a lesson.

"Christian," Ollie started, his voice raspy and broken.

I prepared myself for the worst. He was going to hate me. He now knew that I was the reason Mom was out driving that night. No one really questioned what she was doing or how I saw the wreck from my point of view on the sidewalk. Things were a whirlwind after that night. Mom in the hospital, then her recovery. She was never the same after that wreck. She suffered a mild head contusion, and maybe that was why she was different. Or maybe it was the pills.

Either way, she was never the same. We saw less and less of her at the house. We later found out that she was seeing multiple doctors for her "injuries" and possibly spending time with them outside of office hours, too. Though, I wasn't sure if that was necessarily true—it was just from my assumptions over the years.

"How can you possibly hate Hayley for that?"

My own voice was unrecognizable. It was strained, hardly audible, weak. "Because if I blame her, then I don't have to blame myself."

Ollie scoffed. "Blame yourself for Mom dying? Are you kidding?"

My chest bled a little more. I squeezed the steering wheel. "No."

He shifted beside me, but I kept my gaze on the house.

"It's not your fault, Christian. It's not Hayley's either, but I'm guessing deep down you already know that. You were thirteen years old, worried about your best friend. No one could have predicted Mom would get into a wreck when she followed you. And no one could have predicted that she would get addicted to pain pills. If you blame yourself for her dying, then you might as well blame me, too."

I shot my gaze to him. "Why would anyone blame you?"

He shrugged. "Maybe because after I watched you leave through my window, I told her to follow you." My brows furrowed, and he nodded. "Yeah, I told her to go after you. She wasn't going to. She kept saying you'd turn back around once you got wet enough, but I knew better. I didn't know where you were going, but you were the most determined person I knew, and you never let anything get in the way of what you wanted. Not then and not now."

His words were soothing to the cut in my chest, but it didn't really fix me. Every time I looked at Hayley, I was reminded of that night. That dreadful, rainy fucking night that was the start of something terrible. She was a reminder of all the bad in my life.

Yet, there was still something inside of me that yearned to know she was okay.

It had always been that way with her and me. There'd been five years that we were separated, and every day, the little voice in the back of my head thought of her and wondered where she was.

Ollie's voice brought my attention back. "It's your best quality, you know."

I cleared my throat. "What is?"

"Your determination. It's why we're sitting outside a mansion, trying to find the girl you pretend to hate. You're determined to make sure she's okay, no matter the consequences."

"And what consequences are those?"

Ollie smirked. "I don't know. Maybe walking into this party to snag Piper, knowing very well you're likely to get jumped by a band of pussy-eating Wellington Prep boys because you beat one of their own last weekend." He gave me a side look. "Not your best idea."

Oh, right. *That*. Minor problem. "That's why you're going to go in there and pretend like you're buddy-buddy with Piper."

He laughed. "Can't make any promises." Then, he climbed

out of the car and jogged up the steps, giving me a salute before entering the house.

———

"I can't fucking believe that I fell for that." Piper was sitting in the backseat of my Charger, red hot and fiery. Ollie was sitting smugly in the passenger seat, a big grin etched on his face. "I *knew* not to believe you. The biggest flirt in the school. As if Hayley would really be out here in Christian's car, wanting to talk to me. She wouldn't send you. Ugh." She huffed. "I blame the alcohol."

"Tell me," I demanded, keeping my hands wrapped around the steering wheel. She had been in my backseat for twenty minutes and hadn't budged once.

"I'm not telling you shit, *King Christian*. You hate Hayley. How do I know you're not trying to get info out of me to use against her at school this week?"

I peered through the rearview mirror. "What was wrong with her today? I saw you trying to lift her shirt, and I also saw her wince when she climbed into your car after school."

A coy smile worked itself onto her face. "Wow, for someone who hates Hayley so much, you seem to know a lot about her actions."

"Fucking tell me." I smacked the steering wheel with my hand.

"Nope," she said with a pop on the letter P.

Ollie smirked when he looked back at her. "God, you're even hotter when you're feisty, Piper."

Her face twisted. "Ugh, shut up. I'm still angry with you."

"Tell me right now, or I swear to God, I'll drive right to her house and ask her myself."

Piper laughed, sitting back further into the seat. "Fine,

but you'll have to climb through her window. Maybe then I'll believe you have her best interests at heart."

"Fucking fine, let's go." I turned the ignition, and my Charger rumbled to life.

"Fine! I can't wait until she tosses your ass back out onto the ground for butting into her business!" she shouted.

Ollie twisted back around to me. "Bro, you can't just fucking climb through her window."

My head slowly swiveled over to him. "Watch me."

CHAPTER SIXTEEN

HAYLEY

I CURLED into a ball on my mattress for the third time in twenty seconds, and *yep, still freaking hurts.*

Pete didn't look in my direction once when I had gotten home. Not even when I took a bag of peas out of the freezer and carried them upstairs to my room. Jill wasn't home again, but I really didn't think she'd even care if she knew he had kicked me. She allowed him to hit her, so why would she care if he had hit me?

Piper had emailed me all evening. She'd begged for me to sneak out so I could get away from Pete. She even tried to bribe me with ice cream, but the thought of climbing out of the window with a footprint-sized bruise on my ribs? Yeah, no thank you.

She was worried about me. Her mortified expression imprinted itself into my brain after I had showed her the bruise. Piper knew something was wrong when I whimpered while carrying my backpack that morning. She tried to lift my shirt up in the middle of the hallway, upset that I wouldn't tell her what happened, so I finally dragged her into the bath-room and reluctantly lifted my shirt.

I sighed as I flopped onto my back. The bag of peas was long gone. They thawed hours ago, and then I ate the cold, uncooked peas for dinner because there was absolutely no way in hell I was going back downstairs to see if there was dinner for me. I'd have rather eaten the stuffing inside this shitty mattress before I took anything from Pete.

As soon as I started to doze off, my eyes peeled open. *Did I just hear something?* I lay still, unmoving, my eyes adjusting to the dark room. The moon from the window gave away a soft glow, so I could see small glimpses of shadows along the wall. I focused on my locked bedroom door, fearful that the knob would turn and Pete would stumble in here. *Wouldn't be the first time someone stumbled into my room, hoping to get something that wasn't theirs.*

Placing my hands on the mattress, I slowly sat up, wincing at the bite in my side. And that was when I saw it. A dark figure standing over by the closet door, immobile, lurking in the dark.

Panic seized me, and I rushed to my feet, yelling out with pain. My breath shortened, but I was ready to fight. *Did they really come for me?*

"It's me," the voice said. My brows drew tighter, and I still wasn't sure if I should scream.

"What are you doing in my room?" My voice was a whis-per, but it was dripping with anger. The tiptoeing of my feet padded over to the small lamp on the floor, and I flicked it on, a soft light giving away that Christian was actually in my bedroom.

His gray, stormy eyes pinned me to my spot. He looked at my face and trailed his stare over my T-shirt and bare legs. I flicked my eyebrow up and tapped my foot, waiting for my answer. When our eyes met again, I felt heat trickle across my body. In an alternate universe, Christian would have been my knight in shining armor. He would have been the Flynn to my Rapunzel. He'd whisk me off my feet and out of this awful tower I was locked in, and we'd live happily ever after. Or better yet, he'd storm over to me right now and rip this T-shirt off my body and have his way with me. *Okay, whoa...stop it.*

Almost as if he heard my thoughts, he stormed over to me. Too stunned to do anything, I stood stuck in my spot, my bare feet glued to the old oak floor beneath my soles. I sucked in a heavy breath as I peered up into Christian's face, the storm clouds hooded by thick dark eyelashes. His jaw was shut tightly, the muscles protruding near his temples. He fingered the hem of my long T-shirt, and chills broke out along my naked legs. Heat pooled in my core, but I was too struck by confusion to do anything. Then, he slowly—so slowly I thought I might have melted into a puddle of lust—lifted my shirt up.

When he hissed under his breath, the indifferent look in his eye went back to its normal hardness. "What the *fuck* happened?"

I stuttered, blinking away my bedroom eyes. "Wh—what?"

He pulled on my T-shirt, crashing my body into his hard chest. He lifted my shirt up again, and I realized what he was looking at. I quickly shoved him away and pulled down my shirt, mortified that I had just allowed him to lift my shirt in the first place.

"What the hell do you think you're doing breaking into my room like a stalker and lifting my shirt up?" I kept my voice down low, afraid I'd somehow wake Pete out of his drunken slumber.

"I didn't see you complaining with those fuck-me eyes a

second ago." He squinted one eye. "Better question is, what the hell were *you* doing letting me lift your shirt?"

My face flamed. My cheeks burned with embarrassment. *I hate him.*

"How did you get in here?"

Christian eyed my room. His gaze fixed on the mattress on the floor, my one blanket in a crumpled mess. There wasn't much to the room: a mattress pushed up against the old and tattered, yellowing wallpaper and a small bedside lamp on the floor with the cord trailing across the room like a tightrope. My backpack was tucked away in the corner with my uniform in a bunched-up mess a few feet away. That was it. The only personal item in the room that had any meaning at all was the locket around my neck.

I was certain Christian was comparing his life to mine—his glamorous, entitled, has-everything-he-ever-wanted life, whereas mine appeared like the bottom of a dumpster in an abandoned alley. I had nothing. I was nothing. Those were some of the last words my own mother had spoken to me. That was what sucked about words—they never left you. Bruises faded. But words never did. I'd been hearing her voice for the last few years on a loop in my brain.

"Who did it?" I cleared the thoughts in my head. My fingers fiddled with the locket around my neck, something I did when I was nervous.

"Why do you want to know?" I set my mouth in a firm line. "Want to thank them for doing the job? Give them a medal? Bond over your hatred for me?"

His face twitched. The sharp line of his jaw appeared like steel. "I don't hit girls, Hayley. Whoever did this deserves to have their teeth kicked in."

"And what if it was a girl who did it? I thought you didn't hit girls."

He scoffed. "It wasn't a girl. Whoever did this to you is

bigger and stronger. Or else they never would have gotten a hit in. Now, who did it?"

I leveled him with a stare, shifting on my bare feet. "Did you climb through my window? How did you even know which one was mine?" Christian was wearing jeans, his Vans, and a dark T-shirt—none of which had dirt or even a tiny smudge from climbing. How was that possible? Last time I climbed down the lattice, I tore the hole in my jeans even wider.

"Tell me who, Hayley." Christian's voice was strained, rough like he had swallowed gravel.

I huffed and rolled my eyes, and instead of answering him, I tiptoed over to my bed and lay down, not even sparing him a glance. I covered myself back up with the thin-as-paper blanket Jill had laid out for me the first day I got here and pretended like I was going back to sleep.

I was certain I appeared cool and nonchalant, lazily getting comfortable in my prison-like bed, but on the inside, I was frazzled. My nerves were fried, and my heart was racing. *What does this mean? Why is he here? Why does he care? Why are you excited?*

Part of me wondered if maybe Piper was right. Maybe he didn't hate me like he said.

"You can leave now. I'm not telling you anything," I said, closing my eyes and attempting to calm my heart rate.

Hearing pacing, I peeked an eye and saw Christian storming back and forth in my room. I hurriedly sat up. "Stop it!" I hissed. "You'll wake Pete up!"

He stopped and glared. "Who's Pete?"

"My foster dad, now stop."

The tilt of his head and sinister look he leveled me with had me gulping. "Did *he* do it?"

I flung the blanket off my legs, all hot and pissed off.

"Why do you even care? You have made it *very* clear you hate me and want me gone. So why?"

He looked troubled. His heavy brow furrowed. "Did someone at school do it? I need to know, Hayley. Quit fuckin' around and tell me."

"Please," I hushed. "Keep your voice down."

Nerves were coiling inside my stomach. My hands started to tremble. "Is that what this is about? Wondering if someone at school did this?"

He shrugged, looking out the window. "If someone in my school is hitting girls, I need to fucking know."

And here I thought that he might actually care about me. What a joke. No. King Christian only cared about his stupid, forsaken school. *Why are you so upset about this, Hayley?*

A dire laugh fell out of my mouth. "You can relax; your precious peasants are all following your rules. No one has messed with me since Madeline took my clothes."

"It was your foster dad, wasn't it?" His eyes jerked to my bedroom door, and it felt like a bullet had lodged its way into my spine.

Knowing he was correct, he lunged for the door, turned the knob, and paused. He tried turning it two more times, jiggling it back and forth. Then, he slowly turned around, his broad shoulders pulled back tightly. "Is.." He swept his dark gaze back at the door before leveling it in my direction. "Is your fucking door *locked?*"

I had to admit, this was not how I had planned for my night to go. I was supposed to be sleeping peacefully on my prison cot.

"You better fucking tell me what the hell is going on right now, or I swear to God I'll break down this door with my bare hands and find out for myself."

"Jesus Christ," I whisper-shouted. I walked over to the pile of clothes on my floor and pulled on some jeans. Christian's jaw went a little slack as he watched my every move. It was a nice look for him. Much better than the angry, firm jaw and menacing eyes he often threw my way. I whipped my shirt off, thankful I had a bra on, and threw on a hoodie. I trotted over to my bed, created a dummy-like body lying on the mattress with my pillow and a pile of dirty clothes, switched off my lamp, and trotted over to the window. "Since you're acting like a man-toddler, stomping around and yelling like a freaking Neanderthal, we're going to talk outside. So, let's go."

I didn't wait for Christian to answer me. I was certain he was angry at me for bossing him around, but I thought that might have been just what he needed.

Christian needed a little dose of his own medicine.

CHAPTER SEVENTEEN

CHRISTIAN

HER TINY, yet feisty, body climbed down the lattice like it was a rock-climbing wall that she'd climbed a million times before. The crunch of autumn leaves sounded from below as she hopped down, and I followed after her.

My mind was in a spiral of questions, and my dick was a little hard from seeing her in nothing but a T-shirt. I hated that she had an effect on me. I hated how I lusted after her, and I hated how I was all but salivating at the mouth when I had pressed her body up against mine. Her reaction set off a domino effect in my body: my head spun, my hands itched to touch her, my lips ached to taste hers. The past slipped through my fingers, and I was focused on one thing and one thing only: *her*—here, in the present.

Once she had stepped back out of my grasp, I focused on the real reason I was in her bedroom: the bruise on her side. My blood was bubbling over. An angry heat was prickling the back of my neck. I would fucking kill her foster father if I was correct in my assumptions, and don't even get me started on her locked door. I knew very well she hadn't had the best living arrangements since being in foster care. She'd been through some shit, according to her file, but this? Was this how her life had been since her dad died? Hayley wasn't the same girl from five years ago, and I thought I was beginning to see why.

As soon as my own shoes landed on the soft ground, I grabbed Hayley's hand and spun her body around the old oak tree. The bark was rough as I gently pushed her back against it, caging her in. "I don't like this."

Her soft breath fanned over my skin. "You don't like what?"

Everything in my body froze. Something about Hayley turned off my brain, and my body acted in ways it never had before. She was a magnet, and I was the metal. "I don't like that my fucking head is spinning over a girl I hate. I don't like that I can't figure you out. I don't like that you have all these secrets running around in your head. And I especially don't like that you won't tell me a damn thing."

The pounding of my pulse awakened the muscle inside my chest. It was beating fast and hard. Lust was swimming around the pair of us, my eyes dipping down to her pouty lips. I could see the curve of them even in the dark. I wanted to run my mouth over them. I wanted to shove my tongue in her mouth and drink in every last secret she kept.

Hayley lifted her chin a little higher, our lips no more than a breath apart. We stared at each other for far too long before she whispered, "Don't you know you're not supposed to tell your secrets to your enemy, Christian?" Then, she pushed me away and rounded the tree, taking my breath with her.

I was stupefied—stunned, even. No one had ever pushed my buttons the way she had in the last few weeks. I hated her two days ago, and yet, here I was, following after her like a splinter being drawn to the surface. Why couldn't I stop trailing her? Why did I all of a sudden feel protective over her?

As soon as she crossed the street, she looked for my Charger, which was tucked behind a massive, decked-out Escalade.

"Up ahead," I urged, nodding in the right direction. The lamppost above her head flickered, and she brought her attention to her foster house. I watched her swallow down what appeared to be nerves, and then she let out a breath and walked the remaining distance to my car.

"Are you kidding? Did you kidnap my friend?!" She spun around and glared at me, her dark hair a mess, whipping around her face.

I shrugged and climbed in on the driver's side as she did the same on the passenger side. Her body swung around and landed on Piper, who was sitting with her arms crossed over her chest. Ollie was laid back, looking relaxed as ever, a smug grin on his face. *I didn't even want to know.*

"Did he kidnap you?"

Piper huffed. "Pretty much! He demanded I tell him everything, and when I wouldn't, he said he was just going to drive here. I made him climb the window instead of knocking on the door because..."

Hayley's scowl turned soft, her lips curving upward and her eyes darting down. "Thank you."

"Okay, now fucking talk," I interjected, tapping my fingers along the steering wheel, staring at the ugly square house she called home. Even though being so up close and personal with Hayley muted my anger for a moment and distracted the hell out of me, I was back.

My temper was rearing its ugly head, and ol' *Pete* was about to be the casualty.

"If I tell you, will you leave me the hell alone?" She flew back into her seat, exasperated. "I still don't even know why you care. You've made it perfectly clear the last two weeks that you hate me and obviously blame me."

Ollie stuck his head in between us, resting his elbows on the leather center console. "Yeah, about that. Christian doesn't blame you. His reasoning is whack as fuck."

"Shut the fuck up," I bristled. *Not the fucking time.*

"Yeah, I'll leave you alone." *Not a chance in hell.*

Hayley looked at me from her peripheral vision. The car went silent. Ollie sunk back into his seat, and Piper stopped scowling at him. We were all on edge, waiting for her to explain. Hayley swallowed, the truth ready to spill from her lips. "I fell down the stairs."

I growled and smacked my steering wheel. "Quit fucking around, Hayley. Who the hell hurt you? Why won't you tell me?"

She leveled me with a stare that hit me in my core. "Because I don't trust you. I don't trust anyone."

She looked away, wounded. I flicked my eyes into the rearview mirror, and for once, Piper didn't look angry. She looked sad. The skin around her eyes crinkled, the dark color of her irises pleading with me to keep going. *I must have proven my worth by climbing through the window.*

"So what? That's it? You're not going to tell me anything?"

She huffed. "Absolutely not! Why would I tell you anything? The only thing you've proven to me since I came to English Prep is what a jerk you can be! I know you're used to people bowing at your feet, but I won't be one of them." She was seething now, fuming, her voice louder as each insult flew out. "I know guys like you. Rich, entitled assholes. Just like climbing in my room and demanding I tell you who left this bruise on my side! Or demanding to know why my door was locked. I owe you nothing, Christian. When I first got to English Prep, I thought maybe we could pick up where we had left off, but I was sorely mistaken." My name coming out of her mouth was laced with venom. Like I was a villain. And maybe I was. "You manipulate people to follow you around school with their tongues hanging from their mouths. You can't manipulate me. I'm nothing like the people you surround yourself with. I no longer want to be in your good graces." She sighed heavily. My stomach was tightened, ready for more. "Maybe I did two weeks ago, when I was walking into English Prep blindly, a heart full of hope, but you've said it and your actions proved it. You hate me. We're not the same two kids we were five years ago. So, no. I'm not telling you anything!"

Finally, Hayley was done with her rant. The car felt suffocating. Everything she said had some piece of truth to it. When I looked at her, I saw the past, and it made me want to hate her, but in the same breath, I also saw the future, and it made me want to love her.

Her hand was on the door handle. "Just leave me alone." She glanced back at Piper, giving her a sad smile. "And take Piper back to where you found her." With that, she climbed out of my car and slammed the door.

My fingers were drumming the steering wheel again, my mind going a million miles a second. Piper's voice had me pausing. "Christian, everything she said was the truth. You are an entitled, rich dick who thinks he can control everything and everyone at English Prep. But this?" I flicked my eyes to hers in the rearview mirror. "This is real life. I've only known her for two weeks, and I can tell you right now that she isn't the type of girl to ask for help or to confide in someone—not even when she needs to. And right now, she needs to." She worried her lip between her teeth. "It's not a good situation."

"Was it her foster father?" I asked, keeping her stare.

"Yeah," she answered.

Ollie hissed. "Bro, don't do anything stupid. I can save

your ass at a Wellington Prep party with a bunch of pansy asses, but I'm not so sure about this."

I ignored his protests and climbed out of the Charger. I tried to keep a steady head. *Think this through.* I couldn't be rash.

Or could I?

Hayley was crossing the street as I passed the parked Escalade to my right. Her arms were wrapped around her middle, her hair blowing in the wind.

I stepped over the curb, and she turned toward me quickly. "Jesus Christ." She threw her arms up when she saw it was me. "Take a hint! I don't need any help."

"No, but Pete is about to."

I stormed past her, ignoring her gasp. Right before I got to the bottom step of the house, Hayley sidestepped in front of me, her eyes wide underneath the soft glow of the moon. "Christian, stop! No!"

I snarled, ready to shove her away. Her warm palm landed on my bicep, skin on skin. *I can't believe her own foster father laid his hands on her.* It wasn't my intention to beat his ass when I climbed out of my car and followed after her. My plan was to act like I was so Hayley would stop lying and tell me the truth. But once I got to the bottom step and she looked up at me with fear plain as day in her eyes, something snapped inside of me. A protectiveness of her that I thought no longer existed emerged. *He hurt Hayley. My Hayley.*

"Christian." Her voice pulled me further away from anger, her hand wrapping tighter around my arm. "Don't. Please. I'm begging you."

I paused, wavering for a moment. When I shifted my attention back to the house, she squeezed harder.

"If you ever cared about me at all, please don't do this."

My head tilted; my jaw tightened. What a stupid thing to

say. Of course I cared about her. It was why I was acting so insane right now.

"That's not doing it for me, Hay. Better think of something else to distract me with, because I'm seconds from bashing his fucking face in." I couldn't wait to see his reaction when he opened the door and I punched him clear off his fucking feet. I'll kick him in his side just li—

My breath was momentarily gone. A spark of life went through my body like lightning striking the ground. Hayley's lips were on mine, moving effortlessly, as if they were meant for me all along. Her hands left my arms and weaved into my hair; her soft breath mingled with mine. My heart moved inside my chest as I pulled her in closer. I'd never felt such a tug in my core than I did in that moment. Hayley's ruby lips were mine for the taking, and I took every last breath that she had.

As soon as she pulled away, I was shocked. I couldn't speak. Or move. Hayley dragged me by my forearm, over the dip in the grass and all the way to the tree near her window. I was like a lost puppy being tugged by his collar. Once we were face to face, I watched as her tongue darted out to lick her swollen lips. I stared at her. She stared at me. I blinked once. She blinked back. *What the fuck just happened?* One minute, I wanted to end her, and the next, I wanted to save her. "Are you back? Level-headed? Ready to hear me out?"

Well played, Hayley. Well fucking played. Hayley definitely knew how to distract me, and it worked.

It worked too well.

"I'm ready." My voice was gravelly sounding. It was almost painful to talk after what just happened. *Her kiss. Holy shit.*

Hayley looked up into the starry sky. "Yes. Pete was the one who kicked me. And no, there isn't anything I can do about it. Trust me. I want to take the dullest knife in the silverware drawer and hurt him with it until he bleeds, but I can't, because if I get kicked out of this house, I'll go into a group home."

"So?" I ran my hand through my hair, wanting to tug at the ends to keep myself from grabbing onto her body and pressing my lips to hers again. "So?" she hissed, her legs pacing back and forth in front of me. Twigs and leaves crunched underneath her weight. "I turn eighteen soon! Do you know what they do when you turn eighteen while in a group home?" She didn't give me time to answer. "They kick you out! You're officially out of the system. A big congratu-fucking-lations. You get booted on your ass and become homeless. But"—she turned around and stared at the side of the house—"Jill and Pete and I have it all worked out. I can stay here until college as long as I give them my stipend money from the state and as long as I don't give them any trouble."

"And what if Pete doesn't?"

Looking over her shoulder at me, she asked, "What if Pete doesn't what?"

"Stay out of fucking trouble? He left bruises on your body!" I almost yelled, heating up again inside.

Hayley turned around and walked over to me, peering up into my face. "That's something I can't really wager on working in my favor, Christian. You don't get it. You aren't in the system. Shit doesn't always work out the way it should. It's about survival. And this is me surviving!" An audible groan left her mouth. "This is my last fucking pit stop. If I mess this up, I can kiss the scholarship I want goodbye. Being homeless and still attending English Prep and getting stellar grades would be impossible. And you're not going to fuck this up for me because you have some crazy control issue."

I shook my head. "That's not why I'm butting in. I'm not trying to control you." I was honestly surprised at how calm my voice was. My temper was clanking off every bone in my body as it tried to emerge.

"Then why are you butting in? We're not friends. We're not even acquaintances. Do I need to remind you that you've told me on several occasions that you hate me and want me gone?"

I wanted to punch my fist into the tree, but instead, I gritted through my teeth. "I don't fucking know, Hayley!" I took several deep breaths, running my hand through my hair again. "God, fuck!"

Hayley came closer; this time she was pinning me against the tree instead of the other way around. "I don't need a knight in shining armor, Christian. Especially one who acts as the villain, too." She slowly backed away after invading my personal space. "Now leave me be. I've been taking care of myself for a long time. I've learned to depend on me, and me alone."

My back stayed against the tree as Hayley walked back over to the side of her house and climbed up the lattice. She didn't even look back as she reached her window. Her light never came on, and there wasn't a single peep that came from her house. My lips still tingled long after she disappeared from my sight, but Hayley was right. She wanted me to leave her be, and I needed to listen.

CHAPTER EIGHTEEN

HAYLEY

THE NEXT FEW days were uneventful, especially given the weekend. Something I said to Christian must have stuck. Maybe it was the way I stressed that he needed to leave me alone, or maybe it was the kiss.

The unspeakable kiss. The moment that I kept pretending never happened. And apparently, him too, considering he hadn't glanced my way once since Friday night. I couldn't believe I kissed him. The second I climbed in my window and shut it behind me, I rested my back along the wall and slid to the floor, my chest heaving up and down as I replayed every waking moment since he had climbed into my room. I replayed the part where I undressed in front of him and how I liked watching my effect on him. How he had me pinned against the tree with my heart in my throat. How alive I felt when our lips collided.

There were so many up-close-and-personal moments, each one branding itself into my heart like a memory I'd never forget.

I wished I could forget. It would have been a lot easier keeping my gaze transfixed on the blackboard instead of scolding myself every five seconds.

From what I noticed, it seemed Madeline was outcasted by the popular group this week. Piper said she heard bits and pieces about Christian calling her out at a party over the weekend, and there was word that he told her to stay away from me, too—which was conflicting.

I was half-angry that Christian acted like I needed his help and protection, but the other half of me relished in it.

I was a mess.

And that didn't even touch my home situation. The house felt like one big shard of glass, and if I stepped the wrong way, I'd be cut. It was suffocating. Pete was a ticking time bomb, and I was pretty sure I was the fuse.

Pulling out my notebook and smoothing out my skirt, I got myself ready for Mr. Calhoun's lecture about Shakespeare. I'd been keeping up with the course load just fine at English Prep, and I only had a few more colleges to apply to, plus many more scholarships. A few of the teachers had already pulled me aside to tell me that they were impressed, even after only a few weeks, and they'd have my recommendation letters drafted up quickly. At least one thing in my life was going well.

My skin prickled as the dynamic in the room changed. People hushed; glances were stolen. It meant that Christian and Ollie had walked in. It was like that every morning.

The sounds of conversations about the football game erupted in the room when Eric mentioned that college scouts were coming to watch. A few girls were talking about what they were going to wear, complaining that they just weren't sure. *Oh, how nice it would be for my biggest worry to be what I was going to wear to a football game.*

I was supposed to go to the game with Piper. I had

promised her last week, but it was basically the last thing on earth that I wanted to do, although it did beat being locked in my bedroom.

A word caught my ear as Mr. Calhoun started to write something on the blackboard. It was Ollie's voice. "Yeah, fuck Oakland. They play like a bunch of little bitches."

"Language, Ollie," Mr. Calhoun scolded.

My chest burned. "Oakland?" I turned and looked at Ollie. The entire room fell silent. All eyes were on me.

"She talks!" Eric raised his fist up! "Finally! I was wondering what that pretty voice sounded like."

Ollie ignored him, glancing at me through his thick eyelashes. His voice grew softer with me than when he was talking to everyone else, and in any other circumstance, that would have annoyed me, but right now I couldn't think of anything other than the anxiety rising up. "Yeah, we play Oakland on Friday at home."

Oakland here? Gabe.

I shot up quickly out of my seat, my notebook tumbling to the floor. My words were choppy as Mr. Calhoun turned around to see the commotion. "May I...use...the restroom?"

"Yes, hurry back," he answered, but I was already halfway out the door. My insides sizzled with an undeniable amount of anxiety. There was a touch of anger, too.

Do not let him have an effect on you, Hayley.

Did Gabe even know that I went to school here? I plowed through the girl's restroom. The smell of bleach and a fruity scent did nothing to comfort me. I placed my hands on the cool, tiled wall and dropped my head to stare at my Chucks.

The last words he threw in my direction rang throughout my head when I squeezed my eyes shut. Then came the entire eclipse of that night from not too long ago.

I pulled my eyes open as I felt something beside me. The room was dark except for the moon shining through the lavender, sheer curtains to my left. It took my vision a few moments to adjust, but when they did, I saw Gabe leaning down above my head.

"Gabe? What are you doing?" I tried to sit up, but he didn't move. He just continued to tower over me, his light hair hanging down below his eyes. "Are you drunk again? You're in the wrong room."

His voice was husky, low. "I'm not in the wrong room." Slowly, he took a seat by my feet, and I hurriedly pulled them up out of his way.

"Then what are you doing in here?" I glanced at the clock on the bedside table. "It's two in the morning."

"Did you like the new clothes my mom brought home for you?"

I glanced at the shopping bag near the desk I did my schoolwork on. I shrugged. "I haven't looked at them yet."

Gabe ran his hand through his hair, the ends flipping up around his ears, casting shadows along his T-shirt. "You know, they always wanted a girl after they had me. But Mom couldn't get pregnant anymore. Something with my birth did something to her, permanently destroying any chance to have another child." He looked over at me, and something had shifted in his demeanor.

I considered Gabe a friend, a brother almost. He wasn't, of course. He was my foster brother, and I'd only been placed with the Santiellos two months ago. But they were a nice family. They bought me things, made me dinner every night. Gabe drove me to school every day and yelled at his friends who made fun of my homely attire—which was probably why there was a bag of brand-new clothes sitting on my floor. But tonight, Gabe looked sinister. His voice was eerie. I had my antennae up.

There were a few times over the last couple of weeks that he'd asked me to go to a party with him "to hang out with the cool kids," but I had declined every time. Popular kids weren't my scene. And I didn't want to do anything to jeopardize the roof over my head. After all, they fed me and clothed me. It was the least I could do to follow their rules.

Gabe inched closer to me, and I gulped. "Gabe, whatever you're doing, stop."

He halted, hovering a breath away. My vision was adjusted now, and the look in his eyes was nothing like I'd ever seen before.

"Do you like living here, Hayley?"

At this particular moment, I wasn't so sure. But I answered him. "Yes."

"Then you'll be okay with me sneaking in here every so often, right?"

I bristled at the thought. "Um..." Courage found its way up my throat and out of my mouth. "I don't know what type of foster sister you're used to having, but I'm not like that. So, please go back to your room."

He pounced on me as the words left my mouth. Fear clawed at me, but the anger inside of me shut it down quickly. Gabe wasn't used to being told no—that much was obvious. He muttered things like, "a tease," as he tried to get a hold of me, but Gabe also wasn't used to a girl who had been through hell and back. This wasn't my first foster home, and it surely wouldn't be my last.

I rolled off the bed after giving him a swift knee to the groin. He moaned as I jerked up from the floor, ready to bolt out the door, but he caught my foot at the last second. His large hands wrapped around my waist as he pulled me up and pushed me against the wall.

"Let me go," I rushed out, my hair falling out of my face.

His breath was hot on my skin as he quickly shifted his hands to my flailing arms. Should I scream? Would his parents even hear me on the third floor? Would they even believe me over him? Doubtful.

"Stop fighting this. I know you want it. Walking around the house in those short shorts every morning." Gabe's hands moved quickly as he gathered both of mine in his one. His other hand crept down along my body, curving over my breasts and down the front of my sleep shorts. I fought back the tears and told myself to keep fighting. He didn't get to take something that wasn't his. My body was not for the taking. Once his fingers dipped inside of me, his grasp loosened slightly, which was enough to wake up the fighter girl inside of me. I reared my head back and banged it off his so hard he tumbled backwards, cursing under his breath.

My heart was lodged in my throat, and I could taste the metallic zing of blood in my mouth, but I ran for the door and skipped almost the entire flight of steps before I reached the front door.

Gabe was quick on his feet, his large strides covering much more distance than my short ones. What can I do to make him stop? He was bigger than me. I couldn't outrun him. His parents were upstairs asleep, and I wasn't sure I could trust them to be on my side anyway.

I eyed the garage to my left. I hurriedly skidded over the pebble-lined driveway and jammed my fingers into the code lock. 2-3-0-1-2. The doors started to climb up, and I slid underneath, out of sight. It was dark and smelled of must and engine oil. But I knew where Gabe's baseball bat was. It was tucked away in the corner until base-ball season came around.

The wooden handle felt comforting underneath my skin, my palms savoring the strength the weapon gave me. I heard Gabe's foot-steps, pounding and heavy. I knew he saw me in the corner, lurking near his precious Mustang.

His body was outlined by the deep night sky, the stars and moon glowing behind him. The garage was lit up just enough so he could see me raise the bat.

"I always did like a chase. Stop running from me, Hayley. You keep your mouth shut, spread those pretty little legs, and you can stay living here. Maybe my parents will even adopt you."

"You're sick, Gabe."

He crept toward me, blood trickling from his nose. Good. I made him bleed.

"You won't get the chance to touch me again." I raised the bat higher as his eyes widened. I drove it headfirst into the windshield of his Mustang, causing the alarm to blare, waking the entire neighbor-hood. Rage filled his body. He ran after me so fast I couldn't keep *myself from falling backward into the wall. Various sports balls fell upon our tangled bodies, our limbs getting tangled as he hit me and as I clawed him.*

Gabe got in a few punches that night.

But so did I.

I thought I'd won. His parents ended up coming down and breaking us apart. The neighbors' lights flicked on. We had caused a scene. He lied to his parents, and they bought it.

I was whisked away and sent to juvie, later finding out that his parents dropped the charges. For what reason? I had no clue. I was a little relieved, but the last words Gabe spoke to me had buried themselves into my brain, just like the words of the faceless thugs who killed my father. Before I was shuffled out of the Santiellos' house that night, Gabe leaned into my personal space and spat, "The next time I see you, you'll pay for this."

Heavy breaths escaped my mouth as my hands stayed glued to the tiled wall. I was angry that the recent memory had hit me head-on. I was also angry that I could feel the remnants of fear. I was sweating. Small droplets of salty moisture lined my forehead.

I yelped and fell backwards onto my butt when the girl's bathroom door flew open, revealing a set of gray eyes that resembled the moon versus the normal storm cloud.

Christian's brow furrowed when he found me on the floor. I looked away quickly. Embarrassed. "What happened at Oakland?"

Jesus. He wants to know everything.

I slowly pushed myself up off my butt and took a steady breath. Fear had no place in my body right now. The past was the past. It could affect the future, but it surely couldn't be changed.

"What are you talking about?"

Reaching up and tucking my hair behind my ear, I glanced into the mirror. *Yikes.* My face was pale, slick with sweat. My lips were blood-red from biting down on them.

"Something happened there, and I want to know what."

His voice was demanding and distant but still had a small twinge of warmness intertwined. My head slowly swiveled over to him, and we caught each other's eyes. I begged my gaze to stay fixed on his, but it didn't listen. My eyes bounced down to his set of pale, full lips—the ones that caved in to mine just a few nights ago.

It had felt good to kiss him. Too good.

Things sparked inside of me, which only made me lash out. I brushed past him, needing to get control of myself. "Like I said before..." I stopped right beside him in the doorway of the bathroom. We were inches apart. His fresh, woodsy scent was the only thing I smelled. "I depend on me and only me."

With that, I walked back to class feeling a little bit empowered. Maybe facing my fears would be a good thing. Maybe I should show up to the game with Piper and look Gabe right in the eye, proving that he had no effect on me. *The next time I see you, you'll pay.* Yeah, we'll see, Gabe.

He wasn't the first person to threaten me.

And it was time I stopped being afraid of these empty threats. I'd been through far too much to back down now.

Later that day, I was sitting with Piper during lunch, the pair of us tucked away in the corner, looking out into the cafeteria. I was debating with myself if I should go to the game or not.

I wanted to look Gabe right in the eye and tell him I

wasn't afraid of him, but deep down, I may have been a little. I learned that you couldn't trust someone from the outside looking in—or maybe even if you were on the inside with them. People were unpredictable. It was human nature. Even I was unpredictable at times. Kissing Christian proved that.

With the thought, I looked over at his lunch table. He was picking away at his food, shoving it around his tray. Ollie and Eric were talking animatedly, and everyone else, girls included, were hanging on their every last word. Madeline sat a few seats down, still at their table, but no one was speaking to her.

If it were anyone else, I might have felt bad. But she was mean, and mean girls deserved to be lepers.

Christian's head swiveled toward the lunchroom doors, and I followed his gaze. The dark oak slabs opened, and Headmaster Walton waltzed in, his bright-red tie a focal point. Then, right after him, I saw Ann's bright, straw-colored hair and tired face following him.

I sighed, Piper stopped talking and asked me what Ann was doing here. I shrugged as Headmaster Walton pointed me out, and Ann caught my eye.

"I'm gonna go find out before she sits down at our table like we're all besties."

Piper snickered. "I'll take care of your tray. I'll see you after school to finish our conversation, even though you didn't hear a word I said because you were too busy ogling Christian."

I gave her the side eye but didn't bother arguing with her. She was right. I *was* ogling him.

Before I made it all the way over to Ann's painfully bright smile, I snagged my attention on the popular table again. No one was paying attention; there was too much commotion going on in the lunchroom: lots of chatter, my peers moving through the food line, cafeteria ladies cleaning and replacing food, random teachers grabbing their afternoon cup of joe. But Christian, he was locked onto me, staring, pinning me down with a questionable look.

Ignoring him and the way my chest fluttered, I turned and headed right for the doors. I gave Ann a fake what-are-you-doing-here smile and whisked through the door as she trailed me.

Her heels clanked against the tile floor as she waltzed over to a nearby bench and sat down. I did the same before turning to her and asking, "Why are you here?"

She laughed. "Oh, Hayley. You're one of my favorites." I bristled at the thought, picking at the stray pieces of my tattered skirt end. "I just came to check on things. You know, that's kind of my job."

"Things are fine," I answered truthfully. Things weren't *that* bad. They could always be worse.

"That's what you all say." She shook her hair out and massaged her temples. I knew that being a social worker was a thankless job, but I also knew that not every social worker did their job correctly or with as much heart as others. Ann, though, was beginning to show her worth. I was pretty sure she was one of the good ones. There was something about her that was warm and fuzzy. Motherly. But that didn't mean I was going to divulge in some amazing mother/daughter relationship with her. I wasn't going to suddenly start seeking her advice. *Should I go to the game with Piper? Should I keep pushing Christian away? Should I trust him when he asks me all these questions? Why is he butting in? Why did his kiss brand me? What do you think about Pete locking me in my room? I'm almost eighteen, do you think those men who killed my father are going to show up on my doorstep like they promised so long ago?*

Ann dissolved my thoughts just as quickly as they filtered through. "Who is your friend? The one you were sitting with?"

"Her name is Piper." I licked my lips.

I could feel Ann staring at me, but I didn't meet her eye. "I'm glad to see you have made a friend here. Have you guys hung out outside of school much?"

I shook my head. "Not really."

"And why not?"

This time I turned my attention toward her. "Do you really think she's going to want to come hang out at Pete and Jill's with me? And honestly?" I sighed. "Even asking Pete and Jill to use the washing machine grants me an eye roll and heavy huffs of breath. I don't talk to them unless I have to. The thought of asking them to go to Piper's or to the game this Friday makes my skin crawl."

Ann's small, makeup-covered nose twitched. "Creating these relationships with your peers is important, Hayley. Consider it done. You're going to the game Friday. You're going to be a normal teenager. Your grades are soaring. Headmaster Walton told me that the faculty letters are pouring in and they're excellent. There is no reason why someone as hardworking as you can't have a little bit of fun." She dipped her head down low. "Especially considering the last five years of your life. Pete, nor Jill, will protest when I tell them this."

A rush of anxiety hit me. "Why do you care so much? I'm almost out of the system. Maybe you should put forth your effort with someone younger than me. I don't need your help with Jill and Pete."

Ann's eyes stayed warm, her expression still relaxed. Her lips turned upward just slightly. "I care because you remind me of someone I used to know."

She stood up, smoothing out her skirt. "Go to the game. I'll give Jill and Pete a call. I need to check in with them anyway. I didn't like how things ended last week."

Curiosity piqued me. Angling my head up to her, I asked,

"Who do I remind you of? Another kid who is lost in the system?"

Her expression never changed. It was still warm and comforting. "Was."

"What?"

"She *was* lost in the system."

She started to walk away, and at the last second, before reaching the end of the hall, she looked over her shoulder. "You remind me of me, Hayley. And I'd love to see you come out on top."

Then, she walked out of the doors, leaving me with my thoughts. *I knew she wasn't like all the rest.*

I stood up and smoothed out my skirt when I heard the bell ring. Scooping up my backpack, I was about to walk to my next class when a rough and callous voice rang out. Christian was the first to enter the hallway, everyone else still gathering their things and throwing away their lunches.

"Going to the big game on Friday then, yeah?"

My jaw slacked. "Were you spying on me?"

He tucked his hands into his pressed khaki pants, casually. He looked effortlessly cool in his uniform, whereas I looked like a lost schoolgirl with tangled hair and ratty shoes. "Maybe."

I crossed my arms over my chest. "Why? *Why* are you so concerned with everything I do?"

His jaw tightened, his teeth working back and forth. He began to walk past me as people started to pour out of the lunchroom. Piper caught my eye and lifted her eyebrow, a knowing grin on her face.

As soon as his clean, woodsy scent enveloped me, he whispered, "I have no fucking clue."

CHAPTER NINETEEN

CHRISTIAN

It was funny how quickly things became a part of your everyday, same ol' schedule. Things like brushing your teeth, taking a piss in the morning, running suicides before practice. The things you didn't think twice about. You just did them because you were so accustomed to doing them. You didn't even give them a second thought.

When did they become the norm? At what moment did I decide that brushing my teeth directly after I downed a cup of coffee was the thing to do? At what point did I decide that driving to an entirely different town, in the fucking dumps, to stare at Hayley's house was what I'd do every night?

When did I decide that watching her inhale her food during lunch was my new norm? She was taking over. She was inflicting herself into my bones, seeping her devastatingly broken, yet beautiful face into my brain. I was worried. There was this superego part of me that wanted to be there to save her, to swoop her up into my arms and protect her from everyone who hurt her—including me.

Did she remind me of the past? Yes.

Did that bother me anymore? Maybe if I wasn't looking at her somber blue eyes. Maybe if I wasn't reminded of the bruise on her side. Maybe if I didn't see that tiny bit of fear etched on her features. Because that did something to me. She was the cure to my guilt, whereas before, I thought she was the culprit of it.

The stadium lights were as bright as the sun above my head. We only had two minutes to go; one touchdown stood between us and the winning buzzer. Oakland was three points ahead. I looked up into the stadium briefly. I scanned over to my father, standing up on the bottom bleacher in his nicest suit. This was the first game he'd been to in a long, long time. I knew he'd leave shortly after, and although I didn't want to admit it, him being here made me want to play better. It may have been the desperate little boy inside of me that wanted his father to be proud of him, but either way, I had played my very best tonight.

I flicked my eyes past him as I ran out onto the field from the sidelines. The crowd was roaring, my cleats pounding on the wet grass and dirt, my teammates grunting and hollering all around me, but somehow, my eyes found her.

Hayley was standing with Piper, her dark hair in two braids. She had on a navy bulldog's shirt, and there was an actual smile on her face. Not the kind that she wore in class when the teacher congratulated her on her high test score. Not the kind she wore when she bumped into someone and said excuse me. No, this one reached her eyes. Hayley Smith was having fun, and I hadn't seen her smile like that for a really long time. It made me crave the past, and I was used to running from it.

"Sideswipe," I yelled throughout the huddle. I had a couple confused looks. Ollie nodded briefly through his helmet, and Eric muttered, "Coach gon' kill ya."

"Sideswipe," I repeated. We all clapped and lined the field. Coach was probably having an aneurysm at this point, knowing we were bypassing his safe call, but I knew what I was doing. One long pass to Ollie and we'd have a touchdown. Coach made me captain for a reason, and I'd remind him of that when we beat Oakland at the end of the game with more than a measly field goal.

"Hut."

The ball snapped to me quickly, the pigskin-rubber glued to my palm. I trampled backward, and I zeroed in on Ollie's fast legs trucking down the field. I wound my arm back, knowing I was about to get plowed, and ignited the ball down the field. I swore the entire stadium went quiet. The buzzer was about to go off, and I landed on my back with an Oakland defensive lineman on top of me. He tried to intimidate me with his glare, but it didn't work. I pushed at his heavy body when I heard the crowd roaring. I was hoping it was because Ollie had scored and I didn't blow it. Just as soon as the thought left my head, a few of my teammates appeared above me, pulling the meathead off my body even further. They were smiling ear to ear, black smears underneath their eyes dotted with sweat.

They lifted me to my feet, and I knew that I'd made the right choice. Coach could suck my dick. *That* was how you won a game. Eric and Taylor lifted me up onto their shoulders, yelling and screaming insanities at Oakland's players. I was smiling for once, too, genuinely happy.

Through the celebrations, we were pulled off the field as the kicker came on to do the extra point. Coach growled at me but pulled me in for a back pat in the end. "Little fucker," he said in my ear. "Don't pull that shit in college. You'll be benched no matter how good you are."

I chuckled and pulled my attention away, glancing back up

into the stadium to catch a glance of the little ray of sunshine. My brow furrowed when I didn't see her.

But fuck it. Now wasn't the time to be thinking of Hayley.

After we all barreled into the locker room and started to pull off our pads, everyone was on a high. Eric already had girls heading to the cabin to celebrate, and my dad was already long gone back to the house to catch up on work and get ready for his next business trip, wherever the fuck that was.

Ollie was smiling ear to ear as he pulled me in for a hug. "Glad you knew what you were doing out there, bro. The scouts are going to be sucking your dick to get you on their team."

I laughed as I whipped on a clean T-shirt.

With my back turned to the locker room door, I watched as every guy's expression changed. Ollie pulled back, and his eyebrows drew together. "Piper, what the hell are you doing in here?"

I spun around quickly, my resolve wavering. "Christian." She gulped.

Ollie and I were both over to her within seconds, ignoring the rest of the team. Her face was pale, her body trembling. Her words were rushed. "It's Hayley. Something bad happened, and she won't let me call 911. Hurry."

Ollie and I didn't even bat an eyelash. We ran as fast as we could after her.

CHAPTER TWENTY

HAYLEY

As my face was smashed into the cold, gritty ground, I wondered how I'd gone from standing in a crowd roaring with excitement over a football game to lying in the gravel. Remnants of asphalt were rubbing my skin raw as someone pushed the side of my head down as the other kicked me in the back. Tangy blood filled my mouth, and I held back a whimper. I tried to fight them off. I knew I got one in the balls by the way he had crouched down after, but the other flew on top of me, and now I was pinned.

Their voices were rough, their faces covered in black masks of some sort. It was dark where we were. As soon as I felt them grab me while walking to the bathroom, I knew I should have waited for Piper. I didn't want her to miss the last few minutes of the game, and I didn't want to have to wait in a long line of people as they rushed out of the stands.

With each punch and kick to my body, I wondered if this was a result of Gabe. Maybe he *did* know that I went to English Prep now. Maybe it was a mistake coming here, pretending I was a normal teenager who didn't have threats appearing all around her.

The two hours of fun with Piper and the eye roll of Pete when she picked me up weren't worth this.

Not at all.

"Fuck, people are coming. Is it her? Has he texted back?"

Who?

The guy holding me down spoke. "Fucking shit. He hasn't messaged back. If we got this wrong, he's going to kill us himself. He'll never know he can trust us. Let's just take her anyway. Dump her on the side of the road if it's not her."

The palm that was over my mouth, holding my head down, loosened just a tad. They stopped beating on me when I stopped struggling. *They were waiting for confirmation.* My worst nightmare was coming true. My blood hardened. Fear morphed into anger.

I could sense the nerves rolling off the guys; they were younger, maybe even close to my age by the sound of their voices. The one who inflicted the most pain on me was pacing back and forth, tiny flakes of the ground crunching underneath his boots. People were about to pour out of the stadium. Piper was going to come looking for me. I tried to look around at my surroundings. I couldn't have been too far from the bathrooms, but when you're kicking and clawing while getting taken down with a hand over your mouth, you lose track of time and your awareness.

I heard a phone ping, and even though my body was already hurting in places I couldn't even register, I hastily opened my mouth and bit down on the hand covering my face as he loosened his grip. *Rule number one of the Hayley Fight Club: never let your guard down.* Lucky for me, the bastard underestimated the strength of a seventeen-year-old girl.

He screamed out and withdrew his hand hastily. I spun my body around, gravel scraping my stomach. I screamed bloody murder and hopped to my feet, ready to take off. I didn't dare look back to see if they were running after me. I ran until I tripped over something, losing my balance. I quickly spun around on my hands and looked in the direction I came from.

All I saw was darkness and a few flying insects through a tiny stream of light. I jumped up again and climbed the grassy area, wheezing and unable to catch my breath. My foot slipped twice, and I was just waiting for a hand to wrap around my ankle, but nothing ever came.

I could see the brick-covered bathrooms up ahead with people swarming about.

"Hayley!"

I whipped my head over to Piper, my now loose braids smacking me in the face. My feet took me over to her quickly, and her wide-eyed expression had me turning to look back. *They followed me, and now I just put her in danger, too.*

"Run."

I grabbed Piper's hand and dragged her alongside me. We passed by curious faces, bumping into random people. As soon as we made it to the parking lot and we were in the comfort of other people trying to get to their cars, I leaned my back against her hood and tried to catch my breath. I was gasping as adrenaline ran through my veins.

Piper's mouth was still wide open as her gaze ran all over my body. I tried to catch my breath to explain what happened, but she just kept rambling, "Ohmygodohmygodohmygod." Then, she reached out to touch me but thought twice and, instead, pulled her phone out. "I'm calling 911. You're...you have...there's a lot of blood. Hayley, can you talk? What happened?"

"No!" I yelled before slumping down on the ground. Now that the adrenaline was starting to give way, things hurt. My stomach ached. I could still taste blood in my mouth. It seemed my eye was swelling, because I could only see half of her face. My words were choppy. "I don't have money. No hospitals. Pete and Jill will be mad. And Ann will know."

"Hayley!" Piper bent down, her red hair swaying in front of her worried face. "Oh my God. Okay, um." She covered her hand with her mouth. "Get in the car now. Lock it. I'll be right back."

She helped me to my feet and gently put me in the back-seat. I slowly slumped down, my head resting on the soft fabric. I wasn't sure where she went—maybe to get me some wet paper towels to clean the blood up. At this point, I didn't care. Lying down felt better than sitting against the hood. My body started to come off its high. I trembled and continued to breathe through my nose. A small noise sounded from around me, but I was too tired to open my eyes. It sounded like a whimper.

Oh my God. Is that me?

I reached up and felt my face. It was wet. Sticky and wet.

Am I crying? Why does this hurt so bad?

Suddenly, the car moved a bit, and the door opened up. A cool breeze hit my face, and I clenched my eyes shut. *Jesus Christ, they're back, and I don't have enough fight left in me.*

"Hayley."

My eyes snapped wide as I heard his voice.

Christian.

CHAPTER TWENTY-ONE

CHRISTIAN

THE SIGHT of her felt like I had gotten my throat punched. My knees wanted to buckle. I could barely form words. I covered every inch of her body with my gaze, fear and anger wrapping itself tightly around my windpipe.

She was bloody. Her face was wet, shining under the car's interior lights. The right side of her cheek was red and had small pebble-like cuts dotting the skin. One eye was swollen shut. Her shirt was ripped, and her flat stomach had scrapes down the front.

Hayley squeezed her eyes shut when she saw me. She curled into herself even more, and that sent an entirely new line of fear down my spine. Hayley didn't do that. She didn't cower. She didn't fold into herself, and I was pretty sure she didn't cry. She was far too tough for that.

I immediately went into action mode. I wanted to know who did this and why, and then I wanted to wrap my hands around their neck and kill them. But the most important thing was Hayley. I wasn't going to stand here and argue with her. I wasn't going to try and fish out information she didn't want to give up.

She needed help. She needed *me*.

Piper whispered from beside me, "She wouldn't let me call 911. She said she didn't have money for it."

More rage bubbled within. "I'll fucking pay for it." My hands were squeezing the life out of the car door as I peered down at Hayley. Her face moved slightly, and she croaked, "No." Then she tried to move and cried out.

"Goddamnit. Stop moving." I bent down a little further and assessed her injuries.

"Ollie, you and Piper go to the nearest store and grab all the antiseptic shit you can find. Grab bandages, ice packs, whatever the fuck you see, and meet me back at the house." He nodded once, and I held my hands out to Piper. "Give me your keys. Go with Ollie. Meet back at my house." She didn't hesitate. She slapped her keys in my hand and took off with Ollie, running and weaving through the parking lot. My shit was still in the locker room, but I'd get it later.

Hayley was the top priority here.

As soon as we arrived at my house, I noted that all the lights were off. *Good, Dad was gone already.* That meant I wouldn't have to answer any questions. Not that I'd give a shit regardless.

I opened the backseat, and Hayley was still curled in a ball. Her arm was wrapped around her midsection, and I knew that when I pulled her out, it was probably going to hurt.

I did it anyway, though.

"Wrap your hands around my neck," I said as I reached around her body. She trembled slightly and hissed between her teeth. I was half-expecting a protest from her, but she didn't say a word. She wrapped her warm arms around me and buried her head into my chest.

Once we got to the front door, I bent down slightly and put the code in. She groaned, and I slowly stood upright again and whisked us inside. It was dark as I climbed the steps and passed the five doors until I got to my room. Before I laid her down on the bed, I gently placed my mouth near her ear. "I'm going to fucking kill whoever did this to you, Hayley."

And again, to my surprise, she didn't protest. She opened her eyes, one more squinty than the other, and locked onto me. I felt my heart swell within the deep walls of my chest.

I realized something at that moment. Hayley wasn't nearly as strong as she pretended to be, and I wasn't either.

CHAPTER TWENTY-TWO

HAYLEY

I BASKED in the comfort of Christian's bed for what seemed like hours but, really, was probably closer to ten minutes. He sat at the end with his head hung low for a few minutes before getting up and going through another door.

I glanced around the open space. A small smile tried to find its way to my mouth. Christian's room hadn't changed much since the last time I was in here. So many years had passed, and so many things had changed, but I found comfort in knowing his room hadn't. I felt like I still knew a small part of him. It made it real. The old Christian wasn't completely gone. The memories we shared were still tucked tightly away in my heart.

He came back a second later, holding a towel in his hands. He didn't look me in the eye, and I was glad. If he looked me in the eye, he'd see just how broken I actually was.

I pushed away the thoughts of the last hour and focused on the burning and stinging on my face and stomach.

The bed dipped down low, and I felt the warm towel

softly hit my face. Christian dabbed it a few times before he shifted. I flicked my attention to his, and he was staring at me, jaw set, reddened towel in his hand.

We were locked on one another for eons. My heart thumped. My pulse went haywire. My resolve was slowly slipping. Tears threatened to spill.

I was afraid.

I felt unsafe.

And now, looking at someone that made me feel the opposite of those two things, no matter how badly I tried to forge the truth of them, was breaking me in half.

I wanted to succumb.

It was all too much.

My father.

My mother.

My life.

Foster home after foster home.

Gabe.

Pete.

"Are you okay?" he finally asked, his voice softer than I'd ever heard before.

I almost wished he was mean to me. I wished he had his cold, brooding expression on his face. It would have made things so much easier if I could have been mad, if I could have covered up my fear and pain with anger.

My voice cracked, and my lips felt dry as the word rushed out. "No."

Christian shut his somber, gray eyes tightly. His mouth set in a firm line. He blew out a heavy breath as one single tear rolled down my cheek.

My hand shot out to brush it away before he saw me crying, but he stopped me at the last second. His warm palm enclosed my wrist, and he shook his head lightly. Instead, he took his other hand and swiped the tear away with his thumb.

I couldn't move. I couldn't speak. I was too afraid that I would completely lose the hold I had over my emotions. If I moved or spoke even a syllable, I would break in half.

Christian opened his mouth to say something, but our attention was pulled away to Ollie and Piper flying into the bedroom.

Ollie was carrying several bags, and Piper was, too. I almost laughed at the sight of them. When did this happen? When did I become this person who had people who cared about her? For the last several years, I'd been on my own. If I got a scrape, I was the one who put a Band-Aid on it. If my heart got broken by a stupid boy, I was the one who picked up the pieces. If my mom spent all of our grocery money on drugs, I was the one going through the trailer dumpsters for leftovers. I depended on me and only me.

But now, looking at Piper's worried face and Ollie buried by bags of medical supplies, paired with Christian's tender hand, I somehow morphed into a girl who wasn't as alone as she thought she was.

Piper rushed to my side as Christian's hand left my wrist. I slowly pulled myself up, trying to hide my wince. "How are you? Are you okay? If you ever scare me like that again, I'll kill you! Who did this?" I huffed out a small laugh. Ollie was unboxing things, Band-Aids falling at his feet and landing on the soft carpet. Christian got up and went to get another towel. Water was running in the background.

Piper brushed some of my hair out of my face, her emerald eyes getting serious. "Was it Gabe?"

"Who the hell is Gabe?"

I didn't get to answer Christian before Ollie blurted out to him, "Let's go. Get your keys. It's time someone teaches that piece of shit a lesson."

"Where is he?" The soft voice Christian had earlier was long gone.

I began to shake my head as Piper snatched the towel from Christian and began wiping my face and then my stomach.

Christian interjected. "Don't fucking shake your head at me, Hayley. Do you see yourself right now?" He was pacing back and forth. His broad shoulders were drawn upright. He stopped right in front of the bed, peering down at me. "I know you like to keep your secrets, Hayley. You like the taste of lies on your lips, but this has gone too fucking far. I get it. I was a fucking dick to you. I told you I hated you, but so help me God, if you don't tell me who did this, I'll beat the face of every single *Gabe* in the world until I know he has paid for this."

Piper's hand clenched mine. "You should tell him."

"I'm not so sure it was him," I whispered. Gulping, I thought back to the exchange. It might have been someone Gabe asked to rough me up, but that didn't make sense. The guys said they were going to take me; they were waiting for confirmation that I was who they needed. Chills broke out along my arms, and it felt like acid was boiling in my stomach.

Christian began ripping open antiseptic and Band-Aids left and right, taking out his anger on the medical supplies.

"Then who was it?" Piper asked, her face drawn in a frown.

"You're gonna tell us who this Gabe guy is and why he would do something like this, even if it wasn't him." Ollie was standing in the doorway with his arms over his chest. He was wearing a frown, too, which was unusual for him. His blond hair was tousled, his hard jaw an exact replica of his brother's.

"You need to tell them. Let us be here for you, Hay." I bit my lip as Piper squeezed my hand again.

To be honest, I was scared to trust them as much as my

heart wanted me to. There was nothing like the pain of losing someone you trusted indefinitely. But I was tired. I was so tired of keeping everything under lock and key. For once, I wanted to spill the secrets I had underneath my hard exterior.

I was ready. Tonight scared me enough to let some of my walls fall down.

Christian handed off the antiseptic spray to Piper, still staring down at me as my voice cracked. "Gabe was my old foster brother, but before I tell you,"—I shot an unbending glare Christian's way—"you have to swear that you won't lose your temper and try to be my knight in shining armor again and get me justice."

He clenched his teeth. His lip curled. "I can't promise that."

A groan escaped me. "You will promise me that because this is *my* life and things are different for me." I shook my head, sighing. "I'm property of the state, Christian. I have a record. Things go on that record. If something happens to Gabe, even if I didn't technically do anything, it could be traced back to me, and I'd end up back in juvie. There is no proof that Gabe did this. In fact, I don't think he had anything to do with it. So, promise that you'll listen to me and do as I say. This isn't some little high school game. This is the real world."

Silence passed between all of us. I wouldn't go on until he agreed. I knew he didn't understand. He wasn't from this world. And if you didn't live in the world I lived in, it was hard to wrap your head around it. It truly was. Sometimes I even struggled to wrap my head around it.

"Fine," he finally grunted. He moved to the far wall, just beside the door, and propped his leg behind him and crossed his arms over his chest. He looked hot with all the anger bouncing off him.

"I was in a different foster home before Jill and Pete's. And for once, it wasn't a complete shithole. They were rich." I looked around Christian's room. "Not like you guys are rich, but they had money. They bought me clothes and let me eat dinner with them. Gabe later told me that his parents had wanted to have a girl after he was born, but his mom couldn't have any more children, so they started to foster when he was in middle school." I swallowed, looking down at Piper cleaning the scrape on my stomach. "He thought that since his parents were so nice to me and gave me things that it meant he could take what he wanted from me." A sarcastic laugh fell off my lips. "He was wrong. He tried to..." I worked my jaw back and forth, sweat coating my neck.

"He tried to?" Christian's voice sounded like he had swallowed bark from a tree. Rough and calloused.

"He made a pass at me, and I refused. So, then he tried to force me, and I took a baseball bat to his car. It landed me in juvie. The bruise on my face when I first started English Prep was from our encounter."

Christian's face remained unmoving. Ollie blew breath out of his mouth but stayed in his spot, so I continued with my story.

"The reason I thought he may do something was because he told me if he ever saw me again, he'd make me pay." An escaped groan fell off my lips as Piper laid something cold and gooey on my stomach.

"Sorry," she whispered with a crescent-like smile.

"But," I started again. "I don't think tonight was a result of Gabe."

Christian pushed off the wall. "And why's that?"

Memories from that night five years ago tried to assault me. Tiny images of my father lying on beige carpet with blood pooling around him flashed through my brain. His last look at me still had me shaking to this very day. The black-masked men who killed him and their ugly laughter echoed, as did my mother's shrieking scream that I'd ruined everything.

Licking my lips, I looked Christian in the eye. "Because Gabe isn't the only one who has threatened me before."

CHAPTER TWENTY-THREE

CHRISTIAN

THUMP. Thump. Thump. My heart was crashing against the bones inside my rib cavity. Blood was rushing down my limbs, my fingers tingling to inflict pain on someone.

My shoes stomped against my bedroom floor. Piper took Hayley into the bathroom so she could change her dirty and torn clothes and finish cleaning her up. Ollie was sitting on the end of my bed, staring down at the carpet.

"Man," he said quietly. "What a fucked-up life."

And I was certain we didn't even know half of it.

I didn't say anything. I didn't trust myself not to self-combust.

"Hayley was the girl who always smiled when we were in middle school. Do you remember that?" Ollie shook his head as soon as the words left his mouth. "Of course you do. She always smiled when she was with you. But she was nice, and sweet, always including everyone." She did. Hayley was the nicest girl in our seventh-grade class unless someone messed with her or one of her friends. Ollie shifted on the bed. "You know, I always felt sorry for us. Sorry that Mom died. Sorry that Dad was never home. But this?" My feet stopped moving, and I tore my eyes away from the bathroom door. Ollie smashed his lips together before saying, "I bet you're regretting being a fucking dick to her a few weeks ago, huh?"

I didn't say anything. Because yeah, I fucking did. I was up on my high horse, putting blind blame on Hayley for what? Forcing me to face my own shit? For inflicting the guilt on me that I always pushed away?

The bathroom door swung open, and I had to tear my eyes away after a few seconds. Hayley came out with her braids re-done, two of them trailing down her back. Her face looked a little brighter, some color dotting her cheeks along with the tiny cuts and swelling. She was wearing one of my bulldog T-shirts, and it hit her mid-thigh. That was it. Her jeans and T-shirt were draped in Piper's hand.

When she sat back down on my bed, her bare legs were peeking out from below the shirt, and I had to focus on something else.

"Tell us," I managed to ground out. "Who else has threatened you? And I want to know exactly what they did and said to you tonight."

I cracked my knuckles and tried to calm myself by leaning against the wall again. The slick coolness coated my back through my shirt, grounding me to the spot.

Her tongue darted out to lick her lips, and a flame tore through my body. A reminder of the forbidden kiss came through my head like a wrecking ball. *That would surely ground me.*

"Well, I'm sure you all remember my father was shot and killed in my house five years ago."

No one said anything, and Hayley didn't even bother looking up at us.

"When the men came, my mom and dad were in an argument. They were fighting over money or something." Her eyes crinkled around the edges as she brought back the memory. "I can't remember exactly because a lot of what they said didn't make sense to me, but I was upstairs in the hallway, listening over the banister. The door flew open, my mom screamed, and my father started to apologize and ask for more time. I peeked through the banister slats and saw that the men had black masks on." She shook her head slightly, her voice growing weaker. It took everything I had to stay in my spot against the wall. "There was a lot of yelling, threatening words being thrown around. My father's voice was breaking, and it scared me. I'd never seen my dad scared before, so I called 911." Hayley sucked in a sharp breath. Piper's hand covered hers. Ollie kept his head down low, staring at the carpet. "My heart was beating so fast in my chest while I was on the phone. The operator told me to go hide, but when I got up to do that, large hands wrapped around my upper arms. The man snatched my phone out of my hand and hung up. He saw that it was 911. He dragged me down the stairs and kept a hold of me as he yelled out to the other two men what I had done. They didn't even give my father a chance to explain. Our eyes met briefly, and I still, to this day, can't decipher what he was trying to tell me. They shot him right in front of me. My mom screamed at me. The man held my arm so tight I had a bruise, and my mother didn't even care. She was mad that I'd called the cops. Sirens wailed in the background shortly after they shot him, so they quickly left, but not before they turned to me and my mother. They threatened us. Said they'd be back for everything and that they'd come for me when I turned eighteen for the rest."

Breath escaped Hayley. Her cheeks puffed up as she blew it all out.

"The police ended up freezing all of my father's assets,

which left my mom and me with nothing. We moved to a trailer not long after, and she got a job at a diner and went even further off the deep end. I've only seen her once since CPS took me, and I've never once asked her about that night or the threat."

I couldn't move. I was plastered to the wall as each and every word flew out of her mouth. Ollie didn't move a muscle either.

Piper was the only one who reacted. She scooted up onto my bed and put her arm around Hayley. At first, Hayley didn't move, but she eventually rested her head on Piper's shoulder and teetered her lip back and forth.

The words barely made it out of my mouth. They were choppy, like waves crashing against a shoreline. "You think it was them tonight?"

Hayley's blue eyes peered up at me, so glossy they looked like glass. "Maybe. I don't think they were necessarily trying to hurt me, but I fought them so much they had to hold me down and make me stop."

Rage filled my vessels.

"They took a picture of me as the one guy was holding my head down on the ground." Her forehead furrowed. "The other was waiting for confirmation that I was the right girl. They were going to take me anyway and then dump me if I wasn't whoever their boss wanted." She gulped, and her voice teetered on the edge of hysteria. "Maybe it was Gabe. I don't know. Nothing ever confirmed who wanted me. It could have been Gabe that they were waiting for a text from, but that doesn't make sense."

"Why?"

"Because Gabe was in the game. How would he text them back if he was playing football? Whoever it was probably has a nice gash on their hand from when I bit them. That's when I ran." She trembled, and I ran my hands through my hair.

She's had enough for tonight. I stood there, looking at her as Piper rubbed her arm up and down. Hayley was staring off into space, a blank look on her face. Her lip was turning even redder from the constant biting. The hard exterior she'd formed around herself was no longer there. I was seeing the real Hayley. The one who wasn't hiding behind anger or resentment. The one who wasn't shying away from the truth or hiding behind lies. She was real. She was real, and she was scared, and she was hurt. Emotionally and physically.

I pushed off from the wall and stopped at the end of the bed. Ollie glanced up at me for a moment as I looked to Hayley and Piper. "What do you want to eat?"

Hayley furrowed her brow. "What?"

"I'm going to get us all something to eat. What do you want?"

A ghost of a smile brushed over her mouth. "I tell you that the men who killed my father and threatened me may have sent someone to kidnap me tonight, and you want to know what I want to eat?"

"Yes."

Piper sat up a little straighter, tucking her hair behind her ear. "Maybe we should discuss—I don't know—*calling* the police?!" She looked at Hayley for backup, but she quickly shook her head.

"No. No police. There's no point now. They're gone. I have no clue what they look like, and"—she sighed—"the police don't really take people like me seriously."

"But they'll take us seriously." Ollie finally stood up. "Our father knows plenty of law enforcement; you know he has tons of people in his pocket, lawyers—the police chief himself, if I'm not mistaken."

Hayley laughed. "We are in no way getting your father involved." She threw her head back and looked at the ceiling. "It was a cold case. They never found the men who killed my father." She leveled us with a stare. "Not that I think they put much effort into it. They wouldn't tell me much. My mom ran as fast as she could away from my father's problems. It's a fucked-up situation, but there's not much anyone can do."

Piper looked at Hayley. "We should go to the police."

She shook her head again. "Piper, there's nothing they can do, and I really don't want this on my record."

Piper's voice grew loud, and she flew up from the bed. "So what? You're just going to go about your day and hope no one else tries to kidnap or hurt you again—or worse?"

Hayley's features softened, her pouty mouth smiling sadly. "What are the police going to do, Pipe? Give me my own personal bodyguard? The only thing they'll do is tell me to keep my eyes open and to stay vigilant. To call them if I suspect someone is following me. They don't care about some threat that was made five years ago. Especially since no one even knew who made that threat. No one but my father, and that's not exactly helpful since he's dead."

Piper stood with her hands on her hips, huffing out a breath. Ollie worked his jaw back and forth, thinking, analyzing.

"What do you want to eat?"

Hayley's eyes flicked to mine, and I swore I saw a smidge of gratitude in them. "You don't have to feed me. I'm fine." She slowly swung her legs over the bed, trying to hide a wince on her face. "I think we better get going."

A choppy laugh escaped from deep within my chest. "What do you want to eat?"

She gave me a pointed look, her legs slowly dropping to the carpet. "I appreciate you helping me tonight, but you don't have to do this. I'm fine."

I stormed over to her, put my hand underneath her chin, and angled it to my face. Her warmth hit me head-on. "What do you want to eat?"

"Christian."

I grabbed her face a little tighter, and she bit down on that red lip. I swiped my finger up and released it. Her eyes glossed over. "What do you want to eat? And don't even act like you're about to walk out of my house. You and Piper are both staying here tonight, and I'll be climbing through your window every fucking night until I feel you're safe."

A small growl vibrated in her throat. "I'll eat your food, and I guess we can stay here if Piper is okay with it. But you're not climbing through my damn window every night and staying with me. I can protect myself."

I laughed sarcastically, then I looked over at Piper for confirmation. She shrugged. "We can stay here, *but*"—she glared at Ollie—"don't get any ideas. I'm not sleeping in *your* bed."

Ollie's mouth tugged upward. He gave her the grin that made girls weak in the knees. "We'll see."

"Ugh," she yelled as she plopped down on my pillows. "My first sleepover with Hayley and it's with you two egotistical jerks."

I fought back a true laugh, but I kept a hold of Hayley's face.

"Chicken. I want chicken nuggets."

I couldn't help it. I threw my head back and let the laugh out. "Chicken nuggets?"

She pushed my hand off her chin and crawled back into my bed with Piper. But this time, she pulled the covers down and shimmied underneath.

"What are you? Five?" I asked, dumbfounded.

Her face flushed as she looked at the ceiling. "No, I'm hungry, and they're my favorite food."

It was difficult to keep my face neutral. "Chicken nuggets it is. Let's go, Ol."

He glanced at Piper. "Chicken nuggets for you too?"

She thought for a moment and shrugged. "Sure."

"We'll be back." I turned around once more and glanced at Hayley. "Don't get any fucking bright ideas to leave and go to Piper's while we're out getting chicken nuggets, Hayley. And lock the door behind us."

She tried to fight a grin. "I'm locking my window tomorrow night. This is the only night we will ever spend together. You got it?"

I chuckled. "Yeah, we'll fucking see."

CHAPTER TWENTY-FOUR

HAYLEY

I LAY IN MY BED, underneath the ratty quilt, and stared at the shadows on the ceiling. It was moments like this that I wished I could turn my brain off. I didn't usually think of the past or the life I'd had. When I lay down in bed, I popped my old iPod in my ears and listened to music until I fell asleep. But tonight, my iPod was laying on the ground beside the mattress, and I just stared.

Last night was strange. It felt like a hazy dream, except I had the bumps and bruises to prove that it wasn't. From going to the football game and trying to be a *normal* senior in high school, to getting attacked, then staying at Christian's. It had all felt very surreal.

It felt like something was shifting between us. Not only did he swoop in and save the day, he bought me chicken nuggets, let Piper and me stay in his bed while we watched *Gossip Girl* for hours, and didn't once scowl in my direction. After Ollie made Piper and me breakfast—which according to Christian, he never did much of anything in the mornings

—we left with the threat of Christian staying with me tonight.

Pete didn't say a word about my face. He didn't even glance at me when I walked through the door, and Jill was asleep when I came home this morning. I stayed upstairs in my room the entire day, working on homework and trying not to think about the past, empty threats, or Christian. When I finally caved and went downstairs a few hours ago to grab some water and food, Pete and Jill weren't even home. I had no idea where they were— maybe on a date. I chuckled aloud to myself. *Yeah right.* Regardless, my door was locked at 8pm sharp, so they were back home, and Jill was probably sucking his cock as I lay up here, thinking.

Reluctantly, a certain question kept sliding into my thoughts: *Would Christian really come tonight?* I told him, several times, I was locking my window, so there was no use for him to even attempt, but something in my heart dinged when his gray eyes grew dark and he muttered, *"I'll pop it open."*

Did I want him to climb through my window? *No! Yes! Wait, no!* I slapped my hands over my face and ran them down the sides of my cheeks. I hated that I liked the excitement bubbling up inside of me. I hated that I got butterflies when he took my face in his hand last night. My heart actually bloomed in my chest when he told me he wanted me safe.

The thought of meaning something to someone was new to me, and I liked it. It made me feel warm and safe, and that was very dangerous to feel in a life like mine. Things were constantly changing, revolving. People were in and out. Getting attached to anything or anyone wasn't in the cards for me—until it was.

Now I had Piper, who I'd known for a few weeks now, but she was probably the closest friend I'd ever had. I trusted her. She didn't turn on her heel to save herself when she found me bleeding and terrified. She didn't run when things turned bad, and that said a lot about a person.

Then you had Ollie, who was nice to me from the very beginning, but something about his playfulness made me want to hold onto him forever.

And Christian—the boy who swore he hated me, wanted me gone, said I was part of his mom's death, sent scowls my way in school, had Madeline dump her lunch tray on my chest the first day of school—was, for some reason, demanding I let him in my bedroom at night so he could make sure I was safe. He was now the boy who had wanted to kill Pete when he learned that he had hit me. He wanted to go back and strangle the guys who attacked me at the game. He wanted me to stay at his house, and he tended to my wounds. All those good things pulled me in, and I never wanted to let him go, but the guarded part of myself cowered beneath the surface. Pushing him away might hurt less than losing him in the long run, because I'd already lost him once in the midst of losing everything—and it stung.

A sound jerked me out of my thoughts. I sat up in bed and bounced my attention back and forth from the bedroom door to the window. My heart picked up its pace; butterflies invaded my stomach. I felt giddy, and I couldn't remember the last time I'd ever felt like that.

One long, lean, jean-clad leg tore through my window once it was pulled open, and I stayed ramrod straight in my bed. I felt pathetic that I wore my best band t-shirt and nicest sleep shorts when I climbed in my bed tonight, just in case he followed through with his threat.

I was a typical schoolgirl at that moment. Not caring about much in my life other than a boy who probably didn't carry even a fraction of the feelings I carried. He wanted me safe, but that didn't mean he got excited when he saw me or felt a tightening in his lower stomach at the thought of kissing me.

Once Christian was fully inside my bedroom, he turned around and closed the window. He placed his hands on his hips and kept his body angled toward mine. It was dark in my room, the only light from the nighttime sky filtering through the glass. I couldn't make out his face all together, but I was certain he was wearing a grin.

"Thought you were going to lock it," he half-whispered.

My face flamed, and I was grateful the room was still dark. "I forgot..." I exhaled slowly. "You don't need to be here, Christian. I'm fine. All tucked away and locked in my room. What do you think is going to happen?"

Christian inched further into the room. I watched as he tore his jacket off and laid it on the ground near my laptop. Next, his dark figure walked closer to my mattress, and he sat down with his back resting along the wall. His long legs were pulled up with his arms resting on top.

I could see him clearly now. The sharp angle of his jaw as the moon's light cut through the room, the high cheekbones and straight nose. The only thing I couldn't tell was the color of his eyes, but I knew those by heart: stormy, sometimes lighter and sometimes darker.

His gravelly voice finally broke the silence. "Who knows. Maybe those fuckers know where you live, and maybe they'll climb through your window. Maybe they'll pay Pete to unlock your door. Or"—Christian's voice grew quieter—"maybe Pete will try something. Whatever. I'll be here in case something *does* happen."

I paused. I told my heart to stop beating so fast and made sure my voice wasn't high-pitched and girly when I said, "I told you I can take care of myself, Christian. I'm not asking you to save me or to protect me."

I didn't need to see his eyes to know how serious he was. "You never would, and that's precisely why I'm here."

"To protect me because I wouldn't ask you to?"

"Everyone needs to be saved every once in a while, Hayley. Just let me be the one to do it."

Asking why seemed redundant. He always danced around the reason, which only left me more curious. *Does he have some hidden feelings for me? Did the kiss mean something to him, too? Did he have some strange knight-and-shining-armor fantasy he wanted to act out? Did he realize I didn't have anything to do with his mom's death? Was this guilt for the way he had treated me?*

"Whatever," I finally said. The word sounded so juvenile in this situation. "But you're not sleeping on the bed."

He grunted. "Well, I'm sure as fuck not sleeping on the floor." He poked the side of my mattress. "Though it may be more comfortable."

I rolled my eyes playfully. "Oh, shut up. Not everyone can have a rich daddy like you."

A barely there chuckle escaped him.

"So..." I flopped back on my bed and stared at the ceiling again. "What do you plan to do in the morning? And where does your dad think you are?"

"My dad's never home. And I'll climb out of your window and go home to shower and then go to school."

I played the devil's advocate. "So, what if my kidnappers watch you leave and then come and get me?" Christian didn't say anything, so I rolled on my side and gazed at the side of his face. "I was kidding. I'm not totally helpless." Little did he know I had a steak knife underneath my mattress—just in case.

"You know..." He slowly turned his face in my direction. "Maybe I'll just shower here and drive you to school."

I laughed out loud before I slapped my hand over my

mouth, bringing my voice to a whisper. "Yeah right. Pete times my showers. Six minutes or he will shut the water off. What makes you think he'll allow me to take two showers, assuming he won't know that you're the second shower of the morning?"

"He times your showers?" Appalled, he shook his head and muttered something under his breath.

"Not the point." I rested my head in the palm of my hand. "The point is, there's no way that'll work."

"Unless..." Christian's whispers shouldn't have sounded so appealing and sexy. They sent a shiver down my spine, almost as if he were whispering in my ear with his warm breath hitting just the right spot. "I shower with you. We can both shower within six minutes. Pete will never know."

Two things happened: I felt hot all over—even my core felt like it was in the bottom of a volcano—and my brain screamed the word *yes!*

My mouth, however, did not. "In your dreams, Christian."

He chuckled and mumbled something, but I wasn't sure what. "I guess I'll sneak out when Piper shows up to pick you up. Then, I'll go home and shower and get to school. You two goody-goods get to school way before the first bell rings anyway. I'll have time." His shirt scratched along the wall as he shrugged. "And if I don't, Headmaster Walton will write me a note—anything to keep his star student safe."

My face blanched. "What? I'm not his star student."

"With SAT scores like the ones you have? Having students as smart as you brings in potential donations and future Ivy-League-destined individuals, so trust me, he doesn't want anything to happen to you."

My heart studded to a stop. "How do you know my SAT scores?"

Christian swiveled his head in my direction. We were looking at one another, and even through the blackness of my room, I swore I could feel his stare. "I looked through your file."

I felt the muscles in my face falling. "You...what? My *entire* file?"

He didn't miss a beat. "Yes."

So that's what this is about. Pity. Instantly, I felt my hopes come crashing down. I felt stupid. And worse, I felt ashamed.

"That's why you're here." I said it aloud as I was thinking it. Like he wasn't even in the room.

"I'm here because—"

"Because you feel bad for me." I scoffed and fell back onto the bed. "I don't need your pity. I had a fucked-up life after my dad died. So what? The girl you knew back then is gone. I don't even remember her. I don't need you to save me anymore, Christian."

"You should know by now that I don't give people pity."

"That's why you're here!" I whisper-yelled. "You read my file. Learned all there is to know about me and my life. How my mom is now a crackhead and gave up her rights to me the first time CPS was called, how my dad was murdered because he was a part of some sketchy money laundering shit, how I've lived in seven foster homes, and well, I told you about Gabe, so you know everything there is to know about that." I felt my body shaking with anger. I wanted to scream. The frustration I felt was inevitable. The frustration not only over the fact that Christian knew things about me that I wanted to keep buried, but also because *a lot* of people knew things about me that I didn't want to even think about myself. That was all I was to most people: a freaking file.

"That is not why I'm here."

I shot up, my hair flying past my face, the quilt falling to my legs. "It is! You already told me you hated me, wanted me gone, blamed me for your mom's death, and yet you're here?

Something doesn't add up, Christian. You feel guilty for treating me like shit because my entire life is shit."

A beat of silence passed between us. My chest was heaving up and down beneath my T-shirt. My hands were clenched together in my lap. Sometimes I did this; something small provoked me, and then I just lashed out. Everything seemed to hit me all at once.

Christian's voice was supposed to soothe me, but I was too worked up to allow it. "Let's not bring up my mother's death."

I was too angry and mortified that he had read my file to know what to say. Instead, I rolled over, my back now facing him. "I'm going to sleep. Feel free to climb out my window at any time."

I wanted to grab my iPod in the worst way, but getting up out of the bed felt like I was waving a white flag, like I was backing down from my anger. I wasn't. So instead, I just lay there, fuming, pushing all the thoughts of the past out of my head. I carefully built up my walls and pretended I was in my own world, without the memories or echoes of a gunshot. But soon, I found myself listening to the sound of Christian's breathing, and it somehow lulled me right to sleep.

CHAPTER TWENTY-FIVE

CHRISTIAN

I PARKED my Charger beside Ollie and Eric, my eyes scanning the courtyard for a dark-haired girl who wouldn't even look in my direction.

My neck was stiff as fuck, my back aching, both of which had nothing to do with football. Three days of sleeping up against a wall or on the floor did that to you.

Hayley wasn't speaking to me. I wasn't speaking to her, either.

She was angry that I had read her file, refused to believe that I was at her house for any other reason than pity, and when she said things weren't adding up, she was absolutely right. *What the fuck am I doing?* The golden question. I had no idea. I was supposed to feel guilt and hatred when I looked at her face, just like it was before, but I felt so much more. And it was making me crazy. I climbed through her window every night as if I didn't tell myself hours prior to stay away.

I thought back to the conversation between my father and me this morning and sighed.

"I got a voicemail from Jim. Why did you call him?"

"Because I needed him to look into something for me."

"Hayley Smith? Stay out of it, Christian."

"Why? What do you know?"

"What I know is that it isn't safe for you to be butting into things that are well beyond your years. Let the authorities handle it."

Only they weren't. There were no authorities handling it. The authorities didn't even know that Hayley had been attacked or that there was some threat made several years ago.

She drove me fucking crazy. Her need to survive on her own was frustrating and infuriating all in one.

"Hey, Sunshine." My head jerked to Ollie as he sauntered over to my car. I was thankful he was now waking himself up and stopped partying so hard on school nights. It was one less thing I had to worry about, and I had a hunch he was doing it because he knew I was in over my head. "Rough night? Hayley talk to you yet?"

I slung my backpack over my shoulder, now scanning the parking lot for Piper's BMW. My eyes jumped right over Madeline cowering in her car from my public shutdown a couple of weekends ago, then I passed April and the rest of the cheer squad who were all vying for my attention.

"She's already inside. I watched her and Piper walk in a few minutes ago."

Relief poured over me, which only made me angrier. Why couldn't I stop caring? Where was the old Christian? The one who thought of nothing but football, saving Ollie's ass from drunken shenanigans, and if Madeline was going to suck my dick before the game.

Ollie glanced around cautiously, then he bent his head. "I heard you and Dad on the phone this morning." My teeth clinked together. "I assume you're not going to listen to him. Did Jim find anything?"

Jim was my father's P.I. He hired him shortly after Mom started acting distant, not too long before she died. He was a close friend of my father's, and apparently, I misjudged how close they were since he seemed to have talked to my dad about my request when I specifically asked him not to.

"Jim hasn't said anything to me yet. But he's obviously talked to Dad." Ollie and I began walking over to Eric and the rest of the guys congregating in the courtyard. "I'm going to continue to keep an eye on her. And I'll probe Jim later."

Ollie nodded once, and then the pair of us launched into a conversation about the upcoming game this weekend with the rest of our friends.

It had only been a few days, but people finally quit talking about Hayley's face from our last game. She wasn't as roughed up as she was the first day she came to English Prep, but the scratches on her cheek were evident. I was surprised Headmaster Walton hadn't called me into his office to ask if I knew anything about it.

My head jerked mid-conversation with Eric as I heard someone say the name Hayley.

"And did you see her face? I heard she got them having sex with one of Oakland High's finest during the game. Sex in the gravel or something like that."

Another girly voice.

"Kinky!"

Ollie's eyes caught mine, and he grinned coyly.

I spun around quickly and located my source.

"April, tell your little friends to keep their fucking gossiping mouths shut."

April swung her blonde hair over her shoulder. "What? Why?"

"Because Hayley-fucking-Smith isn't their goddamn concern. And she wasn't fucking someone during the game."

April's head twitched a fraction; her two friends—who I

was certain were underclassmen—looked back and forth at one another.

Ben snickered from behind me. "*But* who was she fucking after? Was it you, bro? You've got it bad. That's twice now you've stuck up for the trailer tra—"

Ollie grabbed him by his school tie and brought him to his knees almost instantaneously. "You better watch your fucking tone and who the fuck you're talking about."

The entire group went silent. Ollie didn't get angry often. I was the hothead when compared. Even when we were younger, he'd let me win all the games because he knew how angry I'd get.

My fist clenched, but I held my ground as Ben peered up into the sun. "Damn, are you fucking her too?"

Snap. Like a rubber band. Before Ollie could wind his arm back, I swooped in and punched Ben's jaw so hard he flew to the side of the grass.

I slowly and calculatedly walked over to his slumped-over body, his button-up jacket now dirty, and peered down. "Keep her name out of your mouth." Then, I turned on the sole of my shoes and passed by my peers who were all looking at me like I'd lost my mind.

I had.

I was certain of it.

Ollie caught up to me quickly, Eric right behind him. "Dude, I fucking had it. I was taking care of it."

"It's not your problem to take care of." I pushed through the doors, and my eyes found her within a second. She was resting her back along her locker, her raven hair tucked behind her ear. She smiled at Piper, and I felt a surge of jealousy go through my body. A smile from a girl like her was rare —so rare I didn't know that I'd ever seen one.

"But it's yours?" Eric moved in front of me and Ollie, no longer trailing us.

I eyed his dark hair and features. His brows were pulled together, his eyes crinkled at the sides. He shook out his hair. "Hear me out; I'm on your side. You don't want people talking to her, that's fine. I'll help ward them off. But what the hell is going on? Are you two a thing?"

I caught Hayley's eye as she began to walk past us. She narrowed her gaze, those blue eyes sucking me in as they locked onto me. She leaned in close to Eric, so close her skirt was touching his pant leg.

"To answer your question, *no.* Christian and I are *not* a thing."

Her words felt like a sledgehammer to my chest, but it was the first time since Saturday night that she'd even looked in my direction. Every time I climbed in and out of her window, she was facing the wall as she lay on her mattress. When she'd get up to shower in the morning, she'd walk right past me, as if I wasn't lying there on her floor.

Anger clawed up my chest. My words were a bite to every exposed part of her body. "Hayley needed my help with something, but she's got it all figured out on her own."

I hated that I couldn't read her expression. *What are you thinking?* Was she glad I was throwing in the towel? Did she want to protest? Was there another lie about to rest on those pouty lips?

Hayley was full of little lies.

I knew she felt better with me in her room every night. She felt safer. Yet, she pushed me away every chance she got. She said she didn't need my help. Well, fucking okay then.

Her tongue darted out to lick her lip. It was as if it were only the two of us. No one else was in the hallway. No one else was on the entire fucking planet. "You're right. I don't need your help—or anyone else's."

I huffed out a laugh, crossing my arms over my chest. "Fine."

She did the same. "Fine."

The bell rang and it startled both of us. We both dropped our fuck-off poses, our arms hanging down by our sides. She brushed past me, and I flared my nostrils, clenching my teeth together.

Ollie and Eric were staring after her and then at me.

Ollie dipped his head in. "That was all part of this game you two are playing, right?"

I ground out. "I'm not playing a fucking game."

Eric chuckled as his eyebrows shot to his hairline. "Oh, you two are definitely playing a game, bro. She's just winning." He smiled mischievously and walked off, throwing his head back. Once he was down the hall, he turned around and cupped his hands around his mouth. "I'm rooting for you, though." The entire school looked at the two of us, and they were, no doubt, wondering what the fuck was going on. The rumors were destined to start.

What exactly was going on with their king and the girl from down the block?

Their guess was as good as mine.

CHAPTER TWENTY-SIX

HAYLEY

"*HAYLEY SMITH GOT CAUGHT banging someone in the gravel from Oakland High at the game last week. Did you see her face?*"

"*Hayley Smith begged Christian for his help with something. He turned her down.*"

"*Ben Jennings got his ass beat for fucking Hayley. Christian was not happy.*"

"*Hayley and Christian are fucking. She's the new queen of the school. Madeline is losing her hair over this.*"

I kinda wanted the last part to happen. Madeline bald? That would surely wipe out all the rumors circulating the school regarding me.

But instead of dwelling on them, I continued to bury myself in homework and papers. Piper tried distracting me during lunch by buying me a chocolate chip cookie, and it actually worked—for a minute. I didn't dare look at Christian or his table of followers. Piper said he wouldn't look at me either.

Which was fine. Maybe he wouldn't climb through my

window tonight. Maybe he'd stop feeling bad for poor little Hayley.

I couldn't deny the pit that formed in my stomach at the thought of his presence not being there tonight. As much as I didn't want to admit it, I anticipated his long body climbing through my window and settling down onto the floor. No words spoken, just an abundance of angry, hot tension lingering in the air between us. I hated the pity, but I loved the comfort. My heart was torn in two.

He had to have known that a small part of me was too weak to put up a fight. I could have locked my window at night, but I didn't. I couldn't bring myself to do it. I blamed it on the damaged twelve-year-old girl inside of me. She wasn't as strong as seventeen-year-old Hayley. She was scared, and worried, and felt helpless in almost every situation of her life. Things were out of her control five years ago, and they were out of control now, too.

"Hey, you ready?" Piper dangled her keys in front of my locker, her backpack slung over her shoulder.

"Yep, let me grab my chem book real quick." I reached in to grab my book and heard her sharp inhale of breath.

"Don't freak, but I think I just saw your social worker." My stomach dropped, remembering my face this morning when I got ready for school. You could still see the marks from the gravel on Friday night. There were tiny scratches all along my cheek, and if you were to lift up my shirt, you'd see some nice scratches there, too.

Piper grabbed my arm in reassurance. "Maybe she just has a meeting with Headmaster Walton."

I shrugged quickly and shut my locker. "Let's go before they come looking for me."

She nodded, and we briskly started to walk down the hall and head for the doors. Right as Piper's hand touched the handle, Headmaster Walton's voice echoed down the hall.

"Miss Smith, a word please."

"Shit," I whispered.

Piper took her pink lip in her teeth and gave me a worrisome look. "I'll wait for you."

Shaking my head, I started to walk backwards. "No, don't you have something going on at home today? Some dinner or something?"

Her face fell.

"I'll take the bus; it'll be fine. I'll see you tomorrow, okay?" I gave her a half-smile and turned around quickly so she wouldn't argue with me. I made my way to the office's oak doors where Headmaster Walton was waiting for me in all his glory.

He didn't come out of his office much. I never really saw him roam the halls. He was securely tucked away in his large, expansive office with hundreds of books lining the built-in bookshelves. I couldn't blame him. If I could hide out in there, I would.

Once I was within spitting distance, Headmaster Walton glanced at the scratches on my face. His brows furrowed as he turned around and walked back into his office. I gave Ms. Boyd a nervous smile, clutching my backpack for dear life, and headed in after him.

Ann was standing near his desk, wearing a skirt and a blouse, with her arms crossed over her chest. She didn't look like her normal, sunshine-y self, and that didn't sit well with me.

Alarms went off in my head. My stomach felt queasy.

"What happened?"

Acting dense, I brushed my hands down my plaid skirt. "What do you mean? I'm fine. In fact,"—I met her eyes—"I got a perfect score on my world language test today."

"Cut the shit, Hayley." Headmaster Walton, now sitting at

his desk, sighed heavily at Ann's choice of words. "What happened to your face? Was it Pete?"

"And who is Pete?" he asked, placing his hands flat on his desk.

Ann answered sharply without taking her eyes off my face. "Her foster father."

"No. It wasn't Pete." I was hoping she couldn't tell I was sweating underneath my uniform. Even the backs of my knees were sweating. "I fell at the game."

She rolled her eyes. "You fell at the football game and got scratches all over your face? I don't think so."

I mean, it technically wasn't a lie.

I huffed. "Do you want a witness?"

"No, I want you to tell me the truth! If your foster parents aren't treating you correctly—which we both know they aren't—I need to know, Hayley."

A sarcastic laugh erupted. "Are we going to do this again?" I evened out my tone, trying to remain calm, but the thought of Ann making this bigger than it needed to be almost sent my nerves through the roof. *I'll be damned if I go to a group home.* "Ann, I'm not lying. Pete did not do this. Things are fine at home. Pete doesn't talk to me. I don't talk to him. Everything is fine."

"I don't believe you." She shook her head and looked at Headmaster Walton. "Have you heard anything? What about that girl that stole her clothes?"

Headmaster Walton sighed. "I haven't heard anything but good things about Miss Smith. Her teachers rave about her. She's quiet, focused, and receives the best of the best grades. She's soaring here. I'd hate to see you take her out of her current placement and take her somewhere else farther away, making it impossible for her to get here in the mornings, given she doesn't have transportation."

My face felt hot. Maybe Christian was right. Maybe

Headmaster Walton truly needed me in his school. What-ever. It didn't matter. He was right. I agreed with him, and what he said basically came directly from my own brain. If she took me out of Pete and Jill's and put me into a group home, it would be a domino effect in ruining my already shitty life.

"I have a witness," I blurted. "Christian saw me fall. He helped me up."

Headmaster Walton eyed me suspiciously, his bushy, graying brows gathering together. "Christian was on the field, playing football, my dear."

Shaking my head quickly, I said, "No, it was right after. Piper was in her car, waiting for me. I had to use the restroom and fell while walking to the parking lot. He was going to the locker room." *Please believe me—or at least play along.* I shot him a look behind Ann's back. *Come on.*

"Well, fine. I want to ask Christian myself."

I almost growled at Ann. "Why are you being so difficult?"

The planes of her face softened. "Because I care about you."

My heart grew. *Why do those words always affect me so much?* Headmaster Walton called Ms. Boyd on the phone and asked if she could locate Christian; he told her he'd likely be on the field for football practice.

Silence coated the room as we waited for him. Awkward didn't even come close to what we were all feeling. It prob-ably took five minutes max, but it felt like five hours with Ann staring at my face and Headmaster Walton pretending he was reading something at his desk.

As soon as the door opened and Christian's face appeared, I felt my body relax. His angular jaw was the first thing I saw, then his gray eyes which immediately found me. At first, his brows drew together, and then he noted Ann, and he put on his cool, blank face that drove me insane because I could never tell what he was thinking.

"Christian, please come in." Headmaster Walton stood up from his desk and ushered Christian inside, shutting the door behind him.

He was no longer in his school uniform, but instead in workout shorts and a tight, white T-shirt. His hair was a little mussed on top, and I found myself swearing under my breath as I peeked at his arms. I was instantly brought back to the time in the stairwell when he found me half-naked. He was dressed the same, ready for football practice. And he looked just as casually sexy today as he did then. The only difference was his eyes weren't full of loathing anger. Today, they were a blank canvas: cool, calm, and collected.

Once Christian took his seat in front of Headmaster Walton, dipping his head in Ann's direction, Headmaster Walton opened his mouth to ask the question, but Ann interrupted.

"Christian?" He turned his head in her direction and raised his brows. I stood back along the books, praying that Christian would corroborate my story. *Once again, saving my ass.* Ann put her hand out and shook his. "I'm Ann, Hayley's social worker. I have a quick question for you."

"Okay," he said, his face still cool as a cucumber. Meanwhile, I had sweat dripping down my back.

"Did you see Hayley on Friday night?"

He didn't miss a beat. There wasn't even a twitch of a muscle on his face. "Yes."

My heart began beating frantically in my chest.

"And did anything out of the ordinary happen?"

His lips turned upward just a fraction, and suddenly, I could feel my hope falling rapidly. *He was going to throw me under the bus.* And what did I expect? I had been giving him the cold shoulder since he told me he read my file. I'd been pushing him away, hoping he'd stop saving me and feeling sorry for me.

Now, I wanted to get down on my hands and knees and beg for him to save me. To keep my secret safe so I could have a chance at a normal life, far away from this city.

"Nothing is ordinary with Hayley." A soft chuckle left his throat.

Ann wasn't impressed with Christian's beat-around-the-bush response, and the only thing it did was confuse me. Where was he going with this?

"Where did you see her Friday?"

Suddenly, I felt like Christian should have been in an interrogation room, under a swaying spotlight, with Ann pacing back and forth, making threats.

Christian leaned back in his seat, crossing his arms over his tight chest. "I saw her at the game, right after it ended."

My hope started to climb, and I wasn't going to wait for him to ruin the half-truth I'd given.

"See!" I threw my hands out, looking at Ann. "I told you, he was there when I fell. He helped me up."

Headmaster Walton smiled proudly at Christian. "Christian is a gentleman; it doesn't surprise me that he helped her."

Okay, relax. I'm not that much of a damsel in distress.

Ann narrowed her eyes in a dubious way. "Christian, is that true? Did Hayley *fall*?" She glanced at me and then back at Christian. "Please be truthful. I have a hunch that Hayley could very well be in danger, and she's too stubborn to ask for help."

I held my breath, waiting, staring directly at Christian. His eyes slowly moved to mine, and we held onto each other in that moment for no longer than a few seconds, but something unspoken was exchanged between us.

"Yes, I saw her trip, and she took quite a fall. I helped her up and then walked her to her friend's car to make sure she was okay."

Relief washed over my entire body. I almost exhaled.

"I told you," I said expectantly to Ann. I straightened my shoulders and made a note to glance at Headmaster Walton's hanging clock. "Now, if we're done here, I have to get going, or I'm going to miss the bus, and Pete will be wondering where I am." *Not true.*

Ann's face fell. "Of course, go. I'd give you a ride, but I have a few more stops in town before I'm done for the day. I'll be back to check on you next week, okay?"

I gave her a thumbs up. "Super." Then, I turned to Headmaster Walton and gave him a small gesture before bypassing Christian.

I hurriedly left the room and tried not to run at a full sprint out of the office. There was no way he was going to let me get away without a word after he just saved my ass—again. But I needed time to think and to decompress.

My steps grew faster when I heard the office doors open and close behind me. At that point, I was almost running, and before I knew it, I was outside, the cool autumn breeze causing my hair to fly around. I blew air out of my mouth and could taste the freedom, but then my heart stopped as a hand snaked around my arm and pulled me back. Christian spun me around and peered those eyes down at me below his thick, dark eyelashes.

I stifled a yelp. My chest was rising and falling quickly.

"Still don't want my help?" His mouth was set in a firm line, but his eyes were playful.

I yanked my arm out of his grasp, even though something in my body yearned for me not to. "I appreciate the help in there." I pointed my head in the direction of the doors. "But I'm fine otherwise."

A sharp laugh rumbled out of Christian's throat. He

turned around and clasped his hands behind his head. A hefty breath sounded from his direction, and then he turned back around, his arms falling. "Are you that damaged that you can't take a little help and protection from someone else?"

I pulled back instantly. "I'm not damaged!" Hurt pierced me. *But aren't you, Hayley?* I knew Ann would be coming out of Headmaster Walton's office any second, so I rounded the corner of the building, knowing Christian would follow.

His footsteps were heavy as twigs and crispy leaves broke with each stride. "You're not? You have some fucking psychos following you and jumping you, threats from years ago coming to the surface, your foster dad locks you in your bedroom and times your showers...but you're fine? You don't need anyone's help? It's bullshit!"

I wasn't sure I'd ever seen Christian so frantic. As kids, even when he was angry with someone at school, or with Ollie for following us around and begging to hang out with us, he still acted collected. Cold, but collected. He never raised his voice. The other night, when he was clearly both-ered by my injuries, and even more bothered by my story regarding Gabe, he didn't visibly show his emotions. But now? His face was red, his hands were clenched into fists, and his gray eyes were like a raging storm brewing over the ocean. He shook his head sharply. "What are you so afraid of?"

A gust of wind blew across the bare skin of my legs. I crossed my arms over my uniform. "I'm not afraid of anything." *Oh, but you are, Hayley.*

The thought assaulted me, and I knew my expression showed it. Christian narrowed his gaze.

I tore my expression away, feeling my walls cracking a little. *Shit. No.* Then, I heard a rattling sound, like the old, beat-up truck that one of my past foster dads owned. My gaze went directly to the parking lot, and I froze.

I recognized that truck.

I recognized that skinny arm hanging out of the passenger side window.

Oh my God.

My attention moved back to Christian, and my resolve fell to our feet. My entire body broke out in goosebumps.

"I lied." My voice sounded like broken shards of glass. Sharp and choppy. Breakable.

"What?" Christian stopped pacing and placed his hands on his hips.

I swallowed and moved beside him. I looked out into the parking lot again, meeting a pair of eyes that matched mine. "I lied." I craned my neck up to Christian, his body heat warming me for a fraction of a second. "When I said I wasn't afraid of anything."

He tilted his head while peering down.

I gulped as my mother climbed out of the rusty, old truck. "I lied."

CHAPTER TWENTY-SEVEN

CHRISTIAN

FEAR PROVOKED OUR WORST BEHAVIORS.

That was why I was acting so unlike myself. I was flustered, angry, baffled, and downright desperate to get Hayley to admit that she needed someone to lean on. I'd never acted so idiotic before—not over a girl, at least.

And then, when she hit me with those blue eyes full of straight, unending fear, I knew I was a goner. It killed me. The thought of Hayley being afraid or hurt sent me straight to the red. It felt like an open wound in my chest, a burn only she could soothe.

"What are you afraid of?" I asked as her hand clenched onto my forearm. She was staring at something behind me, and I craned my neck in that direction, but before I could get a good look, she squeezed my arm and stole my attention.

"My mom."

For fuck's sake.

"Your mom?" I spun around. Hayley's hand stayed glued to my arm, and we watched a woman who I'd seen many years ago—but definitely couldn't have pointed her out in her current state—climb out of an older, beat-up Chevy.

"Christian." The breakage of Hayley's voice had me grinding my teeth. She looked up at me, and suddenly, I was taken back several years ago, looking my best friend in the face after she told me her parents were fighting every night. "I need you to keep your mouth shut but stay beside me at all times."

"Why? Has she hurt you before?" My heartbeat was in my ears.

She shook her head, the pink color of her cheeks fading. "Not physically, but the man she is with?" I locked eyes with the man in the driver's seat. The distance between us was far, but even so, I could tell he was a fucking scumbag. "He's bad news. Don't do anything stupid."

Can't promise that.

Her soft hand squeezed my arm again and brought me back down to earth. "Christian. Please. Promise me." The pleading in her voice almost broke me in half. "I'll do anything. You can stay in my room every night. You can even take the other half of the bed. I don't care. Just don't say a word. I can handle it."

"Fine," I finally answered. As soon as her hand left my arm, I grabbed it and clasped our palms together, interlocking our fingers. She paused, looked down at our hands, and let out a shaky breath.

Then, I let her lead the way.

Her mother looked like shit. Complete and utter shit. If you were to look up the word *death* in the dictionary, Hayley's mother's photo would be beside it. She reeked of stale cigarette smoke, her face was wrinkled, and a too-dark shade of makeup coated every deep crevice on her cheeks. Big bags hung underneath her eyes, and if you lifted her shirt, I was certain you'd be able to count every rib in her body. She wore a pink top that went around her neck and shorts that looked as if they belonged to Daisy Duke herself, except Hayley's mom's spaghetti-noodle legs stuck out from below.

We were only a few yards away from the truck, tucked away on the side of English Prep. Hayley's hand was still clasped in mine, but I could still feel the nerves rolling off her body.

"How did you find me?" She stopped just a few feet away from her mother. I peered around her body and looked at the man in the driver's side of the truck again. His dark gaze was dead set on us. He looked just as ragged as Hayley's mom with a cut-off flannel shirt and a bandana wrapped around his head.

"That doesn't matter," her mother answered, reaching out to touch the bow around Hayley's neck. Hayley jerked back-ward, clenching down on my hand. I squeezed it back, reas-suring her that I was still here.

Hayley leveled her mom with a stare. "What do you want? Money? I don't have any."

Her mom smiled with her yellowing teeth. Her painted-on pink lipstick made my stomach turn. *Desperate much?* She looked like a hooker on meth. "Maybe not, but I bet he does." Her eyes flicked over to me, and I hoped she could read what I was thinking. *Not a fucking chance, you piece of shit.*

I didn't know the entire story of how Hayley had landed in foster care, but I knew it had to have been something extreme if CPS took her on the first call, and judging by the looks of her mom, it was rightfully done.

"Are you that desperate to come begging me and my..."—Hayley looked at me for one second before the word flew out of her mouth—"friend for money after abandoning me? I haven't seen you for three years, and do you remember what I said the last time you came around asking for money?" Hayley's mom sighed as she wrung her hands together. "I told you to fuck off and to never contact me again."

Thatta girl.

It was almost as if her mom didn't hear a word she said. She reached out again and tried to touch Hayley's uniform—with no success—then she glanced at the school behind our heads. "Look at you. All grown up and at this fancy school. You always were smart."

Yeah, no thanks to you.

The more I stared at Hayley's mom, the angrier I grew. How? How did this happen? One day, Hayley was a normal seventh-grade girl, and the next, her dad was murdered, and her mom dragged her away to some trailer park.

Then, she ended up in shitty foster homes for the next five years?

Hayley kept her mouth clamped, and I did too, although it may have been the most difficult thing I'd ever done, next to watching my own mother self-destruct.

"You need to be smart now."

Hayley's body moved a fraction, but I kept us in place. "What are you talking about?"

Her mom bit her lip with her decaying teeth before bringing her bloodshot gaze to Hayley. "I didn't just come for money. You know they're coming for you, right? You're almost eighteen. They want their settlement."

A chill ran over my spine.

"You should come with me and Tank." Her mom looked back and blew a kiss to the man in the truck. "He protects me."

Hayley laughed. "At what cost? Your pussy anytime he wants? Prostitution on the side? Making him money?"

I almost laughed out loud. *Jesus fuck.* What exactly had Hayley seen and been through in these five years apart? Her mouth was a force to be reckoned with. Her knowledge went far beyond the luxury of English Prep and trust-fund babies.

The red in Hayley's mom's cheeks grew brighter. "It's better than those men having me. They'll come for you and do the same. You'll be their little doll to do whatever they want with after they get the settlement."

Now it was my time to squeeze Hayley's hand. I squeezed so hard I heard her small intake of breath. I slowly let go, found my footing, and took a deep breath.

Hayley's voice was near breaking. "Do you know who they are?"

Her mom's eyes lit up like a sparkler on the 4th of July. "Yes, if you give me some money, I'll tell you some stuff that'll be to your benefit since you won't join Tank and me."

Is she fucking serious? Almost as if Hayley could read my thoughts, her hand clamped down onto mine. "I have three dollars. It's all I have."

She had three dollars? That was all? I surely hoped that wasn't true. Hayley let go of my hand and whipped her backpack off her back. She reached into the pocket and pulled out the three dollars, and fuck me, it was in quarters and dimes.

Her mother snatched it out of her hand quickly as I scanned the side of the courtyard for any wandering eyes. It was pretty desolate as school had ended a little while ago. The last thing we needed were more rumors.

"So, tell me and then be on your way. I don't want to see you again. Ever."

Hayley's mom rolled her eyes as she flung her tangled hair behind her shoulder. "Your daddy got into some debt, made some bad investments, and was trying to cover his ass by laundering money through his company." She fidgeted on her feet, and Tank yelled out the window, "Let's go!" She jumped, her blue eyes piercing Hayley. "The cops know who did it; they just didn't have much evidence other than my word.

Watch your back. They're bad people. They make the people I hang out with look like angels."

Then, she turned around and ran back to the truck, hopping in and slamming the door shut. Hayley let go of my hand and wrapped her arms around her middle. She shouted, "What settlement were you talking about?"

Her mom glanced at her once, and then Tank took off, smoke billowing from his exhaust. Once the truck was out of sight, a held breath left her mouth. I stood back with my hands on my hips, completely baffled at the exchange shared with her mom and even more baffled that I was able to keep my shit together.

"Go wait in my car," I demanded, still staring down the road. The truck was long gone, but the achy feeling it left behind was stuck in my limbs. I needed to punch something, or run, or yell. I needed to do something to get this pent-up anger out of my system before I blew up.

"I'll take the bus." Her words were nothing but a whisper in the wind.

"Hayley, goddamnit," I seethed through my teeth. "Don't fucking play with me." I leveled her with a glare, and it only made matters worse. Her eyes were glossed over, and her pink cheeks were as white as her school blouse. "I kept my mouth shut while that piece of shit you share DNA with filled your head with nothing but riddles." I stalked over to her, trying to ground myself before I went ballistic and started running after the truck to demand more information. I put my hand under her chin. She was reluctant to look up at me, but in the end, she did. My voice was softer now, but I could still hear the edge. "Go sit in my car. I'll be back in a few to take you home." She clenched her teeth together and worked her jaw back and forth. Her eyes were watery, but she didn't dare let a tear spill. "And I'm staying in your room and will pretty much be your shadow until this is figured out."

"Why?" her voice cracked. "Why won't you just stop? I don't need you getting mixed up in this. I don't need anyone else butting in."

I kept my voice steady. "Because I can't stop, Hayley. I can't fucking stop. Now go, and lock it when you get inside."

Her brows drew together, but in the end, she huffed out a warm breath, picked up her backpack, and walked away, her hips swaying in her wake.

I growled out loud, angry that I couldn't stop bending over backwards for her and that I couldn't keep my eyes from watching her ass all the way to my car.

I stormed off once I saw her get into my car and went straight to the locker room. I had forty minutes of practice left, and then I was taking Hayley home and making a call to Jim.

My father could fuck off. Someone was after Hayley, and we needed to figure out who.

I was certain the lattice would have broken by now. I climbed it, hearing it crack and bend underneath my weight. All the lights were off in the house, which meant everyone was likely sleeping, but I knew Hayley would be awake. She was awake every time I climbed through her window, even though she pretended to be asleep, all curled up on her side, facing the wall, far away from me.

Ollie smirked every time I left the house but didn't say a word. And thankfully, each morning, when I dragged my ass back home to shower, he was up and had a pot of coffee waiting for me. I guessed that was his way of saying he was there for me—that, along with not partying as much, knowing very well I couldn't have bailed him out at the last second.

When my fingers reached Hayley's window, I found that it was already open. I smirked in the darkness, climbing through until my feet hit the hard floor. It took a few minutes until my eyes could adjust, but I found her in her normal spot, her small body curled in the fetal position, facing the wall with a quilt draped over her body.

The energy in the room was off. It was usually tense the second I stepped in here, both of our anger and annoyance seeping into the walls. And that was the exact energy I left her with when I had dropped her off earlier. Not a word was spoken between us when I drove her home. Not one single word. I was too lost in my thoughts, eager to call Jim, and Hayley stared out the window at the passing trees and houses with her arms crossed over her chest.

But tonight, something was off.

I shut the window behind me, the wooden pane sliding in place with a small creak. My back slid against the wall as I slumped down into my normal spot. The house was eerily quiet. I could hear my own blood thumping in my veins.

And then I heard it.

My neck snapped over to Hayley. I stared, feeling my chest tighten with each passing second.

Was she crying?

No. Surely not. Hayley tough-as-shit-didn't-need-anyone wasn't crying. The old Hayley might have cried, but the new one? *No.*

But she was.

It felt like a knife was lodged deep in my chest. *Why was this hurting me?*

A barely audible, shaky sigh left her mouth, and then I watched the shadow of her blanket move as she wiped an eye. *Jesus fuck.*

I quickly got up, a jolt going through my entire body. I stood there and stared down at her mattress on the floor. Hayley curled into herself even more, hiding her face. She let out another shaky breath, trying her hardest to hide her tears.

In the beginning, all I wanted was for her to cry. In fact, it was my goal to make her cry and for her to go running back to wherever she came from. But now, hearing her cry was drilling a hole into my chest.

My body acted of its own accord. First, my knee landed on the mattress, and she inhaled a breath. Then, my hands hit, and I swung the rest of my body down until I was lying flat on my back. Hayley was holding her breath. It wasn't until she let out a few tiny puffs of air that I snuck my arm toward her and pulled her over. The second I went to pull her body into mine, she crashed into me. Like two magnets that were drawn to each other. Her head landed on my shoulder, her arm went around my body, and mine went around her hip. Her body shook against mine. The taste of blood filled my mouth as I bit down on my tongue, keeping my own emotions at bay.

In between her hiccups and swiping of eyes, she whispered along my chest, "It's just too much."

Nodding, I brought my hand up to her hair and wove my hand through it.

It was too much. All of it. There was a lot of baggage between Hayley and me, but her own personal baggage outweighed ours by a longshot. She was fragile, even when she pretended not to be. And I was so swept up in her that nothing could have pulled me out.

I wanted her to stop hurting. At that moment, I would have done anything in the world to make it stop.

Which is why, when she calmed her cries and breathing

and angled her head up to look at me, I looked down at her with pleading eyes. *How can I make this stop for you?*

Hayley swallowed, her face now dry from salty tears. Her eyes glittered in the darkness, and when they darted down to my lips, a fire erupted in my body.

She shimmied her body closer to mine, her body heat making me burn even brighter. My hand rested along her bare thigh as my dick grew hard. Hayley felt the shift in the air, and if I could have seen her eyes more clearly, I could've guaranteed that her pupils were as dilated as mine.

Is this what you want?

My hand slowly moved along her soft skin, reaching the bottom hem of her shorts. A sharp intake of breath filled the room, and my body ached. I flipped her over onto her back, the dark strands of her hair whooshing out of her face. I came over top of her body, begging my hands to go slow even though all I wanted to do was rip off every bit of her clothing, tear it to shreds, and bury myself inside her.

Hayley's legs parted instantly, allowing me access to tower over her. A thrill went down my spine. *I'm going to make you feel good, Hayley. We're going to put a pause on the past.*

"Is this what you want?" I whispered as my lips hovered above hers.

Hayley licked her bottom lip, and within a second, she was raising her head to kiss me. Our lips touched, and every thought in my head flew out the window. I plunged my tongue inside her mouth, tasting every lie, deceit, and ugly truth that was on her lips. My arms caged her head in, and I moved my mouth over hers over and over again until it was nothing less than a frenzy between our bodies.

I sat up quickly, excitement buzzing through my veins. There was nothing left in my body except for the need to make her feel good. I'd never been like this before. I'll admit, I was selfish in the bedroom, only putting forth the effort so

I could achieve my own finale. But with Hayley, it was different. I was here to please her. In fact, knowing I had an effect on her was enough to get me off right then.

My hand skimmed the top of her shorts as her chest heaved up and down. She was squirming under my touch, and a dark smile found its way onto my face. When I slid my hand under the waistband and into her panties, she bucked her hips up, meeting me halfway.

Yes, Hayley. You're as eager as I am.

Not wanting to waste any time, I pulled her shorts and panties down quickly, throwing them over my shoulder. I stared down at her with the gleam of the moon and was in complete awe.

She was the sexiest, prettiest thing I had ever seen in my life. Her pussy was perfect, and I swore in that moment, it was made for me.

I pushed her legs wide, and Hayley's head fell backwards. My one hand cupped her waist as I hooked one of her legs over my shoulder and bent my face down low.

"Christian." Her voice was breathy and doped up on lust.

My face moved closer, and I inhaled, my dick throbbing in my jeans. *Jesus Christ.* I'd never been so turned on before. If I wasn't careful, I'd bust a nut right here. I was driven by desire, and I didn't give a damn about anything else with her pussy near my face. I blew on her most sensitive spot, and she wiggled underneath me. I tightened my grip on her hip and gave her one swell lick with my tongue. She gasped and fisted the sheets with her hands. I licked again and again, liking that she was putty in my hands. Once her hips started to move along my face with their own rhythm, I took my other hand and reached underneath her shirt. I found her small bud and held back a small groan. I squeezed it with my fingers once before her hips moved even faster. Her breathing was quick, and I peeked up from eating her pussy to watch the ecstasy fall over the soft planes of her face. I licked faster and inched my finger inside her walls. *My God, what a fucking sight.* Her pussy clenched down on my finger instantly, and she moaned something inaudible. I moved my finger in and out one more time while I simultaneously sucked on her clit, and I felt her let loose.

Her pussy sucked so hard on my finger it was almost painful. My dick jerked in my pants, and I had to focus to keep things under control.

I'd never in my life witnessed something so wildly beautiful before. The only thing I could focus on when I pulled myself up and lay beside her again was the feeling inside my body. There wasn't one syllable passed between us as she curled up next to me with her head on my shoulder, yet so much was said.

The last tiny bit of hatred for Hayley was diminished. It had evaporated into thin air. The ugly past no longer existed. The only thing I could think about was her and how her body fit so perfect nestled up to mine.

And that was how I woke the next morning when my phone alarm went off: her body pressed against mine, our legs tangled, my hand still woven in between the strands of her dark hair.

I didn't know when it happened. But the girl that used to repel me in every way, somehow managed to sneak her way into my chest and cuddle right up to my muscle within its walls.

CHAPTER TWENTY-EIGHT

HAYLEY

THE NEXT DAY AT SCHOOL, I avoided looking in Christian's direction. Last night, I was completely shattered and broken beyond repair. My emotions were running high, and I was raw from the inside out.

That was my only excuse as to why I let Christian do what he did. My face flamed at the thought. I wasn't innocent by any means. I'd had sex and fooled around with past boyfriends, but what I did with Christian last night was completely and utterly personal and intimate. There were emotions involved. There was an unspoken understanding between us when we crossed over that line and fused our lips together. He helped me forget, and I all but forced him into it.

I wasn't sure what I was feeling anymore. I was embarrassed he found me crying—and even more embarrassed that I used his shoulder to lean on. Then, he took my brokenness and pieced me back together, at least for a little while. And I wasn't going to lie; part of me was afraid to look him in the eye after last night. He snuck out of my window early, shortly after his alarm went off, and as soon as he was gone, I jumped out of bed and into the shower, only giving myself fifteen minutes to get ready before Piper showed up. She noted my puffy eyes and asked me what had happened yesterday, and I told her the gist of it, leaving out much of what happened with Christian. It felt like he and I were on a whole other planet, and there were ticking time bombs all around us.

He was slowly becoming my safe place, and that was so bad.

"So, do you think you'll be able to stay with me Friday? I promise we don't have to go to the game. I'm sure that's the last place you want to go after the previous one."

I took a bite of my apple that Piper snagged for me—she was still buying more than she needed for lunch, which always resulted in being mine. "Let me work up the nerve to ask Pete and Jill. I think today is Jill's day off, so she should be home. It's easier to ask while she's there."

Piper poked her salad with her plastic fork. There was chatter all around us in the lunchroom. Christian's table was more rowdy than normal, but I kept my eyes glued to Piper shoving lettuce in her mouth. "Jill doesn't seem too bad. Pete, on the other hand... I'd like to stick this fork up his ass."

I laughed, and she paused, her cheeks full of food. Then she laughed too. "Sorry, I just don't like him. I wish you could just stay with me all the time." Then, she dipped her head in low, her ginger hair falling between us. "I know Christian is a no-talk zone, but I feel a lot better that he stays in your room at night."

Me too.

"I don't know what he thinks is going to happen."

She scoffed. "Oh, I don't know. Maybe he thinks some crazy people are going to attempt to kidnap you *again*...."

A chill skidded down my spine as my mother's words ran through my head.

"What's going on with that? Have you heard or seen anything else? Are you being proactive in staying safe?"

I gave her a tight smile. "So far, everything is fine."

I didn't tell her about my mom. I left that part out this morning. I only told her that Ann had come to check on me, and Christian bailed me out with my story about falling. Bringing more people, like Piper, into the situation wasn't only stupid but risky. I had no idea what these men my father apparently used to launder money for were like. But I was betting if they were willing to stay true to a threat about me being their compensation for my father's mistakes, then I was betting they wouldn't mind taking another girl my age, too.

What did they want with me?

I wasn't naive enough to think that scary things like this didn't happen all over the world to all sorts of people. It was easy to think it didn't happen around places like English Prep. Everyone I was surrounded with grew up privileged, tucked away underneath their comfy duvet covers that were miraculously washed and remade by the time their head hit the pillow in the evening.

I'd lived in many places during the last five years. There were drugs, crime, prostitution, gangs—all of that. Most of the girls I was surrounded by in juvie could attest to that. Some were in there themselves for prostitution. They had gotten lost in the system. They found a man who treated them like they meant something, fooled them into thinking they had a family, and ran their bodies for money.

It was sick.

But it happened.

How different would my life be if my father had kept his shit together?

"Hey, you okay?" Piper nudged me with her elbow.

Dazed, I sighed. "Yeah, I'm sorry..."

"Where'd you go? You spaced out. Are you sure you're telling me everything?" Her jade eyes were wide; her face grew worried. "You can tell me anything. You know that, right?"

I smiled softly. "Yeah, I know."

Piper was another safe place of mine. Being around her made me feel normal, and I laughed a lot when we hung out. I was glad I had her on my side in this school. She wasn't like all the rest. Piper had a big heart. "I'm going to go to the bathroom before class. *Gossip Girl* tomorrow if I can get Jill and Pete to let me stay?"

Piper nodded vigorously. "Yes! And lots of snacks."

I laughed as I gathered my bag. "Perfect. See you after school."

She nodded, taking another bite of her salad.

Before I left the table, I glanced back at her eating her food. When she peered up, I smiled. "Thanks for being my friend."

The apples of her cheeks rose. "Of course. And I'll always be your friend...unless you move away like Callie. Don't leave me here alone." A laugh escaped my mouth as I rolled my eyes.

I trotted off to the bathroom without looking in Christian's direction, which was becoming tiresome.

Before I even made it to the swinging bathroom door, a hand wrapped around my waist, and I was pulled into the stairwell. I gasped, ready to swing my leg to swipe the person off their feet, but two cloudy eyes were peering down at me. "Christian," I breathed, fear disappearing. *What is it with us and this stairwell?*

His hands didn't leave my waist, and it felt like his palms were burning a hole right through my uniform. "You okay?"

I gulped as I tried my hardest not to squirm in his hold. *What is he doing?* I stuttered, nerves rolling off my tongue. "I... I'm f-fine." I darted my eyes away quickly, afraid he would see right through me. Vivid images came at me fast, reminding me of what he did last night. I knew my face had to have been red.

I saw a small tilt of his head out of my peripheral vision, and it had me realizing he didn't quite believe me. "Your eyes are still red from last night." I swallowed my nerves and glanced at him. His gaze bounced back and forth with mine. *What is he thinking? Does he regret it?* God. I wanted to smack myself. I looked at his lips, and my core tightened. Those lips and tongue made my toes curl just hours ago.

I shot my attention to the floor again, embarrassed. "Can we act like last night never happened?" My voice was nothing more than a whisper. Christian didn't answer. And he didn't move his hands. I hated the way it made me feel. A hot wave of want ran through me, still running on the fumes of last night. I wanted to bask in his grip.

A choppy laugh escaped him. "I couldn't forget it even if I tried."

I felt myself grow even hotter as I zeroed in on his mouth and those perfect, rose-colored lips. He teetered his jaw back and forth, his dark brows furrowing as he stared back at me. All I wanted to do was kiss him again. I wanted to feel his mouth on my body. I wanted his hands skimming my skin. I wanted to taste him like he had tasted me.

A spark of light jolted me. *What has he done to me?*

"Are you going to the game tomorrow night?"

Why are his hands still on my hips? I swallowed, licking my lips. "No."

His grasp grew tighter, and my entire body grew excited. "No?"

"I'm staying at Piper's."

He thought for a moment, his hands never moving. "I'll be late tonight; I have something to do."

Something to do? Like what? I brushed off my panicky thoughts, angry with myself for even wondering. "I think I'll survive."

His cheek curved. "I'm sleeping in your bed tonight."

Jesus! Why did my heart just soar to Mars and back? Hayley, stop getting so wrapped up in him. Last night was a one-time thing. "Fine," I breathed out, placing my hands on his wrists. Our skin branded together like metal melting on metal, and I realized right then that I was already wrapped up in him. "Don't get used to what happened last night..." I took his hands off my hips, even though my body begged me not to.

He chuckled, his eyes darting down to my lips. I felt my face get hot, and I could only hope he didn't notice. If he were to push me just a little bit further, dip his mouth closer to mine, I wouldn't have cared that I was surrendering to a boy who had hated me just a few weeks ago. I'd forget all about the fact, that had been proven to me over and over again, that needing people made me weak. I wouldn't have cared about anything other than Christian, and I couldn't afford that. I couldn't afford to get lost in him, because if I did, Hayley Smith would be lost forever.

"Whatever you say, Hayley." His breath was minty as the words left his lips and floated down to my level.

I straightened my shoulders, adjusted my skirt, raised my chin, turned on the heel of my Chucks, and walked out of the stairwell. I didn't take a breath until I rounded the corner. The bell sounded, and I couldn't have been more thankful to be lost in a sea of teenagers. Maybe that way, Christian wouldn't find me panting like a porn star from his touch.

"I can't believe we're having our first girls' night!" Piper plopped down on the sofa beside me, wearing a matching PJ set. If it were anyone else, I might have been embarrassed that I was wearing my old sleep shorts and an old band T-shirt, but not with Piper. She seemed to accept me in any form, even beat-up and bruised.

"I know." I tore a Twizzler from the pack laying on the coffee table. "I cornered Jill while she was making dinner last night. Pete was outside, working on his stupid, beat-up truck."

Opening a bag of Cheetos, she said, "Well, kudos to Jill for being nice for once." She crunched on an orange twig and snagged the remote. "Okay, *Twilight* marathon?"

"*Twilight*, like the vampires?"

Piper paused and tucked her hair behind her ears. She slowly sat up from lounging back on the sofa and angled her body in front of mine. "Please, please, pleeeeeeaase tell me you know what *Twilight* is."

I smiled shyly. "Of course." I scanned the rec room we were tucked away in on the first floor of her gigantic house. Her parents were away on another trip to somewhere exotic, so it was just the two of us. "I've just never seen the movies."

"What?" she squealed, covering her face with her hands. "Have you at least read the books?"

I smiled, remembering the first time I had read the books. "Yes, and I'm Team Edward. I'll only watch the movies with you if you're Team Edward, too."

This felt nice. Like I was somewhat normal. Laughing with my friend, watching a girly love movie on a Friday night. This was what teenage girls did, right? I'd never had a girls' night, unless it was with one of my foster sisters, and that wasn't the same thing. Trust me.

Piper pulled her hair up in a ponytail using a scrunchie. "I knew we were meant to be best friends." Once she flipped the lights down low, she started to search the TV for the movie. My eyes were glued to the massive flat screen, not sure I'd ever seen a TV so big. It was as big as a movie theatre screen.

"So, when did you read the books? How long ago?"

I settled back into the couch, pulling the blanket over my lap. "It was shortly after I went into foster care. The first two houses weren't that bad," I began, the memory of being tucked away in a strange bedroom surrounded by books to help me cope with my new life enveloping me. "The Berkshires were an older couple. They were the first house I stayed in. They were attentive to me, nice. Nothing like Pete and Jill." I chuckled, getting sucked into the memory. "My room was all done up in purple with a butterfly quilt. My first thought was that it was kiddish, but then I remembered that I *was* a kid, despite all the growing up I had done in the last year."

"What happened?" Piper's voice almost startled me.

I shook my head, clearing the vision of purple butterflies. "Right after the police froze my father's accounts, my mom moved us to a trailer park in Pike Valley. She was never a good mom, never really attentive to me—my father was the stellar parent of the bunch, even if he did launder money." I sighed. "But after he died, she kinda shut down. Everything happened so fast. My mom got a job at a diner and stopped coming home most nights. Eventually, when she did, she'd sleep for days, or she'd bring men home with her. A lot of bad shit happened that I don't like to talk about. There were a lot of drugs floating around, and we never had money. I didn't eat much. It was...bad. A teacher ended up notifying CPS after a parent-teacher conference, and that was when I was taken to the Berkshires'. Then, Mr. Berkshire got sick, and they couldn't take care of me anymore, so I was moved to my next foster home after a couple of months." I smiled. "They let me keep some books, though. Hence, when I read *Twilight*."

Piper's voice was soft as she pointed the remote to the screen, pressing play. "I'm sorry you had to leave them."

I huffed out a sigh, snagging another Twizzler. "Me too."

Her attention was on me now instead of Bella and her father on the screen. "So, what about the next house? Bad or good?"

I couldn't help the smile slithering onto my face. "It wasn't all bad."

"What does that mean?"

I bit my lip. I'd never told anyone about Kyle. Not a single soul. It was my little secret—and his. I felt a Cheeto ping the side of my head, causing me to look at Piper. "Tell me!" she whined, smiling.

Oh, what the hell.

I pulled the blanket up tighter, letting it rest just below my chin. "The house itself wasn't the best. The family was okay. They weren't nearly as attentive as the Berkshires, but they weren't mean to me by any means. It just wasn't a good neighborhood. But then there was Kyle."

"And who is Kyle?" Piper's face lit up, eager for the rest of my story.

I pictured Kyle's face in my head as I continued on, his blond hair and sky-blue eyes. He was the first boy who had caught my attention since leaving Christian behind. "Kyle was my neighbor. He was a couple years older than me."

"Oh, so an older boy." Piper's eagerness only grew.

I laughed. "Yeah, he made the house bearable, to say the least. We'd hang out on our front stoops, talking until the wee hours of the night."

"So, was he your boyfriend?"

A sad smile crept onto my face as my heart grew warm. I shrugged. "I don't know. Maybe? He went to a vocational school, so there wasn't a point in putting a label on us. We were just"—I shrugged again, thinking—"us."

"Did you love him?"

I laughed again. "No." I kicked her playfully. "You should know by now that I never let myself get *that* close to someone. Not while being a foster kid and being uprooted so much. But Kyle and I were nice in the moment."

Piper smiled before turning her attention back toward the TV. I sensed that she felt kind of bad for me. Her smile didn't quite reach her eyes, and it looked as if she wanted to say something else but held back.

"He took my virginity."

Her head snapped over to mine, and I continued on. *I can't believe I'm telling someone this.*

"In a park tunnel. You know those tunnels that little kids crawl through?"

Her mouth gaped open, and then she threw her head back, laughing. "Are you kidding?"

Giggling erupted from me as my face burned. I shook my head and pulled the blanket over my face.

Before I knew it, she pulled the blanket down. Her smile was still plastered to her face, but hers wasn't as playful. "Don't be embarrassed. I lost my V-card at a Wellington Prep party... and I don't even know who took it. The room was too dark, and it just happened."

My eyebrows raised. *Wow, I definitely didn't peg her as a girl who'd do that.* "Wait, what?"

Shame had her brows furrowing. "I know. I'm a slut."

"What?" I almost yelled. The blanket dropped to my lap. "That does *not* make you a slut, Piper."

She shrugged as a sigh escaped her mouth. "Well, regardless, my story isn't as cool as yours. Sex in a park tunnel with an older guy? Sounds hot."

I stifled a laugh. "It wasn't nearly as hot as you'd think. It was awkward and uncomfortable, but it was the only place we could think to do it without my foster parents or his mom finding us."

Her head knocked to the side. "So, did you guys ever do it again? Somewhere else?"

This time I felt the fire rushing to my cheeks. "Yes."

She squealed and begged me to tell her more, but the doorbell went off. Both of our laughs faded as we locked eyes.

It was well after 11pm. We were alone in a huge house out past city limits. "Expecting anyone?" I asked, my heart jumping to attention.

Piper thought for a moment as she shook her head. Then, she grabbed her phone and dialed someone. The doorbell went off again.

Piper quickly asked whoever she'd called, "Is that you at the front door?"

I could hear the background noise from the call. It sounded like a party of some sort. Piper rolled her eyes and hung up quickly.

"Who'd you call?" I asked, slowly standing up.

She sighed. "No one important."

I wanted to question her further, but knocking erupted from down the hall. "Is this place alarmed?"

Piper ran over to the hallway to look and shook her head. "I forgot to arm it."

Normally, I wouldn't have freaked out, but with last Friday still fresh in my mind, my body was in a frenzy. Adrenaline spiked my blood, and suddenly, I felt my feet carrying me to the front door, the pads of my feet gliding over the plush carpet. Piper stood behind me, both of us proceeding with caution.

She had her phone in her hand, ready to call for help if need be.

I reached up on my tiptoes and peeked through the peephole, expecting to see someone. But no one was there. I turned back around, looked at Piper, and raised my shoulders. *Maybe it was the wrong house?*

Just then, we heard a bang on the window. Piper screamed, and my heart lodged itself into my throat. *What if it's them?*

The doorbell rang again, and this time, my body acted of its own accord. I snatched an umbrella that was resting in the corner and swung the door open. Fury rested on my shoulders, and I was ready to take my attackers head-on.

I poked the umbrella outward like a sword before my eyes even registered who it was.

"What the fuck, Hayley!" Christian bent over at the waist, wheezing. His hand clamped down on the umbrella, and he jerked it out of my grasp. I gasped and was suddenly brought back to reality as Ollie and Eric roared with laughter from behind Christian.

"Sorry!" I stepped further out onto the porch and watched Christian slowly stand back up, one hand on his stomach where I'd poked him and the other gripping the umbrella. "I thought you were—"

His broody stare pinned me to my spot. "I know who you thought I was, and I hate to say it, but a fucking umbrella isn't a wise choice." He shook his head after rolling his eyes. "This is *exactly* why we're here."

Piper crossed her arms over her frilly pajama top. "What exactly are you three jerks doing here? And how do you even know where I live?"

Ollie stepped forward, his blond hair appearing darker than it really was. "We broke into the headmaster's office and looked it up." His cheek lifted. "And nice pajamas." Then he winked. Piper shifted on her feet as her cheeks turned pink.

Breaking up their moment and storing it away in the "ask

about later" part of my brain, I shifted on my feet, wishing my sleep shorts were a little longer. I'd worn these before when Christian stayed over, but I'd always been under the covers and facing the wall when he'd climbed through my window. *What does it matter? He literally had his lips on the part these shorts are hiding.* "What do you want?"

Christian pushed through the door, causing Piper and me to part like the Red Sea. Ollie and Eric followed, leaving us standing there looking like we were deer caught in headlights. She mouthed, *"What the hell?"* to me, but I was just as surprised.

I peeked outside, scanning the dark and desolate road before shutting the door behind me. Piper mumbled, "These jerks are ruining our girls' night—*again.*" I held back a laugh and followed the guys. They acted nonchalant, as if they'd been at Piper's house plenty of times.

"Christian!" I stopped in the doorway of the expansive and newly remodeled kitchen with its sky-high ceiling and sparkling new appliances that probably cost more than Jill and Pete's *entire* house. "What are you doing here?"

When we spoke last night, after he climbed through my window and into my bed (on top of the covers), he asked me again if I was still staying at Piper's. I assumed he was just making sure he didn't need to climb in my window. I snarkily told him to go to Eric's after the game and to have a grand ol' time and enjoy the fact that he wouldn't need to babysit me.

I didn't know why I had said it like that. Jealousy was itching all over my skin at the thought of him going to Eric's with all the girls that drooled over him at school, so I lashed out, but I got a sense that he enjoyed it.

He wanted me jealous of the girls he frequented.

But I wasn't going to make that stupid, schoolgirl mistake again. Christian could do what he wanted. His hands and mouth on my body were a one-time thing. There was too much heavy baggage between Christian and me—too much drama that hadn't been dealt with.

Christian leaned back on the island in the middle of the kitchen, appearing casually hot in his tight black T-shirt, slightly wet hair, and jeans. "You guys are coming to the party with us."

I placed my hands on my hips, my gray Metallica T-shirt rising a smidge. "No, we are not."

His stare deepened as he flicked it down to my bare legs and back. "Yes, you are."

"No." I stood my ground.

"*Yes,*" he snarled.

Piper interrupted our soaring match. "Why the hell do you want *us* to come to your party?" She was looking at Eric now who had remained silent for most of the conversation.

He sighed out a chuckle. "It's not me who wants you there. It's him." He nodded his head full of coal-colored hair at Christian.

I crossed my arms over my chest, annoyed. "I'm not going to some stupid party where you all pass around girls like they're a goddamn bong."

Ollie snickered, trying to hold in his laugh.

"Is that jealousy I hear?" Christian raised an eyebrow, his cool and calm demeanor back in place.

Mortification had me feeling like my body was plunging into a fire pit. I was quick—probably too quick—to say, "Absolutely not. You can fuck any girl you want and pass her on. Why would I care? I just don't want to go."

Christian smirked after staring at me for a second too long. "Piper? Do *you* want to go?"

I glanced over at her in her lavender, floral pjs, and my stomach took a nosedive. *Ugh, she so wants to go!*

She looked at me once and squeaked out. "No."

"Lie," Ollie mused as he threw an arm over her shoulder. She shrugged it off, but a small smile was ghosting her lips.

Be a good friend, Hayley. She wants to go. Eric answered a call on his phone while I contemplated. I grabbed Piper's arm and pulled her into the dining room. We were standing beside a large, crystal-glass dining room table with a huge vase atop full of lilies. By the smell of the room, the flowers were real. "Do you want to go?"

Piper teetered her lip back and forth. "No."

I placed my hands on her shoulders. "We're friends; you can tell me the truth."

Her pale face turned pink again, the few freckles on her nose even more prominent. "I mean, I've never been to one of Eric's parties. They're kind of an English Prep staple, ya know? Even if I'm only being invited because of Christian's infatuation with you, I still kind of want to see the hype."

Ugh. I knew this was a bad idea even before I agreed, but nonetheless, I did it anyway.

"Fine." I turned around and began walking back to the kitchen. "But I need something to wear," I called over my shoulder.

She squealed as she followed me.

"Fine. We will go." I glared at Christian's smug expression. "But don't let me stand in your way from getting laid. I'm not going for you. I'm going for Piper."

Ollie's eyes lit up. "Oooh, can we watch?"

I smacked him in the shoulder on my way past him, Piper hot on my heels.

"Hurry up!" Christian yelled, and I flipped him off.

CHAPTER TWENTY-NINE

CHRISTIAN

MY FINGERS TAPPED on the steering wheel of my Charger as we waited for Hayley and Piper to come out of the house. Eric was still on the phone, tucked away in the backseat, directing someone to grab a keg on the way to his cabin. Ollie was looking out the window into the darkness surrounding Piper's yard.

"So, what exactly is your plan? I thought I heard you telling Kayla you're hers tonight after the game." Ollie shook his hair out, his leg tapping up and down. "I mean, I can't blame you. She's pretty fuckin' hot in her cheerleading uniform, *but*"—he sliced his eyes to me—"I know you have someone else on your mind at all times."

I played it off. "You heard Hayley; she's not there for me."

He held back a grin. "Oh, but *you're* there for her."

Yes, I fucking am, and I'll prove to her she's there for me, too. I kept silent, listening to Parkway Drive play through the speakers of my car.

Yesterday in the stairwell was a minor dip in my cool

facade. My hands around Hayley's waist, the heat I felt fly through my body, the thoughts of the night prior, the exhilaration of her face being so close again—I was ready to kiss her until she begged for more. My dick still throbbed, and my body was in overdrive the rest of the day. I barely slept a wink in her room, even *after* making the pit stop. I surely thought pounding flesh with my bare hands would be a great outlet for everything that was built up inside of me, but I was wrong.

I didn't sleep, played one hell of a football game, and *still*, I was fucking hyped, wound tight like a rubber band ready to snap.

Hayley was under my skin, nestled right inside my ribcage. I wanted to poke her until she felt what I felt. Jealousy. Desire. She wanted to act like I didn't affect her, and we *both* knew that wasn't the case. And, not to mention, I could keep a closer eye on her at the party. For the entire game, every time I'd let my mind wander from Hayley, it felt like a dark cloud resting over my head. I worried when I wasn't near her. Thoughts of Jim's words pierced my mind like sharp, misshapen pieces of rock at every turn; images of her scratches and tears blurred my vision. I felt out of control when I didn't have my eyes on her.

"Fuckin' finally," Eric muttered under his breath as Hayley and Piper descended from her porch. I flicked my car lights on, and it felt like a punch to my gut.

"Oh, hell no," I said under my breath. I quickly climbed out of the driver's seat and stomped my way over to her and Piper as they trotted over to Piper's BMW.

"Go change," I demanded, my eyes burning a hole in her exposed stomach.

She laughed. Hayley laughed right in my face. *What was I thinking?* Telling Hayley to change was only going to make her want to wear the outfit even more. My plan backfired. I was wearing my emotions on my sleeve, and I *never* did that.

"She looks hot." Piper unlocked her car, not looking at me.

I ran my gaze down Hayley's body once more, wondering for a brief second if Eric was right the other day when he said she and I were playing a game—and she was winning.

Because from where I was standing, she *was* winning.

The black top she was wearing was tight and molded to her skin. It hit just above her hips, showing a sliver of soft skin from her stomach. The jeans she had on were glued to her legs and ass, and I had to fight the urge to groan when she turned around to open the door. The ends of her dark hair tumbled down her back, and when she glanced up at me, the lights of Piper's car showcased the planes of her face. I lost my footing. She was wearing makeup for the first time since coming to English Prep, and the only thing it did was enhance her silent beauty. The red lipstick she wore had me tightening my stomach.

"Go fucking change, Hayley. Every guy is going to be following your every fucking move."

Her lips turned upward. "You wanted me at the party. Deal with it." Then, she slid into Piper's passenger seat, and I felt my entire world get rocked.

Fuck me, she *was* winning.

The party was in full swing when we pulled up. Eric hopped out of the backseat like there was a fire under his ass. I knew he was headed to the keg immediately. Eric was a good friend, always had my back, but he had his own issues that he needed to deal with—alcohol being one of them.

Ollie and I waited for Piper and Hayley near the back of my car, and once they descended from her BMW, they headed straight for us. Hayley crossed her arms over her chest and cocked her hip. "So, what exactly is the plan? You wanted us here, so we're here. Do we have a curfew? Can we leave when we want?" She scoffed and rolled her eyes.

I was certain she meant for the question to be rhetorical, but I answered anyway, just to make her mad. "You can leave when we leave."

Hayley sneered. "I was kidding. We will leave when we want to leave. You are *not* our babysitter."

I raised my eyebrows, calling out over my shoulder as I walked up to the cabin. "Says the girl who gets threatened, almost kidnapped, *and* tries to hurt an intruder with a fucking umbrella." I swung around and faced her blanched face. "Face it. You feel safer when you're around me."

Her eyes narrowed, her mouth set in a firm line. I tried to keep myself from gazing down her body, but I failed in the end.

I ground my teeth together. Something was off between us tonight. We no longer hated each other—we hated that we felt something for one another. Something deeper, intimate. She didn't want to admit it, and I desperately wanted her to. It was like a cat-and-mouse chase.

Time to turn the court around and start winning this fucking game.

As soon as I was inside the cabin with Ollie, Piper, and Hayley trailing me, everyone yelled my name in unison. I played a good game tonight, despite my mind wandering to Hayley every five seconds.

"Bro, bro, bro," Ben yelled as soon as I was within earshot. "If it weren't for you, we would have totally fucking blown the game tonight."

Ollie punched his arm, a cup already in his hand. "Fuck

off, I was the one that ran the ball."

Ben nodded. "I know, I know. But I have no fuckin' clue what we're going to do next year when this fucker goes off to college." He nudged my bicep as I leaned over for my own cup.

I didn't usually drink much at these parties—or ever—but tonight, with Hayley looking like she did, I needed something to take the edge off. Otherwise, I'd end up pinning her against a wall and kissing her senseless with everyone as my audience.

There was a warning voice in the back of my head telling me to tread lightly when it came to Hayley. And for that, I wasn't sure why. Maybe it was due to the loss in my life. I had lost my mom, and I had also lost Hayley at one point, too. Not to mention, my father was gone most of the time, so loss didn't come lightly to me, and Hayley felt *just* out of reach. If I did finally catch her, I wasn't sure I'd be able to hold onto her.

There were threats at every corner—literally and figuratively.

"What the hell is she doing here?"

I knew that everyone's eyes were on Hayley. Hayley and I weren't friendly at school. To the naked eye, we didn't pay each other any attention. But to the trained eye, anyone could see that we both snuck glances at each other every few minutes. I was hyperaware of her—and she of me.

Ben continued his questioning after throwing back his cup. "And who is she with? They both look fucking fine as he—"

I glared at him. "Don't finish that sentence. She's off limits."

"Who is?" another fuckwad asked. *What is his name?* Jared? Jeremy? Whatever. It didn't matter. He was an underclassman, and I wasn't even sure who invited him.

"Both." I leveled him with a stare.

Eric, with his smug smile, piped up. "Well, we all know why Hayley is off limits. But why Piper?"

"Because I said so," Ollie interjected before I could answer.

I chugged my beer, the malty flavor coating my tongue. "Leave 'em alone," I said once more before spinning around and laying my eyes on Kayla. I knew where Hayley was before I even looked at her. The entire room gravitated around her. Like she was the sun and we were the planets. She radiated in the room, drew unwanted attention to herself, and I knew it was the very last thing she wanted.

"Hey, babe." I snuck behind Kayla and wrapped my hand around her tiny waist. She smelled of booze and perfume— nothing like Hayley.

Her blonde hair tickled my chin when she tipped her head. Her eyes were glossy and red; she was already tipsy as hell.

"Hey, I was wondering when you'd show. Are you still mine for the night?"

No. "We'll see," I whispered into her ear, nuzzling my head into the side of her neck. As I brushed my nose along her skin, I lazily moved my eyes over to Hayley. I had to fight the urge to smile like a damn fool. Her eyes were hard and ice cold as she stared at Kayla and me. *Does this bother you, Hayley?*

I placed a tender kiss along Kayla's cheek, and I thought Hayley was going to blow a gasket. Her chest was heaving; her fists clenched at her sides. *Are you regretting those words you spat at me earlier?* Hayley told me I could fuck any girl I wanted and pass her right along. *"What do I care?"* she asked.

A laugh bubbled up out of my chest. *Oh, you fucking care.*

I placed my attention on Kayla and grabbed her hand, pulling her behind me to the couch. Once I sat down, Kayla sat on my lap and put her arm around my neck. A new drink was placed in my hand by an underclassman, and I sipped on it while giving some attention to Kayla and keeping my gaze trained on Hayley.

She and Piper stood along the wall for a little while before she couldn't take it any longer. She huffed and rolled her eyes, turning around so she didn't have to see me anymore. My stare returned to her a few times in between keeping up a conversation with a few guys and giving some attention to Kayla who continued to rub her ass on my dick.

It was hard.

But for an entirely different reason.

That might have made me an asshole, but I never claimed to be a saint, and with Hayley involved, I had no shame.

Through a sea of people, I saw Hayley take a drink from Ollie. She tipped it back before swinging her eyes over to me and Kayla. We were stuck in an intense stare-off, and heat flared within. The room felt electrified. It took everything in my entire body not to push Kayla off my lap, stalk over to Hayley, grab her hips in my hands, and assault her with my mouth.

I felt crazy, animalistic. I wanted to rip her clothes off and fuck her into oblivion. I wanted to feel her body in my hands, her lips on my mouth, erase our past and the future.

I wanted to be in the now with her.

I wanted to forget that I had hated her for five years. I wanted to forget about that fucker Gabe laying his hands on her. I wanted to forget about her sleazy mom and her puzzling warning.

Hayley licked her bottom lip, her fervent stare burning a hole in my skin, but then her face fell at the sound of a voice coming from behind her.

"Remember me, Hayley?"

Oh fuck.

CHAPTER THIRTY

HAYLEY

CHILLS COATED MY SKIN. I fought the need to shiver. My heart dropped to the ground at lightning speed. Christian was pushing Kayla off his lap as I turned around and found a pair of familiar, sinister-like eyes glaring at me.

I sucked in a breath at the sight of Gabe standing in Eric's cabin. *What the hell is he doing here? And what the hell happened to his face?* I surveyed the kitchen for half a second before Gabe's voice stole my attention.

"Who is your fucking boyfriend? Huh? Which one of these fuckers jumped me?"

Oh my God. I'm going to kill Christian.

I felt Christian's presence behind me like the devil sneaking up to take me to hell. Everyone in the room stopped talking. The music was cut to an abrupt stop. Gabe stood there with his face bruised and swollen, a few of his friends that I recognized stood behind him for backup. They were all wearing Oakland T-shirts with the wildcat logo in the center.

"I don't have a boyfriend, Gabe," I answered calmly. On

the outside, I was sure I looked unphased, but on the inside, my stomach was tied in knots. I was angry with Christian, jealous of his little show with Kayla that was still brewing in my mind, annoyed that the party was now centered on me, and a whole lot fearful, looking Gabe in the face.

"Bullshit," he growled, taking a step toward me. I was instantly blocked by Ollie, Eric, and Christian within a matter of seconds. Piper stood beside me with wide eyes.

I pushed through Christian and Ollie, stepping in front of them. I glared at Christian. "I don't need your help." Then, I seethed under my breath, "And I know this is your fault."

I crossed my arms over my tight shirt. "Whatever happened had nothing to do with me." *How did he even know I was here?*

Gabe snarled like a dog. His nostrils flared; his pupils dilated. The only thing standing between us was the keg on the kitchen floor. "Oh really?" His voice was full of cynicism and sarcasm. "Then tell me why, once they vandalized the fuck out of my Mustang, they grilled me about you all while throwing punches every five fucking seconds. And two against one? How fucking fair is that?"

"About as fucking fair as you sticking your hand down my pants when I told you not to. Now get the hell out of here."

"You dumb bitch."

"That's enough." Christian was all but foaming at the mouth as he slid up beside me. I wanted to knock him off his ass almost as much as I wanted to knock Gabe off his.

Gabe's head ticked to the side, sparring off with Christian. I glanced at Piper who was bouncing her eyes back and forth between me and Gabe. I mouthed, "*Record this*," and she hurriedly reached into her back pocket and whipped out her phone. Once she had it in place, I started to probe.

"So, why did your parents drop the charges?" I knew I was setting myself up for humiliation with almost all of

English Prep's finest watching. I could already hear the rumors forming, but my pride didn't stand a chance against shutting Gabe down. Except, he didn't take the bait; his glare was still set on Christian. "Did they realize I was telling the truth? Didn't want me to run my mouth about their precious prodigy being a rapist?" I laughed in his face, inching toward him. "It's no wonder they took in strays like me; they probably needed a distraction from the type of person their son was." Gabe clenched his fists and narrowed his eyes even further. His rosy lip curled up on the side. "Did they believe you when you said you didn't try to rape me, Gabe? Huh? What did they do? Ground you for the weekend?" I laughed again, and it seemed to work in my favor.

"Fuck you, Hayley. You wanted it." He came closer to me, and I met him halfway.

I glared up into his fucked-up face, my pulse racing underneath my skin. "Is that what you have to tell yourself to sleep at night? In what world does the word *no* mean to keep going? Go on, Gabe. Tell everyone what happened when you didn't stop."

The room was quiet. Gabe clenched his teeth together, his jaw working back and forth. I could feel Christian's body heat beside me, reminding me that I wasn't alone.

"Tell them. Tell them how you stuck your hand in my pants after I said no, and how you ended up on the ground, wailing like a little bitch."

Gabe's friends looked back and forth at one another, and I got the confirmation I needed that Gabe had lied to them. I smirked, knowing my plan was working.

"Don't act like you didn't tempt me at every fucking corner, wearing those short shorts and playing hard to get." Christian stepped forward, but I sent him a glare, and that had him halting. Gabe continued on, inching closer to me with a gleam in his eye. "You fucking wanted me to touch you. You saying no only turned me on further."

At the last second, Gabe's hand came around my wrist, and he squeezed, but I had anticipated his move and snatched my arm out of his grasp at the same time I brought my knee up to his balls. He grunted and grabbed onto his dick, gasping for air. Before I knew it, I was kneeing him in the chin, which caused his unsteady body to tumble backwards. I reared my foot back to kick him in the stomach, but someone wrapped their arms around my torso, causing me to stop. I took a deep breath and inhaled Christian's scent. *Shit.* I glanced at Piper and remembered my original plan.

"Put me down."

Christian landed me on my feet but kept his hands on my hips. He whispered in my ear, "Calm down."

I let out a shaky breath, and even though I was still angry with Christian, I knew I needed to listen. I was certain everyone thought I was some type of rabid animal.

Once Gabe staggered to his feet—without the help of his two friends who stood looking at him with disgust—I snarled.

"Leave or I'll leak this video through Oakland. Every single person will know what a disgusting pig you are." I glanced at his two buddies. "That is, if they don't tell people first."

Gabe wafted his gaze around the room. The energy was bound tightly. Girls were scrunching their faces at him, and every guy looked ready to kill him on the spot.

Realizing he'd lost, he glared at me once more before leaving. "Fuck you, *bitch*."

Christian's hands left my waist quickly as he went to follow him, but I grabbed his arm at the last second, holding him in his place.

Now that I had Gabe taken care of, I now had to address the other elephant in the room.

I was still high with adrenaline as I watched Gabe and his two friends stagger out the door. The room erupted in hoots and hollers, but it did nothing to sooth my anger.

"Are you freaking kidding me?" I shouted, dropping my hand from Christian's. "I told you not to get involved—for a very good reason, might I add—and what the hell do you do?"

I was fuming. My body trembled with unshed anger. *Why does he insist on saving me?*

"Who said it was me?"

Oh, nice freaking try.

I grabbed his arm roughly and brought his knuckles between us. I had no idea what was going on in the kitchen around us. I wasn't sure if people were staring or if they were going about their usual party business. As soon as I locked eyes onto Christian, regardless of the situation or our surroundings, everything else faded.

"This tells me!" I dropped his red and scabbed hand with force. I wasn't sure how I didn't notice his cut knuckles before. "Ugh!" I yelled, storming away to the stairs.

I was mad. So mad.

This could have gone a lot worse. It still could. Gabe's parents could find out who beat Gabe's ass and vandalized his car, and it could lead right back to me, which would get the police involved, which would then lead to the judge, and I could kiss any hope of a scholarship or roof over my head until graduation goodbye.

I was aware I had other things to worry about, like a looming threat on my life from my dead father's mistakes.

But a problem was a problem, no matter the size.

My feet pounded along the wooden steps as I climbed the stairs. I had no idea if Christian or Piper followed me or if anyone was talking about what had just gone down, but I didn't really care. I needed space. I needed to be alone to calm down and think rationally. The only thing I wanted to do was scream.

I went into the first room in the hall and slammed the door. I kept the lights off, knowing the darkness would likely calm me faster.

Several breaths escaped me as I paced. *It's fine. Gabe won't go to his parents. I basically have a confession on video. He's smarter than that.*

"Hayley."

I sliced my head over to the crack in the door. "I'm going to kill you!" I yelled, stomping over to Christian. He pulled himself farther into the room, shutting the door behind him. This time, I turned the light on. The switch flicked, and I glared at him. His jaw was set, the sharpness drawing my attention to it.

"Is that why you came to my room so late last night? You went to Gabe's house? To what? Teach him a lesson?"

I was pacing again, feeling like I was going to explode.

He shook out his dark hair. "That wasn't my intention when I got there, no."

"Ugh!" My feet stomped over to him, hovering near the wooden door. "You know what? I don't even care. Just go back downstairs and back to fucking that girl. You two were putting on quite a show. I'm sorry Gabe had to ruin it."

As soon as the words left my mouth, I wanted to suck them back in. Christian and his minion were not important, and I hated that I sounded like a desperate, jealous girlfriend.

"What if I don't want to?" Christian pulled himself away from the door and stalked over to me. I stood my ground, my stare never wavering.

"You looked like you wanted to before Gabe showed up. Don't let me stop you." *God. Why was I acting like this?*

"Does it bother you? Seeing me with Kayla?"

The lie tasted bitter on my tongue. "Not one bit."

His head cocked to the side. His hooded gray eyes almost had me backtracking my words. The way he was looking at me had me forgetting I was angry with him. I wanted his lips on mine in the worst way.

On cue, I heard a girly voice slur from the hallway, "Christian? Christiannnn, where *are* you?"

Jealous rage crept along my limbs. The thought of Christian sticking his mouth anywhere near Kayla made me want to rip her hair out. *Oh my God. It does bother me. So much.*

I panicked with the thought. I rushed over to the door and put my hand on the doorknob, ready to shove Christian out, right into Kayla's arms. Maybe then I'd have no choice but to ignore my feelings, and maybe I could stop bending all my rules and remember how difficult it was to heal your heart when someone close to you was ripped away.

The metal knob twisted in my grasp, but Christian's palm landed on top of my hand. He spun me around so my back rested along the door. The click of the lock sent a thrill all the way to my toes. His brooding eyes were hooded as they lazily dropped to my mouth. *Do it. Kiss me.* My heart thrashed in my chest.

"Let's stop playing this game, Hayley."

"I'm not playing a game."

His arms caged me in, each one resting beside my head. His knee found its way in between my legs, and I had to fight the urge not to move my body. Everything felt hot. A surge of energy fanned over my skin.

"You are. We've been playing a game since the moment you kissed me outside of Pete and Jill's." The memory was something I replayed almost daily. Any time my mind would wander, it'd end up right there: me kissing Christian. It was like hitting the tip of an iceberg.

I swallowed, my resolve slipping with him being so close. *No.* "You're the one playing games." I tipped my chin even higher to meet his stare. "You tell me you hate me, try to torment me at school, swoop in to save me—even when I tell you not to—sneak into my bedroom every night, cause me to forget my name, then ignore me at school, followed by an eye-fuck whenever we're in a moment like this, and *then* you start kissing another girl right in front of me, your hands skimming her body." My voice grew as my list went on, feeling more and more agitated. "I hate you," I muttered, my eyes dipping to his mouth. I knew what his lips felt like on mine. They made everything disappear—morphed hate into love, and sadness into happiness.

"I hate you, too," he groaned before dropping his hands onto my face and smashing his lips onto mine.

My heart jumped to my throat as his mouth covered my lips. My hands wrapped around his neck, going into his hair as his tongue flicked my upper lip to give him access. It roamed over mine, and I deepened the kiss, seeing sparks ignite behind my eyes. Christian groaned into my mouth, and I got off on the sound. I liked him at my mercy. I liked that I affected him as much as he affected me. Every longing stare, every scorched touch, all the pent-up energy we held every single night in my room was coming to light.

He was feral, kissing me as if he were branding me.

And for once, with a clear head, I was submissive. When we had let our guards down the first time, I blamed my heightened emotions. I told myself I wasn't thinking clearly. But that was how it always was with him. My emotions were always standing straight up when he was around. And I real-ized I had it wrong the other night. Christian didn't cloud my judgment between right and wrong; he made me divulge in whatever felt right, and this—this right here—felt right. It felt good. *He* felt good.

Christian's hands moved under my butt, and he lifted me up. My legs automatically wound around his hips, and I felt his hardness rub against me. Heat spread all the way up to my throat.

"Too long," he grunted, pushing me up against the wall. "It's been two days since I've touched you like this, and it's been too fucking long."

I couldn't speak. I just needed more of his mouth on mine, silencing every thought.

I moved my body up and down on his, and he swore under his breath. He walked us over to the bed, dipping his head into the crook of my neck and sucking my tender skin. Goosebumps covered my body.

Christian slowly lowered my body, his dark stare scorching me on the way down. His fingers reached the hem of my shirt, and he slowly lifted it up and threw it across the room. He descended down on top of me again, my body his to do whatever with. The reins were in his hands. I liked the feeling it gave me. I liked feeling handled by him. For once, I didn't want to be in control. Christian made me feel wanted, and that was something I didn't feel often.

His warm mouth moved from my swollen lips over to the delicate side of my ear. I reached up and grabbed his biceps, the feel of his skin making me hot all over again. Once his head dipped down to my shoulder, kissing the bare skin, he slipped his finger under the strap of my bra and almost ripped it off.

"I want to savor every bit of this, but I just can't." His words came out rushed, and before I knew it, I was lying on the bed without a bra on. His pupils dilated, and when his head dipped down to suck, I saw stars.

"Christian," I breathed, arching my back.

I felt wild. The pressure in my core needed a release before I lost my mind. I wiggled in his grasp, trying to move below him as he teased and sucked my bud. His hands finally moved to my jeans, and with the undoing of my button, we heard the music come to a stop downstairs. He paused, his fingers ready to pull the denim from my legs with his mouth hovering over mine. We were both panting. His neck was red and splotchy from our heat meshing together. Then, we heard yelling and the brief shout of, "COPS!"

My heart fell to the ground, right there along with my bra.

CHAPTER THIRTY-ONE

CHRISTIAN

THE FEAR in Hayley's eyes had me snapping to attention. So close. I was so close to giving in to what we both wanted *and* needed. Kissing her again felt like I had gotten a slice of heaven. My body was moving in ecstasy.

"Christian. I can't be caught here with drugs and underaged drinking."

Hayley flew off the bed and slipped her bra on. Her fingers were trembling and fumbling over the clasp. I rushed over, still in a daze from kissing her, and clasped it. She was rambling. "I can't get caught. I'll go into a group home. Maybe back to juvie. Shit. Shit. *Shit.*"

I put my hands on her upper arms to calm her. "I'm not going to let that happen."

Her eyes were wide, the blue in them even bluer than before. The doorknob jiggled as partiers tried to hide—which wouldn't work. The only way not to get caught by the cops was to get the hell out of the house.

"Christian. What are we going to do?"

Fuck. I don't know. I eyed the window, and Hayley's eyes lit up. She ran over and pushed it open, leaning her body out to peer down. "Let's go." She looked back at me for a second before getting ready to jump.

I rushed over and pulled her back. *Jesus Christ.* "What the fuck, Hayley? You'll break your goddamn neck."

"I'd rather break my neck than go to a group home and age out." Her words were rattled, eyes wide and fearful. "You don't know what it's like, Christian. I can't get into trouble." She peered up at me, fear clouding the fire I saw in her eyes moments ago when she was grinding her body against mine.

I knew at that moment I'd do anything for her. The last five years didn't matter. Thirteen-year-old Christian was back, and Hayley was his whole world again.

"Go get your shirt." Hayley looked down at her chest, confused that she wasn't wearing her shirt. She quickly ran past the bed and searched frantically. I leaned my body out the window, the cool air grounding me for a moment. *That's a long jump.*

"I can't find it!" Hayley was still searching for her shirt, but we no longer had time. I heard the pounding footsteps echoing in the hall. Ripping my shirt off my back, I flung it over to her. She slipped it on within seconds, the hem hitting her mid-thigh.

"I'm going first, then you'll jump after."

"You can afford to get caught." She rushed over, moving past me. "I can't. No sense in you breaking your legs. You have football to worry about."

So stubborn. I pulled her back by my shirt. "Hayley, for fuck's sake, stop being so independent! Let me help you. This is fucking sixth grade all over again."

She bounced back on the heels of her feet. "I jumped then, and I can jump now!"

She is so fucking infuriating and hot and sexy and...

I moved her quickly, spinning her around my back. Pushing her away, I leaned one leg out the window, the wood resting under my weight, then the other. My chest broke out in goosebumps from the crisp autumn air. "Once I land, jump, and I'll catch you. Then, we run like hell."

"What about Piper?"

"Ollie will take care of her. Now let's go."

I jumped and held my breath as I braced for landing. *Jumping for Hayley. How did I end up here?* Once I felt the ground below me, I tucked and rolled, jumping back to my feet quickly. The jump wasn't nearly as bad as I thought. I glanced up and saw the light around Hayley's head appear when she slipped back from the window. Then, I saw her legs, and within a second, she was jumping from the window.

She landed in my arms with a whoosh, and I couldn't help but notice how her hands automatically wrapped around my neck. Perfect. Our bodies fit together like that was how we were meant to be for life.

"Let's go." I put her back on her feet and grabbed her hand. We ran like hell through the darkness. Thankfully, I parked at the end of the gravel road since we were the last to get here, which would make it easy to leave.

Hayley ran alongside me, her shorter legs somehow keeping up with mine. "What about Piper?" she asked again.

"Ollie has her." She tugged on my arm.

"But how do you know? I can't leave her!"

In the chaos of it all, a smile tugged at my lips. Hayley— even as much as she wanted to be selfish and save her own ass —was still worried about her friend.

"I'll call Ollie once we're in the car. Go, hurry. They'll be coming to check cars soon."

I knew how this worked. It wasn't the first time I'd been busted at a party. This was definitely a first for Eric's cabin, though. Someone had to have tipped the cops off. The cabin was tucked away on the outskirts of town, deep in the forest. I was certain it was Gabe.

Once Hayley and I were beside my car, I dragged my gaze around the cabin, watching people scramble out the two doors that likely had cops posted beside them. I unlocked the car, the lights probably drawing attention as we shuffled inside. My back pressed along the cold leather of my seat as I tossed Hayley my phone.

"Call Ollie," I demanded, hearing the rumble of my engine.

I tore down the gravel road fast, pebbles flying past my wheels.

"There's a text from him." Hayley held onto the handle above the door as I sped around the curves and dips of the road. "It says, '*I have Piper and Eric. Did you guys get out?*'"

"Tell him we will meet him at Piper's in a few hours."

"A few hours? Where are we going?"

I slowly inched my neck in her direction. "To finish what we started." Then, I pressed my foot on the pedal and sped like my life depended on it.

When we pulled up to my house, the car was jam-packed full of sexual tension. Neither one of us dared to even speak a syllable on the way over in fear it would ruin this thing we had going.

I hesitated with my hand on the door handle as Parkway Drive tumbled through the speakers. I could feel the thump of the bass within my chest. I ground my teeth, trying to figure out what to do. *Fuck.*

"My dad is home."

Hayley shifted in her seat. "Okay, so..."

"I need to tell you something before we go inside."

She rested her back along the passenger seat and gave me her full attention. Her dark hair was messy as it rested along her shoulders. The dash lights casted shadows across her high cheekbones. She kept her face solemn, blank. *She was so hard to read sometimes.*

"I didn't go to Gabe's with the intention of losing it on him."

"Then why did you go?" Her anger was back. She crossed her arms over her chest—the chest my mouth was on not too long ago.

"I went because the night you got attacked at the game, the cameras near the bathroom caught a car speeding off shortly afterwards. I wanted to make sure it wasn't his."

Her face flattened. "He was *in* the game. It wasn't him."

I shrugged. "I wasn't convinced. I needed to know for sure."

"Wait. There were cameras? How did you even get access?"

And here comes the part I didn't want to get to.

"I hired a P.I."

She blinked. Once. Twice. Three times. "What?"

I gazed out the windshield, noting my father's Porsche and Jim's Range Rover. "I hired a P.I., and instead of waiting for him to run plates and figure out if the car was a clue to all of the fucked-up shit you've been through, I decided to pay Gabe a visit." I shrugged, clenching my knuckles tightly as I grasped the steering wheel. "Once I saw him, I lost it. I kept thinking about his hands on you and how scared you must have been, and it shook me."

I risked a glimpse at her face, and her brows were furrowed. "How do you even have access to a P.I.?"

"It's my dad's. It was the P.I. he used after my mom..." I shook my head, clearing my thoughts. "It doesn't matter. He's been looking into the case with your father, trying to figure out who attacked you, who made threats against you."

Her mouth opened, but I didn't wait for her protests. I opened my door and climbed out. I went to her side, opened the door, and peered down at her, resting my arms on top of the door. "I don't care that you don't want my help. Let's go." I inclined my head toward the door.

I knew she wouldn't go down without a fight. She'd protest, get angry again, and repeat that she didn't need help, but in reality, we both knew she did.

To my surprise, Hayley didn't say anything. She climbed out of my car and pushed her hair behind her ears. She looked so innocent and downright beautiful. The scowl she often wore and directed toward me made her appear strong, which was definitely hot, but I liked this side of her too. She looked fragile, breakable, and the only thing I wanted to do was wrap her in my arms and fight off every last threat that could break her in half.

"Christian." *I spoke too fucking soon. Here come the protests.* "I'm wearing your shirt."

"What?" I looked down at my bare chest as a gust of wind brushed along my skin. "Oh. So?"

She looked around the driveway nervously. "So...won't your dad...you know...think we had sex or something? This looks bad. I don't want to walk in there and have him think the worst of me. I've never met your dad."

I couldn't help the smile that had my face lifting.

"What?" she huffed.

"It's cute that you want to impress my dad. Careful now, or I'll think that you actually like me."

Even with the moon being our only light, I could see her cheeks tinting with embarrassment.

She pushed past me quickly, heading for the door.

Before I caught up with her, I took a deep breath and

leveled my thoughts. I had a hunch I was walking into a war zone, but nonetheless, I was more than likely on the winning side. My father and I didn't see eye to eye, so this wasn't necessarily anything new to me.

Once Hayley and I were inside, I grabbed her hand and walked us down the hall, past the large living room, and down a step, onto the tile floor of the kitchen. I spotted my father and Jim sitting at the breakfast bar.

"Christian." His voice was laced with anger, but his tone wasn't loud. "I told you to stop with the Hay—" His tired eyes darted to Hayley, and he snapped his mouth shut.

Jim stood up with a coffee mug in his hand, wearing something similar to my father: dress slacks and a button-down. My father appeared much more disheveled, though. His hair looked as if he'd run his hands through it a few times, and his shirt was unbuttoned on top, his sleeves rolled up.

"Hi, Hayley." Jim gave Hayley a warm smile that I'd never seen before. He barely even addressed me most of the time.

Hayley's cheeks were still dotted with a pinkish hue, and a weak smile appeared. *Is she being shy?*

I chuckled, and she shot me a glare.

There she is.

"Hello, Hayley," my father said curtly, looking back and forth between my naked torso and my shirt draped on her body.

"Hi, Mr. Powell."

He dismissed her quickly and set his eyes on me. "We need to talk."

Hayley was quick to add, "I'll just go upstairs and call Ollie and Piper to make sure they got home okay." Then, she spun around and darted to the stairs, clutching my phone in her hand.

Something about the way my father was looking at me and the fact that Hayley left my side had me feeling uneasy. I felt like a caged animal, ready to attack the first person who came near.

"What's this about?"

"Christian, I told you to stay out of that girl's business."

That girl? As if she didn't have a name.

"You mean Hayley? Yeah, I know."

He grunted, running his hand through his hair. Jim sat back down and sipped on his coffee as my father continued to talk. "Yes. Hayley. Digging around in her life isn't smart. And Jim"—he gave him a pointed look—"is officially done feeding you information."

My chest felt tight. "And what the hell do you know about her life?" I walked farther into the kitchen. "What the hell do you care if Jim looks into things?"

He stomped over to the cabinet and pulled out a bottle of bourbon, snagging a glass. "There are things that you don't know about her. There are things *she* doesn't know."

"Like what? Because I know plenty. I know her father was murdered. I know her mom is a junkie and left Hayley to fend for herself. I know her foster dad has abused her and that he fucking locks her in her room at night. I know her old foster brother tried to rape her. I know there are men that think she's theirs for the taking because of something her father did. I know plenty, Dad. And guess what? I care. I'm not just going to turn my back on someone because they have problems in their life—unlike you."

His heavy brow furrowed. His jaw clenched. *I see where I get it from.* "What does that mean?"

"Oh, come on!" I threw my hands out, the blood in my veins rushing to the tips of my fingers. Anger was seeping out of every possible outlet. "You knew Mom was struggling. You knew she was abusing her pills." My voice was growing louder and louder, but I couldn't seem to stop yelling. "You turned your back when things got messy. She was fucked-up, and you left Ollie and me here with her. I mean,"—I rounded the island, Jim's eyes bouncing back and forth between my father and me—"I fucking found her body, and it took you twelve fucking hours to come home."

It felt like the bomb inside my chest that had been ticking since Mom died had finally exploded. My pain from the memory was quickly morphed into unmatched anger. I'd kept things locked away for years, but as I grew older and understood things more clearly than my thirteen-year-old self could, it pissed me off to oblivion.

I kept going as my father stood and stared at me, his gray eyes burning holes in my chest. "For the last five years, I've blamed myself." I let out a sarcastic laugh. "Actually, I blamed Hayley. That night Mom got in the accident?" My father and I were inches apart now. My feet continued to drag my body closer to his as if yelling at him from across the room was no longer working for me. "It was my fault. Hayley called because her parents were fighting, and then she wouldn't pick up the phone. I knew something was wrong, so I asked Mom to take me over so I could check on her, but she wouldn't, so I got angry and darted out the door and onto my bike. She was out looking for me when she got in the accident." Another harsh laugh fell out of my mouth. I dropped my head and looked at my shoes, feeling as small as the boy who inevitably watched his mother self-destruct to the point of death.

Pulling my attention from my feet, I leveled him with a stare. "This whole time, I'd been putting the blame on myself for going out that night, for not seeing the signs before it was too late, but it's not my fucking fault." My finger hit his chest. "It was your fault. I never should have had to find her. I never should have had to make sure Ollie and I were taken care of when she was too drugged up to get out of bed. You should have been here." I pushed my finger into his chest even harder. I was ready for him to lose it, to show me that temper that I'd inherited. "It's your fault. I won't turn my back on Hayley just because her life is hard, so don't ask me to."

He dropped his head, staring at my finger. His voice nearly shook when it exited his body. "You're right."

I dropped my hand slowly, almost annoyed he wasn't sparring with me. I didn't want to be right. I didn't want him to be submissive. What I really wanted was this entire fucking mess to disappear. I wanted the nervous feeling deep in my stomach to dissipate. The knots were tied around and around like a tangled bundle of cords.

"But can you blame me for wanting to keep you safe? I lost your mother. Do you think I want to lose you too? Or your brother?"

"What are you talking about? You mean with Hayley?"

"Yes, I mean with Hayley!" He slapped his hand onto the marble counter. His neck turned in Jim's direction, and that must have given Jim the push he needed, because he stood up and started to explain.

"I have to stop looking into the threats and the attack." My teeth ground together so hard I thought I might have broken some. "It's dangerous, and not to mention, if I dig any more, I could be lawfully convicted. It's an undercover sting. They know who killed Hayley's father. They know a lot about him and his gang. They're responsible for the majority of crime in the city. Probably one of the biggest drug runners in our state." Jim darted his attention to my father and then back to me. He rubbed his tired face, the scratch of his five o'clock shadow the only sound in the kitchen. "This isn't my first time running into them, per se. I've watched them before."

My eyebrows dipped. "When?"

My father answered. "Before your mom got into the crash."

The beats of my heart tripled. My words came out callous. "What do you mean?"

My father's head tipped upward, and he stared at the ceiling. When he leveled me with a stare, I could see it plain as day: *guilt*. I could see it

clearly because it was the same look I'd had for the last several years. "The crash wasn't what caused your mom to become addicted to narcotics."

I kept my face unmoving in fear that even a small twitch would make me break everything in half.

"Christian,"—my father's gaze swept the room—"your mom was using pills well before the crash. And she got the majority of them from the drug dealers that Hayley's father was laundering money for."

The word sounded strangled as it came out of my mouth "*No.*"

"I hired Jim before the crash to look into things because your mother seemed off." He began to pour bourbon into his glass cup. "She liked to party in college and before we got married and had you boys. I knew the signs; I was just too afraid to face the truth."

My chest grew tighter with every word that passed his bourbon-stained lips. Anger had my neck tensing. My hands held on to the bottom edge of the counter, my knuckles white from the pressure.

"Once it was confirmed, I confronted her. She denied it. And then she got into the crash a week later." He dropped his head down low, I'm sure full of regret. "After she got past the hump of her injuries, she seemed like she was back to normal, so I didn't press any further. I buried myself in work. I ignored the signs again." He shook his head, not meeting my eye. He was lost in his own memories. "Maybe because I didn't want to believe them. I even lashed out at Jim when he came forth with what he'd found. And then..." It almost pained him to say it. "And then, she overdosed, and I will never forgive myself for not paying attention. For leaving you and Ollie here to fend for yourselves. For believing her lies and deceptions."

My voice was on the edge of breaking. *I* was on the edge of breaking. "So, you knew? You knew she was getting high off pills before the wreck, and you thought it was smart for the doctors to give her *more* narcotics for her injuries?"

My father's face was full of uncertainty. His hard brow line dipped, and he clutched his glass tighter in his hand. "They didn't give her narcotics. The doctors weren't the ones who prescribed her that kind of pain medicine. In fact, I don't think 90% of her injuries were even real."

My nostrils flared. I was losing my grip on my sanity. "Are you saying she made it up?" *No. Fuck that.* I refused to believe a word that was coming out of his mouth. I saw the crash. I was there. The broken headlights, the way the metal of the car was bent. She was injured. I saw her.

"I think she had injuries, but I don't believe they were as severe as she made them seem."

And there it was. My breaking point. I rounded the corner and got in his face. We were the same height; I might have even been a little taller. "No! No! You can't try to turn this around on her! You can't make her out to be the bad guy. I saw her! I saw the way the fucking car bent with her inside. You weren't there."

"Christian." Jim's stern voice caused me to snap my head over to him. "He's telling the truth. I dug. I dug deep after she passed. The doctors did not prescribe her narcotics. There were no doctor's appointments a month after the accident. They cleared her on a clean bill of health."

"Why do you think no one was held responsible for her death? It's because the doctors didn't prescribe her those pain pills. Your mother had an addiction. She sought out dealers on her own and got in over her head." The smell of my father's alcohol-ridden breath had me cringing. "It wasn't your fault. With or without the accident, your mother would have found her way to the same end."

My eyes were burning. My throat was tight. My anger from the grief was slowly fading away. My father's eyes were pleading. Jim was staring at me expectantly. It felt like small shards of glass were cutting into my chest and carving out the last bit of respect I had for my mother.

No.

I swung my arm out and swooped my father's bourbon and cup off the island. It was a small slip of my temper, but it still felt good. Once I heard the glass shatter onto the floor, I stormed my way to the back deck, needing the fresh air to hopefully bring my sanity back.

CHAPTER THIRTY-TWO

HAYLEY

I'D BEEN in this exact position before, cowering on the landing above a column of stairs, plush carpet underneath my body as I crouched down with my head peeking through the slats of the railing. Only this time, instead of watching my father die, I watched Christian storm off through his house and out the back door.

I heard bits and pieces of the conversation with his dad, but with my attempt to give them privacy, I couldn't hear everything.

I wasn't sure what Christian needed at this point, but something had me standing up and slowly creeping down the stairs of his house in search of the boy that somehow found his way into my heart.

I cared.

I paused with my hand hovering over the doorknob, blinded by my last thought. *I cared.* It seemed as if a waterfall of warmth washed over my body. My neck felt warm; my fingers were tingling. My heart skipped a beat. I cared about Christian.

As soon as I opened the door and the air cooled my warm face, I found him. He still didn't have his shirt on. His smooth, bare back was facing me as his arms were resting in front of him on the deck railing. His head was bent low, showing off the muscles along his shoulders. Images of us kissing came back to me, but I shook them away, knowing this wasn't the time.

"So how much did you hear?" he asked without moving.

I crept a little closer to him. "Not much. Just some bits and pieces."

And that was the truth. I heard my name a few times, some yelling about his mom, but that was all. There were huge gaping holes of information left out.

And the strange thing was, I didn't really care to know them, even if they were about me. In this moment, all I cared about was him.

"Are you okay?" I slipped up beside him, looking out into the backyard. It was huge. The treehouse we used to play in still sat up in the oak tree off to the right. I could see other large homes in the distance, just past the fence, and if I moved over a bit, I bet I could see the tall front arch of my old house.

"I don't know."

I nodded. I understood that. "I'm sorry."

His head turned. I could feel his stare on the side of my head. "For what?"

Slowly, I took my gaze off the sparkling lights of the homes that were still awake and placed them on Christian. His dark brow line was heavy, his lips almost calling out to me. My insides twisted as I stared at them. "I'm sorry about your mom. I still haven't said that since being back, and I am sorry."

His face softened. The worry lines on his forehead relaxed. "I'm sorry I blamed you." He shook out his hair before running his hands through the short strands. "I think after that conversation with my dad, I should have put more blame on her."

My hand itched to cover his. "Why *did* you blame me?"

He let out a heavy breath, his head jerking over to the treehouse. "The night your father died, you called me. Do you remember that?"

My heart picked up its pace even with the small mention of that night. "Honestly, I try not to think about that night. Ever."

He nodded. "Fair enough. But you did. You remember how we used to talk on the phone for hours, somehow not really talking at all?"

A small laugh escaped me as I tucked my hair behind my ears. "Yeah, I remember."

"Well, you said your parents were fighting."

"Talking to you always made me feel better."

"You said your parents were fighting, and then you hung up. I kept calling you over and over again, and you wouldn't answer, and I got worried. I asked my mom to take me to your house so I could make sure you were okay, and she said no because it was raining."

The rain. I remembered the rain. I remembered standing outside my house with flashing blue and red lights. I was happy it was raining so no one could tell that I wasn't crying.

I struggled with that often. I didn't cry when my father was murdered. It was like a switch was turned off. He died, so I wasn't able to produce tears anymore. I learned, in a group therapy session that I was forced into by a past social worker, that it was a form of shock. But still, to this day, I didn't cry often. Which was why it was so alarming to me when I cried in Christian's arms last week.

Christian's voice carried me away from the past. "I was angry, so I left anyway. Got on my bike and started to race to your house. My mom followed me in her car, and then she got in a car accident right in front of me. I watched the car basically bend in half with her inside it."

I covered my mouth, not sure what to say, but the pain in his voice made my stomach hurt.

"That's not what killed her, though," I whispered. "She overdosed."

He turned his head to mine. "Yeah, and up until tonight, I thought it was the pain medication she got from the doctors that got her addicted. But according to my dad and Jim, that's not the case. She was addicted before the crash; she just used her new injuries as a clutch for more."

I swallowed a lump in my throat. "I'm so sorry."

"For the last five fucking years I've blamed myself."

"And me."

He nodded, looking out into the distance again. "And you. *Us.* I told myself it was your fault that I left that night. I was so infatuated with you that I didn't care about anything else. And then she got into the wreck, and it caused a spiral of things to happen, leading to her overdose." His head dropped along with his voice. "I blamed you because I didn't want to blame myself. Which, ironically, only made me hate myself more. I blamed us both for so long."

I bit my lip hard. "I know what that's like, you know— blaming yourself for a parent dying." Christian's head snapped over to mine so fast I was forced to meet his eyes. "It hurts and it's heavy." I swallowed back another lump, our stares locked and loaded with crickets chirping in the background. "I don't like to think about it. I go back and forth with wanting to forget and wanting to remember. If I push it away, it'll save me grief and guilt, but if I push too hard, I'm afraid I'll forget him." My eyes somehow found my shoes.

"I'm afraid I'll forget the color of his eyes, or his chuckle when I'd tell a silly joke. I'm afraid I'll forget the way he used to read me bedtime stories when I was little. He was a good dad."

Christian's black shoes somehow ended up in my line of sight, the toes of our shoes hitting each other. The pad of his finger touched the bottom of my chin and forced my face up to his. He was blurry, and it took me a second to realize that my eyes were watering. I was on the verge of tears again. Something about Christian made my walls tumble down.

I could see the gray in his eyes clearly now that we were so close. The charcoal specks glittered when he opened his mouth. "Let's just forget for tonight, okay?"

My heart beat wildly in my chest when he dropped his hand and laced our fingers together. He pulled me behind him, leading me down the steps and onto the crunchy grass. I wanted to ask where we were going, but I already knew.

Christian climbed up the old, rickety wooden ladder of the treehouse nailed onto the tree stump, and I quickly followed, eager to be back in our safe place. We had spent many summer evenings here, playing card games with Ollie and hoarding snacks, only for them to disappear by morning when critters swooped in.

Once I reached the top peg, Christian's large hand wrapped around my wrist, and he hoisted me up and over the edge. I wondered if it was even sound enough after all these years to be up here, but once I got one glance at Christian's face, I didn't care.

The treehouse could have fallen and tumbled to the ground with us in it, and I wouldn't have known the difference. It might have even lit on fire with the way he was staring at me, and I wouldn't have cared.

His hands found my waist fast, and he picked me up and wrapped my legs around his hips. He lowered us to the wooden floor, the old rug we had in here years ago still laid perfectly in the middle.

Once my back was on the floor, Christian bent over and placed his lips on mine. At first, his kiss was gentle and caressing. His lips coaxed my body to relax, but his tongue slipping through the gates had my core bursting with flames. My hips moved unknowingly, and he sucked in a breath. "Patience."

I felt desperate to get things moving, my body still burning from earlier, but he was right. I wanted to savor this.

Christian's hands found the button of my jeans, and with the flick of a finger, he managed to unbutton them and began pulling the zipper down. I angled my butt up, almost panting as he shimmied them off my legs. His hand traveled up the inside of my thigh, and shivers broke out on every inch of my skin. My hands found their way to the back of his neck, and I pulled his face closer, our lips melding together to the point that I was in a state of bliss.

His mouth did that to me.

It made me forget everything bad in the world. His kisses were full of good and love. *I felt loved.*

"What are you doing?" I asked as Christian pulled himself up and peered down at me.

"I like you like this. Hot but beautiful. Wild but tamed." I all but combusted when he dipped down to kiss me again. His lips were warm and gentle, but his hands were all over my body. I arched my body up to his when he broke our kiss. His mouth quickly descended down to my belly. He pulled my shirt up and over my head, and I shivered. His warm whisper brushed against my skin. "Are you cold?"

A harsh laugh fell out of my lips. "No. I'm hot. Really, really hot."

I felt him smile along my torso as he began trailing kisses over my hips and legs. Once his warm breath hit my center, I felt my body tighten. Things wound up in my body that hadn't been wound in a long time. Maybe never. I'd never felt like this. I was vulnerable and at his mercy. I gave him all the control, and I liked it that way.

Christian slowly moved my underwear to the side with his finger, and the slip of his tongue had me bucking up to meet his face. The warm lapping he did caused a familiar pressure to build, and all I wanted was more.

"Christian." My voice was more like a dog panting, but I didn't care. Us here, in this treehouse, was *everything*. Nothing else mattered. Him and me. That was it.

Christian shushed me as his finger found its way inside of me, and with the mix of his warm mouth, I was left breathless. It didn't take long for ecstasy to wash over my body. I muttered something as I came, but I had no idea what.

I pulled myself up onto my elbows, and I felt a fire burning me from the inside out. Christian was right. I was being wild. I'd had sex before, but not like this. It was purely driven from passion. It felt like the last several weeks were some sort of foreplay. Christian in my room at night, listening to his breathing. The small touches he'd give me. The shared kisses full of fragility and denial.

I descended on him like a cat on its prey. I kneeled in front of him, both of us on our knees, and my hands found his shoulders. I pushed him back lightly and straddled his lap, my hair falling down to his shoulder as I bent my head and laid my lips on his. His tongue flicked mine as his fingers unclasped my bra. He palmed my waist and moved my body over his jeans, scratching at the fabric of my wet underwear. My body grew even hotter as our tempo picked up and Christian's breathing was fast and loud. I stopped moving my hips for a moment, his eyes scorching me as I crept down his body and found the button of his jeans.

"Hayley," he groaned, throwing his head back.

"Shh." His pants were down quickly with his help, and as soon as my hand inched inside his briefs, he let out a groan. I moved my hand up and down him slowly, enjoying the show of watching him let his guard down. I almost couldn't take it. I felt a buildup in my own body just by watching him. Brooding, hot Christian who never showed his emotions was letting go. He was letting me work his body, getting lost in my touch, and I liked it. I liked it a lot.

I pumped my hand up and down a few more times before my mouth found him.

"Jesus Christ," he groaned, straining against my lips. His hand found my head, and he wove his fingers through my hair as my mouth bobbed. *Why is this so hot?* My core was tight, and I almost wanted to reach my fingers down to get my own release as I gave him his.

But Christian didn't let me get too far. Instead, he grabbed onto my biceps and pulled me to his face. He wore a carnal look, his jaw taut, his eyes hooded as he trailed his gaze to my naked chest and legs. Suddenly, I was whipped around, and he was back on top. The fabric of my panties was ripped down my legs and thrown somewhere in the treehouse.

"Hayley." Christian's voice was gravelly, and I felt it all over my skin. "I'm going to ask you something, and all I want is for you to give me a simple answer, and then we're never going to talk about it again. Okay?"

"Okay," I whispered back.

"Are you a virgin?"

My heart stopped. I swallowed before I answered him. "No."

I couldn't read his expression. There was a small tick of his eye, but that was it. I knew he wasn't a virgin—that much was made clear the first day I stepped foot into English Prep.

"So, I don't have to go slow and gentle?"

My mouth curved. "Don't you dare."

And just like that, his mouth was back on mine, but this time, it was urgent and hungry. Our mouths tore into each other like our lives depended on it.

I felt his slick skin at my entrance as we moved up and down. Before things got too heated, he snagged his jeans and pulled out a condom. I watched in awe as he slipped it on, nervous excitement blooming in my chest.

He was back on top of me within a second, and I spread my legs wide, locking onto his eyes. It took a little while, but once he was inside, I finally let my breath out.

"Is this okay?" he asked, towering over me.

I nodded slowly, pivoting my hips up to get a better angle. "Perfect."

"You are," he whispered, moving in and out of me slowly. "You are perfect." He bent his face down to mine and kissed my forehead, but soon, his slow thrusts turned into fast, hard ones. I matched his body and met him with each stroke. I felt all my worries wash away. I felt all my insecurities disappear. My hard exterior turned soft with each touch of our lips. I finally felt, after five dreadful years, I was safe.

The pressure built up inside of me, and I withered underneath Christian. His tempo picked up, my back arched, and as soon as his lips touched my neck, I reached my limit. My hands squeezed his biceps as I braced myself for the fall, and not a second later, he paused on top of me, falling just as fast as I had.

For a few moments, he just rested on top of me, his slick forehead on mine, our bare chests smashed together. Unspoken words were shared between us, and I never ever wanted to live without him again.

Once our breathing finally slowed, Christian rolled off of me. I shivered as the sweat on my skin began to dry, but Christian was quick to put his shirt back on me. A small smile found its way onto my lips.

"Is that a real smile I see? Was that all it took? Sex with me?"

I smacked his shoulder. "No. I was smiling because you were being a gentleman when you put your shirt on me because I was cold. It was nice."

Christian shrugged as he pulled his pants back on. His arms reached out, and he pulled me over into his lap as he rested his back along the wood. "I've been nice this whole time. You just kept pushing me away."

I looked up at him. "The *whole* time?"

He peered down at me through his dark eyelashes. "Fine. I've been nice recently. Is that better?"

I softly laughed. "Yes."

My gaze roamed around the old treehouse, a blissful state settling within my bones. "Did you ever expect this?" I took his hand and wrapped it around my middle. "Us. Here. Naked in your old treehouse?"

Christian's chest tumbled behind me. "On more than one occasion, yes."

I threw my head back and laughed. A real, genuine laugh. "What? When?"

"I was a horny fuck in middle school. Of course, back then it freaked me out, thinking those things about you, but I still thought them and indulged in them while in the shower."

"Oh my God!" I covered my face with my hands, feeling my cheeks burn.

He laughed again, and soon, both of our shoulders were shaking with laughter.

Once we caught our breath, Christian intertwined our hands together. My heart swelled in my chest. I was giddy. Happy. And for once, I wasn't trying to run from it.

"Now, if you would have asked me in the last five years if I'd thought you'd be mine, I would have growled."

My cheek lifted. "Who said I'm yours?"

His hand left mine, and he brought it under my chin to tip my head back. His eyes were dark and intense, passion blazing throughout. "I did."

A sense of excitement ran through my veins. Nervous jitters bounced in my stomach. I liked this. I *wanted* to be his, more than I had ever wanted anything in my life, and that was scary.

His face fell for a moment. "You are mine, aren't you?"

Without hesitation, and before my mind could stop me, my heart answered, "Yes." Then, I paused and narrowed my eyes, still looking up at him. "But I'm still mad at you about the Gabe thing."

His mouth curved upward, and I rolled my eyes, snuggling back into his chest. The truth was, I was annoyed about the Gabe thing. He shouldn't have gone over to his house and let his temper get the best of him, but what was done was done, and there wasn't much that could ruin this moment with him —especially not Gabe.

I stared out of the treehouse window, the crickets still chirping a melody in the background. A gust of cold air wafted around us as I saw a light flicker off in his house. "Do you think your dad is going to come looking for us? Because if I thought he was going to think poorly of me showing up in your shirt, he's *really* going to think poorly of me seeing me in your shirt with no pants on."

Christian's finger traced the inside of my thigh, and I felt my body heating up again. I kept my breathing even, but I was simmering underneath. "I don't care."

"But I do!" I swatted at his hand.

His hand froze as his large palm laid on my leg. "We need to talk about something."

I paused. "What?"

I heard him swallow, and my chest grew tight.

"It's about something Jim said when we came home.

Before I got into the argument with my dad."

An uneasiness settled on my shoulders.

"He said that the police know who killed your father. They've been tracking the group for a while. It's some sort of undercover sting."

I sat up straight and turned around to look at Christian. He was leaning back on the wooden side of the treehouse in jeans. His brown hair was tousled on top as if some stylist actually came and laid every strand to look messy and sexy. I locked eyes with him.

"An undercover sting?"

He nodded. "He told me to stay out of it and he had to, too. Obviously, interfering would cause the sting to go wrong. The same men who killed your father are, apparently, some of the biggest drug dealers in the city. They're more than likely the ones who sold my mom her pills."

A weird sensation washed over me. Relief? Relief that my father may get some sort of justice. Or was it a feeling of hope? Hope that the authorities would put those men away for a long time. The threat they spewed years ago would be gone, and I wouldn't have to have this little voice in the back of my head telling me to tread lightly, to be careful, and to watch my back. I hoped that Christian's family would get some sort of justice, too.

"Tell me what you're thinking." Christian's soft voice tore my gaze from the tattered rug.

"I'm thinking..." I bit my lip, teetering it back and forth between my teeth. "I'm thinking I'm glad I'm not alone in this anymore."

My heart felt full inside my chest. So full that it might just explode. His arms reached out and he pulled me into his body. His hands found my face, and his lips sealed the deal.

This was real.

Christian and I. We were real.

CHAPTER THIRTY-THREE

CHRISTIAN

"CHRISTIAN," she hissed under her breath as my hands toyed with the top of her underwear. "Stop it! If we wake up Pete, I'll have to shove you out the window, and then you'll die, and then I'll go back to being alone."

I smiled along her soft skin. Her hair smelled good; *she* smelled good. "Let Pete find me. I don't care."

She giggled underneath me.

We should have been sleeping. We had school tomorrow, and it was already almost three in the morning. I snuck in here hours ago, and after promising Hayley I'd let her study for a few, (and to be honest, I needed to study some, too) I finally talked her into fooling around. I couldn't help myself. After Friday night, this girl was branded onto my skin, my heart, and my brain. She ran laps around my head all day long.

Last night, she made me promise I wouldn't interrupt her girls' night with Piper this weekend, since we never ended up going back to her house Friday night. After the treehouse,

Hayley and I finally climbed down and went back inside to my dark house. My father had gone to bed and then left early the next morning with things unsettled, like usual.

Hayley made a good point that morning when I brushed off his disappearance. She came up behind me as I made coffee, trying to hide my resentment. My father was a runner at best, constantly running from tough shit.

When her arms hit my middle, burying her head into my back, my body stilled. I wasn't used to affection. Even with Madeline, or whoever it was that I was fucking, we never got affectionate unless it was some sort of foreplay, but Hayley was different. It felt right. It felt serene. I basked in her warmth, and I'd been thinking about her words since the moment they left her lips. *"Remember how you felt when you thought it was your fault that your mom died? That you and I caused the wreck and were the ones who started the domino effect? Every time you looked at me, you felt immense guilt, right? Well, that's how your dad probably feels when he sees you or Ollie. He probably feels like he failed you, and sure, in a way he did, but everyone deserves a second chance. Let last night sink in, and maybe he'll come around and face his issues. After all, you did, didn't you?"*

Hayley. She was what I was missing in life.

"Christian," she quietly moaned as my finger slipped inside her wet folds. My dick grew stiff; my balls tightened. I'd never wanted to taste someone so much before. I couldn't get enough of her, and it was downright ridiculous that I thought I'd ever be able to resist this girl.

"Tell me you like it," I whispered in her ear before taking her lobe with my teeth. She moved her hips up to meet my finger and worked herself to the point of oblivion within seconds. I sucked on her flesh as my other hand traveled to her nipple. She had lost her bra a while ago, right after I interrupted her studies.

"I..." Her breathing was ragged, her nipple tightening as

her hips moved faster. I slipped another finger in, eager to please her. It was the biggest turn-on of all. Watching Hayley let loose, her hair messy, her mouth parted. It was my own fucking porno. "I..."

I stopped moving my fingers. "Tell me," I said again, my mouth hovering above hers.

Her eyes flared with lustful need. "I like it." Her hips bucked upward, and my cocky grin fell back in its place. Pausing like that seemed to work in my favor, because as soon as I pulled my finger out and back in once more, Hayley came. I sealed her mouth with mine to drown out her moans.

Once she calmed down, she pulled my fingers out of her pussy and pulled me on top of her. My dick was hard, yet tucked away within my pants, but I moved over her anyway, loving her warmth.

Hayley licked her lips as her hand found itself in my pocket, pulling out a condom and ripping it open with her teeth. She pulled my pants down quickly, and I kicked them off, pulling my shirt off, too. Being naked with Hayley was a sort of heaven I didn't even know existed. It was intimate with her. Different. It wasn't just sex. I wasn't just in it for the receiving part. I wanted to give. I wanted to make her lose her mind like she did to me.

Hayley's fingers found my dick, and she rolled the condom on and took charge on angling me into her pussy. A heavy breath escaped my mouth as I found her warm walls. Her legs widened; her breasts pushed up in my face. I moved on top of her slowly, my hands wrapping around her tiny body. I buried my face into her neck, pumping in and out nice and slow. The build-up was fast, as always, and I was certain that I'd never have to conjure up a porno in my head to get myself off with fucking her. One touch of her lips had me unraveling.

"Fuck," I muttered, thrusting faster and faster. Hayley's

hand slipped in between our bodies to rub her clit, and I begged myself not to look because it would inevitably cause me to come within a second, but I couldn't fucking help myself. She made me lose my mind. All bets were off when it came to her.

I growled as my eyes found her finger circling herself, and within ten seconds, we were coming together. My hand slapped over her mouth, and she bit my palm, trying to drown out her moan.

Fucking Christ.

I lay on top of her until my breathing settled, and once I was off and deposited the condom, her warm body curled up beside mine. I was too large for her bed—if you wanted to call it that—as my legs hung down below the mattress edge, but I didn't care.

"I'm never going to get used to this," she whispered, hooking a bare leg over mine.

"What? Sex with a king?" I teased.

She giggled as she slapped my chest. "No, this. Us. You and me like this." She shook her head against my chest. "I didn't let myself think of us like this because I was so afraid to let you in." She paused. "And plus, I kind of thought you'd hate me forever."

"I fought against my feelings for a while." I placed my lips on top of her head, wondering when I turned into a guy who did that sort of thing.

Her body began to relax in my arms, and I felt my body falling into slumber. What a strange turn of events the last few weeks had been.

"What are we going to do about school tomorrow?"

My voice grew tired, raspy. "What do you mean?"

Her head angled up to mine, but I kept my eyes closed. "I mean, are we going to tell people? I don't really like attention, and you're all anyone really cares about at English Prep."

"Oh, people will know, regardless of whether we tell them."

"Why is that?" Her hold on me grew tighter.

"Because now that I've had you, I'll never be able to keep my hands off you again. You're mine now, Hayley. There are no take-backs like in sixth grade."

"I'm not your property, Christian." If I were to look at her face, I could guarantee she was rolling her eyes and scowling.

"Maybe not, but I'm yours."

And with that, we both fell asleep until her alarm went off the next morning.

The following morning started off with a bang—literally. I talked Hayley into letting me shower with her at Pete's. A six-minute shower shared by the pair of us wasn't a feat, but keeping myself from bending her over the tub was.

Once we got back into her room and successfully shut the door before Pete or Jill descended from their room, it took us seconds to have our mouths on one another.

I'd never been so lust-crazy before.

Even now, an hour later, as she pulled up in Piper's BMW in the school parking lot, the only thing I could think about was her lips. Both sets.

Ollie sauntered up beside me and stared in their direction. "So, I talked to Dad."

"Mmhm," I mumbled, swiping my lip with my thumb. Hayley climbed out of the passenger side with her hair still damp from the shower. Her skirt somehow appeared sexier than ever, and I was certain it was because I'd tasted what was underneath.

"He told me about your talk on Friday. Is everything okay with you?"

"Mmhm," I mumbled again.

"Dude!"

I felt a shove to my shoulder. "What?" I asked in a daze.

Ollie's mouth split in two, and then he started to laugh. Our group of friends all stopped what they were doing and stared. "Dude, I've never ever seen you like this."

"Like what?" I asked, keeping my eyes off Hayley.

"Fucking shit... I don't even know."

Eric popped up beside Ollie. "I think the word he's looking for is...not a fucking asshole."

I shrugged. "I'm not always an ass."

"You surely aren't right now, which means..." His line of sight left mine. "Does this mean what I think it means?"

"Does this mean what?" April, along with her catty friends, sauntered up, all of their faces burning my irises. *Did I really find any of these girls attractive before Hayley?*

"Christian?" Eric snagged my attention, and I gave him a small flick of my head.

Hayley doesn't want unneeded attention, and I understood that. I respected it. I told her I'd try my hardest to keep things level on my end when it came to us. Keeping things under wraps for now was okay with me.

I wasn't going to stop staring at her, though.

And it probably wasn't going to stop me from sneaking in touches every chance I got.

But I'd try.

For her.

CHAPTER THIRTY-FOUR

HAYLEY

CHRISTIAN WAS ABSOLUTELY awful at keeping his distance from me at school. It'd only been two days since the treehouse incident, and basically, the entire school knew something was up.

I smiled more, and Christian wasn't his usual, brooding self.

We'd get caught staring at each other, and someone would make a comment. Christian wouldn't correct them, and neither would I. I was at a point where I didn't care much about high school drama. Madeline's secret dirty looks in PE did nothing to faze me. April and a few other girls rolled their eyes at me or made comments about my uniform being too worn, but I only shrugged.

Things were good.

Christian snuck in kisses and forbidden touches under the stairwell at school, and afterwards, when his hands would leave my waist because the bell rang and soon students would start pouring through the hallways, I felt indifferent.

Unwanted attention was something I'd always been against.

But now that it stole Christian away from me, I was second-guessing my decision. I didn't care if people knew I was a poor foster kid, and I shouldn't care if they knew I was with Christian. Most girls would have been flaunting it everywhere, if they were me. But that was the difference between me and other girls my age. I didn't want to flaunt it for them; I wanted to flaunt it for me. I didn't want to hide him, because I actually felt better with him by my side.

I *wanted* him by my side.

Just as the thought escaped me, a large hand wrapped around my waist and pulled me around the hallway corner. I yelped and spun around, exhilarated. "Hi."

Christian's lip tipped upward. "Hey." Then, his hands wrapped around my face, and he kissed me. He swooped his tongue into my mouth, which left me breathless.

I pulled away quickly, butterflies floating in my stomach. My hands clasped onto his wrists.

His brow furrowed. "What's wrong?"

I swallowed, my gaze bouncing back and forth between his gray eyes. "I don't think I want to hide this."

Christian's head tipped to the side. We were tucked away near the library, hidden in the corner at the far end of the hall.

"You don't?"

I slowly shook my head.

His grasp grew tighter on my face. "So, what does this mean then?"

I shyly shrugged. "I don't really know."

Christian's hands dropped from my face as he reached up and grabbed the straps of his backpack. "I don't either." He licked his lip. "Let's just do what feels right. Yeah?"

"What feels right to you?"

Christian looked away for a second before pinning me with an intense look. "Honestly, I don't know. I've never done this. I've never been this way before." He looked away again, and I could have sworn his cheeks grew pink for a second. "The old Christian, from five years ago, was completely infatuated with you. Then, I grew to hate you and everyone around me. My feelings were superficial at best. Girls hung on my arms, but it was all for show. My heart didn't beat for them." Christian stepped closer to me, his body heat enveloping me. He swallowed roughly, his Adam's apple bobbing up and down. "I know there's been a huge gap of time between us, and other constraints of the past, but this..." Christian took my hand and placed it on his chest. I could feel his heart thumping against my palm. "This has always beat for you. Even when I wanted to hate you, it beat for you."

My eyes glossed over at his words. I gulped back a lump as I watched the hope gleam in his eye. He was waiting for me to say something. He wanted confirmation that I was feeling the same way.

Three days of accepting my feelings and my heart was already attached to his like it was when we were barely teenagers.

"What are you thinking?"

A smile found its way onto my face. I hurriedly grabbed Christian's large wrist and pulled him down the hallway. The farther we moved from the corner, the more our peers appeared. Every one of their faces was stricken with confusion. I kept pulling Christian until we were outside the school doors. Mostly everyone was getting ready to leave for the day, slowly walking to their overpriced cars or mingling in the courtyard, gossiping.

I stopped just a few feet away from Christian's group of friends. My hand slipped from his wrist, and when I peered up into his face, a gust of crisp autumn wind blew leaves around us. I reached up on my tiptoes and placed a long, full-of-life kiss on his lips. My mouth moved over his languidly as his hands wrapped around my waist. I was pulled into his body roughly, and somehow, everything and everyone disappeared. This kiss wasn't for them. It was for us. I wanted to show him what felt right to me. And it was him.

He felt right.

As soon as we broke our embrace, we stood and stared at each other. He smiled first, and then I followed suit. We didn't break our stare until people started clapping, which caused the both of us to chuckle.

"There," I said, still staring up at him. "That's what feels right to me."

He tipped his chin once, grabbed onto my hand, and pulled me over to his group of friends. I may not have fit in right away, but nothing seemed impossible with Christian being mine.

Nothing at all.

CHAPTER THIRTY-FIVE

HAYLEY

THE NEXT WEEK AT SCHOOL, things changed dramatically. Dynamics were shifted. Some stared; others gossiped; teachers were shocked. Even Headmaster Walton came out of his office to see if the gossip mill was being truthful.

Christian, the unattainable king, was no longer single. And to everyone's surprise, the girl to snag him was one from the wrong side of the tracks.

Whenever Piper and I would pull up a chair at his lunch table, the room would grow quiet, as if people lost their sense of verbiage. It was funny, but a bit unnerving.

It did nothing to affect Christian and me, though. All the stares and curious whispers behind our backs didn't bother us a bit. We sat together, walked the halls together, and kissed when we felt like it. Butterflies swarmed my stomach 24/7, and they were the good ones. Not the dreadful, ominous ones with black wings.

It was like that all the time now. I fluttered around the school and Pete and Jill's like I was a butterfly myself. Even

Ann noticed a change when she'd stopped by to check in the other day. And it was a damn miracle that Pete and Jill hadn't caught on to Christian and me yet. If they were to pay a little more attention to me, they'd know something was different. I was surprised they hadn't caught him in my room yet, either. He popped in through the window around nine every night, which was a rule I laid out so I could still get my homework and studying done (there was absolutely no hope with him near), and we'd either end up talking for hours or stripping down underneath the covers. It was usually a bit of both. We'd gotten out of hand a few times now, but still, no one came looking.

One week of being Christian's and it felt like no time had passed between us at all. The hate was gone. The past was in the past. Every day with him felt like the start of forever.

"Madeline is staring again." Piper bent her head down to me as we all sat at Christian's lunch table. His hand was resting on my knee as he casually talked to Ollie and Eric about this week's game. I slowly swiveled my head to Madeline and caught her thick-mascara-laden eye. I flicked an eyebrow up, and she glared.

My ears felt hot, but I told myself not to engage in her catty behavior. A feud with Madeline was the last thing I needed. Things were finally calming for me—at least at English Prep.

A small squeeze of my knee had me glancing up at Christian. His sexy grin was plastered on his face. "You're coming to the game, right? With Piper?"

"Piper is *definitely* coming." Ollie's grin matched his brother's.

Piper's head swung forward. "I'm not coming for you, Ollie—in either sense—so I don't know why you're so excited."

He rolled his eyes. "We'll see about that."

"We'll see what?" she asked, but I tuned their argument out as I glanced back at Madeline. She was still staring.

"Want me to say something?" Christian's whisper hit my ear.

"No. I can handle it on my own."

I could tell he was grinding his teeth back and forth.

"What?" I asked under my breath.

His stormy gaze found mine underneath his thick eyelashes. He messed with the tie hanging around his neck. "I'm your boyfriend. I'm supposed to stick up for you."

I bristled at the thought. "Not to someone like Madeline." I glanced around the table, and thankfully, no one was paying any attention to us. "She's just jealous that she could never truly snag you."

"If she bothers you, let me know. I don't like the idea of someone messing with you."

A ghost of a smile touched my lips. I leaned in closer to Christian, my knee touching his. "I can handle much more than you give me credit for."

His tongue darted out to lick his lips. "Trust me. I know."

My core started to tighten, but I ignored it.

"Then let me handle Madeline. A scowl or two from her is nothing compared to the real threat out there."

Christian's lips formed a straight line as the reminder of my father's past lingered in the air. It was something we both tried to push away, but it never truly left our minds.

"I know," he finally said as the bell rang for class.

"I'm gonna go to the bathroom real quick," I said, reaching up and planting a small kiss on his lips. Piper and Ollie were still in some sort of feud, so once I said my brief goodbye to them, I headed for the navy doors, clutching my books in my hand.

"Hey, wait." Christian pulled me back by my shirt and whipped me around. Our peers were walking past us slowly, pretending not to sneak a glance at their king with his girlfriend.

"What?"

Christian's hands wrapped around my face as he brought his lips down to mine. My entire body grew warm as his tongue swiped over mine. All the breath left my body when he pulled away.

"I just wanted to kiss you."

Butterflies flew around in my belly when he winked at me and started to follow his friends. I shyly glanced around the hallway and met the eye of several people. The girls' mouths were hanging open, and the guys were all shaking their heads, wearing grins.

My face was still flaming as I entered the bathroom and even as I washed my hands afterwards.

The whole boyfriend-girlfriend thing was new territory for me. I thought I wouldn't like it. I thought the attention would bother me. But turned out, not much bothered me with Christian by my side.

My head swung to the left as the bathroom door opened, and soon, my light and fluttery feeling disappeared.

Madeline's eyes dug right through me. *Here we go.*

I continued to wash my hands as she stared at me, blocking the door like a bouncer at a bar. *Doesn't she know I can knock her flat on her ass in seconds?*

"Well, spit it out, Madeline. I know you have something to say."

Her foot tapped the tiled floor as she waited for me to look at her. I took my sweet time drying my hands and gathering my books, knowing very well I was going to be late to class.

"So, how does my pussy taste?"

I couldn't help the laugh bubbling up my throat. "Are you serious? That's the best you've got?"

Madeline's face wavered for a moment as I stepped closer to her. "Madeline, I'm not that dense; I know that you and Christian used to fool around and have sex." Although, the thought made me recoil inside, the past *was* the past. "But for you to stand here and act like he just fucked you this morning and I got your sloppy seconds is a bit desperate. Don't you think?"

She growled, "You took everything from me." Madeline paused for a moment before darting her glistening eyes away from me. *Was she crying?* A small part of me felt bad almost instantly. She didn't deserve it. But I did feel a little bad. Something had to have made her this way: cold, detached, craving everyone's attention at all times.

"Madeline, you did this to yourself. Take a step back and evaluate your actions. Your motives. No one wants to be friends with someone who's conniving and mean." I walked over and stood beside her until she finally moved out of the way. The late bell rang above our heads. "I think you should know that better than anyone."

She held her chin up high. "What's that supposed to mean?" Her voice dripped of unshed tears.

I shrugged, placing my hand on the door. "Someone made you feel inferior once; that's why you are the way that you are."

Her face twisted and grew red. "You know nothing about me. You're the one that feels inferior."

I laughed sarcastically. "You're damn right. I've been put down more times than I can count." I turned around and pushed through the door, but not before I said over my shoulder, "But at least I can admit it."

Then, I left her to think about what I'd said. Madeline was mean and callous—conniving, at best—but I knew people weren't born that way. Something or someone caused her to do the things she did. I knew better than anyone that there was more than met the eye when it came to one's actions.

"I can't believe they crushed them that badly." Piper laughed as she pulled onto the highway.

My fingers fiddled with the holes in my jeans as we drove out to Eric's cabin for the after-game party. "I know. I've only been to a few football games—ever." I laughed. "But that was, by far, the worst beating I've ever seen."

Piper glanced over and smiled. "Christian probably played so well because he knew you were watching."

"Oh, whatever." I laughed. Then I cocked an eyebrow. "I wonder why Ollie played so well..."

Piper grunted.

"Is something going on with you two?"

"What? No!" Her voice squeaked at the end of her sentence, and I couldn't decide if she was hiding the truth or if it was a coincidence. "We're just thrown together a lot because of you and Christian." Piper quickly tried to change the subject. "By the way...how are things with you two? People *still* haven't gotten over seeing Christian act so...*happy*."

I smiled as my body grew warm. "It's weird, you know? But in a good way." I shrugged, tucking a braid behind my shoulder. "I don't know how to explain it. There's just this comfort with him, but excitement, too. One curl of his lip gives me butterflies and makes me feel wild, but his hugs calm me almost instantly." I shook my head a little. "It's hard not being so independent with him, though. I'm used to being alone and relying on myself, and now he's there, wanting to fix all my problems. Even Madeline."

Piper didn't say anything, so I paused my thoughts of Christian and glanced at her. Piper's eyes were bouncing back and forth between the windshield and her rearview mirror. My back flew into the passenger seat as she pressed down on the gas. "Piper, what's wrong? Why are you speeding like that?"

She didn't look at me. "Speaking of... You don't think Madeline would ride my ass on the way to Eric's, would you?"

"What?" I quickly turned around and saw headlights glaring into the back of Piper's BMW. My heart instantly started to race. "How long has that car been following us?"

"A while. But it just now started to ride my ass. I'm going twenty over the speed limit."

My eyes darted down to the speedometer, its lights illuminating the interior. "Jesus, you're going almost eighty miles per hour."

Piper gulped. "I know." Her voice was on the edge of hysteria, and I was feeling it, too. "Hayley, what do I do? You don't think..."

My hands fumbled to grab her phone out of the center console. "Try to slow down, and see if they pass."

As soon as Piper let off the gas, the car jolted forward, and she screamed. My throat began to squeeze as I frantically scrolled the contacts on Piper's phone. I found Christian's number and dialed quickly.

Piper's voice rang out as I pulled the phone to my ear. "Hayley! What do we do?"

Run. My body's natural response to fight or flight in this situation was to flight—and to flight fast.

"Drive faster."

Christian picked up on the first ring.

"Hello?"

"Christian." My own voice surprised me. I was scared. Really, really scared. Even more so when I heard his voice.

The car jolted forward again, and Piper's scream filled the air.

"Hayley? What's wrong? What the fuck is going on?"

My heart began to sink as I grabbed onto the handle above my head. The yellow lines on the road were blurring faster and faster.

"Christian, I think they found me."

CHAPTER THIRTY-SIX

CHRISTIAN

MY FOOT PRESSED onto the gas. My chest was constricted as I gripped the steering wheel with one hand, the other holding the phone up to my ear.

"Bro, what's wrong?" Ollie yelled from beside me as I tried to catch my breath.

"Hayley, where are you?" My voice came out sharp and bleak.

Piper screamed again in the background, and I could hear Hayley's labored breathing.

"Hayley!" I yelled, and this time my voice had an edge of anger to it—sinister sounding.

"Route 55. Piper is going almost one hundred miles per hour, and they're somehow still catching up to us. If they hit us again going this fast, we'll wreck."

My head whipped over to Ollie as I pushed the "speaker" button on my phone. "Call Eric. See where he is. Someone needs to fucking get to them now."

"What the fuck is going on?" Ollie whipped out his phone and was dialing Eric before the words even left his mouth.

"Christian, what do we do? Do I call the police?"

Fuck.

"No, stay on the phone with me." I looked at Ollie out of the corner of my eye. "Tell Eric what's going on, then hang up and call the police, and tell them that a BMW is being tailgated on Route 55, going around one hundred miles per hour."

Ollie didn't bat an eyelash. He did exactly as I said.

"Hayley? Talk to me." My heart was damn near exploding in my chest. It was going a mile a minute. My foot pressed harder on the gas pedal, and my Charger all but came to life as it weaved in and out of traffic on the highway.

"They're still following us." Her breaths were short. I heard her comforting Piper. "You're doing fine, Piper. Just try to stay calm."

"I'm almost to you; I just turned onto Route 55."

"You're not going to catch us. We're going ninety-three."

"My car is faster; I will catch you." *Jesus, will I, though?* My stomach burned with acid. The thought of someone hurting Hayley made me go crazy. I was going as fast as my Charger would take me.

"Eric just turned around. One of us will get there. Just focus, bro."

The center white lines were zipping in front of us, and I'd passed nearly all the cars going their normal speed, and now it was just my Charger on the road.

"Hayley, you okay?" I asked as my hands tightened on the steering wheel.

Piper screamed in the background, and Ollie's head snapped over to mine as he was on the phone with the police operator, giving them the details I'd told him.

"We're okay. Piper went off the road a little. I see a car up ahead."

"It's probably Eric; just keep driving. Don't you dare stop." If she stopped, they'd fucking take her. I knew it. That black storm cloud was no longer in our rearview mirror at every turn. It was right above our fucking heads.

"Okay, but—" I heard Hayley's scream, along with Piper's.

"Drive faster!" Ollie yelled, and I ground my jaw. I felt like I was going to puke.

"Hayley?" I yelled, my fists aching from my grip on the steering wheel.

Ollie snatched my phone off my lap. "Hayley!"

The only thing we could hear were random bits and pieces of Hayley's voice. It was static. She was losing service, or I was. It didn't matter. I couldn't hear a damn thing.

"I swear to God," I gritted through my teeth. "This shit has to stop. I can't take it. The minute I let her out of my sight, something fucking happens."

Ollie tried dialing Piper's number again, but it wouldn't pick up, so I kept driving.

My foot ached to go faster, but I was going as fast as I could. We were nearing the end of Route 55, and I didn't see any taillights in the distance.

Where the fuck are they?

CHAPTER THIRTY-SEVEN

HAYLEY

My HANDS SMACKED the dashboard when Piper and I came to a sudden stop, but I popped back up almost immediately, the phone still clutched in my hand.

"Get out and run to that gas station. Now!" I shouted at Piper as we both whipped our seatbelts off. We were able to get a little ahead of the car following us, but not by much. We both tumbled out of her car and dashed for the lone gas station. Our feet slapped against the concrete as we heard screeching tires behind us. Piper grabbed onto my hand when we got to the glass door. The bell jingled above our heads, and the gas station clerk looked startled. He looked up from his phone with furrowed brows. I pulled Piper over to the counter, panting. I didn't want to look behind me, afraid of who I'd find, but I did anyway. My heart dropped to the ground as I let out a gasp. I saw Eric jump out of his Range Rover. He looked at our car, met my eye through the glass door, and then turned around, waiting for the other car.

"Uh, can I help you girls?" the clerk asked as Piper and I stood back along the counter, still holding hands.

I squeezed her hand as I shut my eyes tightly. My body was shaking with adrenaline. My pulse was still racing under my skin. I'd been through some scary shit before, and I'd found myself in several compromising situations over the last few years, but nothing had ever been like this. The speeding, the bumper hitting, the panic in Christian's voice, the uncertainty of what to do. It was all too much.

The bell chimed, and I popped my eyes open and met Eric's icy eyes. "Are you guys okay?"

Piper dropped my hand and crouched down to rest her head among her jean-clad knees. Her head moved back and forth, her red hair swishing. She took several deep, loud breaths. I stood rigid straight. My hands were still shaking. My legs were tingling with fear.

The gas station clerk sounded from behind me. "Yeah, I'm kind of wondering the same thing. Are you girls okay?"

I couldn't find my voice to answer either of them. Instead, I put my hands on top of my head and shut my eyes. *Breathe in and out, Hayley*. I had to catch my breath. I needed to calm myself down. Fear was still slithering up my back like a snake. *Why is this happening?* I wanted to curse my father in his grave. I *knew* who was chasing us. Just like, deep down, I knew who attacked me at the football game.

I'm almost eighteen. They said they'd come for me when I was eighteen. The threat made years ago was coming to the surface, and I felt as if nothing in the last five years had prepared me for it.

"Christian's here."

My eyes flew open, and I instantly searched through the glass to find him. The Charger came to a sudden halt right beside Eric's Range Rover, and he was out of the driver's seat within half a second.

I held my breath until I got to him. I ran past Eric and took off through the door, hearing the little jingle above my head. I ran until I felt his arms circle around me. I buried my head into his chest, taking small gasps of air, breathing in his woodsy scent.

"It's okay, it's okay. I'm here. I'm sorry I didn't get here faster." I could feel his heart drumming through his chest, thrashing just as hard as mine. My eyes started to well up, but I squeezed his waist harder. Christian pulled me away just a fraction and wrapped his hands around my face. The loose strands of hair from my braids fell on top of his knuckles as he caged my cheeks in. "I don't fucking like this, Hayley. I don't like this feeling."

"What feeling?" I breathed out, still holding on tight. My chest was still heaving; my body was still trembling.

"This fucking feeling of my heart being torn in half at the thought of something happening to you." He brought his head down, resting his forehead on mine. "I fucking love you, Hayley. And I know that probably makes you recoil because you're not used to being loved and cared for, but I do. I fucking love you, and we're going to figure this out. Whatever it takes. I'm not letting someone take you away from me. I've already lost you once. I'm not doing it again."

Tears fell down my face as Christian continued to ramble. His jaw was sharper than ever; his tone was like a knife being sharpened. He listed everything he was going to do in order to fix my father's mistakes so I would be safe.

He loved me. Christian loved me. And I loved him. There was no other way around it.

That was what made the threat that much scarier. Now I had something to lose. I had *someone* to lose.

"Christian," I whispered, pushing my body closer to his. "Stop."

"I'm not going to stop. I'm never going to stop until I

know you're safe." He shut his eyes, still resting his head on my forehead. "I feel like I'm losing my mind."

"Christian," I whispered, clenching his T-shirt in my hands. He finally took a breath and opened his eyes. The gray depths sucked me in. "I love you, too."

He nodded his head along mine for several minutes. We just stared at each other and held one another under the buzzing gas station lights. "We're gonna figure this out, okay?"

I nodded. "Okay."

CHAPTER THIRTY-EIGHT

CHRISTIAN

HAYLEY, Piper, Ollie, Eric, and I all sat around the breakfast bar with our heads huddled low a couple of days after the chase. We each had a copy of the police report from when Hayley's father had died—courtesy of Ollie working his magic at the records office and flirting incessantly with the registrar.

Piper's BMW didn't have much damage, and she told her parents it was a hit-and-run accident at the football game, so no questions were asked. We still weren't sure if the police had gone out on Route 55 when Ollie had called and told them about the BMW being tailgated, but nonetheless, they never came to the gas station that evening, so no one knew anything of the matter.

Except us five—and the fuckers driving the other vehicle.

I told Hayley I was done fucking around. Her mother's half-assed, puzzling warning was on a loop in the back of my head, along with the threat from five years ago, and I was sick of feeling like a weight was on my shoulders whenever Hayley wasn't around. I felt sick to my stomach, as if there was a rock laying inside, getting heavier with each day.

"So, why can't we go to the police?" Eric leaned back in his seat, his black hair ruffled on top from running his hand through the strands. Eric demanded to know what was going on after he'd found Hayley and Piper at the gas station. Hayley didn't want anyone else involved, but he was already knee-deep in, and to be honest, the more the fucking merrier. We needed to get this sorted out.

Hayley's hand wrapped around mine as she looked at Eric. "Because Jim said that it's an undercover sting and we shouldn't get anyone involved. Because if the cover is blown or they know we're looking into them or start asking questions, it could be ruined, and the last few years of work will go down the drain. Thus, there would never be an end to this." Hayley took a deep breath. "I'm just ready for this to be done so I can breathe."

Piper spoke up now. "But who are *they*?"

"That's what we need to find out first," I answered coldly. "We need to read through these papers and see if they mention it or give us a clue." I glanced at Ollie, still holding Hayley's warm palm in mine. "Ollie, you Google the shit out of drug runners and cartels that do business in Pike Valley and beyond. We'll read these." I dangled the papers in my other hand.

"Alright," he answered, opening his laptop.

Hayley's hand squeezed mine one last time before she let go and pulled the papers close to her face. She tucked a strand of dark hair behind her ear and let out a hefty breath. I knew this was bothering her. Not only were we reading things about her past and her father, but she was adamant against people helping her. It made her nervous and fearful. But what she didn't realize was that we were all fearful, too—even Eric. Hayley had the ability to make everyone around her fall in love with her. She radiated in a room, drawing loud attention to her quiet beauty.

I loved her. Ollie loved her. Piper loved her. And I was pretty certain Eric was starting to love her, too. Or maybe not. Maybe he was only helping because he knew I'd go ballistic if something happened to her. Either way, Hayley had woven her way into our iron-clad circle.

The severity of the situation wasn't far from our minds. We were all on edge. In fact, for the last two nights, when I'd snuck into Hayley's room, we didn't talk. She curled up on her side and rested her head on my chest, both of us too caught up inside the tangle of fears inside our heads to do much of anything other than hold onto one another.

"Does Pete think you're staying at Piper's?" I asked Hayley as I tried to distract her from the paper in her hand. Her leg was bouncing up and down underneath the breakfast bar.

"Yeah, I told him we had a project to do. He grunted at me, so I assumed that was him saying it was okay."

I nodded as she went back to reading the police report. I knew what was in there, and I knew what she was coming up on. I had scanned it before she came over. The dispatch conversation she had when she'd called the cops was in there, word for word. It was horrific to read—at least for me, knowing I hadn't been there for her.

"Are you hungry?" I took her hand in mine. My chest felt like it was splitting open because I knew she was hurting.

Hayley slowly swung her gaze to me and stared. "Are you trying to distract me?"

A twitch of my lips had hers inching up. "Maybe."

"Christian, I'm fine."

You're not, and that's okay.

"I'm hungry," Piper announced out of nowhere. Everyone turned their attention to her. She had her red hair tied in a high ponytail on top of her head, and she met my eye briefly. *I know what you're trying to do,* she silently said.

I gave her a slight nod, and she jumped out of her chair. "Let's make the boys some food while they look for clues." She grabbed Hayley's hand and pulled her out of the chair.

Hayley stood and placed her hands on her hips. "Don't think I don't know that you two are teaming up on me right now. It's not gonna work. I have cartel men trying to kidnap me; we need all hands on deck."

"There doesn't need to be four out of the five of us looking at the same document." Eric sighed, flipping through another paper without looking up. "Plus, you lived through it. There isn't anything in this report that you don't already know. We need fresh eyes."

Hayley didn't say anything for a few moments. I watched her tiny body go from angry to calm in a matter of a few seconds. She didn't like being pushed away or told what to do, but in the end, she knew it was the truth.

"Let us handle this part, okay?" I said softly, reaching out for her hand again. Hayley's head dropped a fraction, but then she squeezed my palm and nodded once.

"Fine, but as soon as we're done making food, I'm back in the ring. Got it?"

"Yes, ma'am." I winked at her.

A small piece of relief fell upon my shoulders, but it did nothing to take away the dull ache in my stomach.

CHAPTER THIRTY-NINE

HAYLEY

I FIDDLED with the locket around my neck as I silently sat at Christian's lunch table. Everyone was talking around me, except Christian, Ollie, Piper, and Eric. We all five remained quiet, wondering what our next move was.

It'd been several days since Piper and I were chased, and just a few hours ago, the five of us sat around Christian and Ollie's breakfast bar, staying up way too late, trying to come up with some out-of-thin-air idea to get a drug cartel off my back. We were in over our heads. There was nothing a bunch of teenagers could do. In fact, there wasn't much anyone could do. The cartel had been around for many, many years, according to the information Ollie had gotten off the internet, and not even the FBI had been able to stop them.

Jim said there was some sort of undercover sting going on, and I couldn't help but feel like I was in the center of it all. I felt like I was the missing piece. I was the shiny, golden ticket that the FBI was dangling in front of some of the world's most dangerous men.

I didn't know what to believe.

I didn't know much of anything, other than my father had fucked with the wrong people, and his daughter was about to pay for his sins.

"You're almost eighteen. They want their settlement." Those words. They kept coming around, full swing, in my head. My mother's nails-on-a-chalkboard voice scratched the walls of my brain. Why now? Men like the ones who killed my father and who worked for a drug cartel wouldn't wait until I was of age to kidnap me for vengeance unless it had something to do with my age. It had something to do with me being eighteen. It was significant for some reason, and I was pretty sure there was only one person who I could ask that would know.

I just didn't know how I was going to get to her without Christian knowing.

It wasn't that I didn't want him by my side at all times. I did. I just knew that if he went around her again or saw where I used to live—the living conditions—he'd go nuts. His temper would get the best of him. What was that saying? It was better to ask for forgiveness than it was to ask for permission?

I didn't need his permission to go see my mom, but I had a feeling the boy who held my heart in his hands so delicately wasn't going to see it like that.

He wanted to protect me at all costs, and that was exactly why he couldn't come with me.

My eyes sliced over to Eric's for a brief second, and when he caught my gaze, he silently tilted his head in question.

Eric.

Yes.

"Absolutely not."

"Eric, *please*. I know what I'm asking of you, but it's either you go with me or I go alone. I can't bring Piper. I need someone who's going to look threatening enough so that no one bothers me while I try to fish information out of her."

He threw his hands up and raked them through his dark hair. Eric's looks were dark and mysterious, and I wasn't sure if I'd ever seen him smile. He was brooding, much like Christian. He stood tall—at least six feet—and he was built wide. He drew attention to himself, but not the good kind. Eric looked like a bad boy who wasn't afraid to knock someone on their ass. Which was precisely why I needed him. "Christian will fucking kill me, and he's my best friend. No fucking way. I can't betray him like that."

"Even if it means saving his girlfriend in the end?" I countered.

That had him thinking, so I kept going. "If I bring Christian, he will lose it with the first rude remark my mother makes, because he's already going to be trying to keep it together when he sees where I used to live. You know this; I know this. His temper will get the best of him. He'll drag me out of there before I can even ask my mom about the settlement." I dropped my voice, remembering that we were in the library. "There is something significant about me being eighteen. Otherwise, it doesn't make sense, and if I'm going to be dangled right in front of the cartel by the FBI, I want to know why. I need to know what I'm walking into. I turn eighteen tomorrow! It's obvious they're going to keep coming after me."

Eric sighed and rested his back along one of the bookshelves. "How the hell will we even pull this off? And if Christian kills me, it's your fucking fault."

I almost squealed and wrapped my arms around his neck in relief. Eric and I barely knew each other, but there was something about the two of us that worked. He was level-headed, and I liked that about him, and not to mention, we both cared about Christian, so there was that.

"How do you feel about skipping school?"

Eric's lip curled. "Wouldn't be the first time."

My hands started to sweat at the thought of ditching school. *Or maybe...* "Are you close with Headmaster Walton like Christian?"

He shrugged. "Close enough, why? What's the plan?"

"Follow me."

"I can't believe that worked."

Eric and I jogged to his car after I faked getting sick in our calculus class. Mrs. Simmons allowed Eric, who *bravely* volunteered, to take me to the office. Headmaster Walton jumped on the opportunity of Eric taking me home since the bus would have taken forever.

"Headmaster Walton likes me because I'm smart, according to Christian. I had a feeling he'd be okay with it, especially since he likes you."

Eric started up his Range Rover and darted his eyes to the clock. "We have an hour and twenty minutes before we have to be back here for the end of last period. Otherwise, Christian will know."

"Then let's go."

I could hear my heartbeat in my ears the entire drive to the trailer park, even over Eric's loud, heavy-metal music. He checked his phone a million and one times, and each time, I was fearful that Christian's name would pop up. He was going to be livid, but hopefully, in the end, he'd understand. I hated doing something without him, and that was a huge change for me. I was independent beyond belief, and now I found myself longing for Christian to be by my side.

"Pull up there." I nodded my head to an abandoned gravel drive where a few dumpsters sat. I couldn't even count the amount of times I had to dig through the garbage for something to eat. Far too many to have only lived here a few months before CPS came and got me.

Once Eric and I climbed out of his car, he locked it, and we began walking down the overgrown, weed-infested dirt road lined with broken and ugly trailers.

Eric kept his mouth shut the short walk to my mom's. We had to have looked strange. We were both in our school uniforms in the middle of the day, the sun directly over our heads, but I highly doubted anyone even knew what time it was. Most of the people in this trailer park were still asleep from the banger they had the night before.

As we rounded the bend where my old home sat, I grabbed onto Eric's forearm. His sleeves were rolled to his elbows, so my nails dug into his skin. "Try not to say anything while we're in there. She's probably going to be nasty to me. I just need you here in case one of her creeps is with her."

Eric glanced to my hand on his arm and then back up to my face. "I've got you. Let's go."

With a single nod and hefty breath from my lips, I stepped up onto the broken porch and swung the door open wide.

Here goes nothing.

"What the fuck! Shut the goddamn door and get that light out of here," my mom yelled from the couch as sunlight streamed through the filthy living room. My nose scrunched up at the smell of urine and old booze, but I kept my shoulders pulled back and my head on straight.

The door slammed behind Eric and me, and we both stood in the small area, staring at my mom on the couch with her hand holding a plastic vodka bottle. "Hayley? Is that you?"

I clenched my teeth. "Yes."

"What do you want?" She tipped her head back and took a big gulp of the clear liquid, swallowing it without even so much as a blink.

There were dirty-looking bed sheets hanging from the windows in the living room to block out the daylight, and I could see a pile of dirty plates stacked high in the sink. But instead of letting harsh memories of this place come to surface, I got right down to business.

"I want to know what the settlement is."

I inched inside the trailer a little more, getting closer to her. I watched as her eyes turned into slits. I felt Eric slide up beside me. Thankfully, it seemed my mom was alone, but I knew we needed to hurry before her scummy friends came to pay a visit.

"What do you have to offer?"

Everything had a price when it came to her.

"You know I don't have money," I answered, grabbing onto Eric's arm to let him know I had this under control. "But you can pawn this for some cash." A soft exhale left my lips as I reached up and grabbed the gold chain hanging around my neck. My heart all but broke at the thought of giving it up. My eyes grew watery, but a locket was material-istic at best. Just because my father had given it to me, and I was giving it away, didn't mean I'd forget him. *It's just a neck-lace. That's it.*

My mom waited a beat before I dangled it in front of her. Then, she angled her head to the side so I'd lay it on the table closest to me. I stepped forward and took in her appearance. Days-old—or maybe even weeks-old—makeup was smeared on her face, and her yellow hair was knotted on the ends and looked as if it hadn't been brushed in months. She definitely looked worse today than the other day when she had paid me a visit.

"I thought you said you never wanted to see me again."

I ignored her statement.

"What's the settlement?"

My mom took another gulp of her vodka before rolling her eyes. "You are."

I shook my head, anger rolling in quickly. "Why when I'm eighteen? What's the significance of me turning eighteen?"

My mom stared at me, evil lurking in her eye. It made my stomach hurt the longer we held each other's stare. How did she become this woman? My mother was never a good mother. She wasn't attentive. She hated giving me attention when I was little. She sent me to my room more times than I cared to remember, but how did she end up like this? CPS took me away soon after she began to wither away into nothing, but as I stared at the woman in front of me, I couldn't even see a tiny sliver of the woman I used to call mom.

"A trust fund."

My head jerked. "What?"

She sniffed. "Your father set up a trust fund for you. When you turn eighteen, you get it. He wrote it in his will before he was murdered." She laughed sarcastically. "You got a trust fund, and I got nothing. The dumb bastard didn't care what happened to me. Only you."

My voice was near breaking. "I thought all of his assets were frozen because of the laundering."

She shrugged, glancing at the necklace I had laid on the table. "Your father had a way around some things. He was smart in some senses."

"So, they want my trust fund so they can technically be paid back what he lost?"

A small amount of comfort washed over me. I'd gladly give them the money in exchange for my freedom. They could have every penny! I would willingly hand it over. They didn't have to kidnap me!

I had nothing left to say to my mother, and I had no time to waste. I came for information, and I got it. She could have the locket and pawn it for drug money. Or maybe she wanted to buy a few more of those cheap plastic vodka bottles. I didn't care. I got what I came for.

"Let's go." I grabbed onto Eric's arm, and we walked over to the door. As soon as I let some sunlight in, my mother chimed from behind. "They'll keep the money *and* you...just so you know. Your father fucked us both over."

My heart dropped slightly, but I refused to believe her words, even though, deep down, I knew they were true.

Eric's arm dropped from my grasp as he turned around and stalked back through the trailer. "Eric, what are you doing?"

I watched as he ripped my locket off the table, and as he leveled my mom with an enervating stare. "You don't fucking deserve this. And you know it."

To my surprise, my mom didn't say a word as Eric tore past me. I jumped at the sound of the door slamming behind me. "You're right. Christian would have lost his shit in there."

I nodded as my shaky legs climbed down the wooden steps after him.

Eric was rushing so fast to get back to his Range Rover, still clutching my locket in his hand. As soon as we climbed inside, he handed it to me and said, "He knows."

My head snapped over to him as I held the chain of my locket in my hand. "What?"

His Range Rover purred to life. "He knows, and he's pissed."

Great.

CHAPTER FORTY

CHRISTIAN

I STOOD with my back against the side of my Charger, waiting. I was fuming, *livid*. My arms were crossed over my school
tie, and my knuckles itched to punch something to release
the anger.

When Headmaster Walton called me down to the office
to let me know Eric would likely be running late for practice
and for me to inform Coach that it was fine, I was confused.
Then, when he told me *why* Eric was running late, I almost
snapped Headmaster Walton's desk in half.

I was impressed that I kept it together while in his office.
My face stayed calm and collected, but on the inside, I was all
but frantic.

*Where are they? Why did she ask Eric to take her home? She isn't
sick. What the fuck is going on?*

My hand shook as I tried calling Eric again. He wouldn't
answer. All I got, thirty minutes ago, was a text that read,
She's fine. We are on our way back.

I think the thing that bothered me the most was that she didn't tell me what was going on. *What the hell* was *going on?*

I snapped my attention up when I heard approaching wheels. Eric's Range Rover came into sight, and my heart went into triple speed. Half of me was eager to see her so I could wrap my arms around her, but the other half was ready to demand answers.

They stayed in his car for a second too long, both of their eyes on me. I cocked an eyebrow, and that gave Hayley the notion to finally open her door and step out. Her head was hung low, her dark hair hanging in front of her face. As soon as she was in front of me, Eric hanging back by his Range Rover (probably because he knew I'd lay him flat on his ass), she tilted those blue eyes up to me, and I almost forgot I was angry.

She looked tired. Sad. A little detached.

"*I'm sorry*," was all she said.

I stood unmoving, my shoes planted to the ground, and stared at her. "Where were you?"

She nibbled on her bottom lip, and I ached to remove it from beneath her teeth. "I went to see my mom."

My chest grew tight. "You...what? Why the fuck would you *ever* go see her?"

Hayley sighed as she avoided my eye. She looked out past the school into the wooded area. "I needed some more answers. I wanted to know what the settlement was and what it had to do with me."

I scoffed, feeling myself grow even angrier. "And you thought to ask your crackhead of a mother? Come on, Hayley. You're smarter than that." I pushed off from my car and ran my hands through the short strands of my hair.

"Bro, go easy on her."

My eyes lasered onto Eric. I was seconds from plummeting my best friend to the black asphalt. "And you! What the hell were you thinking? You didn't think to fucking tell me that my girlfriend was going to a trashy trailer park to talk to her doped-up mother?" I shook my head, seething. "Instead of telling me, you fucking take her yourself?"

"Christian, calm down!" Hayley shouted as I started to meet Eric halfway. Eric was my best friend, but I wanted to plow him to the ground. I was pissed. I wasn't sure if I'd ever been so angry.

"Why?" I turned around and glared at her. "Why did you ask Eric? And not me?"

"Well, I think you freaking out like this is a good enough reason as to why I didn't ask you."

"So, what? You don't trust me?"

The planes of her face softened. "Of course I do."

"Then fucking why?" I didn't shout at her, but the tone of my voice portrayed just how upset I was. Not only was I bothered that she had Eric take her to the trailer park in Pike Valley, but I was also hurt beyond belief that she didn't think to even tell me.

"Because she knew you'd fucking flip out if you saw where she had lived. She was afraid you'd lose your temper and her mom wouldn't be willing to give forth any information."

I turned away from Eric and faced Hayley again. "That's bullshit. If it was important, I would have kept my mouth shut. I did the first time she came around, didn't I? Do you not trust me? Because if you don't trust me, I don't even know why we're standing here right now."

Hayley rushed over to me and wrapped her arms around my middle. I stood much taller than her, but I didn't dare look down. Instead, I turned my head and clenched my jaw.

Why doesn't she trust me?

"I do trust you. I trust you with my entire life. I've never had anyone love me the way you do."

"Then why?"

I heard Hayley swallow, and when I looked down at her, the blues of her eyes looked like glass. "I was ashamed."

My brow furrowed. "What?"

Her chin quivered for a brief second before she found her footing. "I was embarrassed for you to see where I used to live. What type of life I had before coming here." Hayley's hair flew into her face with a gust of wind. "I didn't want you to see what my own mother chose over me." Her head dropped a fraction, and my heart felt like it was falling down a rocky slope. "She didn't love me enough to take care of me, and it hurts. I don't like showing my weaknesses, not even to you, and the second you saw that trailer and the way my hands shook when I walked inside, you would have known. I couldn't risk you trying to swoop in to save me this time. I couldn't risk you yelling at her or trying to drag me out. I needed answers. So, I took Eric with me so I'd have someone to help me if I needed it. That's why. That's why I didn't tell you."

Jesus Christ. I pinched the bridge of my nose to keep my emotions in check. She was right. The second I would have seen her hurting, I would have done anything to make it stop —whether that was by dragging her out of that trailer, or making her mom feel like the piece of shit that she was. Whatever Hayley felt, I felt too, but ten times deeper.

And not to mention, I knew a little of what she felt. My mother chose something over me, too, and it did hurt. It hurt like hell.

The bell sounded from inside the school, and soon, people would be pouring out the doors to get to their cars to go home. I pulled Hayley from my body by the tops of her arms and peered down at her.

How can I be angry with her?

She licked her lips, keeping her tears at bay as I slowly leaned in to give her a quick kiss on the forehead. "Let's just talk about this later, alright?" I whispered as I pushed her away.

She nodded once and let out a shaky breath.

"Piper is taking you home, right? And then bringing you back to my house in a couple of hours?"

She nodded again.

"Okay, stay on the main roads at all times. Surround yourself with lots of traffic. Don't take any shortcuts."

"I know, I'll see you in a few."

"Alright."

As Haley began to turn around, I grabbed her by her arm and pulled her small frame back to mine. I planted a long, hard kiss on her mouth, pouring my feelings into her. When she pulled away, I said, "I love you." And her soft smile instantly made me feel ten times better.

"I love you."

Then, she walked away and headed for Piper's car.

Eric came to stand beside me, and I asked, "Was it that bad?"

He let out a sigh. "Yeah. It was bad."

CHAPTER FORTY-ONE

HAYLEY

"Wow." Piper pulled up to the curb and put her car in park. "So, how much is it?"

I just got done filling her in on my trip with Eric and the fight I had with Christian. Apparently, the whole school saw us arguing in the parking lot. Someone snapped a picture and put it on Twitter within seconds. *The joys of high school.*

"How much is the trust fund?" I shrugged, gathering my backpack. "I don't know, but if they're willing to kidnap an innocent girl, I'd say a lot."

Silence encased the car. My mind was spinning. I thought back to the last few hours, and before I knew it, I was busting up laughing. My hand found my stomach as I continued to laugh. Piper was looking at me like I was crazy, and that only made me laugh harder.

"What are you laughing about?" Her eyes were huge, her delicate eyebrows shooting up to her hairline.

In between laughs, I managed to get out, "My....life..."

More laughing. "Is this seriously... my life?" I shook my head as I wheezed. "I have a fucking drug cartel after me."

Piper let out a small giggle and asked if I had lost my mind. I had. I had completely lost my mind. But if I didn't laugh, I was certain I'd cry.

So, we sat there in her car, laughing for a solid ten minutes before I finally regained my breath and looked over at her.

"I can't believe you're still my friend."

Her cheeks rose. "Always. Even with a drug-running cartel after you."

A sigh left my mouth, and I was feeling a little better after laughing for so long. "Okay, pick me up in a couple of hours? I want to get some homework done before we head to Christian's."

She nodded and then said, "Wear something cute."

My hand paused on the door. "Why?"

She smashed her lips together. "Just do it."

My lip twitched as excitement tore through my chest. "As my best friend, you have to tell me what's going on."

"He's throwing you a birthday party."

"A party?!"

Piper shook her amber locks out. "It's just a few of us. Relax! But he's gone all out for it. It's actually kinda sweet how much effort he has put into it."

My face fell into my hands. "Now I feel even worse about earlier. He was putting together something for me, and I went off with Eric behind his back."

Piper's hand touched my arm. "Don't be so hard on yourself. I think he gets it."

The fight with Christian was too fresh in my mind for me to put it on the back burner. I was glad I had gotten the information from my mom—although I had no idea what to do with it—but I hated how I had to go about it.

I was all jumbled up inside. I didn't like feeling out of

sorts. The unknown was lurking in the shadows, and the thought of Christian being upset with me only made them that much darker.

"Yeah," I finally answered. "Okay, I'm gonna go get started on homework. I'll see you in a few." I opened the door and climbed out of her car. "Be careful on your way home."

"Don't worry. I check my mirror every other second. The other night is forever embedded into my brain."

I huffed out a laugh and slammed the door, giving Piper a tiny wave.

Once I reached the porch of Pete and Jill's, Piper sped away. I watched her taillights disappear around the parked black Escalade that was *always* sitting beside the curb like some type of street ornament. As soon as I stepped through the threshold of the house, the hairs on my arms stood erect. My heart dropped. I could feel my pulse in my fingertips.

Something wasn't right.

After five years of living through hell, you started to learn the signs that pointed to evil. It was too quiet. I quickly scanned my surroundings, noting Pete wasn't in his green La-Z-Boy in the corner. My eyes dropped to the lampshade that was turned on its side and to the remote that was several feet away on the floor, as if it were thrown.

My first thought was to retreat. I took one step back, the door still open with my arm on the handle, but when I inched my head to the street, my throat began to close.

A short, bald-headed man with tattoos decorating his scalp was leaning against the hood of the black Escalade, staring right at me. His arms were crossed over his leather jacket, and they only moved when he put a cigarette up to his lips to puff out smoke.

My heart sunk.

I shouldn't have been surprised, but I was.

The harsh truth of my past was coming straight for me,

and I stood there, acting like a deer in the headlights.

My feet inched farther inside, and I let the door slam behind me. There was no use in being quiet. They were here. They finally found their opportunity, and I was cornered.

I wanted to run and never look back, but then I would have been giving up the things in my life that made me happy —that made me *want* to live. And I couldn't run forever, and who knew if I'd even make it down the road before they caught me.

This needed to end. I wasn't sure how it would end, and I wasn't sure if I'd make it out alive, but I had to have some form of hope.

There were two things on my side: the inside guy—the one who was undercover, according to the P.I.—*and* the fact that I'd put up absolutely no fight in handing over my trust fund. They could have it. I didn't want any part of it.

I kept my heart rate as steady as I could when I dropped my backpack down onto the floor. My Converse slapped against the wood as I walked through the house, heading to the kitchen.

I halted as soon as I saw Pete sitting in the kitchen chair, his big potbelly hanging over his pants as blood trickled out of his nose. I expected his eyes to flare with distaste when they landed on me, but they didn't. Instead, they showed something I'd have never ever expected from him: *worry*.

"So, you finally found me." I stared at the two men standing behind Pete, one of their hands clamped down on his shoulder.

Their expressions stayed immobile. "We've been following you for years. We were instructed to wait until you turned eighteen."

I swallowed before I snarled. "Well, Happy Birthday to me."

I locked stares with Pete for a moment before I raised my

chin and glanced back to the man holding his shoulder. "So now what? You kill my father and come for me? You want this big settlement from me that I don't even have yet?"

The men didn't answer me. Pete's eyes darted around the kitchen like he was planning on doing something, but it was no use. These men had weapons; I was sure of it. Pete would end up dead, and as terribly as he had treated me, no one else deserved to die for my father's mistakes.

Not even Pete.

"Well, what are you waiting for?" I asked, anger filling my veins. For five years, I'd thought of this moment. Fear was always present. I always imagined I'd cower, and cry, and beg them not to take me, because I knew once they did, I'd never ever be the same girl as I was now. I'd be this empty shell of the girl I used to be. But for some reason, standing here, looking at them, I wasn't scared. *I was pissed.*

My life was just getting good.

I just learned what love was.

What friendship was.

I wouldn't go down without a fight, and one way or another, I'd fight like hell to get back.

Just as the thought passed through my mind, the back door opened. The man with the tattooed head peeked in. He first landed his gaze on me, and his eyes held onto mine for a fraction too long. The subtle twitch of his cheek had me wondering who he was. He wasn't like the others. He didn't have a vengeance in his eyes. He didn't reek of death.

"The car is ready. Coast is clear. Let's go."

The burly man with his hand on Pete's shoulder stayed put as the others stalked toward me. I kept my gaze straight on Pete as the man came closer to me. He was tall, so tall I'd have to incline my head if I wanted to get a good look at him, but I didn't. I kept my stare on Pete. *Don't do anything stupid, you old drunk.*

"What are we doing with him?" the burly man asked.

The man who now had his hand wrapped around my bicep snarled in their direction as he half-dragged me past. "I don't care. Make sure he doesn't call the cops. Kill him if you have to."

My throat shut tightly. The fear was back, and it threatened to pour out of my mouth, but I dug deep into the girl I was molded into from the last five years. "He won't call the cops. He doesn't give a shit about me, do you?" I glared at Pete and prayed to God he was catching on. "Plus, he has his own demons to hide from them." The man's hand tightened on my arm, and I bit my tongue not to cry out. I heard the punches and grunts as he pulled me through the door, following after the scrawny man who led us across the street.

The good news was I didn't hear any gunshots as we crossed the quiet street. I thanked God that Jill wasn't home, because things could have gone a lot differently if she were.

The grip on my arm was loosened just a bit as I was pulled closer to the man. He smelled like tobacco and gunpowder. My nose flared when we reached the Escalade.

"So, what exactly is your plan with me?" I asked, probing him for answers. "Prostitution? Payment? Sex trade? Gonna try to make a buck off me?"

He glared at me, his eyes forming slits. The tattoo-covered man warned me with his eyes, which only perplexed me further.

"If you're going to kidnap me, at least tell me why. Is it for the settlement? You can have it whenever I get it."

"Your father owes us that settlement and more."

A sarcastic laugh fell off my lips, and I couldn't stop myself from mouthing off. Maybe it was the hidden fear that I kept pushing away so I didn't scream at the top of my lungs, or maybe it was some sort of defense mechanism.

"Get her in there. I'm gonna smoke before we take off."

The burly man passed me off to the smaller man with tattoos. I jerked my arm, but I knew it was no use. They had guns. They could shoot me if I ran. I needed a different plan. A smarter one.

As soon as the tattooed guy all but threw me into the Escalade, he climbed in after, scooting beside me. I eyed the door on my right, but he put his hand on my knee.

"Don't."

I slowly swung my gaze from his hand to his face, and when his eyes met mine, they squinted. My breathing picked up, and panic started to set in. Suddenly, I felt like I was losing. I wasn't the badass girl from the trailer park who'd been perfecting this tough facade for the last five years.

I was trapped. My chest started to grow tight, and my throat felt like it was constricted. I tried to think of Christian and the way he made me feel safe, but it wasn't working. That only made me panic more.

"Just breathe," the man whispered, squeezing my leg.

My eyebrows dipped with confusion. He eyed the men outside the vehicle. The big one, still smoking, was now joined by the other man who had taken care of the Pete problem. When his eyes swung back over to me, he mouthed the words, "Just keep him talking."

What?

He gave me a cautious look.

I was lost. Confused, scared, pissed, leery of every single person I was surrounded by. But after five years of being around sketchy people, untrustworthy people, people who gave me a sinking feeling deep in my stomach with one look, I'd obtained quite a skill. I knew right off the bat if I could trust someone, and I knew, without a doubt, that this man wasn't bad.

I could trust him.

And I hoped with everything in my body that I was right.

CHAPTER FORTY-TWO

CHRISTIAN

"WHAT TIME ARE THEY GETTING HERE?" Ollie, with his school shirt untucked and unbuttoned at the top, held a purple streamer as he balanced on the counter to attach it to the ceiling.

"Any minute, so hurry up."

He scowled at me.

Hayley turned eighteen at midnight, and I knew it was a big deal, even if she didn't want to admit it. Turning eighteen meant she was free. She could, technically, leave Pete and Jill's if she wanted and stay somewhere—anywhere—else until college. I wanted to drain my account and buy her an apartment with a top-notch security system and put her in there without taking no as an answer, but I knew she'd be pissed and refuse, so a small birthday party was going to have to do for now.

Not only were we celebrating her eighteenth birthday, but we were also celebrating the last five birthdays. There was a separate room for each birthday that Hayley didn't get to celebrate because of being in foster care. As each hour passed, we'd go into a different room and celebrate that particular age.

I'd been planning this party for a week now. What I wasn't expecting was a massive punch in the gut from her earlier road trip with Eric, but that wasn't something I was willing to simmer on. I promised her we'd talk about it later, and we would, but for now, Hayley deserved this.

"What's all this?" I switched my attention to my father walking through the kitchen with a briefcase in tow.

I was shocked, to say the least. "What are you doing here?"

A deep chuckle escaped him as he laid his briefcase on the island. "I live here and pay the bills."

I snorted. "You barely live here."

"Yeah, well, I'm going to work on that."

I flicked my eyes to meet his and stared. We still hadn't resolved anything since the last time we had talked. In fact, I didn't think there had been more than a sentence or two shared between us since then.

It wasn't difficult to avoid him. My days were spent at school and then practice soon followed. Then, I was with Hayley for the rest of the night with the occasional stop to talk with Ollie.

"So, what is this? What's up with the black and purple?"

Ollie was the one who answered. "It's Hayley's birthday. We're throwing her a party."

"You know I don't allow parties here."

"How would you even know if we threw parties here?" I gritted my teeth. The more I stared at him, the angrier I got. "And this isn't a party. It's just a few of us."

My father stared at me from across the island. His dark features relaxed. It was like looking at a reflection of myself. We were similar in every aspect, and that irked me because it was the last thing I wanted. He was the only parent I had left, but we were so disconnected that I knew nothing about him. I half-expected him to give me another lecture about Hayley, but before he could say anything at all, my phone rang.

I saw Piper's name flashing and answered it quickly.

"You on your way?"

"Christian." Her voice had my chest constricting.

I dropped the black streamer. "What's wrong?"

Her words were fast through the line. "It's Hayley. Something...something's wrong. Pete..." She sucked in a heavy breath of air, and it suddenly felt like I had none. "Pete is hurt. I think they took her." Piper was crying now, and I braced myself on the island, clutching the phone hard in my hand.

"What's going on?" The words barely came out. It felt like I'd swallowed my own heart.

Piper choked on her words. "I don't know. Pete is bleeding and won't wake up." I heard some shuffling and then, "Wake up! Please wake up!"

I dropped the phone, and my chest started heaving up and down. I couldn't hear a word being said by Ollie or my father. The only thing I could hear was the quick pace of my heart beating wildly in my chest. I watched as Ollie picked up the phone and began talking, his green eyes widening as he locked onto me. My eyes squeezed tightly together.

There is no fucking way someone was taking Hayley from me. My Hayley. Every possible scenario of someone putting their hands on her filtered through my mind, much like they had every night since she got attacked at the football game, and I suddenly felt out of control. Hayley was strong. One of the strongest, most obstinate people I knew, but I also knew that, deep down, she was scared. There was still a part of her that was the old Hayley—the bright, happy, naive girl that had her head in the clouds. She formed a thick skin over the last few years, but no one was invincible.

I cursed myself for not taking more precautions. She convinced me that she was fine at Pete and Jill's house for the few hours that I had football practice, and she did her homework every night. She said, *"You can't be with me every single second of every day, Christian."* Fuck football. Fuck school. I shouldn't have let her out of my sight.

"Son!" My head jerked as a hard hand gripped tightly onto my jaw. I clenched my teeth, finally taking breath, and stared at my father's troubled face. "You need to take a breath."

"I...I can't." The words were forced; my lungs were constricted. The feeling was familiar. Flashes of my mom's lifeless body flew through my head as I tried to hold on for dear life. *No. Not now.* My father's hands wrapped around my head. "You can. Just look at me and breathe. We will figure this out. She's going to be fine."

She's going to be fine. Hayley.

I forced another breath as I continued looking at the worry lines on my father's forehead. Another puff of air came out, and I slowly felt my chest loosening with oxygen.

"Ollie, call Jim and tell him it's an emergency. Tell him to get his ass over here and to call Scott on the way."

"Who's Scott?" Ollie asked, searching for Jim's name.

"He's on the force. Call him. *Now.*" I'd never heard my father's voice so calm but demanding at the same time. Ollie quickly walked away after glancing at me and put the phone up to his ear.

"Are you with me now? I need you to pull yourself together so we can figure this out. You hear me?" My jaw ached from both the pressure of clenching my teeth and my father's hand squeezing my jaw.

"I'm..." The words were lodged in my throat. "I...I'm not going to lose her like we lost Mom. I won't."

The situations were vastly different. My mother had a choice when it came to leaving me. *Us.* She could have gotten help. She could have grasped onto her love for us more than her love for her addiction, but she didn't, and that was a regret I was sure she'd have if she were here. But Hayley didn't have a choice in this matter. She wasn't willingly leaving me. The choice wasn't hers. It was her father's. Hayley was the casualty in her parents' choices, and I was going down right with her.

"You won't lose her. Do you want to know why?" My father's hands dropped from my face as he took a step back and rounded the island. "You won't lose her because you're fighting for her. And when a Powell man fights for someone he loves, he always wins." My father started to roll up his sleeves as if he were ready to fight someone. "I fought for your mother once, and I won. The problem was, I stopped fighting."

He bent his head, and I was unable to form words. The whites of his knuckles matched his dress shirt as he squeezed the edge of the kitchen island. His head slowly came back up, and he pinned me with a lethal Powell stare. "Don't you ever stop fighting for the person you love, Christian. Do you hear me?"

I swallowed back a rough lump in my throat. "I hear you."

"Then get your shit together so we can get her back."

I dipped my chin, and we walked through the kitchen together, ready to do whatever it took to get my girl back.

CHAPTER FORTY-THREE

HAYLEY

I HAD ALWAYS IMAGINED that an Escalade would feel like riding in a luxurious limo of sorts. It was big and sleek—fancy, for lack of a better word. But each time we'd go over a bump, I'd bang my head off the side of the door.

My hand itched to try the shiny handle on the right, but even if my captors were dumb enough to leave the door unlocked, we were going so fast I was likely to die or have serious injuries if I jumped. I kept glancing at the man beside me, the one I felt that I could trust—although, I wasn't sure to what extent. I replayed his words in my head, '*Keep him talking.*' I didn't really have time to dissect the *why* in this situation, so I just went with it. I had nothing else to lose.

We rounded a curve, heading for the highway, and my stomach twisted with each jerk of the vehicle. I shifted in my school skirt, glancing at the two men up front and then to the man beside me. His tattooed head stayed straight, but his eyes moved to the corner of his eye.

I turned my head to the front and tried my best to keep

my voice steady. "So, what *exactly* did my father do to land me in this lovely seat?"

The burly and most frightening of the men sliced his eyes to mine in the rearview mirror. He grunted and then turned his gaze back to the road. *Okay, well, that didn't work.* I decided to keep probing. "So, what? You're just gonna kidnap me but not tell me why? How is that fair? Is it the settlement? My trust fund, right?"

Still no answer. "That *is* what you're doing, right? Kidnapping me? Wait, is it called kidnapping if I'm not really a kid anymore?"

There was a small twitch on the tattooed man's mouth and a barely noticeable nod of his head. I took that as a confirmation that I was doing something right.

"Seriously, guys. What gives? Were you the ones who killed him?" I chuckled, glancing out the window at the passing trees for a second. "I bet it was you, huh, big man?"

The driver sliced his eyes to mine again, and I met his cold stare. "Was it you? Do you remember me cowering on the steps in my house? Scared out of my mind?"

His jaw worked back and forth, clearly agitated.

"Or was it you?" I leaned forward a little, breathing into the ear of the man sitting in the passenger seat.

"No," he answered quickly, not nearly as annoyed or irritated as the burly man.

"Maybe it was this guy?" I asked, pointing my head to the tattooed guy.

My heart was beating recklessly in my chest but not from fear. I was eager, anxious, and excited. I *wanted* to push these men over the edge. I felt like I had a smidge of control. I was causing a reaction, and when there was time for hasty reactions, there was time for error. If he let his guard down, I'd run like hell. Undercover sting or not, I was done being a piece in their game.

"Will you shut the fuck up?" The driver whipped his head back to me for a brief second, and I jumped with the loudness of his voice.

I didn't let it deter me, though. I kept poking the bear. *If I go down, he's going down with me.*

"Just tell me. Was it you?"

"Goddamnit!" he yelled, craning the wheel over to the right. My head smashed off the window, and the tattooed man's hand reached out and clamped onto my leg. He quickly removed it when the vehicle came to a stop.

The burly man opened his door and jumped out, slamming it behind him. My stomach dipped with fear, but I kept my guard up, unable to let the fear shade my bravery.

"Now what do we do?" The man in the passenger seat flipped around to stare at the tattooed man and me.

"Fuck," tattooed man mumbled, looking at me wide-eyed. "Keep him talking about your father. We need him to confirm the kill."

"W-what?" I stuttered. But before I could get an explanation, my door flew open, and I was dragged out by my arm. The pain radiated down my wrist, and my feet barely touched the loose gravel below my body as the devil himself pushed me up against the side of the Escalade. The door was still open, and I was thankful. At least when this man killed me, I wouldn't necessarily be alone.

Christian's face flashed through my head, and it was like I was instantly taken back to that awful night, five years ago, when all I wanted was him. I remembered hiding on the steps, watching a black-hooded man kill my father right in front of my mother in the middle of my living room. When I squeezed my eyes shut to block out the scene, all I could see was Christian. His playful smile, his gray eyes. He was my light in the darkest time of my life, and it was still true today. Christian was my safe place. He had always been my safe place—*my person*. My heartrate calmed a fraction as Christian's face continued to flood my brain. His cocky smile, the smoothness of his cheeks, the defined jawline and relaxed muscles when I'd peek at his sleeping face.

A slap across my face had Christian's face fleeting from my vision. Anger flew to my limbs. "Yes, I fucking killed your pathetic fucking father." I sucked in a breath as his hand wrapped around my neck. He wasn't squeezing yet, but the pressure was building, and I was suddenly losing my grip on my courage. "He was a narc and had to be dealt with, and you're just collateral damage." His hand squeezed harder, and I began panicking. I couldn't breathe. He was choking me too hard for me to do anything. I clawed at his hands and kicked my feet against the side of the tire. A venomous laugh escaped him. "Jimmy and I were the ring leaders, and then your father came in and started calling shots left and right and switching up the way we did business. Little did our boss know, your father was working with the feds. I killed your father because I knew he was a rat, and on top of all that, he was stealing money on the side, too. *For you.* We know all about the little trust fund he made you, and once you accept it, it'll be ours." An ugly laugh rested among his lips. "Of course, the money is all Franco cares about, but he gave me free rein to do what I wanted with you. And, pretty girl...*you are mine.*"

His hand left my neck, and I fell quickly, my bare knees landing in the gravel. I gasped for air as I held my stomach. After a few heavy breaths, I heard the other two men climb out of the Escalade, but it was no use. Burly Man was still on his high horse. I coughed and sputtered as I tried to regain my breathing, but he pulled me up by my hair. I stared into his dark eyes, and an unyielding amount of fear choked me. His eyes were void. It was like looking into a cold and dark, empty grave. "I killed your father, and I would have killed your mama too if the cops hadn't shown up." He pulled my head up higher, and my eyes got blurry, glistening with unshed tears. "And now that you're mine, I need you to obey and learn how to keep those beautiful lips shut." He dropped me to the ground again, and before I could protect myself, he kicked me in the stomach, knocking the wind out of me. I heard the footsteps of the other men getting closer, and I hoped that they would save me. It was the first time I'd ever had the thought, and it almost stunned me.

I wanted to be saved. I wanted help.

Then, a hard kick came to my face, and everything went black.

"Come on, Hayley. Wake up." Something cold landed on my face, and I felt my eyebrows draw together. "That's it, open your eyes."

Slowly, one of my eyes peeled open, but the other one seemed to be stuck. My eyelashes fluttered against my skin as I focused on the person talking to me. When I saw who it was, I yelped and tried to scoot away.

His face turned from happy to worried. He threw his hands up. "Relax, you're safe. It's okay. I'm not going to hurt you." I continued rubbing my back along the gravel, not caring that it was scratching me. "Hayley," another voice sounded, and I turned my head. It was the tattooed man. Both he and the man from the passenger seat were crouched down beside me with worried lines on their faces. For some reason, they didn't look scary anymore. The tattooed man never truly did look scary. He had tattoos, lots of them, but his deep-brown eyes were calming and almost comforting.

"But you...you hurt Pete." My voice was raspy as I looked

at the man closest to me. He was the one who had to deal with Pete when they first took me. "I heard you hitting him."

He nodded and looked at his friend before bringing his attention back to me. "I did, but he's fine. I knocked him out once and left him there. I had to, or our cover would've been blown." He chuckled. "Plus, your foster dad is a fucking asshole. He deserved a good knockout."

True.

I stopped moving my body on the gravel to get away from them, mainly because I was inching closer to the road, and if another vehicle drove down it, I'd be run over.

"Hayley, it's okay. We're the good guys." He smiled down at me. "And you...you were the missing piece we needed all along. You just helped put this guy behind bars for a long, long time, and not to mention, you've helped unlock many more doors." I sliced my eyes over to Burly Man who was crouched down by the car, clearly unconscious, with his hands bound together with what looked to be zip ties. Sirens wailed in the distance, and I hoped they were coming for me.

"You're a fighter, just like your old man."

I slowly sat up and tried to get to my feet. Tattoo Man was beside me within a second, grabbing my arm gently and pulling me up.

"I don't understand," I finally said after taking several even breaths. It hurt to breathe, but my need for answers far outweighed my injuries.

The other man, who was now standing close to Burly Man, spoke first. I took a step back, releasing my arm from the tattooed man's grasp. "Hayley, your father was an informant for us five years ago. He got caught laundering money, and instead of doing prison time, we offered him an informant job. He was helping us take down one of the biggest drug cartels in our area. You just helped us take down Franco's right-hand man, giving us probably the biggest piece of missing information that we needed to start dissembling the cartel's activity in the surrounding areas. We're finally getting to him." He shut his weathered eyes tightly. "Fucking finally. You just hit the tip of the iceberg, Hayley. This is how we get Franco to sink."

Tattoo Man stood in front of me as several police cars and an ambulance pulled up behind the Escalade. "I promised your father that if something ever happened to him, I'd watch out for you. I'm really glad I was able to keep my promise."

I felt many things in that moment. So many that I couldn't even decipher the feelings pouring out of me. I felt everything deeply. Raw emotions pooled in my eyes, and they swept down my cheeks gracefully. I allowed myself to feel and to cry right there in front of two men I'd never met before and a dozen officers and EMT workers. For so long, I'd been afraid to feel. I'd been afraid to be hopeful. I'd been afraid to let my guard down. I'd been afraid to think back into the past where I had a father who loved me. Everything changed the night he died. The love he showered me with was destroyed. He put me in danger, and my mother let her grip on reality slip away along with her role as a mother. I was betrayed, and up until a few weeks ago, I felt unlovable. Christian showed me what love was again, and this moment here, knowing at least one of my parents looked out for me, was the start of my healing.

CHAPTER FORTY-FOUR

CHRISTIAN

I WAS silent as I sat in the police station's waiting area. Orange and gray seats were filled with family members of criminals, whereas I was there for Hayley. The girl who somehow helped take down one of the biggest drug cartel's hitmen.

I didn't know all the details, even though Jim thoroughly explained them to me as we all sat around my kitchen, waiting for news. Even Ann, Hayley's social worker whom I'd met briefly, showed up. Apparently, Pete finally came to, after being knocked out, and grew a heart. He called the police and Ann to tell them what had happened to Hayley in hopes of finding her.

My heart had never thumped so violently as we waited hours for someone to let us know that she was okay. I had to keep my memories in check as my mind kept drifting to the night of my mom's accident. I waited hours for Hayley to call back that evening, and she never did. It was eerily similar tonight. Ann was the first to get a call that Hayley was safe, and she and I immediately jumped in our vehicles and headed to the police station where we have both been for over an hour now.

Tonight felt like it had lasted years. From the second I found out something was wrong to now had taken actual years off my life.

My knuckles were bruised from taking my fear and anger out on the hallway wall, and oddly enough, my father was the one who got me to calm down. I found that to be ironic, considering he was usually the one who got me riled up. Ollie didn't speak a word as we waited. Instead, he sat with Piper's head in his lap as she curled into a ball on the couch and dozed in and out of sleep.

Shaking my head, I bounced my leg up and down as I stared at the one door keeping me from Hayley. They needed to question her and get a statement before she was released—as if she hadn't already been through enough.

Part of me felt guilty. I felt like I had failed her. I had wronged her when she first came to English Prep. Tormented her, bullied her. And now, after I found my way back to her heart, I let her walk right into danger.

She needed me five years ago when her father died right in front of her eyes, and she needed me tonight as the same danger hit her head-on, and I wasn't there.

I swore to myself, after pacing my living room hours ago, that if I got her back, I would spend the rest of my life making it up to her.

The door jerked open from across the waiting area, and I leapt to my feet. I growled silently as I realized it wasn't Hayley, but instead a fat man with a gnarly beard. His girl-friend jumped to her feet wearing nine-inch heels and a skirt showing entirely too much of her saggy ass and swarmed him with sloppy, full-of-tongue kisses.

I was almost thankful he came out of the door instead of

Hayley, because if I had to continue listening to his methed-up girlfriend ramble on at the speed of light about their love story, I was going to commit a crime just so I could land on the other side of the steel door and away from her annoying voice.

Actually, that wasn't a bad idea. *How can I get to the other side of that locked door?*

The man was still halfway in the doorway as his girlfriend jumped on him and wrapped her legs around his middle, her tiny legs barely fitting because of how large his circumference was. They were gross, but they'd serve as a great distraction for others as I tried to slip past, so kudos to them. The police officer who escorted the man out cringed with disgust as he turned his back to walk down the hall, and that was when I slowly stood up.

"What are you doing?" Ann leaned forward, putting her phone back in her purse.

I shrugged. "Going to get Hayley." The moment was fleeting, so I took another step, and Ann hissed.

"Sit down! You're going to get yourself into trouble."

"I don't care," I answered quickly, keeping my eye on the woman behind the glass and the slowly shutting door. "She's been back there for hours. I'm going to get her."

"Christian," Ann huffed as she glanced at the closing door. I raised an eyebrow. *Sorry, Ann. You can't stop me.*

Ann must've seen the look of determination on my face. Her furrowed eyebrows softened. "Don't get caught, and if you tell anyone I helped you, I could lose my job, so don't."

Ah, I think I like Ann.

I strode over to the door, slipping past the couple in their gross embrace as Ann stood and walked to the glass window. I stuck the toe of my shoe in the inch-wide opening, keeping the door open for a fraction longer. As soon as I heard Ann ask the receptionist a question regarding

Hayley, I slid inside the threshold and helped it latch quietly.

If there was anything I'd learned in my eighteen years of life, it was to act as if I belonged even when I felt like I didn't. If you looked suspicious, you likely were, but if you acted like you knew where you were going, no one would bother you.

The officer who escorted the man to his annoying girl-friend shot through the large metal door at the end of the hall without looking behind him, which was good for me. I craned my neck around the corner where I knew the receptionist was and listened to her and Ann still in mid-conversation. I was certain there were cameras all around me, but I was hoping no one would be paying attention as I crept down the hall. My shoes pounded right along with my heart. It was as if my actual heart beat for Hayley. Every thump it made, my brain chanted her name at the same time. I blamed it on the fear from earlier, but I knew that was unlikely. I breathed Hayley in and out of my body like she was my only source of oxygen.

Slowly and meticulously, I searched the sliver of window along each door that lined the walls to see if I could find her. The first room had two men who wore suits and held Styro-foam cups in their hands, likely full of burnt coffee. The next two were empty. And then, the last one on the right had my limbs feeling like they were full of electricity.

There she was.

My hand touched the doorknob, and I opened and closed the door quietly and quickly before anyone bothered to find me.

"Christian!" Hayley jumped back from the metal table, the chair scraping along the floor. She was still wearing her school uniform, but her knees were bandaged, and the white of her shirt was stained with dirt.

Before she made it over to me and crashed her body into mine, I caught a glimpse of her face, and I almost doubled over and vomited. *She was hurt.*

"I'm here," I whispered as I wrapped my arms around her torso, bringing her into my chest. We both inhaled at the same time, breathing each other in.

"You're here," she whispered back. We stayed like that for a long time, her body glued to mine, my arms locked around her. It almost felt like torture letting her go. I brought my hands up to her cheeks, softly touching the bruise on her eye. "I'm going to fucking kill whoever did this to you."

She chuckled into my hand, bringing those baby blues up to my face. "He's arrested and going to prison for a long time."

I shook my head. "I don't care. I'll break into the prison."

A soft laugh escaped her. "You can't break into prison."

I cocked an eyebrow, peering down at her. "Wanna bet? I just broke into here."

"What?" she squealed, her grip on my wrists growing stronger.

I shrugged. "They were taking too long. I've been sick to my stomach for hours, worrying about you, and it's been fucking torture, sitting in that waiting area, knowing you were a short distance away, needing me."

The apples of her cheeks rose, a pink dotting touching them. "Who said I needed you?"

The thump of my heart beating was so loud she could probably hear it. The feeling of anxiety wormed itself into my chest. "You may not need me, but I need you. I've always needed you."

Hayley swallowed, her cheeks falling. She inched a little closer to my face, standing on her tiptoes. "I don't like the feeling of needing someone. I want to be able to make myself happy and be able to save myself when needed...but"—her warm breath fanned over my face, and I dug my fingers into her hip—"you've always been the one to save me, Christian. You've always been my safe place, the one person I could think of when the sky grew dark. When all the little lies tasted bitter on my tongue, you were the one truth I couldn't hide from. It's you. It's always been you."

My lips dipped down to hers, and once they touched, the feeling of solitude bound us together. We were one. A vine of lies, truths, hurt, and sunny memories wrapped around our bodies, and there was absolutely no way it was ever going to break. I loved her. I'd always loved her.

The door swung open as our lips moved on one another, but neither one of us broke apart. I didn't give a fuck who walked in. My tongue swept inside her mouth, and she happily obliged. Someone cleared their throat, and I finally broke my face away from hers, but I didn't pull her body even a fraction of an inch away.

A man with an impressive mustache glared at me. "Who let you in here?"

My mouth twitched. "Myself. You need to get some better security. I walked right through the doors and found Hayley —the *victim*—still in her dirty school uniform from hours ago, without so much as a cup of water, sitting in this cold fucking room." My nostrils flared as the man's scowl disappeared. "This is absolutely unacceptable. I'm taking Hayley home, and if you have any further questions about her statement, you and your corrupted force can come to my house and get it from her." I grabbed Hayley's hand and began to walk out of the dimly lit questioning room.

The man called after us, "You can't just leave. We aren't finished."

"Like hell you aren't," I called back, Hayley's hand still tucked in mine. "You have Hayley in this bleak questioning room, alone, after she's been through hell and back, treating her like *she's* the criminal." The man kept his mouth shut and dropped his eyes to the floor, realizing his mistake. "Now, if you need anything else from her"—I turned around, putting my back to him—"feel free to call me or her social worker. I'll leave both of our numbers up front."

Hayley looked up at me with unshed tears in her eyes and a hidden smile on her face.

"What?"

"I think I like it when someone sticks up for me."

I cocked my lip. "Good. Get used to it."

She smiled and walked alongside me until we made it through the doors of the station. Ann was quick to pull Hayley into a hug. I watched as Hayley's face changed from surprised to relieved. She wasn't used to people caring about her, and that was just something else she was going to have to get used to.

EPILOGUE

HAYLEY

I CLUTCHED my backpack with both hands as it rested on my shoulders. My stomach was a jumbled mess of nerves and excitement. This wasn't an ordinary situation, to say the least, but I was excited.

For once, I was letting myself accept help as it poured all around me. Since Christian and I left the police station, with Ann trailing us, everything had been a whirlwind.

I had detectives and FBI agents taking my statement every other day it seemed and, unfortunately, making me relive the past. I had to give them a recount of everything that had happened in the last five years, especially touching on everything that had happened in the last few months. Tattoo Man came to visit me once, too. Apparently, he and my father worked closely together when he was an informant. It was nice to know that my father was trying to make right in the end instead of throwing his family to the wolves.

As for my mother, she was still living her best life in the trailer park. The only thing she was concerned with was her next high. My father left her nothing but the scraps of our old life, and when my father was murdered and the FBI wanted to help us, she refused, which was why they had to get creative and pretty much wait until the cartel came after me for the settlement.

"So, what do you think? You can paint the walls if you want, any color." Ann stood in the middle of my new bedroom, wearing jeans and an old T-shirt. Her blonde hair was in a bun on her head, and I couldn't remember ever seeing her this relaxed.

"It seems silly to paint my room when I'm going off to college in the fall."

Ann smiled softly. "But what about when you come back for breaks? Christmas?"

A sinking feeling hit me. "Ann, I appreciate it, but just letting me stay here until September is plenty. I can stay at school for my breaks, or go to Christian's, or even Piper's.

And then when summer rolls around, I can get an apartment until fall semester starts back up."

Apparently, the feds couldn't prove that my trust fund money was stolen. My father had covered all bases and invested a lot of his early savings into it, so it was mine to do whatever I wanted with it, but for now, I was saving it for college—that was, unless I got a scholarship. Until then, I was saving it until I got my admissions letter(s) and staying with Ann.

Since I was eighteen and, technically, out of the system, it was okay for me to live wherever. That was when Ann all but begged me to stay with her. It beat staying with Pete and Jill, who were surprisingly happy to know I was okay, and although Christian wanted me to stay with him, I got the feeling that wasn't a good idea.

We were still trying to figure out how to be boyfriend and girlfriend *without* a major threat looming over our heads. Living with him seemed insane, even if I really wanted to.

"Well, if you decide you want to paint or...you know, stay here on breaks and during the summer, you can."

I stared at Ann as she raked her gaze around the room she had set up for me. She had gone above and beyond. The walls were a pale coral color, the bed looked fluffy with a big white duvet, and there was even a headboard attached. Tucked away on the far wall was a dresser and a desk with a pretty lamp on the edge.

My throat closed for a second before I regained myself. "Thank you, Ann."

Her attention snapped to me, and her cheeks rose in a smile. "You're welcome. I want you to feel safe here. And I want you to know that you are not alone." She paused. "Mainly because your boyfriend won't leave your side for nothing."

A laugh escaped my mouth. "It took a lot of convincing to get him to leave me for the night."

Christian's dad let me stay at their house for the last week as things got sorted out with my statement, and not to mention, the feds wanted to make sure things were safe since they'd taken down one of the cartel's biggest drug runners. But it was time Christian took a second to himself instead of following me around like he was my shadow. Not that I was complaining; I just felt bad that he was constantly worrying.

Even at school, he walked me to and from each class. Everyone talked quietly about what they thought had happened to me. It was kept out of the papers and the news, but my face was beat up again, so rumors started to spread.

"Well, I hope you both know that you're safe here. You two deserve a little normalcy in your lives."

I nodded as I took another step inside my new bedroom. My first thought was, *this is too good to be true*. But I was working on changing that mindset. This *was* good, and that didn't mean it couldn't be true.

"I'll let you settle in; I'm going to go finish dinner. Do you like pasta?"

I nodded as my heart warmed. She was cooking me dinner? I hadn't had someone actually cook me dinner for a long time. A really long time.

My stomach growled as I began unpacking my books and a few articles of clothing. I slowly walked over to the closet to pull out a few hangers to hang my school uniform on when I heard a tapping. My head craned to the right, and I saw a figure standing at my window.

My breath caught, but when Christian leaned his face down and grinned, I let out all my breath.

"What are you doing?!" I asked as I pushed the window up.

He told me to back up some, and soon, his long leg was stepping through. "I missed you."

I laughed. "Christian, there is a perfectly fine front door that you could have used. It's seven in the evening. I think Ann would be okay with you stopping over."

He shrugged as he stood before me wearing jeans and a crisp white T-shirt. "I wanted to see how easy it was to climb through your window." He raised his eyebrows as a grin played along his mouth. "I have to say, it's a lot easier now that your bedroom is on the first floor."

I smacked his chest as a smile snaked its way onto my face. At the last second, he grabbed my hand and pulled me in close. "I love you."

I angled my chin up and locked onto his dark gaze. "I love you, too. Always."

He nodded. "Always."

His lips hovered over mine, and butterflies filled my stomach. I breathed in his woodsy scent and found comfort.

Before he pressed his mouth on mine, Ann knocked on my door. "The pasta will be done in about ten minutes."

I held in my laugh as Christian and I froze. "Okay!"

Then, through the door, she said, "And tell Christian he's welcome to stay...as long as he uses the front door next time."

Christian chuckled as a bad-boy grin covered his features. "Will do," he shouted before pulling me in even closer. He bent down a fraction and hovered his mouth over my ear. His warm breath had chills breaking out along my arms. "Not a chance in hell. I'm sneaking through your window every night, because there's no way I'm sleeping without you."

"Good," I answered before letting out a soft laugh. But soon, my laugh was drowned out by his kiss, along with everything else in the world.

The End

ALSO BY S.J. SYLVIS

English Prep Series

All the Little Lies

All the Little Secrets

(Ollie and Piper)

All the Little Truths

(Eric and Madeline)

St. Mary's Series

Good Girls Never Rise

Bad Boys Never Fall

Dead Girls Never Talk

Standalones

Three Summers

Yours Truly, Cammie

Chasing Ivy

Falling for Fallon

Truth

All books can be found on Amazon or at sjsylvis.com

ABOUT THE AUTHOR

S.J. Sylvis is a romance author who is best known for her angsty new adult romances and romantic comedies. She currently resides in Arizona with her husband, two small kiddos, and dog. She is obsessed with coffee, becomes easily attached to fictional characters, and spends most of her evenings buried in a book!

www.sjsylvis.com

ACKNOWLEDGMENTS

As always, I would like to shout out my amazing family for making me smile daily and for always supporting me and my dream. I love you forever and ever. <3

To my author friends (I can't list you all. I would feel too bad if I accidently left someone out, so you know who you are!!)—where would I be without you? To our daily voice messages, shares, likes, encouraging words, and writing sprints—I love you all SO much and I am so grateful for your friendship. Here's to many more books!

To my Betas (Andrea, Danah, Emma, & Megan)—Thank you SO much for helping me with plot holes, confusing scenes, and for reminding me that I need to flip imposter syndrome the bird. You four helped me in ways you don't even realize. Xo.

To my Editor, Jenn, Thank you for always making my work shine. I would not be where I am without you and your amazing grammar knowledge!

To my Proofer/PA, I honestly have no idea where I would be without you, Mary! Thank you for reminding me to do things that I forget about, for picking up my slack, and for everything else. Xo.

To my readers, bloggers, ARC readers, any one who helps spread the word about my books—WOW. You are the reason I can make this writing gig an actual career. Without your support, reviews, & shares, I wouldn't be where I am today. Thank you so incredibly much for everything you do. It does not go unnoticed.

Xo,

SJ

Lightning Source UK Ltd.
Milton Keynes UK
UKHW012357231222
414383UK00006B/468